PAM WEAVER

# There's Always Tomorrow

D1344620

**AVON**

This novel is entirely a work of fiction.
The names, characters and incidents portrayed in it are
the work of the author's imagination. Any resemblance to
actual persons, living or dead, events or localities is
entirely coincidental.

AVON

A division of HarperCollins*Publishers*
77–85 Fulham Palace Road,
London W6 8JB

www.harpercollins.co.uk

A Paperback Original 2011

1

First published in Great Britain by
HarperCollins*Publishers* 2011

Copyright © Pam Weaver 2011

Pam Weaver asserts the moral right to
be identified as the author of this work

A catalogue record for this book is
available from the British Library

ISBN-13: 978-1-84756-267-8

Set in Minion by Palimpsest Book Production Limited,
Falkirk, Stirlingshire

Printed and bound in Great Britain by
Clays Ltd, St Ives plc

All rights reserved. No part of this publication may be
reproduced, stored in a retrieval system, or transmitted,
in any form or by any means, electronic, mechanical,
photocopying, recording or otherwise, without the prior
permission of the publishers.

**Mixed Sources**

Product group from well-managed
forests and other controlled sources
www.fsc.org  Cert no. SW-COC-001806
© 1996 Forest Stewardship Council

FSC is a non-profit international organisation established
to promote the responsible management of the world's forests.
Products carrying the FSC label are independently certified
to assure consumers that they come from forests that are managed
to meet the social, economic and ecological needs
of present and future generations.

Find out more about HarperCollins and the environment at
**www.harpercollins.co.uk/green**

# Acknowledgements

To Eve Blizzard, ever there with an encouraging word, my amazing editor, Kate Bradley, and my agent Juliet Burton – Juliet, you're the best!

This book is dedicated to David, my husband, my lover and my best friend, who never stopped believing in me.

# One

Dottie glanced at the clock and the letter perched beside it. It was addressed to Mr Reg Cox, the stamp on the envelope was Australian and it had been redirected several times: firstly 'c/o The Black Swan, Lewisham, London', but then someone had put a line through that and written 'Myrtle Cottage, Worthing, Sussex', and finally the GPO had written in pencil underneath, 'Try the village'.

Australia . . . who did they know in Australia?

She picked it up again, turned it over in her hands. Holding it up to the light, she peered through the thin airmail paper at the letter inside. Of course, she wouldn't dream of reading it. It was Reg's letter – but she couldn't help being curious.

There was a name on the back of the envelope. Brenda Nichols. Who was she? Someone from Reg's past perhaps? He never talked about his war experiences, but perhaps he'd done some brave deed and Brenda Nichols was writing to thank him . . .

There was a sudden sharp rap at the front door and Dottie jumped.

Nervously stuffing the letter into her apron pocket, she opened the door. A boy with a grubby face stared up at her. 'Billy!'

'Mrs Fitzgerald wants you, Auntie Dottie.'

Billy Prior wiped the end of his nose with the back of his hand. His face was flushed, a pink glow peeping out from the mass of ginger freckles, and colourless beads of perspiration trickling from the damp edges of his hairline. He was very out of breath.

Dottie smiled down at him but she resisted the temptation to tousle his hair. She knew he wouldn't like that any more. Billy was growing up fast. He'd take the eleven plus next year and maybe he'd be clever enough to go to grammar school. As he stood there twitching for an answer, she guessed why he'd come. There was obviously some hitch back at the house and he'd run all the way, keen to do an errand regardless of whether he might get a sixpence for his trouble. He was a good boy, Billy Prior. Conscientious. Just the sort of son any mother would be truly proud of.

'She says it's a pair of teef that you come,' Billy ventured again.

Puzzled, Dottie repeated, 'It's a pair of . . . Oh!' she added with an understanding grin, 'you mean it's imperative that I come?'

'S'right,' he nodded.

'You can go back and tell Mrs Fitzgerald I'll be there directly.'

'If you please, Auntie Dottie . . .' Billy began again, as she turned to go back indoors. 'Mrs F said it was urgent.'

Dottie's fingers went to her lips as she did some quick thinking. Should she leave a note on the kitchen table and go back with Billy? Her mind raced over the preparations she'd already made for the wedding party taking place the next day. Everything was under control; she'd left nothing to chance. Whatever Mariah Fitzgerald wanted, it couldn't be anything serious. Dottie smiled to herself. People like her always needed to feel in charge. To Mariah, any slight hitch seemed like a major disaster. Dottie looked down at Billy's anxious face and her heart went out to him. 'Has there been a fire?'

'No.'

'Did you see an ambulance at the house?'

Billy frowned. 'No.'

'In that case, Billy,' she said, 'the message is the same. Tell them I shall be there directly.'

Billy sniffed and wiped the end of his nose with his hand, palm upwards. He seemed rooted to the spot.

'Off you go then.'

He turned with a reluctant step. 'It's urgent,' he insisted.

'I know, I understand that. It'll be all right, Billy. I promise I will come as soon as I can.'

She watched him go back down the path, worried in case he walked too near the old disused well. Even though Reg had put a board over the top, and weighted it down with a stone, she didn't like anyone walking too close.

Billy's shoulders slouched, so as he reached the gate she called, 'Just a minute, Billy.'

He turned eagerly, obviously expecting her to run all the way back with him. Instead, she went back inside and reached up onto the mantelpiece where Reg kept his Fox's Glacier Mints in a tin. She took it down and looked inside. There were still plenty. She'd filled it up the day before, but he'd been busy last night so most likely he hadn't had time to count them yet. Should she risk it? He could so easily fly into one of his rages if she touched his things. She could hear Billy kicking the doorstep as he waited anxiously, scared of getting into trouble. Should she? Yes . . . she'd take a chance. She went back to the door and held the tin out in front of the child. 'A sweetie for your trouble.'

Billy's face lit up. By the time he'd reached the gate again, the treat was already in his mouth.

'And don't throw the paper on the floor,' Dottie called after him. She chuckled to herself as she watched him quickly change the position of his hand and slide the paper into his pocket.

The clock on the mantelpiece struck five. She'd better get a move on. Reg would be back home soon, another ten minutes or so. If she had to go back to the doctor's house, she'd be there half the night. She'd better tidy up her sewing and shut up the chickens right now. Reg would see to the vegetables after he'd had his tea. With all the rain they'd had lately, they might not even need watering. According to the wireless, 1951 had seen the coldest Easter for fourteen years, the coldest Whitsun for nine years and, with the height of summer coming up, things didn't look so promising for that either. Everybody grumbled and complained – everyone except Reg. He didn't seem to be too worried.

'All this rain is good for the celery,' he said. 'And it'll help keep down the blackfly on the runner beans. Save me buying Derris dust this year.'

Dottie folded away the pink sundress she was working on and put it in her sewing box. The potatoes were beginning to boil. As she grabbed a handful of chicken feed from the tin by the back door, she turned down the gas and hurried down the garden.

Dottie had lived in their two-up-two-down cottage on the very edge of the village for eleven years. At sixteen, she'd come to live with her Aunt Bessie and now, nearly two years on from Aunt Bessie's tragic death, she lived here as Reg's wife. She smiled as she recalled her wedding day. How handsome he'd been in his uniform. He'd been so nervous, his hands had trembled as he put the ring on her finger. If she had been tempted to practice philosophy, Dottie would say that in life some are the haves and others the have-nots and, despite the sadness of the past, she was still one of the haves. She had come from nothing and now she had a nice little home, good health and – if she was careful – Reg was all right . . . Apart from the times when his horrible moods got on top of him, and he couldn't help that, could he? What was it Aunt Bessie always used to say to her? 'You make your bed and you must lie in it.'

She opened the gate leading to the chicken run and closed it behind her, calling as she went. The chickens clucked contentedly around her ankles, clearly recognising her position as provider.

'Chick, chick, chick . . .'

She opened the door of the henhouse and threw in the seed. Most of the hens scrambled inside straightaway. She had only

4

to coax a few stragglers to go in before she closed and locked the door. They were still noisy and agitated, but they'd soon roost on the perches and quieten down. Satisfied that all was well, Dottie turned back to the house. She saw that Reg had arrived and was putting his bicycle into the shed. Her heart beat a little faster. He had lost some weight since his illness but he still had his good looks and his hair was still as black as jet. She paused, waiting to see what kind of mood he was in.

'Got the tea ready?' he said cheerfully.

With a quiet sigh, Dottie relaxed. Thank God. He was in a good mood tonight.

'Of course,' she smiled.

'What are you grinning about?'

She punched the top of his arm playfully. 'Just pleased to see you, that's all, silly.'

Something flickered in his eyes and she knew she'd gone too far.

'Oh, silly, am I?'

Her heart sank and she chewed her bottom lip anxiously. 'I didn't mean it like that, Reg.'

As she brushed past him, he grabbed her left breast and pushed her roughly against the back door. His other hand was already up her skirt, his fingers pressing into her bare flesh above her stocking top. His breathing became quicker as, with one deft movement, he undid her suspender. She felt her stocking slip. As his urge became more acute, he pressed his body against her and she heard a crinkling paper sound coming from her apron pocket. Her heart almost stopped. She still had his letter! Her mind went into overdrive. He mustn't know. Please, please don't let him feel it. Please don't let him ask, 'What's that noise . . . What have you got in your pocket?' She could feel it getting all creased up. If he found out, what would she say? How on earth would she explain?

He was kissing her so hard she hardly had time to draw breath.

His tongue filled her mouth and she could feel the rough stubble on his chin rasping against her face. She tried to respond to him – he got so angry if she didn't – but she couldn't. Her only thought was the letter.

The door latch was digging into her side and it took all her willpower not to push him away. Another thought came into her mind. He wasn't going to make her do it here, was he? Not here by the back door, out in the open, where anyone could come around the side of the house and see them? What if Ann Pearce looked out of her bedroom window? She'd never be able to look her in the face again.

'Come on,' he said hoarsely, pinning her to the door with one hand and fumbling with the buttons on his trousers with the other. 'Come on.'

'Reg . . .' she pleaded softly. 'Let's go inside.'

He pushed her again, banging her head painfully against the door as he lifted his knee to prise her legs apart. All at once, he stopped fumbling with his flies and slid his hands over her buttocks. Her skirt went up at the back.

'No,' she pleaded. 'Not here, not under Aunt Bessie's window.'

He froze. She looked up and he was staring at her coldly. His lip curled and he punched her arm.

'Oh bugger you then,' he snarled as he walked into the house.

Dottie grabbed the window ledge to steady herself. 'I'm sorry,' she whispered. She stayed where she was for a couple of seconds, her knees trembling and her hair dishevelled. Lifting the hem of her skirt, she pulled at her suspender to secure her stocking again. The back of her head was tender but thankfully there was no sign of blood. She glanced into her apron pocket. The letter was completely crumpled. She couldn't give it to him now. He'd go loopy.

Taking a deep breath, Dottie tugged at the front of her dress to pull it straight and held her head high as she walked back inside. She knew what was expected. Business as usual. They never

6

discussed it when it happened. He didn't like talking. Five minutes later, her apron and the letter hanging on the nail on the back of the door, she placed his plate on the table.

He put down his paper. 'Got plenty of gravy on that?'

'Yes, Reg.'

He got up from his chair and sat at the table.

'I've got to go back to the house,' she said, aware that she was treading on eggshells.

'Oh?'

'She sent Billy Prior up with a message.'

'Won't it keep until morning?'

'I doubt it,' Dottie said, risking a little laugh. 'You know what she's like. She'll be in a right state. Josephine's wedding is the *wedding of the year.*'

'I can't imagine there's anything left to do,' said Reg, pulling up his chair to the table. 'Not with you in charge.'

She wasn't sure what to make of that remark. Was there a note of pride in his voice, or was it sarcasm? She decided not to ask and went to fetch her own plate.

'Well, you'd better get over there right away then, hadn't you?'

'We'll eat our dinner first,' she said, adding her own note of defiance. 'She'll send the doctor with the car before long.'

'How do you know that?'

She shrugged nonchalantly. 'You'll see.'

'I dare say I'll look for any sign of mildew in the strawberry beds,' he said, mashing his potato into the gravy and spilling it onto the tablecloth, 'and then maybe I'll take myself off to the Jolly Farmer for a pint.'

'So it's all right for me to go then?' she said.

He looked up sharply. 'Got any brown sauce?'

Just as she'd predicted, Dr Fitzgerald, a small man with a shock of frizzy light brown hair, walked up the path about twenty minutes later. Pushing his thick-rimmed glasses further up his

7

nose, he curled his top lip at the same time, something he always did when he was slightly embarrassed.

Dr Fitzgerald had always admired the simplicity of Dottie's little cottage. Reg kept the garden looking immaculate. The neat rows of carrots, cabbages, beans and peas kept the two of them well fed and healthy. He knew from the various occasions when he'd been called out when Reg was ill that the inside of the cottage was neat and tidy too.

Some would say he was nosy but the doctor made it his business to know all about his patients. Taking umpteen cups of tea by the fireside had enabled him to discover that, born and raised a gentlewoman in the last century, Elizabeth Thornton, known to everyone as Aunt Bessie and the original owner of Myrtle Cottage, had incurred the wrath of her father by marrying beneath her station. Cut off from the rest of the family, she and her beloved Samuel had amassed a tidy fortune in the twenties and thirties by running a string of small hotels, but sadly they remained childless. The frequency of the doctor's visits had increased slightly in 1940, when her only living relative, orphaned by the Blitz, had come to live in the village. A terrible thing to happen to a young girl, but he couldn't be sorry: Dottie had brought a very welcome ray of sunshine back into Bessie's life.

He found the back door open. In the small scullery, Dottie's pots and pans gleamed and glinted. He wondered vaguely where she found the time. He was well aware that she was in great demand in the village. On Mondays and Tuesdays, she worked for Janet Cooper, owner and proprietor of the general store in the village, and on Thursdays and Fridays she was at his own house. Dottie wasn't the usual sort of daily help, all frumpy and with wrinkled stockings – she was attractive too. Damned attractive. Her figure was trim and her breasts soft and round. If she had one fault, it was that she wore her copper-coloured hair too tightly pulled back in a rather severe-looking bun, but now and then a tendril of hair would work itself loose and fall over her small forehead. He wasn't supposed to, but he noticed things like that. And when she laughed, her clear blue eyes shone and she lit up the whole world. He sighed. Oh to have an uncomplicated life like hers . . . to have an uncomplicated wife like her . . . Mariah's agitated face swam before his eyes.

Dr Fitzgerald cleared his throat. 'We sent the Prior boy up, but we weren't sure if you'd got the message,' he began apologetically.

Dottie gave no hint one way or another. Oh dear, oh dear. He dared not return without her. 'Um,' he went on, 'my wife . . . that is . . . we wondered if you could spare an hour or two tonight, Dottie?'

'I told Billy to tell you I would be there directly,' she said in her usual unhurried manner.

'I see . . .'

'I had to take care of my husband first.' Although her tone was mildly reproachful, the doctor envied Reg Cox – not for the first time. When was the last time Mariah put him first in anything?

'Yes, yes, of course,' he said hastily. 'Um . . . I was just wondering . . . . um . . . if you are able to come straight away, I could give you a lift.'

'Well, that's most kind of you,' she said in a surprised tone. 'I'll just do this and then I'll get my coat.' She picked up the bowl and wandered past him to throw the washing-up water onto the garden. 'And,' she added as she walked past him a second time, 'I'm sure you wouldn't mind dropping Reg off at the Jolly Farmer on your way, would you?'

If the doctor was annoyed by her presumption, he wasn't about to make a fuss. He wasn't stupid. He knew that in her quiet way, Dottie controlled all their lives and for the sake of his own sanity and peace of mind, it was important for him to get their indispensable daily woman back to his wife as soon as possible.

\* \* \*

9

By the time they arrived at the house, Mariah Fitzgerald was in a complete flap. She'd got Keith running in and out of the house and into the marquee (a large ex-army tent set up on the lawn), with the large dinner plates from her best service, as well as some plates she'd found on the larder floor.

'Don't drop them, whatever you do,' she'd screamed at her already nervous son. Keith tripped over the guy ropes and she almost had a fainting fit.

'You forgot the china, Dottie,' she said accusingly as Dottie stepped out of her husband's car. 'It's a good job I went into the marquee to check. The tables were bare.'

Dottie said nothing but she was bristling with anger. Dr Fitzgerald disappeared somewhere in the direction of the surgery and she heard a door closing. She hung her coat on the peg on the back of the kitchen door and looked around in dismay. She'd expected interference to some small degree but not on a scale like this. Her beautifully organised kitchen was in total chaos.

Mrs Fitzgerald had been going through everything, even the tins in the pantry. The lid of the tin containing the strawberry shortcake was on the draining board, the tin containing the brandy snaps had the lid from the love-all cake on the top and vice versa. The tin of butterfly cakes had no lid at all. Dottie couldn't even see it. When she'd left that afternoon, the dinner plates, on hire from Bentalls in Worthing, had been in their boxes under the shelf in the pantry. They had since been pulled out and the shredded paper used as packing was now strewn all over the kitchen worktops and the floor.

With an exaggerated sigh, Dottie set about putting things to rights. The bread bins were open and some of her carefully counted cutlery was missing from the drawer. What was the point of asking someone to do something and then changing it the minute her back was turned? Mrs Fitzgerald usually trusted her implicitly. What on earth had changed, for goodness' sake?

Keith came in and bent to pick up some more plates.

'You can leave them,' Dottie said tartly.

'But Mother says . . .' he began.

'I'll deal with your mother,' she said, her tone a little less edgy. After all, it wasn't the boy's fault. He stared at her with wide eyes. She smiled and said softly, 'You go and have your bath.'

'I told her you wouldn't like it,' Keith muttered as he turned towards the stairs.

Dottie set off in the opposite direction, towards the garden and the marquee.

'I shouldn't have to do this, Dottie,' Mrs Fitzgerald wailed as she saw her coming.

'And you don't have to, Madam.' Dottie's tone made her employer look up sharply. There was no insolence on her face, but she needed to let her see she wasn't happy.

'There'll be so much to do in the morning,' said Mariah Fitzgerald. 'Why didn't you think to put the plates out? It would save such a lot of time, you know.'

'They need to be washed first.'

'Washed?'

'I have no idea who had the plates before us, Madam,' said Dottie. 'I didn't think you would want to use them unwashed so I've arranged for Mrs Smith and Mrs Prior to come first thing in the morning.'

Mariah Fitzgerald's jaw dropped slightly. 'Well,' she flustered, as she strove to recover her composure, 'the cutlery needs sorting out.'

'That's right, Madam,' Dottie agreed. 'And I've arranged that Mrs Prior will bring her little niece Elsie to do that. She'll polish everything for ten bob.'

Mariah Fitzgerald went a brilliant pink. The napkin she was holding fluttered down onto the table. She looked around help-lessly. So did Dottie. She should have come sooner. Right now, she was wishing with all her heart that she hadn't bothered to wait for Reg when Billy Prior had knocked on the door. Now she'd have to collect up all that cutlery, take all the plates back to the kitchen and tidy up at least forty napkins before she could go back home. She might even have to iron some of them again.

Their eyes met.

'Yes, well . . .' said Mariah, patting her hair at the back. 'I have to be up very early in the morning. The hairdresser is coming at nine thirty.'

Dottie didn't move.

'So . . . so I'll leave you to it, Dottie.' Mariah said, mustering what little dignity she could find. 'As usual, you seem to have everything under control.'

Dottie watched her as she crossed the lawn and sighed. It would be at least another hour before she had everything back to the way it was before.

Reg was all set to spend the evening in the corner of the Jolly Farmer with his pint of bitter. Usually there were plenty of people still willing to buy a pint for an old soldier, but tonight the bar was almost empty. He didn't mind. It had been a long day – Marney and the station master had had him running from pillar to post.

Marney's chest was bad again. Too much smoking, everyone said, but Reg reckoned it was something to do with the POW camp he had been in. Germany somewhere. You could pick up some weird germs in those places. Marney probably lived week in week out on the verge of starvation as well, and that couldn't have helped. Reg might not have been in a palace himself, but his 'rest of the war' was nowhere near as bad as Marney's. Even if it *were* the ciggies that made his cough, who could blame the poor old bugger? He probably only smoked them to forget something.

As Reg stared deeply into his pint, Oggie Wilson drifted back into his mind. He'd never forgotten poor old Oggie, and when he heard what had happened to him, he'd felt as sick as a pig.

12

Reg never spoke of his own experiences of course. Better to let sleeping dogs, and all that, but when he'd married Dot in '42, he knew he'd fallen on his feet. A nice little place right near the sea, two women at his beck and call – what could be better? Dottie had stuck by him all through the war and it was only the thought of coming home to her that kept him sane while he had been stuck in that bloody prison. He'd finally come back in '48. She'd given him quite a homecoming too. Some of his mates had come back from POW camp to find their missus had given up on them. Jim Pearce's wife had presumed him dead and when he came home he found her shacked up with somebody else. A fine how-d'you-do that was, and the woman had no shame. Reg knew what he'd have done if he'd found any woman of his cheating on him. Not Jim. He'd cleared off and she was still living next door, bold as brass.

Dottie wasn't like that. Dottie had waited and she'd been faithful. Reg took a long swing of his beer. Nah, Dottie would never do anything bad. She was perfect. Too bloody perfect, that was her trouble. Taking her on the doorstep would have added a bit of spice to life. Why did she have to go and mention the old trout? Bloody Bessie with her silly hats and passion for cowboy films, she ruined everything. Even the thought of her made his stomach turn.

He'd had the shock of his life when Aunt Bessie had died and he'd never felt the same since. It had done for his marriage as well. He'd tried to get it together but he just couldn't do it any more. Before the war, he could keep it up for hours, especially if he knew Bessie was listening on the other side of the paper-thin walls. He was a bit rough at times but he'd had enough women to know most of them liked it that way. But ever since . . . well, since then he just couldn't do it any more. Not with her, anyway.

Dottie had never reproached him for it. She was too anxious to please. Sometimes he wished she would. He took another long drink. Trouble was, she never fought back. Whatever he dished out, she just took it. Well, that was no fun, was it? She was beginning to bloody annoy him all the time now.

'Hey up, Reg. You coming outside?'

He put his empty glass down and looked up. Tom Prior from the Post Office was leaning in, holding the door open. 'We're bowling for a pig,' he cajoled.

'A pig?'

'Nice little thing,' Tom went on. 'Fatten him up and he'll be a lovely bit of bacon when Christmas comes.'

Taking in Tom's weedy frame, the thought crossed Reg's mind that he could do with a bit of fattening up himself. Naturally skinny, he and that fat cow Mary looked like Jack Sprat and his wife.

Reg shook his head. 'Nah, I'll settle for a bit of peace and quiet.'

'Peace and quiet!' Tom chortled. 'You'll get plenty of that when you're in your pine box and staring at the lid. Come on, man. Let's be havin' you. I'll stand you another pint and it's only two bob a go. All in aid of the kiddies' home.'

Reg rose from his chair. 'I don't know why I listen to you, Tom Prior,' he grumbled good-naturedly. 'I never bloody win anything.'

Dottie had worked hard and now she was very tired. The marquee was almost back to the way it had been and the kitchen was nearly straight when Miss Josephine, the bride to be, came downstairs in her dressing gown and wearing slippers.

She wasn't exactly a pretty girl. Her nose was slightly too long and her mouth definitely too wide; but Dottie knew that just like any other bride she would look radiant in the morning. Right now the whole of her hair was kiss-curled, each one pinned together by two hair grips crossed over one another. Her face was white, and the Pond's Cream, thick enough to be scraped

14

off with a palate knife, hid every blemish on her skin. She was wearing little lace gloves so she'd obviously creamed her hands and, to judge by the puffiness of her eyes, she'd been crying for some time.

'Are you making some cocoa, Dottie?'

'I can easily make some for you, Miss.'

Dottie went to fetch the milk and a saucepan. Josephine sat at the kitchen table. 'Oh, Dottie,' she sighed.

Dottie was tempted to ask, 'Excited?' but the tone of the girl's voice led her to believe her sigh meant something altogether different. 'What is it?'

'Can you keep an absolute secret?'

'You know I can,' said Dottie, striking a match. The gas popped into life and she turned it down.

'I'm not sure.'

'Not sure of what, Miss?'

'That I can go through with all this.' Josephine produced a lace-edged handkerchief from her dressing-gown pocket and wiped the end of her nose. 'I tried to tell Mummy, but she just got cross and shouted at me. Then she said she didn't want to talk about it because she'd forgotten to do something really important in the kitchen.'

Ah, thought Dottie, careful not to let Miss Josephine see her lips forming the faintest hint of a smile. Mrs Fitzgerald had sent for her, not to sort out a few stray plates, but to stop her daughter from calling off the wedding.

Dottie reached for the Fry's Cocoa, mixed a little of the powder with some cold milk in the cup, then added the boiled milk. She kept her voice level, unflappable, as she asked, 'What's the problem?'

'I don't know,' Josephine wailed. 'And before you tell me it's just nerves, let me tell you it's not.'

'Do you love Mr Malcolm?' Dottie put the cup and saucer in front of her, still stirring the cocoa.

'Yes, of course I do!' She dabbed her eyes again. 'How can you ask such a thing? It's just that I don't . . . I can't . . .' Her chin wobbled. 'Oh, Dottie, supposing . . .'

'Every young woman is nervous on her wedding night,' said Dottie sitting down at the table with her. 'But if you love him . . .'

'I do, I do!'

'And he loves you?'

'He says he does. He's so . . . Oh, Dottie, you're a married woman . . .'

Dottie thought back to her own wedding night. All those old wives' tales her friends teased her with. They only did it because they knew her innocence. What they couldn't know was that their teasing fed her fear of the unknown, the fear of failure, the dread of being hurt. But back then, all her worries had been blown away by her feelings for Reg. Poor lamb, he'd never known real love. He'd never even known a mother's love because he'd been brought up in a children's home. When she saw him waiting at the front of the church on her wedding day, her heart had been full to bursting. Now at last, she would be able to show someone how much she cared and as they'd walked into her honeymoon guesthouse, her one and only thought had been that she would be giving him something he'd never had before. Something very precious . . .

'Haven't you ever?' she began, but one glance at Josephine's wide-eyed expression told her what the answer was. Dottie reached out her hand in a gesture of affection. 'Mr Malcolm knows you've never been with anyone else,' she said gently.

'But I won't know what to do,' Josephine wailed. 'Supposing I fail him? Supposing being married doesn't work?'

'Of course it will work,' said Dottie. 'Even if it's difficult to begin with, you'll make it work.' That's what we women do, she thought to herself. Men pretend everything is fine or go down to the pub, but we get on with it and *make* it work.

Josephine leaned forward. 'Dottie . . . . do you mind? I mean . . . would you tell me? What happens when you and

Reg . . .? Oh, I shouldn't ask that, should I? It's not nice. But what happens . . .? I mean, exactly . . .?'

Dottie glanced up at the clock. What should she say? If she told Josephine how things really were between her and Reg, there would be no wedding. Mr Malcolm seemed a nice enough man. A bit of a chinless wonder as Aunt Bessie would say, but he clearly loved her. Reg had been good and kind in the beginning. Her wedding night had been a little . . . rushed . . . but she knew he loved her really. It was only the war that changed him. All that time he was away, she'd dreamed of what it would be like to have him back home again. It wasn't his fault things weren't the same. Aunt Bessie was right. She always said, 'War does terrible things to people.'

'Dottie?'

Josephine's voice brought her back to the present. She leaned towards her employer's daughter as if she were about to whisper a secret. She wouldn't spoil it for her. She wouldn't tell her how it was, she'd tell her how she'd always dreamed it would be.

# *Two*

When at last Dottie walked outside into the cool night air, Dr Fitzgerald came out through the French windows.

'I'll take you home, Dottie.'

She was startled. 'There's no need, sir. I'm quite happy to walk.'

'Nonsense!' he cried. 'You've got a big day tomorrow. You'll need all your strength. Hop in.'

He was holding the passenger door of his Ford Prefect open as if she were a lady.

'Everything set for the reception?' he said as he sat down in the driver's seat.

'Yes, sir.'

'You're an absolute marvel, Dottie.'

'Not at all, sir,' she said. 'I'm only doing what anyone else would do.' But in the secret darkness of the car, she allowed herself a small smile. Yes, let him appreciate her. It was only right.

Reg still wasn't back from the Jolly Farmer when she got indoors. It was unusual for him to be out this late on a weeknight. Still, he had a half-day off tomorrow. He'd be back home at lunchtime.

She put the kettle on a low gas while she pinned up her hair and put on a hairnet. By the time she'd finished, the overfilled kettle began to spit water so that it coughed rather than whistled. She filled the teapot and sat at the kitchen table. It was lovely and quiet. The only sound in the room was the tick-tock of the clock. Then, all at once, there was a knock at the kitchen window and she jumped a mile high. 'Who's there?'

'It's me, Reg.'

Dottie pulled back the curtain. 'Oh, Reg!' she gasped clutching her chest. 'You scared the life out of me. What are you doing knocking on the window?'

'Come here, Dot. I've got something to show you.'

Remembering how he'd grabbed her when he came home earlier that evening, her heart beat a little faster. She shivered apprehensively. 'I'm very tired, Reg.'

'It won't take a minute.'

What was he up to now? And what was that under his arm? Slipping her feet back into her shoes, she made a grab for her coat hanging on the nail on the back of the door. As she lifted it, her apron hanging underneath swung sideways and the pocket gaped open to reveal Reg's creased-up letter. Oh flip! The sight of it made her stomach go over. She'd forgotten all about it.

'Hurry up,' he shouted from the other side of the door.

Dottie grabbed the apron, rolled it up and stuffed it into the drawer. 'Just let me get my coat on.'

As she stepped outside into the cool night air, whatever he was holding under his arm moved. Dottie cried out with surprise.

'Take a look at this!' he said, flinging the jacket back.

It was a small piglet. The animal wriggled and squealed.

'Where on earth did you get that?' she gasped.

'I won it,' he laughed. 'Tom Prior persuaded me to have a go at skittles and I was the only one who got them all down with one throw. I got the first prize. The pig.'

'But you never win anything,' Dottie said.

'That's what I bloody said,' Reg agreed. 'But this time I did.'

'But what are we going to do with it?'

Reg shrugged his shoulders. The pig protested loudly so he covered it with his coat again.

'Well, we'll have to put it in the chicken run for now,' she said. 'They're all shut up for the night. Has it been fed?'

He shrugged again. 'Shouldn't think so.'

'There's some potato left over from last night, and some peelings in the bucket waiting to go on the compost heap. I'll do a bit of gravy and you can give it that.'

'If we fattened him up,' he said, leading the way down the garden to the chicken run, 'he'd be a nice bit of bacon by Christmas.'

They put the pig in the chicken run and, while Reg pulled an old piece of corrugated iron over the tree stump and the edge of the fence to give it a bit of shelter if it rained, Dottie ran back indoors to get some food.

Later that night, as they both climbed into bed, Reg said, 'I reckon I'll get ten bob, a quid, for that pig if I'm lucky.'

'We'd need a proper pigsty,' she challenged, as she switched off the light by the door and fumbled her way into bed. 'It'll upset my chickens.'

'Blow your chickens,' he snapped. 'You think more of them than your own bloody husband!'

With that, Reg turned over, snatching most of the bedclothes. A few minutes later, he was snoring. Dottie lay on her back staring at the ceiling. First thing in the morning, she'd iron that letter smooth and put it back beside the clock.

Josephine Fitzgerald's wedding day dawned bright and sunny. Dottie was up with the lark, but Reg had already gone to work. He had to be at Central Station in time for the 5.15 mail train in order to help load up the mail bags from the sorting office in Worthing.

As soon as she was dressed, she got out the iron. She had to stand on the kitchen chair in order to take out the light bulb and plug it in, then she switched it on and waited for it to warm up.

Somebody knocked lightly on the kitchen window. She looked up in time to see the tramp scurrying behind the hedge. He'd been here many times before but Dottie hadn't seen him for ages. In fact, it had crossed her mind that perhaps he'd died during the cold winter months, or maybe moved on to another area.

Whenever he turned up, Aunt Bessie always gave him something, a cup of tea or a piece of bread and jam. They all knew Reg didn't like him around so he planned his visits carefully.

Dottie popped out to the scullery to put on the kettle to make him some tea, and to get the rolled-up apron out of the drawer. Taking out the letter, she held it to her nose. It smelled of nothing in particular, but now that it was close up, she could see it had more than one piece of paper inside the thin envelope. There was a white sheet of paper but she could also see the edge of a smaller yellow sheet. Dottie turned it around in her hands. Who *was* this Brenda Nichols? Why was she writing to Reg?

Dottie and Reg first got together in 1942, on her sixteenth birthday. They'd met at a dance in the village hall and they had married after a whirlwind courtship. Aunt Bessie had paid for them to honeymoon in Eastbourne, no expense spared.

Once the wedding was over, Dottie had come back to the cottage to carry on living with Aunt Bessie, while Reg, who was in the army, had been sent to Burma. Perhaps Brenda was someone he'd met out there? All Dottie knew was that his unit was part of the Chindits. They were well respected and very brave but she had to rely on the newsreels at the pictures to give her some idea of what it must have been like for Reg because he never talked much about his experiences.

When he'd returned home three years later than most of the boys from Europe, little more than a bag of bones, Dottie had been glad to nurse him back to health. She wished that he and Aunt

Bessie had got on a bit better but, try as she might, there was always a frosty atmosphere when they were together in the same room. Reg had eventually recovered physically but his war experiences left him with black moods and Dottie had to be very careful not to upset him. Was it possible that Brenda was one of the nurses who had looked after him? If she were, she would have to write and thank her.

With great care, Dottie ironed the letter flat and put it back beside the clock.

The kettle began to whistle. The tramp's tin can with the string handle was outside on the step but, instead of being empty, there was a note inside: *I did it! Thanks*.

How strange. Whatever did that mean? She looked around but he was nowhere to be seen. With a shrug of her shoulders, Dottie scalded the old tin and filled it with tea the way Bessie always had. Then she cut a doorstep slice of bread and smeared it lavishly with marrow and ginger jam. She put it on the window-sill as she went down the garden with some outer cabbage leaves for the pig and some chicken food.

Motionless, the pig watched her as she let out the chickens. At first they were a little alarmed when they discovered they had a new living companion, but after a few squawks, plenty of grunting and some running about, things settled down into an uneasy truce.

When she got back to the house, the tramp's tea and the bread were still there. Where was he? Perhaps he was afraid Reg was still around. Then she saw Vincent Dobbs, the postman, walking up the path. Obviously the tramp was waiting until the coast was clear.

'Morning, Dottie,' said Vince. 'You look as if you've lost something.'

'I was just wondering where the tramp was. I made him some tea.'

Vince shook his head. 'Haven't seen any tramps,' he smiled, 'but I did see some chap coming out of your gate.'

'Who was that?' asked Dottie, puzzled.

'Never saw him before,' said Vince. 'Smart, though. In a suit.' He handed her a letter.

'Oh, it's for me!' she cried, eagerly tearing open the letter.

The letter was from her dearest friend, Sylvie. The tramp and Vince forgotten, Dottie walked indoors, reading it as she went. Sylvie was asking to come and stay for a few days when Michael Gilbert from the farm got married. Dottie had already written to tell Sylvie that Mary and Peaches and the other ex-Land Girls would be coming. Michael and Freda's wedding, scheduled for three weeks time, might not be half so grand as the stuffy affair Mariah Fitzgerald was laying on for her daughter today, but it would be much more fun. Sylvie said how much she was looking forward to meeting up with everybody at the wedding. Dottie smiled. She was looking forward to it too. It would just like old times.

*I can't believe that the war's been over for five and half years,* Sylvie wrote. *This will be a golden opportunity to get together again. I never stop thinking about you all and the fun we had on the farm and all that blinking hard work!*

Dottie laughed out loud when she read that. While everyone else had been slogging their guts out in the fields, Sylvie spent most of her time sloping off for a kip in the barn.

*Write and tell me all about Freda,* Sylvie wrote. *What's she like? How old is she? How did they meet? Oh, Dottie, I can't imagine our little Michael all grown up.'*

Dottie felt exactly the same way. Although there was only two years' difference in their ages, Michael still seemed a lot younger. Freda, his bride to be, was only eighteen. Dottie didn't know where they'd met but they had made their wedding plans very quickly; Dottie suspected that Freda might already be pregnant.

Dottie sighed. Sylvie led such a glamorous life with all those parties and important people she met, but she'd have to pick her moment to ask Reg if she could stay and that wouldn't be easy. She knew only too well how Reg felt about her. 'Snobby, stuck-up bitch,' he'd say.

Dottie glanced up at the clock. 8.30. Time to go. She shoved Sylvie's letter into her apron pocket to read again later then, humming softly to herself, she put a couple of slices of cold beef on a plate with some bread and pickles and put it in the meat safe for Reg's dinner.

Just to be on the safe side, she propped Reg's letter in front of the teapot on the table alongside her own hastily scribbled note – *Dinner in meat safe* – so that he couldn't miss it. Then she packed her black dress and white apron into her shopping bag and set off for the big house.

# *Three*

Mary Prior's niece sighed. 'Nobody's coming yet.'

'Good,' said Dottie happily. 'It must be time to put the kettle on, Elsie.'

Peaches and Mary sat down at the table.

The wedding reception was being held in the marquee on Dr Fitzgerald's lawn. Caterers from some posh hotel in Brighton had handled all the food, but the women in the kitchen had been kept busy with unpacking and washing up the hired plates and glasses. Dottie had asked her next-door neighbour, Ann Pearce, to help out but she couldn't find anyone to look after the kids.

Dottie looked around contentedly. She loved being with her friends and nothing pleased her more than helping to make a day special for someone.

The wedding itself was at 2pm, and once the bride had set off for the church some of them took the opportunity to pop back home. Peaches had wanted to check that her little boy, Gary, was all right with his gran. Mary wanted to get her husband, Tom, some dinner and she took Elsie with her. Dottie stayed at the house: after last night's fiasco, she wasn't going to leave anything to chance.

As soon as the wedding party returned from the church, the waiters began handing round the drinks and some little fiddly bits they called *hors d'oeuvres*. Until everyone went into the marquee for the meal, Peaches and Mary were kept busy with a steady stream of washing up.

The marquee had been set out with twelve tables, each with eight place settings. Each table was named after a precious stone – diamond, ruby, sapphire, amethyst, amber, opal, and so on – and in order to avoid family embarrassments, there was a strict seating plan. Guests were to eat their meal to the gentle sound of a string quartet.

The top table, at which the family wedding party sat, was tastefully decorated with huge vases of fresh flowers at the front, and the toastmaster was on hand to make sure that everything was done decently and in the correct order. Mariah Fitzgerald knew her daughter's wedding would be the talk of the golf club and county set for months to come, so Dr Fitzgerald and the best man would not be allowed to move until the toastmaster had given them their cue.

The catering company had a separate tent on the other side of the shrubbery where a small team of cooks was already busy producing the meal with all the efficiency of an army field kitchen. All the washing up was to be done in the house kitchen and the team of waiters and waitresses would bring in the dirty crockery. They would send it back to Bentalls once it had been washed and repacked in the various boxes.

Dottie gave her little team a piece from one of her cakes and they sat down for a well earned cup of tea. They had been friends since the war years when they had worked together on the farm. Their friendship had deepened when Mary was widowed. It was ironic that Able had gone all through the war, only to be killed on his motorbike near Lancing. Billy was only just over five at the time and Maureen three and Susan eighteen months. Dottie and Peaches pulled together to help Mary through.

'Well, at least the rain held off,' Dottie said.

'They say it'll clear up in time for the Carnival,' said Mary.

'I could do with this,' said Peaches, sipping her tea. 'I still don't feel much like eating in the morning.'

'Not long now before the baby comes,' said Mary.

'Seven weeks,' said Peaches leaning back and stroking her rounded tummy. 'I can't wait to get into pretty dresses again.'

'I bet it won't take you long either, you lucky devil,' Mary said good-naturedly. 'I looked eight months gone before I even got pregnant. Five kids later and just look at me.' She wobbled her tummy. 'Mary five bellies.' They all giggled.

'And your Tom loves you just the way you are,' said Dottie, squeezing her shoulder as she leaned over the table with the sponge cake.

'Our Freda is getting fat,' said Elsie. Her eyes shone like little black buttons and Dottie guessed this was the first time she'd been included in 'grown-up' conversation.

'I wouldn't say that when Freda's around,' Dottie cautioned with a gentle smile. 'She'd be most upset.'

'I can't wait for the wedding,' said Elsie.

'Michael has certainly kept us waiting a long time,' Mary agreed.

'But I wouldn't call him slow,' Peaches said, half under her breath. The baby kicked and she looked down at her stomach. 'Ow, sweet pea, careful what you're doing with those boots of yours, will you?'

Elsie's eyes grew wide. 'I didn't know babies had boo . . .'

'It's hard to imagine Michael old enough to get married,' Dottie said quickly.

'Come on, hen,' Mary laughed. 'He's only two years younger than you!'

She was right, but somehow, in Dottie's mind, Michael had always remained that gangly fourteen year old in short trousers who had followed them around on the farm. It was hard to believe he was almost twenty-five.

'I can't wait to be a bridesmaid,' said Elsie.

'It's very exciting, isn't it?' Dottie smiled. 'I'm sure you'll look very pretty.'

'Are you doing the dresses, Dottie?' Mary asked.

Dottie shook her head. 'Not enough time.'

The older women gave her a knowing look and she blushed. She hadn't meant to say that and she hoped no one would draw attention to her remark in front of Elsie. She poured Peaches some more tea.

'I think Freda will make Michael a lovely wife,' said Dottie.

'Oh!' cried Peaches. 'This little blighter is going to be another Stanley Matthews.'

'Pretty lively, isn't he?' said Mary.

'Can I feel?' asked Elsie.

Peaches took her hand and laid it over her bump.

'What's it like, having a baby?' Elsie wondered.

'I tell you what,' laughed Peaches. 'I won't be doing this again.'

'Why not?'

'That's enough, Elsie,' her aunt scolded.

Elsie pouted and took her hand away.

'Who did you say was looking after your Gary, hen?' asked Mary.

'My mother,' said Peaches. 'She can't get enough of him.'

'Tom's got all mine,' grinned Mary. 'That'll keep him out of mischief. At least you don't have to worry about who's going to look after the kids, Dottie.'

Dottie bit her lip. Oh, Mary . . . if only you knew how much that hurt . . .

'Did I tell you?' she said, deliberately changing the subject. 'I had a letter from Sylvie yesterday.' She took it out of her apron pocket and handed it to Peaches. 'She's coming to Michael's wedding.'

Peaches clapped her hands. 'Sylvie! Oh how lovely. She's so glamorous. I really didn't think she'd come, did you? We'll have a grand time going over old times. Remember that time we put Sylvie's fox fur stole at the bottom of Charlie's bed?'

Dottie roared with laughter. 'And he thought it was a rat!'

'Jumped out of bed so fast he knocked the blinking jerry over,' Peaches shrieked.

'Good job it wasn't full,' laughed Dottie.

'Which one was Charlie?' asked Mary.

'You remember Charlie,' said Dottie. 'One of those boys billeted with Aunt Bessie and me. The one that went down with The Hood.'

'Dear God, yes,' murmured Mary.

'And is your Reg all right with her staying at yours?' Mary wanted to know.

'Haven't asked him yet,' said Dottie. In truth she wasn't looking forward to broaching the subject.

Mary glanced over at Peaches and then at Dottie. 'Why doesn't he ever bring you over to the Jolly Farmer, hen?'

Dottie felt her face colour. She never went with Reg because he said a woman's place was in the home. Mary's pointed remark had flustered her. She brushed some crumbs away from the table in an effort to hide how she was feeling. 'I've never been one for the drink.'

'But we have some grand sing-songs and a good natter,' Mary insisted.

Dottie took a bite of coffee cake and wiped the corner of her mouth with her finger. They'd obviously been talking about it. 'I usually have something to do in the evenings,' she said. 'You know how it is.'

'You should come, Dottie,' said Peaches. 'You don't have to be a boozer. I only ever drink lemonade.'

'I can't think what you get up to at home,' Mary remarked to Dottie. 'There's only you and him, and that house of yours is like a shiny pin.'

'She does some lovely sewing, don't you, Dot,' said Peaches. 'You ought to sell some of it.'

'I do sometimes,' said Dottie.

'Do you?'

Yes I do, thought Dottie. She was careful not to let Peaches see her secret smile. And one day she'd show them just what she could do. One day she'd surprise them all.

Mary leaned over and picked up the teapot again. 'What are you doing next Saturday?' she asked, pouring herself a second cup.

'Having a rest!' Dottie laughed. What were they up to? This sounded a bit like a kind-hearted conspiracy . . .

'Tell you what,' cried Peaches. 'Jack is taking Gary and me to the Littlehampton Carnival in the lorry. It's lovely there. Sandy beach for one thing. Nicer for the kids. Worthing and Brighton are all pebbles. Why don't we all go and make a day of it? You and Reg and your Tom, Mary. There's plenty of room. We can get all the kids in the back.'

'That sounds wonderful!' cried Mary. 'My kids would love it. Are you sure?'

'I don't think Reg . . .' Dottie began. She knew full well that Reg would prefer to spend a quiet day in the garden and then go down to the pub. She didn't mind because it left her free to work out how to do her greatest sewing challenge so far: Mariah Fitzgerald's curtains.

'You leave Reg to me,' said Peaches firmly. 'You're coming.'

'Can I come too?' Elsie wanted to know.

'Course you can,' said Peaches. 'The more the merrier.'

'I don't think you can, Elsie,' said Mary. 'Your mum and dad are going to see your gran over in Small Dole next week. She told me as much when I asked if you could help out today.'

Elsie stuck her lip out and slid down her chair. 'I hate it at Gran's,' she grumbled. 'It's boring.'

Peaches had gone back to Sylvie's letter. "All the hard work . . .'?" she quoted.

'Eh?' said Mary.

'She says here, "I never stop thinking about you all and the fun we had on the farm and all that blinking hard work!" I seem to remember she spent more time on her back than she did digging.'

They all giggled.

'My dad says Mum ought to do that,' said Elsie innocently. She was sitting at the opposite end of the table, her face covered in strawberry jam and cake crumbs.

'But you haven't even got a garden,' said Mary walking round behind her to top up the teapot.

'Not digging, Auntie! Lying on her back.'

Peaches choked on her tea as Mary made frantic gestures over the top of Elsie's head.

'Dad said it would do her good to lie on her back every Sunday afternoon when we go to Sunday school,' Elsie went on innocently. 'But Mum says she hasn't got the time.'

'Lovely bit of sponge this, Dottie,' said Mary, struggling to regain her composure. 'Elsie's really enjoying it, aren't you, lovey?'

'Auntie, why are you laughing?'

'What are you going to do with your ten bob, Elsie?' Dottie interrupted.

Elsie smiled. 'When the summer comes, me mum's taking me over to me other granny's for a holerday,' she said. 'She says I can keep the money for then.'

'That's nice.'

'She lives near Swanage,' Elsie was in full swing now. 'I can go swimming in the sea.'

'While your mum's lying on the beach?' muttered Peaches, starting them all off again. Desperately trying to keep a straight face herself, Dottie nudged her in the side. Elsie looked totally confused.

The door burst open and a waitress dumped a pile of dirty plates on the draining board.

31

'Time to get started,' said Dottie standing to her feet and straightening her apron. 'Get that cake and our cups off the table, will you, Elsie? We shall need all the space we can find now.'

The next hour was a frenzy of activity. The washing up seemed endless and they were hard pushed to find space for both the clean and dirty dishes.

At around four thirty, Elsie came running back. 'They're all coming out!'

The women gathered by the back door to watch.

Josephine Fitzgerald looked amazing and very happy. Her dress, made of organza and lace, was in the latest style. The V-shaped bodice was covered with lace from neck to the end of the three-quarter length sleeves while the skirt was in two layers. The white organza underskirt reached the ground while the lace overskirt came as far as the knee. The whole dress was covered in tiny pearls. Dottie had studied it very carefully. She knew it had cost an absolute fortune, but with a little ingenuity she knew she could make one for less than quarter of the price.

Malcolm Deery looked even more of a chinless wonder than ever in his wedding suit but, Dottie decided, they were well matched. Josephine would lack for nothing. After a couple or three years, there would be nannies and christenings. In years to come, she'd become just like her mother, going to endless bridge parties, and playing golf. She'd buy her clothes from smart shops in Brighton or maybe go up to London to the swanky shops on Oxford Street and, if Malcolm's business did really well, Regent Street.

'Ahh,' sighed Peaches. 'Don't she look a picture?'

'Must be coming in to get changed before they go off for the honeymoon,' said Mary.

Dottie didn't want to think about the conversation she'd had the night before. Had she betrayed that girl? She hoped not, but only time would tell.

'Second wave of washing up will be on its way in a minute,' she said to her companions. 'Better get back to work, girls.'

As if on cue, two waitresses hurried out of the marquee, each with a tray of glasses, followed by a waiter with a stack of dirty plates.

Mary grabbed a small sausage from the top of the pile of dishes and shoved it into her mouth as she pushed more dirty plates under the soapy water.

'Ma-ry!' cried Peaches in mock horror.

'I need to keep my strength up,' said Mary, her cheeks bulging.

'Dottie, would you come and help Miss Josephine?' Mrs Fitzgerald's sudden appearance made them all jump. Mary choked on the sausage and Peaches put down her tea towel to pat her on the back.

'Yes, Madam,' said Dottie, doing her best to steer her employer away from her friend before she got into trouble. Mariah Fitzgerald could be very tight-fisted. Dottie could never understand meanness. Why put food in the pig bin rather than allow a hard-working woman like Mary to have a little something extra? But she knew her employer was perfectly capable, at the end of the day, of refusing to pay Mary if she caught her eating.

Thinking about pig bins, she was reminded of the pig in her hen run. How was it getting on? She'd have to ask if she could take some leftovers for him . . . or was it a her? How do you tell the difference, she wondered.

As she followed Mrs Fitzgerald upstairs, Dottie decided – nothing ventured, nothing gained. 'Excuse me, Madam. About the leftovers.'

'Put them in the pantry under a cover,' said Mariah without turning around.

'And the plate scrapings?'

Mrs Fitzgerald stopped dead and Dottie almost walked into her. 'The plate scrapings?' She sounded horrified.

'Only my Reg has a pig,' Dottie ploughed on, 'and I was wondering if I could take the scrapings home to feed it.'

Mrs Fitzgerald was staring at her.

'He hopes to fatten it up for Christmas.' Dottie swallowed hard. 'He says it would make a nice bit of bacon.'

'What an amazingly resourceful man your Reg is, Dottie,' she said, walking on. 'Yes, of course you can take the scrapings. And when Christmas comes, don't forget to bring a rasher or two for the doctor, will you?'

They'd reached the bedroom where Josephine was struggling with the buttons on the back of her wedding dress.

'I've told Dottie to help you, darling,' said Mrs Fitzgerald. 'I'll have to get back to the guests.'

As they heard her mother run back downstairs, Dottie gave the bride a conspiratorial smile. 'Are you all right now, Miss?'

'Oh, Dottie,' Josephine cried happily. 'It's been a wonderful, wonderful day, and I know, I just know, tonight will be just fine.'

'I'm sure it will, Miss.'

'Mrs,' Josephine corrected her dreamily. 'Mrs Malcolm Deery.' She gathered her skirts and danced around the room, making Dottie laugh.

Between them, they got her out of the wedding dress and into her going-away outfit, an attractive pink suit with a matching jacket. The skirt was tight and the jacket nipped in at the waist. Her pale cream ruche hat with its small veil set it off nicely. She wore peep-toe shoes, pink with white spots and a fairly high heel. She carried a highly fashionable bucket-shaped bag.

Mr Malcolm, who had changed in the spare bedroom, was waiting for her at the top of the stairs. He was dressed in a brown suit and as he waited, he twirled a brand new trilby hat around in his hand. The newlyweds kissed lightly and, holding hands, they began to descend. Halfway downstairs, however, Josephine broke free and ran back.

Dottie was slightly startled as she ran to her, laid both hands on her shoulders and kissed her cheek. 'Thank you, Dottie darling,' she whispered urgently in her ear, 'thank you for all you've done.'

'It was nothing,' protested Dottie mildly.

'Oh yes it was,' Josephine insisted. 'And if I'm half as happy as you and your Reg have been, I shall be a lucky woman.' With that she turned on her heel and ran back to her new husband and they both carried on downstairs.

As soon as she'd gone, Dottie went back into the bedroom. As happy as you and your Reg have been? Had they been happy? If they had, it was all a very long time ago. She could hardly remember their courtship, but they had been happy in the beginning . . . hadn't they?

Even her own wedding day had been rushed. The phoney war was over by then and Reg was nervous, afraid he'd be sent abroad. Under the circumstances, Aunt Bessie had been persuaded to let them marry by special licence on August bank holiday weekend. The gossips had a field day. She knew the rumour was that she was pregnant, but she was a virgin when Reg took her to bed that night.

Remembering all that the boys had gone through at Dunkirk, when Reg wrote to say he was being posted to the Far East, she'd been pleased. 'At least he'll be out of all this,' she had told Aunt Bessie.

But after he'd gone, she'd felt bad about saying that. She had little idea what happened out there, but if the newsreels were to be believed it looked far worse than what happened in Germany. He didn't want to talk about it when he came back, at the end of '48, and he had been a changed man. His chest was bad and he needed nursing. Reg didn't seem to want her for ages but when he recovered and tried to make love to her, he was so rough she hated it. It was hard not to cry out with Aunt Bessie next door. And that was another thing. He and her aunt didn't see eye

35

to eye but funnily enough, when she died, Reg had been deeply affected. The shock of it left him with another problem: he couldn't do it. She wished she had someone to talk to, but it wasn't the done thing, was it? A married woman shouldn't talk about what went on behind the bedroom door.

Dottie sighed. She was still only twenty-seven and if things went on the way they were, she was destined to be barren. There would never be any babies.

She put Josephine's wedding dress on a hanger and, hanging it on the front of the wardrobe door, she spent a little time smoothing out the creases, until the overwhelming need for tears had passed.

# Four

It was cool in the shed. Reg pulled the orange box from under the small rickety table behind the door and sat down. He kicked the door closed and the soft velvety grey light enveloped him. This was his haven from the world and, apart from the occasional passing chicken that might have crept in to lay her egg under the bench, he knew the moment he shut the door he would be left alone. Dot would never come in here uninvited. This was the place where he kept his pictures. She didn't know about them of course, but when the mood came over him and she wasn't there, he'd come out here and have a decko. They were getting dog-eared and yellow with age but he wouldn't part with them for the world. Although he still burned for the love of his life, he might have forgotten what she looked like if he didn't have the pictures.

They weren't the only pictures he had. He'd still got the ones he'd bought off some bloke at the races. Now they really got him going. Those tarts would pose any way the punters wanted them. They got him all excited and when Dot was around, doing her washing or something, he'd watch her through the knothole on the shed wall and have a good J. Arthur Rank. It wasn't as exciting as the real thing, but he liked it when there was an element of danger. And with the way things were at the moment, he wasn't getting much of that either.

But looking at his pictures wasn't the reason why he'd come

out into the shed today. He positioned the box near the small window and next to the place where the pinpricks of sunlight streaming through the wood knots in the boards would give him plenty of light to read the letter. Dot had propped it on the table but he hadn't opened it. He'd shoved it straight into his pocket while he ate his dinner. He wanted to be alone when he read it, somewhere he knew he wouldn't be disturbed.

First he took out his tobacco tin and his Rizla paper and box. As he lifted the lid, he took a deep breath. The sweet smell of Players Gold Cut filled the musty air. Putting a cigarette paper in the roll, he shredded a few strands of tobacco along its length. Then he snapped the lid shut and a thin cigarette lay on top of the box. Reg licked the edge of the paper and rolled the cigarette against the tin. He pinched out the few loose strands of tobacco from the end and slipped them back inside for another time. The years spent 'abroad' had made more than one mark on his character. Reg was a careful person. He hated waste and he always knew exactly how much of anything he'd got. That's how he knew Dot had been eating his Glacier Mints. There had been twenty-four in there when she gave him the new bag. Now there were only twenty-three.

Putting the thin cigarette to his lips, he lit up and the loose strands at the end flared as he took his first drag. He laid his lighter and the Rizla box onto the bench and reached into his back pocket for the letter.

The envelope was flimsy. Airmail paper. The stamp was Australian. He stared at the handwriting and a wave of disappointment surged through his veins. It wasn't what he thought it was. Now that he looked carefully, the sloping hand was unfamiliar. He turned the envelope over for the first time and stared at the name on the back.

Brenda Nichols – who the devil was she? He ran his finger over the writing and sucked on his cigarette. A wisp of smoke stung his eye and he closed it. The address on the front said 'The

38

Black Swan, Lewisham'. He dug around in the recesses of his mind but he couldn't place it.

Reaching over to the jam jar on the shelf under the tiny window, he took out his penknife. The smoke from his cigarette drifted towards his eye again and he leaned his head at an awkward angle and closed it as he slid the knife along the edge of the envelope and tore it open. There were two sheets of paper inside the wafer-thin, transparent blue airmail envelope. The larger was white. A letter.

Reg's hand trembled as he read slowly and carefully.

*Murnpeowie. June 1951*

*My dear Reg*

*I need your help. I never told you but in '43 I had a child. Her name is Patricia. She's eight now. You'll love her. Everybody does. She's a very good girl and she will be no trouble. I cannot look after her any more. The doc tells me it's only a matter of time. I have left Patricia with my friend Brenda Nichols but she can't look after her for long. Her husband is sick. Please come to fetch her. I hope that deep down, you can find it in your heart to forgive me for running out on you like that but I thought it was for the best, things being the way that they are. I'm sorry for keeping this from you, but in my will I have left everything to you and I hope you will give her a good life.*

*God bless you,*

*Sandy.*

There was a codicil at the bottom of the page, written in the same hand.

*This letter was dictated by Elizabeth Johns to Brenda Nichols, who nursed her until she passed away peacefully in her sleep on July 15th 1951. Signed Sister Brenda Nichols.*

\*　　\*　　\*

39

His first reaction was panic. A kid? He didn't want kids. That was what put him off Dot – her incessant bleating on about kids. How long he held the letter he had no idea. It was only when he realised that his cigarette was far too close to his lip that Reg stirred. He took it out, threw the dog end to the floor and ground it into the earth.

He threw the letter contemptuously onto the workbench and reached for the tobacco tin again. There was no way he was going to take in some bloody Australian bastard. He rolled another fag and stuck it between his lips while he fumbled in his pocket for the lighter. Taking a deep drag, he picked up the letter and read it with fresh eyes.

If he refused to take the kid, someone might go digging around in his past. Elizabeth Johns was dead. She'd left everything to him. That was a bit of luck. He'd need extra money if he was going to bring up a kid. Nobody would bat an eyelid if he took it. Running his hand through his own thinning hair he grinned to himself and squeezed his crotch. Yeah, he was still safe. As far as everyone knew, he was the kid's only living relative and she was eight. She wouldn't have a clue. What harm would it do?

Pity it all went belly up back then. He didn't like to think about what happened when he'd got caught, and when he'd got out he was scarcely more than skin and bone. He could hardly remember those first few days of freedom. He'd been a dumb thing, beaten, exhausted, bewildered . . . It had been a close call, but it was worth the risk. Thank God for bloody Burma. Before the regiment was sent there, he'd never even heard of the place.

He'd written a letter to Dot telling her he was on a secret mission and given it to Oggie Wilson. Oggie owed him a favour. He'd heard after the war that Oggie had ended up on that bloody railway. When he got out, Reg tried to trace him but he couldn't. Then someone said that they'd been forced to leave men by the roadside because the guards refused to allow them to bury the dead.

He reckoned that's what happened to Oggie Wilson. A bit of luck as far as Reg was concerned. No one left to blab. He sighed. All the same, it didn't seem right leaving a man like Oggie out there in the open. He should have been buried, decent like. The thought of it made him shudder. If he hadn't been caught, maybe he'd have been sent out to that bloody jungle himself, and if he had, he'd be lying beside poor old Oggie Wilson.

Putting Elizabeth John's letter in his lap, Reg unfolded the yellow sheet of paper. It was another letter, written with a child's hand, complete with a couple of ink stains on the page.

> *Dear Father,*
> *I hope you are well. I am well. I went to MULOORINA*
> *with Mrs Unwin in her truck. We ate ice cream. I am nearly*
> *nine. I can count up to 500. That's all for now.*
> *Your ever loving daughter,*
> *Patricia.*

Patricia . . . Reg leaned back on the orange box and closed his eyes. A letter from Patsy. He liked Patsy better. His stomach was churning, the way it always churned when he was nervous. An old ITMA joke slipped between the sheets of his memories. 'Doctor, Doctor, it really hurts when I press here.' 'Then don't press it.' He'd have to stop thinking about the past. It only made him angry. Put it out of your mind and get on with it. That's what the screw had told them. He'd bloody tried but he couldn't. It was the guilt mainly. He never told anyone, but sometimes he did feel bad about what happened. He felt a draught in the back of his neck and turned his head sharply, afraid that someone was standing behind him, but he was quite alone. He re-lit his cigarette and forced himself to relax.

Lifting the envelope, he put the letter back inside. Something weighted the corner. He tipped it upside down and a small photograph fell onto the workbench. Just one look at that mop

41

of blonde hair and it was obvious why she was called Sandy. She was standing outside a bungalow. It was a sunny day and there were some funny-looking flowers growing beside the door. She was wearing a nurse's uniform. Her hair was loose and cut short. He couldn't make out the detail of her face – the camera was too far away – but she was holding a bundle in her arms. Bloody hell. This must be Patsy.

He was aware of his heart thudding in his chest. His mouth had gone dry. How long he stared at the small photograph he never knew. What did the kid look like now? He squinted at the bundle. Tom Prior, weedy as he was, was the father of twins and stepfather to the three others from Mary's first husband. He always made jokes about Reg and the lead in his pencil. If everyone thought this was his kid, he'd have no trouble from now on.

In the beginning, he'd been quite pleased to get Dot. She wasn't a bit like the sort of woman he was used to but she was all right. He'd never gone in for all that soppy stuff, but until he'd met Dot, he'd never had a virgin either. It wasn't all it was cracked up to be. He'd tried to get her to do what he wanted, but she wasn't having any of it. Yet she was desperate for a kid, even wept about it sometimes. She was careful not to do it in front of him but he'd heard her in the scullery. He didn't even want her now. Since the old aunt died, she bored him.

The more he thought about being a father the more he liked it. The word sounded good. He was somebody's dad. He had a daughter. Patricia. A nice name, Patricia, but he still preferred Patsy.

*I have left everything to you . . .* With a bit of luck Elizabeth Johns was well off when she died. For all her wealth, bloody Aunt Bessie hadn't left him a bean. Well, this could be the big one. The only problem was Dot. She might not take too kindly to having his kid around. He didn't want her to rock the boat so he'd have to play this one carefully. Plan it all out. And when

42

he'd won her round, he'd have a nice little nest egg. After that, the future would sort itself out.

He opened the drawer again and took out his favourite photograph. The woman smiled up at him, her back arched and tits thrust out. She was better than Diana bloody Dors any day. He squeezed his crotch again. Right now he needed someone like her. Just the thought of her made his pulse race. She'd give him what he wanted . . . and more . . . He ran his tongue along her naked body and then shoved the photograph back in the drawer.

Taking another drag on his cigarette, Reg pulled out a writing pad and cleared a space on the worktop. For once he didn't have to word his letter carefully in case other people read it first. All the same, he didn't want anyone to start asking awkward questions. Licking the end of the pencil, Reg began to write.

# *Five*

Dottie didn't finish at the house until late. She was worn out. All she wanted to do was to get home and put a bowl of warm water on the kitchen floor to soak her poor tired feet. She was just about to set off for home when Dr Fitzgerald came into the kitchen.

'A marvellous day, Dottie.'

'Yes, sir.'

'Have you seen my wife?'

'I believe she's gone upstairs to lie down.'

'And you're off home?'

'That's right.'

'I'll give you a lift.'

'There's really no need,' Dottie protested. She rolled the plate scrapings in newspaper for the pig and put it into the shopping bag.

'Oh, but I insist,' said the doctor. 'It's starting to rain again.'

They drove in silence, but this time Dottie didn't feel very comfortable. The doctor seemed tense. He stared at the road ahead and his back was very straight. He's probably driving like that because he's had too much to drink, she thought, but it gave her little comfort. The only sound in the car was the whoosh, whoosh of the windscreen wipers.

He pulled up outside her place and as he put the handbrake on his hand brushed her leg. She gathered her shopping bag, anxious to get out of the car as quickly as possible. 'Thank you, Doctor,' she said curtly.

'Allow me,' he said reaching across her to open the passenger door. Their hands met on the door handle and he pressed himself against her. 'Oh, Dottie,' he said huskily. 'Dottie.'

Dottie was both shocked and surprised. 'Dr Fitzgerald!' she cried as his other hand squeezed her thigh gently.

'Just a kiss,' he was pleading. 'One little kiss.'

His face was right in front of hers and his mouth was open. She could smell his whisky-soaked breath. She turned her head away and dug him in the ribs with all her might. Her bag fell to the floor and everything spilled out. 'Get off me,' she hissed. 'How dare you!'

The wipers were still going and through the windscreen she could see the curtain in Ann Pearce's bedroom moving. They didn't get many cars in their street so obviously the sound of a motor drawing up had brought her to the window. The doctor accidentally touched the car horn and the loud and sudden noise seemed to make him come to his senses.

'Oh God . . .' he began. 'Mrs Cox, I'm sorry . . .'

As he slumped back in his seat, Dottie scrambled to get out of the car. The door swung open and the light went on. As she stepped into the road, she looked up. Ann let the curtain drop, but Dottie knew she'd seen everything. Breathless and still panicking, she ran up the path. Behind her, the doctor's car turned around in the road and drove off into the night.

She burst through the back door into the darkened kitchen and slammed it behind her. Thank God, Reg must still be at the pub. Heaven only knows what he'd do if he found out. Putting her head back, she leaned against the door and breathed a sigh of relief. 'Dirty old man . . .'

'Dot?'

She jerked open her eyes and jumped a mile high. She swung

round to see a dark shape in the chair. Dottie put the back of her hand to her mouth and let out a small cry. She fumbled for the switch by the door and the room was flooded with light. It was Reg. He had a bottle of beer in his hand and as he rose to his feet, the only thing that registered in her mind was the deep frown on his forehead.

'What the hell happened? You look as white as a sheet.'

Dottie felt herself sway slightly. She hadn't expected Reg to be sitting here in the dark. She wished now that she hadn't put on the light. She must look a right mess.

'Dot?' he said again.

She felt her mouth open but nothing came out. She was shaking. He was going to be angry with her, she knew he was. She never should have accepted the lift. And yet she'd been in the doctor's car hundreds of times and he'd never so much as looked at her. Not in that way, anyway.

He came slowly towards her. She still had enough of her wits about her not to tell Reg what had happened. He was the type to do something stupid and face the consequences later.

'What's that all over your skirt?' he accused.

She glanced at her clothes. Lumps of half-eaten wedding cake and salad cream hung from her dress and she had a big blob of egg on her stocking.

'I . . . I . . .' she faltered and swayed again. She felt sick. Whether it was the sight of the pig food or the memory of what happened she wasn't sure. The room was going round and round.

He grabbed at her arm and she flinched.

'Come and sit yourself down,' he said kindly. 'You've obviously had a shock.'

Now she was bewildered, confused. Doctor Fitzgerald's actions were hard enough to deal with, but it was a long time since Reg had been so considerate.

'Did something frighten you?' He had his head on one side and was looking at her for an explanation.

'Yes,' she said quickly. 'Yes, that's it. Someone came up behind me and I dropped the bag of pig food.'

'Pig food?'

'Mrs Fitzgerald gave me the plate scrapings for the pig, but I dropped them.'

'Who came up behind you?' he demanded. 'Did you see him?'

'I don't know,' she said touching her forehead with her hand. She felt something cold and gooey; looking at it, she saw, she'd got pig food on her hand as well.

'I saw an old tin full of tea on the windowsill today,' he snapped. 'Have you been feeding that bloody tramp again?'

'No!' she began. 'Well . . . yes, but I'm sure it wasn't him.'

'I've told you before not to give to them scroungers,' said Reg. 'Let them work for their bloody living, like I have to.' He snatched up the poker.

'What are you doing?' Dottie cried out, horrified.

'You stay here,' he said as he ran outside.

'But it's raining!' she called after him. 'He'll be gone now.'

But Reg was in no mood to listen. For one heart-stopping second she thought the poker might be for her but now he'd gone off in search of the tramp. Thank God the street was empty.

She got up wearily from the chair and put the bowl on the table. There was a little hot water in the kettle so she poured it in and began to wash herself. The fingers on her left hand were swollen and painful from when Doctor Fitzgerald had pressed them against the door handle. Although she knew he was long gone, she still trembled. What on earth had possessed him? It was so unexpected.

As she washed off the pig food, she pondered what to do. She couldn't say anything to Mrs Fitzgerald. The woman probably wouldn't believe her anyway. He was the village doctor, for heaven's sake, and besides, Mariah Fitzgerald wouldn't tolerate even the smallest whiff of scandal. She'd give her the sack for sure and that would have a knock-on effect. If she wasn't good enough for the doctor's wife, most likely her other employers would ask her to leave as well. And there was no way she could tell Reg what had really happened either. She'd have to think up some yarn for when he got back indoors. And then there was Ann Pearce. She must have recognised the doctor's car. What if she told Reg? Dottie's heartbeat quickened. No, she told herself, she wouldn't. There was no love lost between those two. They weren't even on speaking terms. Ann had been living with another man when Jack came back home and Reg was so angry about it, he'd reported her to the welfare people as an unfit mother, an accusation which was totally unfounded but which caused a great deal of heartache. For a time, Ann had been the subject of gossip and innuendo in the village.

'She's doing the best she can,' Dottie told him but Reg made no secret of his dislike.

Reg reappeared at the back door. He was holding the soggy newspaper with the remains of the pig food inside. 'I found this in the hedge just up the road a bit,' he said. 'I reckon the tramp must have fancied it and come up behind you. You running off like that, must have scared him. Obviously he didn't want the law on him so he ran off.'

She gave him a faint smile. 'Yes,' she said. 'You're right, Reg. That's it. That's what must have happened.' It seemed safe enough to blame the tramp. He never came near the cottage when Reg was there anyway. The doctor must have thrown the pig food into the hedge as soon as he'd turned the car around.

'You sit yourself down, love,' Reg was saying, 'and I'll make us a nice cup of tea.'

He lifted the bowl of dirty water and took it outside to throw over the garden while Dottie plonked herself down in the easy chair. Reg was making her very nervous. She couldn't face it if he wanted her tonight but he got so angry if she let him lose the urge when it came. Somehow or other, no matter what she did or didn't do, he lost it every time, and then he'd get angry.

When he came back, she watched him busying himself with making her a cup of tea. Why was he being so nice? It should have been lovely being spoiled, but she couldn't relax. It wouldn't last. As sure as eggs is eggs, there would be a payback time.

# Six

Reg was in a good mood when he arrived back home for Sunday lunch. Dottie was busy carving the joint but he put his arm around her and gave her a beery kiss on the cheek. 'That smells good.'

'Sit yourself down,' she smiled.

He belched in her face. 'You're bloody marvellous.'

She felt disgust at his crudity and yet a glow of pride at his compliment. It wasn't often Reg said something nice to her. The people round here thought Reg a good sort, helpful and friendly. Good job no one saw what went on behind closed doors.

'It wouldn't be half as nice without your wonderful vegetables,' she said modestly.

The meal, roast lamb, mint sauce, new potatoes and runner beans, with gooseberry fool to follow, was Reg's favourite. They ate with the radio on and *Two-Way Family Favourites* and the *Billy Cotton Band Show* in the background.

'I was talking to Jack Smith in the pub,' said Reg as he made for his armchair and the Sunday paper. 'I told him we ought to do something while the weather's nice.'

'Did you, Reg?' Dottie hid her smile. So, Peaches had done it. She'd invited him on the outing.

'The weather might have picked up by Saturday.'

'About time we had some good weather,' said Dottie putting the kettle on for some tea. 'What shall we do?'

'How about a trip to the seaside?'

'Ooh, Reg,' she cried, enjoying the pretence. 'That would be lovely.'

'I reckon we could all get in that lorry of his,' Reg went on. 'You and Peaches will be all right in the back with Gary, won't you?'

It was on the tip of her tongue to say 'but Peaches is pregnant', but she knew he'd be annoyed – perhaps even change his mind. 'Of course we will.'

'I've offered him some petrol money,' said Reg, settling down for a doze before he read the papers. 'You'd better get round to Mary Prior's to talk about the sandwiches.' He yawned. 'She's coming too.'

Dottie hummed to herself as she did the washing up. An outing. How exciting! She hadn't been on an outing since . . . since . . . well, she could hardly remember. It must have been before Reg came back home. Things were definitely on the up. Everyone needed a bit of cheering up. This year's harvest had only been fair to middling and the August bank holiday had been a total wash-out with torrential rain. The papers said it was the worst on record and what with the train crash at Ford which killed nine people and injured forty-seven the Sunday before, a general air of gloom hung over the village.

Never mind, next Saturday was going to be wonderful. She'd got eighteen pounds, four shillings and eleven pence saved upstairs, and that was quite apart from what she had in her Post Office savings book. She could take a couple of quid and buy all the kiddies an ice cream.

The washing up finished, Dottie picked up the bowl to throw the dirty water onto the garden.

'Coo-ee, coo-ee.' Ann Pearce was leaning over the garden fence.

Dottie's heart sank as the full horror of last night came flooding back. What did Ann want? She was smiling. What was she going to say?

51

Dottie tried to appear unruffled. 'Lovely day.'

'Smashing,' said Ann. She noted Ann's lank and greasy hair, fastened to the side of her head with a large hairslide. Dottie thought it a pity that she didn't make more of herself. She wondered if she should offer to give her one of those new Sta Set Magicurls like the one Mary had tried a few months ago. It only cost ninepence and it was really successful. Ann was an attractive woman but it seemed she had given up on herself. Dottie supposed it must be because Ann had lost everything when her husband came home almost two years after the war had ended. There was an ugly scene and both Ann's husband and the man she was living with had cleared off.

Ann raised an eyebrow. 'Having a good day today?'

'Er . . . yes, thanks,' said Dottie, slightly flustered.

Ann smiled. 'How did the wedding go?'

Dottie felt uneasy. She didn't want this conversation to continue. If Reg came out and saw her talking to Ann, she'd never hear the last of it. 'Excuse me,' she said. 'I think I can hear Reg calling.'

'Before you go,' Ann called after her. Her smile was too bright, too eager. Dottie's stomach churned. 'I don't like to ask, but I seem to have run out of money for the gas.'

Dottie relaxed. This was the first time Ann had ever actually asked her for anything directly. Usually, Dottie had to resort to subterfuge to offer her a helping hand.

'I wonder if you could help me out,' she'd said to Ann on more than one occasion. 'I seem to have made far too much casserole for just the two of us. Reg would go mad if he thought I'd was wasting good food, but he doesn't care to have the same meal two nights running.'

Grudgingly, and only to 'do her a favour', Ann would take the dish, making sure to return it, clean, when Reg was at work. For the sake of her pride, Dottie couldn't do it very often. It wasn't like Ann to actually ask for something.

52

'I meant to have got some change when I went down the village yesterday,' Ann went on, 'but I clean forgot all about it when I bumped into *Doctor Fitzgerald*. It was such a *struggle* getting away from him. Well, you know how it is.'

Dottie could feel her face begin to flame.

'So,' Ann continued, 'if you could spare a few shillings for the gas . . .'

The sun went behind a cloud. 'Yes,' said Dottie weakly. 'How much do you need?'

'Ten bob would do nicely,' said Ann.

Dottie turned to go inside. 'I'll just get my handbag. Ten bob, d'you say?'

Ann nodded. 'That'll do . . . for now.'

# *Seven*

Saturday August 25 was indeed what the papers called 'a scorcher'. When the lorry arrived outside Dottie's cottage, the back of it had been transformed by an assortment of blankets and cushions. Mary was perched on top of a pillow laid on a crate of beer and fizzy pop, looking every bit the carnival queen. Tom sat at her feet while all around them the kids were bursting with excitement. Billy had a firm hold on little Christopher and Mary was cradling Connie on her lap. Susan and Maureen sat side by side next to their mother.

'Don't you look lovely, hen,' Mary said as Dottie came down the path carrying a big bag. 'You'd better sit here in the cab with that pretty dress on.'

'What, this old thing?' laughed Dottie, although in truth she was wearing her sundress for the first time. A friend had given her the material because it was too pink. The sleeveless bodice was tight, and she had made a belt to wear at the top of its calf-length full skirt. Luckily she'd been able to match it with some other pink material with tiny white daisies to make a small bolero top.

'You're so good with a needle,' said Mary. 'Me, I'm hopeless.'

Reg nudged Dottie's arm. 'I can't sit in the back, love,' he said. 'I'm afraid if they can't shove up and make room for me on the seat, I shan't be going.' He lowered his voice for Dottie's ears only. 'You know I couldn't face the back of a lorry, not after what happened during the war.'

54

'Of course not, dear,' she smiled. 'You sit next to Peaches, I'm quite happy at the back with Mary and the children.'

She watched as Peaches, dressed in a voluptuous tent-like dress to hide her bump, pulled Gary onto what was left of her lap and Reg, his Brylcreemed hair flopping attractively over one eye, climbed in beside her. Gary looked a little pale and he was complaining a bit.

'I'm not so sure we should be taking him,' said Peaches.

'He'll be as right as ninepence when he's down on the beach,' said Jack.

Dottie walked around the back and, grabbing hold of Tom's hand, clambered over the side of the lorry. 'Poor little Gary still doesn't seem very happy,' she said as she sat next to Mary. 'What's the matter with him?'

'Peaches reckons he's got a bit of a cold,' said Mary, shaking her head. 'He's been like it since Saturday.' And turning to one of her children, she said sharply, 'Put your arm in Susan. If you hit something while we're moving you'll do yourself a mischief.'

Maureen had gravitated to Dottie's lap. It felt good holding her. Dottie enveloped her in her arms, enjoying the feel of her warm little body and the faint vinegar smell of her shiny clean hair, soft as down next to her cheek. The old yearning flooded over her again. If only she could have a child of her own . . .

'I love you, Auntie Dottie,' Maureen lisped.

'And I love you too, darling,' said Dottie with feeling.

The drive to Littlehampton was very pleasant. They all sang silly songs, 'Ten green bottles, hanging on the wall, Ten green bottles, hanging on the wall, and if one green bottle should accidentl'y fall . . . there'll be nine green bottles hanging on the wall,' was one and the other was 'There was ten in the bed and the little one said, 'Roll over, rollover.' So they all rolled over and one fell out, there was nine in the bed and the little one said . . .' and they clung to each other, laughing whenever Jack took a corner fast.

Forty-five minutes later, they pulled up on the seafront. Tom was the first to jump down. He helped Mary and the kids and then lifted Dottie down. Everybody, except Reg, grabbed a bag and they made their way onto the sand. The warm weather and the Carnival had brought everyone out. The beach was already very crowded. In fact it was difficult to find a stretch of sand big enough for all of them to be together, but eventually they did and luckily it was fairly near the promenade. Dottie pointed out the toilets beyond. 'Handy for the kids,' said Mary, giving her a nudge.

Tom and Jack brought some deckchairs down and the adults made themselves comfortable. As for the children, they couldn't wait to get into the water. Mary stripped them down to their little ruched bathing costumes and knitted swimming trunks and let them go. 'Make sure you look after them,' she told Billy.

Knowing they'd soon get bored, Dottie went up top and bought six buckets and spades from the kiosk along the promenade. The children were thrilled to bits.

'You shouldn't have spent all that money, hen,' Mary scolded. 'They must have cost you a fortune.'

'They were only one and eleven each,' said Dottie happily. 'And besides, it was my pleasure.'

'What do you say?' Mary demanded of her children.

Five happy faces looked in her direction and chorused, 'Thank you, Auntie Dottie.'

Reg gave Dottie a dirty look but just then Jack and Tom appeared with the crate of beer and fizzy pop.

'Hope you've remembered a bottle opener,' Reg remarked as he tied a knot in each corner of his handkerchief to make a sun hat. He had already bagged a deckchair and placed himself on the edge of the group.

Everyone looked helplessly from one to the other until Peaches rummaged in her handbag and produced one. 'Thank the Lord for that,' laughed Jack as he set about offering the bottles around and removing the tops.

When it came to her turn, Peaches shook her head. 'I'd sooner have a cuppa.'

'Then look no further,' smiled Dottie, reaching for her Thermos flask.

In the end, the men had beer, the women had a cup of tea and the kids shared from a big bottle of cherryade with a replaceable glass stopper.

'Can I take the empties back to the off-licence and get the tuppence, Mum?' asked Billy.

'We haven't emptied the buggers yet,' laughed Tom.

'Language,' said Mary.

'Whoops, sorry love.'

The deckchair attendant turned up. Reg appeared to be asleep, so Tom parted with three bob. 'He didn't waste much time,' he grumbled good-naturedly.

The sea glistened in the bright sunlight and the air was filled with the happy shouts of excited children. Dottie kicked off her shoes and let the sand get between her bare toes. Mary's kids kept themselves amused for hours, making sandcastles and running to the sea with their new buckets to get water for the moat.

Little Gary joined in for a while but it was obvious he wasn't really feeling well. It didn't take long before he was all curled up on Mary's lap with his thumb in his mouth.

At one o'clock they ate their lunch: egg sandwiches, bloater paste sandwiches and cheese sandwiches; but no matter how hard they tried, they all ended up with a little sand on them. Mary handed round some of her fruitcake and Dottie offered them some Victoria sponge. Then they made the kids lay down for a rest. The little ones were shaded by the deckchairs or a blanket suspended between the chairs as they lay underneath.

'I reckon you should have gone in for the Miss Littlehampton,

Dottie,' said Tom holding out his newspaper. 'You're better-looking than that June Hadden any day.'

'Oh, Tom,' laughed Dottie. 'I'm a married woman!'

'So is she,' said Mary. 'She's a mother of two.'

'Have a go at the Miss Sussex competition.' Tom encouraged. 'That feller from Variety Bandbox is going to crown the winner. Derek Roy.'

'I don't think Reg . . .' Dottie began.

'Reg won't mind, will you, Reg?'

Reg had been lying back in the deckchair with his eyes closed. He opened them to find everyone staring at him, willing him to agree.

'What, and make a fool of herself?'

'Your Dottie is a real smasher, Reg,' Tom protested.

'Come on, Reg,' said Mary. 'Be a sport.'

Reg's eyes narrowed and Dottie laid her hand on Mary's arm.

'Who's for ice cream?' said Jack and a chorus of little voices, all wide-awake now, cried out, 'Me, me!'

'Good timing, Jack,' grinned Peaches.

After their ice creams, Gary, Connie and Christopher slept for upwards of an hour while Susan and Maureen managed half an hour. Billy was allowed to go to play by the water's edge as soon as the others were asleep. Dottie walked with him, not only to keep an eye on him, but also to have a bit of a paddle herself.

She and Billy had a special relationship. He was only little when his dad died but until Tom Prior came along, he'd so desperately tried to do what everyone told him and be the man of the house. He was fiercely protective of his mum. Dottie had never ever told Mary how he'd cried the day of their wedding. His mother and Tom were off on honeymoon – an afternoon at the pictures in Brighton – and Dottie was looking after Billy, Maureen and Susan in their new home. The babies were sleeping and she'd thought Billy was quite happy playing with his toy farmyard but all at once he'd burst into tears. At first she'd thought it was because he was jealous of Tom: after all, he'd had his mother to himself for most of his life. Up until the time Billy's father was killed, the war had meant that, apart from a couple of periods of leave, Billy had hardly ever seen him. But as she comforted him, Dottie realised the child had taken his 'job' as 'man of the house' so seriously, that the tears were tears of relief. Now at last Tom could have the responsibility of looking after his mother.

As she and Billy paddled in the water, Reg, his trouser legs rolled up to his calves, came to join them.

Earlier that morning, Dottie had been thinking about that letter from Australia again. She kept forgetting to say something about it and, although he'd obviously taken it and read it, Reg still hadn't said anything about it. It was probably of no consequence. A letter from the wife of an old army pal or something . . . but it was funny that he hadn't mentioned it again.

She was about to ask him about it, when he said, 'You'd make somebody a good little mother.' His remark caught Dottie by surprise. She stared at him, unsure what to say. How odd. Was he feeling the urge again? Oh dear. Could he hang onto it until they were home, or was he going to suggest they go somewhere?

As they all paddled together, Dottie felt she couldn't be happier. The sun, the sea, the lovely weather, their friends on the beach and Reg . . . She wanted to tell him so, but she couldn't embarrass him in front of Billy.

Picking up her skirts, Dottie ran further into the water. Billy followed and the two of them splashed about a bit.

'Fancy a quick look around Woolworths?' Mary suggested when Dottie and Billy came back. Reg was already back in his deckchair.

'Ye-ah,' said Billy.

'What about the kids?' asked Dottie.

'I'll stay and keep an eye on them,' said Peaches.

'The men can look after them for five minutes, can't they?' said Mary.

'Reg?' Dottie asked.

'I'm reading the paper.'

'Can I come?' said Billy.

Tom and Jack waved them away. 'Go on, get on with you and enjoy yourselves.'

'And me?' Billy tried again.

'You heard your mother,' said Tom. 'Us men'll have to look after the kids. About time you took our Christopher over to the toilets, isn't it?'

'Aw, Dad!'

The three friends set off for the town. As they walked along the promenade, Peaches fluffed out her blonde hair with her fingers. Dottie linked her arms through theirs and they began an impromptu dance until Mary slipped and trod on some man's toe.

'Oi!' he shouted.

'Sorry,' Mary called as they all dissolved into laughter.

'He'll have a flat foot now,' said Peaches. 'Step – flip, step – flop . . .'

It was all very silly but Dottie laughed until she held her sides. 'I haven't had a laugh like this for ages.'

They stopped off to look at the exhibits in the big marquee on the green.

'I'll tell you what,' said Mary, holding a prize-winning jar of lemon curd up to the light, 'your preserves are every bit as good as these, Dottie.'

Dottie blushed happily.

'And I tell you what,' said Peaches. 'I'm busting for the toilet again. Let's head towards the town.'

The friends linked arms once more and set off to find the public conveniences. Outside again Peaches said, 'I'll be glad when this one comes and I can have some fun again. Fancy coming to Brighton with me once I get my figure back? I can't wait to get some new things.'

'Let me make you something,' said Dottie.

'Be nice if we could all go shopping though, wouldn't it?' Peaches remarked.

'Count me in,' said Mary.

'You're on,' said Dottie with a smile.

'How come you haven't got any kids, Dottie?' asked Mary. 'Doesn't Reg want any?'

Dottie felt her face colour. 'It just never happened,' she faltered.

'Oh darlin', I'm sorry,' said Mary. 'Me and my big mouth.'

'It's all right,' Dottie quickly reassured her.

'My cousin Nelly was like that,' said Peaches. 'In the end she went to the doctor and he said she and her husband wasn't doing it right.'

'What the 'ell were they doing then?' said Mary, agog.

'Just touching navels.'

There was a moment of silence then Mary said, 'Was that all?'

They all burst out laughing.

'Perhaps your Reg needs some coaching,' said Mary, giving Dottie a hefty nudge.

'You volunteering?' grinned Dottie and they all laughed a third time.

'What about cousin Nelly?' Mary asked.

'Whatever the doc said to them worked,' said Peaches. 'They've got three kids now.'

'All the spitting image of the doctor,' roared Mary. Peaches enjoyed the joke, laughing heartily. Thank goodness they *didn't* know about Doctor Fitzgerald, thought Dottie as she joined in. Thankfully the subject of babies, and the lack of them, didn't come up again.

'Here we are,' said Mary as they found the shops.

They wandered around Woolworths and Peaches bought herself a bottle of Lily of the Valley. Mary got each of her brood and Gary a 3D stick of rock with 'Littlehampton' printed through it to take home. 'Clever how they do that,' she remarked.

Dottie bought a new comb for Reg.

Reg flipped through the pages of the *Littlehampton Gazette*. Nothing much there. He was just about to fold it up when Connie tottered towards him, a long candlestick of mucus and sand hanging from the end of her nose.

Alarmed, he cried, 'Tom!'

'Cor, love a duck,' said Tom as he saw her.

Lifting her half-filled bucket towards her father, she said, 'Eat tend cakey, Daddy.'

'Hang on a minute, sweetheart, let Daddy clean you up first.' With the practised hand of an expert, her father put one hand on the top of her blonde head to hold her steady while he fumbled in his pocket for his handkerchief. Connie sneezed and the candlestick grew longer.

Jack, who was cuddling Gary on his lap, laughed aloud. Reg shuddered with disgust.

'Tend cakey, Daddy?' Connie said as her face emerged from under the voluminous handkerchief.

'I'd love to,' said Tom, pretending to take a piece. 'Ummm, delicious. Don't forget your Uncle Jack and Uncle Reg.'

'Yum, yum,' said Jack obligingly.

Connie turned towards Reg. 'Not for me,' he said quickly.

Tom ruffled the child's hair. 'Uncle Reg is full up,' he said. 'But I could eat *you* up!' He growled and, snatching her in his arms, he kissed her neck. Connie giggled happily and when he put her down again she wandered back to the area of sand which served as her kitchen.

'Not up to sand pie, Reg?' Tom said good-naturedly.

'Looking after kids is woman's work,' Reg muttered.

'Rubbish,' said Tom. 'I love being with all my kids. I'm a dab hand at changing a nappy too.'

Reg shook his paper disapprovingly and hid behind it again. Thank God Patsy was well past that stage. His lip curled at the thought of changing nappies, and as for dealing with snotty noses . . . You'd better keep well away from me, thought Reg sourly. But a couple of minutes later, the little brat was on her way back. Reg glanced around helplessly. The other two men were gone: Tom was doing something with Christopher and Jack was walking Gary towards the sea where the other kids were splashing about at the water's edge.

'Clear off,' Reg hissed.

But Connie was on a mission. Holding out her bucket of sand, she struggled to steady herself, tottered and made a grab at his trousers. She stumbled against him and fell. At the same time, Reg noticed a wasp crawling along the sand nearby. As Connie pulled herself to her feet again, Reg glanced around to make sure nobody was watching him, and then gave Connie a good shove with his leg. She sat down heavily on top of the wasp. A few seconds later, her heart-rending screams brought the others running.

By the time the girls got back, the kids were sitting further down the beach, watching a Punch and Judy show. Billy had his arm around Connie who was sporting a large white bandage on her leg. Mary listened in horror as Tom explained about the wasp.

'Good job the St John Ambulance people were so close,' he said, pointing to the first aid post a little way along the beach.

'Poor little mite,' said Dottie. 'Couldn't you have stopped her?'

'She fell,' said Reg, re-arranging the knots in the handkerchief on the top of his head. 'Couldn't do a thing about it, love.'

The Punch and Judy show over, Gary was looking very listless again.

'I think you'd better take him to see Dr Fitzgerald tomorrow, hen,' Mary told Peaches.

Peaches nodded miserably.

'Get Dottie to run over and fetch him when we get back,' Reg suggested.

Dottie turned her head away. Oh God, she couldn't possibly face Dr Fitzgerald again. Not after last Saturday night. Whatever was she going to do?

'You'll go and get the doc for Peaches, won't you love?' Reg insisted.

She turned her head and everyone was looking at her. 'Yes, yes, of course I will.'

They arrived back in the village at six thirty. Jack dropped Reg off at the Jolly Farmer and then went on to Mary's place. It took a while to get all her sleepy kids off the back of the lorry, but they all called out their goodbyes.

'It's been a wonderful day, hen,' Mary told Peaches. 'Now don't you worry about your Gary. He'll be all right.'

Jack took Dottie, Peaches and Gary home. The little boy kept whimpering as if he was in pain and Jack had to carry him indoors. As soon as they were safely inside, Dottie and Jack drove to the doctor's.

'You'll wait for me?' she asked.

'Of course,' he smiled.

Dottie was relieved. She'd been frantic with worry. She didn't really want to face the doctor again. Not so soon. But she couldn't refuse a friend, could she? Not when her child was so sick.

She drew some comfort from hearing the engine still running as she walked up the garden path to the big house. Dottie rang the doorbell and waved to Jack. All at once, he drove off. She almost panicked and ran after him, crying, 'Come back . . .' but then she realised he was only turning the lorry around. She turned to face the door. The glass panel grew dark and she knew someone was coming.

It was Mrs Fitzgerald. 'Dottie!'

'I'm sorry to bother you, Mrs Fitzgerald,' Dottie began, 'but is the doctor here?'

'He's not on call today,' Mrs Fitzgerald said crisply. 'You'll have to go to Dr Bailey over at Heene Road.'

'Who is it?' said a voice behind Mrs Fitzgerald.

'It's Dottie.'

'It's all right,' said Dottie quickly. She could hear Jack's lorry drawing up outside the gate again. 'We'll go to Dr Bailey.'

Dr Fitzgerald snatched opened the door and Dottie jumped. She couldn't look at him in the eye and was immediately tongue-tied. 'I didn't know it was your day off . . . um . . . I wouldn't have . . .'

'Is it your Reg?' he asked all businesslike and formal.

'It's little Gary Smith,' Dottie gabbled. 'Peaches and Jack are really worried. We thought it was just a cold and a bit of sunshine would do him good so we've been to the beach all day at Littlehampton. He's been too poorly even to join in with all the other kids.'

'I'll get the car,' said the doctor.

'It's your day off,' Mariah reminded him.

'Don't trouble yourself,' said Dottie at the same time. 'Jack's here. He'll run us over to Heene Road.'

'I'll just get my bag,' Dr Fitzgerald insisted.

Dottie hurried back up the path. She wanted to get into the lorry before the doctor suggested taking her as passenger in the car. Jack was leaning anxiously out of the cab. 'He's coming,' she said, swinging open the door and climbing in beside him.

'Thank God for that,' said Jack with feeling.

Dr Fitzgerald followed them to number thirty-four where Jack and Peaches lived. It made Dottie feel uncomfortable knowing that he was right behind them. She'd have to deal with this. She had to find a way of making it clear that his advances were totally unwelcome, and then they would both know where they stood.

'You will come in with us, won't you, Dottie?' said Jack as they pulled up outside.

'Well . . .' Dottie began.

'Peaches would be glad of a friend.'

When they all got inside the house, Gary was already in bed. Dr Fitzgerald, Peaches and Jack went upstairs and while they were all gone, Dottie busied herself making some tea for when they all came down. After a few minutes, she heard Peaches cry out, 'Oh no, *no!*'

Dottie dropped the lid of the teapot and raced upstairs, her heart pounding with fear.

Peaches was sobbing in Jack's arms. Little Gary was lying very still on the top of his bed while Dr Fitzgerald was pulling down his pyjama top. For one awful second, Dottie feared the worst, but then she saw Gary move his arm very slightly. 'I'll go back home and telephone for the ambulance,' Doctor Fitzgerald was saying.

'What is it? What's happened?' Dottie gasped.

'I'm going with him,' said Peaches.

'I'm afraid that will be impossible, Mrs Smith,' said Dr Fitzgerald, shaking his head. 'Not in your condition.'

'But I'm his mother!' Peaches wailed.

'What's wrong with him?' said Dottie looking wildly from one to the other.

Dr Fitzgerald closed his bag with a loud snap. 'I'm not one hundred percent sure,' he said, 'but it looks to me like poliomyelitis.'

# *Eight*

Billy didn't have the energy to run all the way back to Aunt Peaches. He was much too tired.

It had been a grand day. Memories of the Punch and Judy show, paddling in the water and that huge ice cream Uncle Jack had given him kept going over and over in his mind. It had been his best day ever. Even better than the day Phil Hartwell let him hold the dead frog his cat had killed.

It was late. It was already way past his bedtime when Mum came back downstairs after she'd put the twins and Susan to bed and said, 'Run over to your Aunt Peaches and find out how Gary is.'

He'd said, 'Aw, Mum,' but he'd known it was no use arguing. Tom looked at him over the top of his evening paper. He didn't say anything. He didn't need to: the look was enough. Billy walked as fast as he could all the way there without stopping.

Uncle Jack's lorry was parked outside the house and the cab door was wide open. The doctor's car was there too. And right in front of the house, there was an ambulance as well. Billy hung back. If the adults saw him, they'd be bound to send him back home again.

'This is no place for nippers,' Uncle Jack would say.

The ambulance door was wide open too. Billy could see the bed and all sorts of boxes and things. He tried imagining what it was like to be an ambulance driver. It was bound to be exciting.

He might see squashed people . . . that would be better than a squashed frog the cat killed any day. He sat down on the kerb and gripped an imaginary steering wheel.

'Neee-arrr,' he said as he careered around the corner at top speed to save his patient.

He heard the front door open. Dr Fitzgerald came out with his doctor's bag and the ambulance man, dressed in his dark uniform and cap, followed him. The ambulance man was carrying someone in his arms. The someone was all wrapped up in a blanket and although Billy couldn't actually see who it was, judging by the way he was screaming, and the fact that Aunt Peaches was right behind him crying her eyes out, he knew it had to be Gary.

Auntie Dot came out and gave Aunt Peaches a kiss on the cheek. 'Try not to worry,' she said. He liked Auntie Dottie a lot. She was nice.

He thought back to the time when they'd paddled in the sea together. He'd been wearing his knitted cossie. Auntie Dottie didn't have one but she had picked up her skirts and walked into the water until it was right up to her knees. No other grown up had done that. And she hadn't minded getting wet either. She'd kicked the water all over him and when he'd done the same to her, she didn't get cross and yell at him. She'd splashed him back and she'd laughed. He liked to hear Auntie Dottie laugh. She didn't do it very much but when she did, her whole face lit up. He could tell by the anxious look on her face now that she wasn't very happy.

'You will stay with him, won't you?' Aunt Peaches wailed. 'He'll be so frightened.'

'I'll stay as long as they let me,' Auntie Dottie promised. 'The ambulance man says they have very strict visiting hours, but I'll be there until they kick me out.'

'I should be there,' cried Aunt Peaches. 'I'm his mother.'

Auntie Dottie hugged her again. 'You have the little one to think of. Now leave Gary to me. Until he's back on his feet, I'll be his mum.'

Aunt Peaches blew her nose in her hanky. 'I don't know what I'd do without you, Dottie.'

'Don't be daft,' smiled Dottie. 'What are friends for?'

Uncle Jack appeared behind her. 'I'll follow the ambulance in the lorry and bring Dottie home.'

'Come along now, Madam,' said the ambulance driver. 'The sooner we get him to hospital the better.'

'Someone ought to tell Mary,' Dottie said as she climbed into the back of the ambulance.

Billy stood up and ran to the open door. 'I'll tell me mum, Auntie Dot.' But the other ambulance man pushed him away. 'Off you go now, sonny. This is no place for you.'

'Tell your mum Gary is in hospital,' Auntie Dot called to him. 'Tell her he's got poliomyelitis.' The ambulance man shut the door, banged it twice and walked round to the front and climbed into the driver's seat.

Billy watched as the ambulance raced down the road, its bell ringing like mad. He was confused. What was that she said? Polo-my-light-us? What was that?

Aunt Peaches was going back into the house.

'What shall I say is wrong with Gary, Aunt Peaches?'

'Gary is very ill,' sniffed Peaches. She put her handkerchief to her mouth and closed the door. A second later, it opened again. 'And don't you come round again. It's too dangerous. And tell your mum, none of your family is to come either.'

Billy stared at the closed door. Why couldn't he go to Aunt Peaches? What had he done wrong? He turned and walked down the road scuffing his shoes and trying to work it out.

'Hey-up, Billy. You coming on the swings?'

It was Paul Dore on his bike. He pulled up beside Billy.

'I got to go home,' said Billy miserably. His mum would go spare when he told her he'd upset Aunt Peaches. He'd get a walloping for sure.

'Aw, come on,' Paul cajoled. 'I'll give you a lift on me bike.'

It didn't take much to persuade Billy to put off the moment he faced his mum. When they got to the playground, they didn't have a swing, that was for babies, but the scrubland along the edges of the park was great for a game of Cowboys and Indians.

There was a whole crowd of them there including Mark and David Weaver. Everyone wanted to hear about his day on the beach.

'Lucky devil,' said David as he told them about the Punch and Judy man and his big ice cream. 'Bags I'm John Wayne.'

'It's my turn,' said Mark.

'You did it last time,' Billy protested.

In the end, Billy's day out was forgotten as they had a scrap about who was going to be John Wayne and David Weaver won. Then they whooped around the bushes shooting Indians until it began to get cold and the light was failing. Paul Dore gave Billy a lift back on his handlebars as far as the road next to his and Billy, knowing that he was bound to be in trouble, walked slowly home.

'Where the devil have you been?' his mother demanded as she opened the door. She clipped his ear as he walked past. 'I've been worried sick.'

'Gary's gone to hospital,' said Billy quickly. 'He's got . . .' He froze. He couldn't remember what it was called. 'And Aunt Peaches said none of us should come to her house ever again and she was so upset about it, she sent Auntie Dottie off in the ambulance with him.'

His mother put her hand to her throat. 'Don't tell me he's got polio,' she said quietly.

The isolation hospital was rather grim. It smelled of carbolic soap and disinfectant and it was dimly lit because most of the patients were asleep. Dottie followed the nurse who wheeled Gary onto the ward on an adult-sized stretcher. He looked so small and vulnerable. Wordlessly, they took him to a cot and the nurse drew the curtains around him, leaving Dottie on the outside.

'Are you the child's mother?'

Dottie shook her head at the doctor who had walked up behind her. 'His mother is eight months pregnant,' she explained. 'Her doctor was worried about infection so he told her not to come. I'm a close friend.' The hospital doctor said nothing. 'Gary's father is here,' Dottie went on. 'He's parking the lorry.'

The doctor parted the curtain and went inside. Gary was whimpering.

'If you would like to wait outside,' said Sister, pulling little white cuffs over the rolled-up sleeves of her dark blue uniform. 'I'll come and speak to you later.'

Behind the curtain, Gary, obviously in pain, began to cry.

Dottie hesitated. 'I promised his mother I'd hold his hand,' she said anxiously.

'We have to examine him,' Sister said, 'and the doctor will have to give him a lumbar puncture. It's not very pleasant, I'm afraid, but it has to be done. We need to know what we're up against. Now if you would like to wait outside . . .'

It was as much as Dottie could do to fight back the tears as she waited in the corridor for Jack to arrive. She stared hard at the green and cream tiled walls and the brown linoleum floors until she thought she knew every crack. Beyond the peeling brown door Gary's cries grew more heart-rending. Jack hurried towards her, turning his cap around and around in his hand anxiously.

'How is he?'

Dottie shook her head. 'The doctor's with him now.'

Jack sat beside her and ran his fingers through his hair. 'Oh God, oh God . . .'

She put her hand on his forearm. 'Try to keep calm, Jack,' she said gently. 'They're doing their best.'

'Yes, yes, I know,' he said brokenly. 'Oh Dottie, that boy is my life. I don't know what I'd do if I lost him.'

Mercifully, at that moment they heard Gary stop crying.

'Don't go thinking like that, Jack. He's a tough little lad. He'll pull through.'

Jack leaned further forward and wept silently. Dottie placed her hand in the centre of his back and did her best to fight her own tears. After having such a lovely day, she couldn't believe this was happening. If Reg were here, even he would be upset.

They waited for what seemed like a lifetime until the brown door opened and the ward sister came out. 'Are you the child's father?'

Jack rose to his feet, and wiped the end of his nose on his jacket sleeve. 'Yes.'

'There's no point in beating around the bush and there's no easy way to say this but I'm afraid your son definitely has polio.'

Jack flung his arms around himself, squeezed his eyes tightly and turned away.

'What happens now?' Dottie asked. It cut her to the quick to see how hurt Jack was, but Peaches would want to know every last detail.

'It's best if you leave him now,' the sister said matter-of-factly. 'Mum can visit him in a week or so.'

'*A week or so?*' cried Dottie.

'We keep visits to a minimum,' the sister continued. 'Normally we would allow his mother to see him for twenty minutes or thereabouts, but as you say, she's pregnant.'

'I could take her place,' Dottie said, 'at least until his mum is in no danger.'

'At this highly infectious stage,' the sister went on, 'it's best for the patients to remain calm. Family visits are very unsettling for young children. They cry for hours afterwards.'

'Can we at least see him now?' Dottie asked. 'I want to put his mother's mind at rest.'

'Is he going to die?' Jack choked.

'It's always possible,' the sister said, 'but personally I think he'll be more stable in a day or two.'

'Please God,' Jack murmured.

'I tell you what,' said the sister, her tone softening, 'pop in now, just for a minute to see him settled and you,' indicating Dottie, 'can visit him on Monday.'

Dottie couldn't hide her gratitude. 'Thank you, oh thank you.'

'But when you do come, it can only be for twenty minutes,' the nurse cautioned. 'No more.'

'I understand,' said Dottie gratefully.

They followed her back onto the ward and tiptoed to Gary's cot. His eyes were closed and although his face wore a frown, he certainly looked more peaceful than when they'd brought him in. He was still very flushed and a young nurse was sponging his face with water.

The sister picked up the temperature chart at the foot of the bed. 'His temperature is one hundred and four degrees fahrenheit,' she said.

Dottie touched Gary's fingers. 'Night, night, darling,' she whispered. 'See you in the morning.'

Jack leaned over the cot and kissed his son's forehead. 'Night, son,' he wept.

Gary started to cry again.

'Come along now,' said the sister briskly. 'It's best not to upset the little lad again.'

# Nine

It was quarter to ten when Dottie finally got home. As Jack dropped her off at the gate, she saw Ann Pearce's curtain twitch. Nosy old cow, she thought irritably. She'd probably think she could get even more money out of her now. That last time . . . it was blackmail, wasn't it?

As Dottie walked indoors, Reg scowled. For one sickening second, Dottie thought Ann might have been round and told him about Dr Fitzgerald.

'How long does it bloody take to go to the doctor's house and ask him for a visit?' he demanded. 'I've been waiting for hours for my tea.'

'They took little Gary to hospital,' she said.

Reg's expression changed. 'Hospital?'

Dottie slipped off her bolero and reached for her wrap-over apron. 'I'm afraid Gary has been admitted.'

Reg lowered himself into a chair. 'Admitted . . .'

'It's a bit late for cooking,' Dottie said matter-of-factly. She was angry that he'd sat there all that time, helplessly waiting for her to come home. Couldn't he have got his own tea for once? 'Shall I do you a couple of fried eggs?'

He nodded and she set about gathering the frying pan, the eggs from the bucket of cold water on the scullery floor and the dripping from the meat safe.

'What's wrong with him?'

Heartened that Reg was so concerned, she forgave him immediately.

'He has polio,' she said, cracking an egg over the melted dripping in the pan. 'But they seemed to think he'll be a bit better in a day or two.' She filled the kettle with water and put it on the gas.

'Peaches staying with him, is she?'

'No,' said Dottie. 'They wouldn't allow it. It's too dangerous, what with her being pregnant and all. That's why I went.'

His eyes flashed. 'You?'

She cut a slice of bread and put it into the hot fat. 'And I promised Peaches I would visit him until she's allowed to go.'

'You're not to go.'

'Although how I'm going to fit it all in I don't know,' she said turning the bread over.

'I said,' his tone was harsh, 'you're not to go.'

She gave him a puzzled look. 'But I promised.'

'I don't bloody care! You're not going.'

She put the eggs and fried bread onto his plate and put it in front of him. Then she filled the teapot and sat at the table with him. She wanted to throw the supper at him. She'd have given anything to scream at him, 'I'll make my own decisions and I don't need you to tell me what to do.' But she knew she had to tackle this calmly. He was getting wound up and if she upset him too much, he'd be horrible for days.

'Look, Reg,' she said quietly. 'I know you're worried about me, but really, I don't think I'll come to any harm and Peaches is upset that Gary won't have anyone he knows.'

He glared at her and stabbed the air with his fork. 'I don't care about bloody Peaches. I'm telling you now, you're not going and there's an end to it.' A splatter of egg yolk ran down his chin.

'But she's my friend.'

He carried on eating. She poured his tea and one for herself.

75

She had to make him understand just how important this was. She didn't have many friends around here and Peaches was one of the best. She'd been there for her when Auntie Bessie died. She and Mary had virtually done the whole of her wake: Dottie had been in such a state, and Reg wasn't much help, so she'd been glad to leave it to them. Their friendship went way, way back. Peaches, Mary and Sylvie had kept her going for many a long and lonely month while she'd waited for news of Reg during the war. Other women had been allowed to write to their husbands but Reg had been on a top-secret mission so she had to wait it out with no word from him at all. Peaches, Mary and Sylvie had been there for her which was why it was so important not to let Peaches down in this, her hour of need.

'Reg,' she tried again, 'don't worry. I'll be perfectly safe.'

He slammed his knife and fork onto the plate, making her jump. Then he leaned back and, reaching into his pocket, drew out a piece of paper.

'No, it's not bloody safe,' he cried. 'And there's the reason why you can't go.'

He threw the paper onto the table in front of her. Dottie's heartbeat quickened. The letter from Australia! She'd forgotten all about it. She'd had what Aunt Bessie would have called a presentiment that it wasn't just any old letter the moment she first set eyes on it. Now it rested on the table between them, small and rectangular, and yet it seemed as big as a house.

She stared at the sloping handwriting, the stamp and the strange postmark, and her blood ran cold. This must be serious, but what on earth did it say? She shivered and looked up at her husband.

'Well, go on,' he said with a note of triumph in his voice. 'Read it. I know you're dying to.'

Her hand was trembling as she picked it up. So flimsy and yet heavy with destiny. It was going to change her life, she knew it . . . she just knew it.

She took it out and read it slowly. *I never told you but in '43 I had a child. Her name is Patricia. She's eight now.* Her eyes filled with tears and she swallowed hard. 1943? He had been with some other woman almost as soon as they had been married? He'd been sent abroad just four weeks after their wedding and straight after that, the very next year, he'd been unfaithful?

*Please come to fetch her,* she read on, *I hope that deep down, you can find it in your heart to forgive me . . .* She laid the letter on the table and looked up at him. He was smiling.

'See?' he said triumphantly. 'You think I can't bloody do it, but I can see? I've got a kid of my own. She gave me a kid. She knew how to turn a man on. She knew what to do. Not like you, you bloody cold fish.'

His words cut her into a thousand pieces but all she could think of was that he had had a child with another woman. He had a child . . . and she didn't. Why couldn't he make love with her? Other people thought she was attractive but he was always calling her a cold fish, even though she really tried. She did everything he wanted her to, even things she didn't like.

'For God's sake, stop that snivelling,' he said sharply and Dottie suddenly realised that she was crying. She reached into her apron pocket and pulled out her hanky. Then she blew her nose quietly and dabbed her eyes. She shouldn't have done that. It must have been the shock of seeing Gary.

'I want to get her over here,' he was saying. 'I want my little girl here, living with us.'

'Living with us?' she said faintly.

'Why not?' he challenged. 'She's mine. Why shouldn't I have her here?'

Dottie stared at him, her brain refusing to function. This was all too much for one day. Foolishly she'd always thought he'd been as faithful as she'd been. It never crossed her mind that he'd even had the opportunity. No, she hadn't thought about it.

She'd just presumed . . . but how wrong had she been? He had a child, a daughter. And now he wanted her to come over here?

Her stomach churned. All at once she felt sick and jumped up and ran to heave over the slop bucket in the scullery.

'That's right,' he bellowed after her. 'Always got to be the centre of attention. Get yourself noticed. Let's have the drama queen.'

She steadied herself and wiped her mouth on her hanky, then she walked back into the kitchen.

He was sitting with one hand on his head and the other holding the photograph. 'I want her here, Dot,' he said. 'I want my little girl.'

She couldn't speak. She wanted to be happy for him, but his joy was her misery. He didn't seem to care about how she was feeling. She couldn't think straight. Her eye was drawn to the woman in the photograph.

'Don't you see, you daft bat?' he said looking up at her. 'This is your chance too. You've always wanted to be a mother. Well, now's your chance. A little girl. Patsy. Nice name, Patsy. We'll be a family.'

'But I want a family of my own!' she blurted out.

Reg leapt to his feet and struck her across the mouth. Dottie tasted blood as her lip split under the force of his blow. 'Maybe this is the closest you're going to get,' he snarled. 'I can do it with a real woman, but I can't do it with you. I can't do it in this house. Doesn't that tell you something? Eh?'

Dottie leaned against the dresser, utterly crushed.

'We're going to get my baby over here,' Reg said sitting back down again with the photograph, 'and we're going to be a real family. Me, Patsy and you.'

Dottie opened her mouth but no sound came out.

He turned and glared at her again. 'That's why I don't want you going near that Gary see? I can't have my Patsy getting polio.'

78

# Ten

'You're very quiet today, Dottie.'

Janet Cooper, Dottie's Monday and Tuesday employer, gave her a concerned look as she filled the kettle for their afternoon break.

Dottie had been miles away. She couldn't get the events of the previous weekend out of her mind. Worried about little Gary and upset by Reg's revelations and rantings, she had gone about her work as quickly and as quietly as she could. She hadn't stopped for her mid-morning break, neither had she stopped to eat the sandwich Janet had prepared for her as she closed the shop for the lunch hour. Dottie didn't want to be drawn into a conversation in case she said something she might later regret. She was glad today was Monday and not Tuesday. Dottie helped in the shop on Tuesdays and it was easy to be drawn into long conversations between customers. Janet loved a little gossip. Starved of excitement in her own life, she thrived on the misfortunes of others and had a clever way of weeding juicy bits of gossip out of someone, no matter how reluctant the person might be to part with them. Had it been Tuesday, Dottie would have told her about their day in Littlehampton and little Gary's illness and, before the day was over, it would have been all over the village. Fine if Peaches told friends and neighbours, but Dottie didn't want people to hear it from her lips first.

Janet cut across her thoughts again. 'I see Ellen Riley's daughter is on the bottle again.'

Dottie gave her a quizzical look.

'There was a definite bulge in her coat pocket when she came into the shop this morning,' said Janet, clearly enjoying her tasty morsel of gossip. 'Want a biscuit with your tea?'

Dottie shook her head and wished Janet a million miles away.

'It's the kids I feel sorry for,' Janet went on. 'If you can't be a responsible parent, you shouldn't have children, that's what I say.'

Dottie switched off. Monday was the day she cleaned the Cooper house from top to bottom. Upstairs, she changed the beds, hoovered the rooms and dusted. Then she'd come down and spend the rest of the morning putting the dirty sheets in the washing machine. You had to stand over it when everything went through the wringer, but it was a great help and if the weather was kind she would end the day by ironing the same sheets she had changed in the morning.

With the washing on the line, the afternoon was spent cleaning and dusting downstairs. It was one of her heaviest days and yet with the weight of everything on her mind, she hardly noticed the time passing.

She'd been up early that morning. Reg was still in bed when she'd left for the Coopers. After another outburst about not seeing Gary the night before, she had poured him his usual cup of tea in the morning, but instead of making sure he was awake, she'd crept upstairs, being careful not to disturb him. She'd left the tea on the bedside table. He'd groaned and rolled over when she put the cup down and she'd panicked, but she stood very still and almost immediately he'd begun to snore again. Dottie hurried downstairs and out of the house. She didn't want . . . couldn't face talking to him again. Why did she always take him a cup of tea anyway? It had started when he first came home.

He was ill then. He was fine now. Well, he could get his own tea from now on, she told herself defiantly.

All day long she'd gone over and over the things he'd said and she was surprised to realise that, for the first time in her whole life, she resented the idea of looking after someone else's child. If Patsy was already eight, there was no way she could pretend the child was hers. What was she going to say to the people in the village? She hated the thought of everybody talking behind her back.

'Of course, you know that poor Dot Cox can't have any children.'

Dottie bristled at the thought of being an object of pity.

'Can't blame a man for wanting his own child, can you?' they'd say.

And what about the child? When she had been conceived, she and Reg were already married. Everyone would know he'd been with another woman. War or no war, what sort of a man goes with another woman within a year of his marriage? What did that say about her? And what about the child herself? Poor little thing. She didn't ask to be born, did she?

'Dottie . . .' Janet said.

Dottie frowned. She refused to feel sorry for the child. Why should she? But while she was ironing, she found herself wondering what she looked like. Reg had black hair but only out of a bottle to hide the grey. The woman in the picture was fair. She imagined Patsy all peaches and cream, a little Shirley Temple with pretty blonde curls, who smelled of talcum powder and Gibbs toothpaste. Dottie folded and shook a sheet viciously and banged the iron down on it. She had to stop doing this. She didn't want her. She didn't want Reg's kid. She wanted her own child. And another thing, why should he rant and rave on like that, expecting her to like the idea? She'd be nothing more than an unpaid servant. She was his wife, for goodness' sake. Why should she open her home to his . . . his bastard!

'Dottie!' Janet Cooper's voice brought her abruptly back to the present. 'You've ironed that sheet to death. Sugar in your tea?'

'Er, no. I'm sorry,' Dottie said. 'I was miles away.'

'So I see,' smiled Janet. 'Nothing serious, I hope?'

'I was wondering . . .' Dottie began hesitantly, 'would it be possible for me to go early today?'

Janet Cooper looked at the clock. Normally her cleaner left at four. It was now ten to three. She frowned. Dottie didn't usually ask favours but she'd have to be careful. Give these people an inch . . . the last thing she wanted was Dottie taking liberties.

'I came in at eight instead of nine,' Dottie pointed out, 'and I haven't taken any breaks.'

Janet hesitated. 'Is it Reg?' she asked.

Dottie chewed her bottom lip. She didn't like telling lies but she could see by her face that Janet Cooper needed a good reason to let her go. 'Yes.'

'Oh my dear, why didn't you say so? Of course you must go. We can't do too much for those of our brave boys who came back. Yes, put the rest of that ironing away and off you go.'

Fifteen minutes later, Dottie, feeling somewhat ashamed and guilty, was hurrying to the next village. Durrington was easily a mile and a half away and she decided not to catch the bus that stopped outside the shops. She didn't want anyone from the village telling Reg they'd seen her catching the bus. It was a bit of a rush, but she was fit and knew she could do it.

'How was the trip to Littlehampton, Reg?'

Marney handed him a chipped enamel mug of tea. Reg was acting as ticket collector today, although there were few passengers on a weekday afternoon. He put the steaming mug to his lips and slurped in a mouthful of tea. 'Not bad.'

'Kids enjoy themselves?'

'Reckon so.'

'The wife wanted me to take her over for the torchlight procession and the fireworks,' Marney went on, 'but our Jean and her hubby came by. We all got chatting and then it was too late. Was it good?'

'We were back before 8.30,' said Reg. 'Mary's boy wasn't looking too clever, so Peaches and Jack took him to the doc's.'

'Shame,' said Marney. 'All right now, is he?'

'Suppose so,' Reg shrugged.

'A bit of a fuss about nothing, I expect,' Marney observed. 'It usually is where kids are concerned.'

Reg grunted.

'Still,' Marney ploughed on, 'I expect Dottie enjoyed herself.' Reg gave him a puzzled look. 'Well, the girls like a bit of a get-together, don't they? Have a bit of a chat and a laugh. It does them good.'

They could hear the 3.32 in the distance and Marney turned to go. The door of the ticket office clicked shut behind him, leaving Reg alone on the platform. He frowned. Another day out? Oh, no. Of one thing he was perfectly sure, he wasn't going to be putting up with another day like that in a hurry. He only agreed to it to butter Dottie up. Well, enough was enough. From now on, Dottie would have to understand that her place was in the home, not gadding about with the likes of Peaches and that fat cow Mary.

As the 3.32 was pulling onto the platform of West Worthing station, Dottie was heading into the Isolation Hospital.

'Visiting hours are 2 to 2.30,' said the sister haughtily as Dottie arrived. The clock hanging on the wall behind her said a damning 3.25.

Her heart sank. 'But I couldn't possibly come then,' she said. 'Please let me see him. Just for a moment.'

'I'm sorry, but it's against the rules,' said the sister. She began to walk away.

'Sister, his mother isn't able to come because she's expecting,' Dottie called after her. 'She's relying on me to help her out. I've been at work all day and I've had no meal breaks whatsoever in order to make sure I could get here to see Gary. Please. I can't let his mother down.'

The sister pursed her lips and gave Dottie an irritated frown. 'This is most irregular,' she sighed. 'The child has only just stopped crying. I'm not sure that a visit will be in his best interest.'

'I would hate him to think we've abandoned him.'

The sister gave Dottie a long hard stare. 'Very well.'

Dottie smiled with relief. 'Thank you, Sister.'

'But only five minutes and it mustn't happen again.'

'Of course. I understand,' said Dottie. 'How is he?'

'He's making progress,' said the nurse. 'Hopefully we can start his rehabilitation with the other children by the end of the week.' She pointed down the ward. 'He's down there, next to the girl in the iron lung.'

Dottie hurried down the ward. In daylight, the ward seemed even gloomier than she'd remembered from the Saturday before. The dark green and cream paintwork was pretty cheerless and some of the tiles on the walls were cracked and chipped. But at least somebody had made an effort: although the curtains at the windows were dark blue and faded at the edges, the curtains on the screens that went around the beds had bright nursery rhyme pictures on them.

There seemed to be few toys. Of the children who were sitting up in bed, some were reading comics and others simply stared at her as she walked down the ward. One little girl standing at the end of her cot held her arms out as Dottie walked past.

Gary was as white as a ghost but he seemed more peaceful than before. He saw her coming and whimpered, 'I want my mummy.'

His plaintive cry tore at Dottie's heart. She touched his

forehead and brushed back his damp hair. 'I know, sweetheart, I know. Mummy can't come today, so she sent me instead.'

Gary's chin quivered.

Dottie reached into her bag and drew out two small bears wrapped in dark blue tissue paper. She had bought them the previous year when the whole country had been captivated by the story of Ivy and Brumas and early that morning she'd sneaked them out of their hiding place.

In 1949, Ivy, a polar bear at the London zoo, had surprised everyone by giving birth to a son, Brumas. The following Christmas, just about every child in the land had an Ivy and Brumas bear in their stocking. Dottie had bought a pair, and after wrapping them in tissue paper she had put them in Aunt Bessie's wardrobe alongside Aunt Bessie's cowboy hats and boots, and all the other things she couldn't bear to throw away.

Dottie had always imagined that one day she would put the bears in the cot of her own baby but after what Reg said last Saturday, that day seemed too far away to matter. She realised that if Reg knew about them, he would make her give them to his child and she wasn't prepared to do that. No, she'd sooner give them to someone more deserving and in the present circumstances, who could be more needy than Gary?

He watched her unwrap the bears. 'Where's my mummy?' he whimpered again and a tear rolled down his cheek.

'Mummy can't come today,' said Dottie gently as she put both bears on the bed. 'But Mummy told me she misses you very much.' She was willing her voice not to break. 'So I'll tell you what I'll do.' She fondled Gary's hair again. 'I'm going to give Brumas to you to cuddle and I'm going to put Ivy down here at the end of the bed.'

As Gary tried in vain to move his head in the direction of the bear, the full extent of his paralysis became a chilling reality. Dottie bit back her own tears.

'Ivy loves Brumas very much,' she went on, 'just like your

mummy loves you. She'll be watching Brumas all the time, see?'

She placed the larger bear in his direct line of vision.

'You look after Brumas and all the time you see Ivy watching him, you'll know your mummy is thinking about you too.'

She lifted his limp arm and placed Brumas next to his body. 'Is Ivy watching him?'

'Yes,' Gary whimpered.

'See?' said Dottie. 'Ivy is watching Brumas so your mummy must be thinking about you.'

Gary looked up and gave her a weak smile.

'Sister says it's time to go,' said a young nurse, coming up to them. 'We have got to get all these children ready for bed.'

It was a ridiculous statement, but Dottie knew what she meant. She leaned forward to kiss Gary goodbye but the nurse held her shoulder. 'No. Not too close.'

Dottie kissed her own fingers and touched Gary's forehead. 'I'll come back as soon as I can, darling.' The lump forming in her throat felt like it would choke her. She had to keep strong. She mustn't let Gary see her cry. 'Mummy will come along another day.'

She left him watching Ivy. 'Thank you, Nurse,' she said as they reached the door.

'No,' said the nurse, taking a furtive glance over her shoulder, 'thank you. I'm sure he'll be much happier now. That was a nice thing you did.' And with a rustle of her starched apron, she was gone.

Dottie made her way outside, her whole body racked with sobs. As she stood in the bus shelter, she wiped her eyes and blew her nose. Poor little lamb. Just three years old and not allowed to see his mummy. It wasn't fair. What was going to happen to him?

'Dear Lord,' she prayed through her tears, 'don't let him be paralysed all his life.'

86

The bus came and she got on. Thankfully she couldn't see anyone she knew. As she looked out of the window, she allowed herself a small smile as she recalled Brumas under the sheet and Ivy watching him. She'd go round and tell Peaches all about it later this evening when Reg had gone to the pub. It wasn't much but it would certainly put her friend's mind at rest. Careful that she mustn't do anything to let Reg know where she'd been, Dottie got off two stops before she needed and walked the rest of the way home. The fresh air gave her a chance to clear her head and to compose herself.

# Eleven

It was a mad rush to get the tea ready before Reg got home and the potatoes still needed another ten minutes when Dottie saw him parking his bike against the wall. She wondered what sort of a mood he was in; but she needn't have worried. He was feeling cheerful. He handed her a bunch of sweet peas.

'Ooh, Reg!' She couldn't hide her surprise. He seldom gave her the flowers from his station garden, preferring instead to hand them out to his passengers. In between his station duties, he'd built up a reputation as an expert nurseryman, cultivating flowers and even a few vegetables on the strip of land alongside the station ticket office, and collecting a great many ardent admirers along the way. It was well known in the village that if you had a gardening problem, Reg was the man to ask.

She held them to her nose and sniffed them loudly. 'They're lovely.'

'The fence is covered,' he said proudly. 'A really nice show this year.'

He sat in his chair and took off his railwayman's boots, then went upstairs. A few minutes later he came down in his gardening clothes. 'Just going out to dig a few spuds,' he said. 'Dinner nearly ready?'

'Five more minutes,' she said as she arranged the sweet peas in a vase. Their heady perfume filled the kitchen and she could

88

tell they were his prize blooms by their big, perfectly formed petals. They were the talk of the village.

'No one can grow sweet peas like your Reg.'

'He ought to go enter the flower show with those blooms.'

'Magnificent. What's his secret?'

She was back in the scullery putting the runner beans in a colander when she heard a footfall outside the back door.

'I'm just dishing up, Reg,' she called.

'Dottie, it's me.'

Dottie swung round to find Peaches in the doorway. She looked drained. Her face was pale and she wore no make-up. There were dark circles under her eyes. 'I'm sorry to burst in on you like this, but Jack and I couldn't wait. How is he? Did he look any better?'

Dottie grabbed her arm and pulled her inside. She'd have to be quick. She have to say her piece before Reg came back up the garden.

'What's she bloody doing here?' He was already sitting at the kitchen table. He rose to his feet. 'Get out of here, Peaches Smith. You're not welcome.'

Peaches stared at him aghast. 'Not welcome . . .?' she said faintly.

'No . . .' Dottie began. 'What Reg means . . .'

But Reg stepped between them, pushing Dottie aside. 'Look, no offence,' he said, his tone a little less harsh, 'but Dottie's afraid she'll get it, see?'

'Wait, Reg . . .' Dottie protested.

Peaches gave her a stricken look.

'Listen, Peaches . . .' Dottie gasped. 'Let me explain.'

But before Dottie could start, Reg had taken Peaches' arm and was manoeuvring her back through the door. 'It's best if you don't come round for a while.'

Peaches stared at him. 'Why are you doing this?'

'Hang on a minute . . .' Dottie began again.

Peaches rounded on Dottie. 'You promised to go and see my Gary today. Didn't you go?'

Dottie saw Reg's back stiffen and her heart almost stopped. What was she going to do now? If she said yes, he would have one of his moods. If she said no, Peaches would be distraught. For a second, her brain refused to function. Think, she told herself desperately, think. Say something. Say the right thing. They were both facing her now, one staring at her with a helpless expression and the other with that dark look in his eye.

'Look, Dottie can't help the way she feels,' said Reg, his eyes unmoving as they stared into her face. His words soft and measured.

'But you did go and see him, didn't you, Dottie? You saw my baby?'

Dottie turned away. She lowered herself into a chair. She'd have to lie. To placate Reg, she'd have to lie. She'd go round to Peaches later, like she planned, and she'd explain why she had to do it. Peaches would understand.

'Dottie?'

'I'm afraid Reg is right,' Dottie said quietly. 'I didn't go.'

'But you promised,' Peaches wailed. 'My poor baby. All alone . . .'

'It's not that she doesn't care for the boy,' Reg said, his voice as smooth as silk.

'Oh yes,' said Peaches her voice turning brittle, 'everybody cares.' She snatched her arm away from Reg. 'If I'd known you weren't going,' she shouted at Dottie's bowed head, 'I could have arranged for my mother to go. At least then my Gary would have had *somebody* with him. I'll never forgive you for this, Dottie. Never.'

As she swept out of the back door, Dottie put her hands over her face and closed her eyes.

'Don't upset yourself, Dot. It was for the best,' Reg said as they heard the front gate banging shut. 'You did it for my Patsy.'

'Patsy, your Patsy,' Dottie burst out. 'You don't even know when she's coming. Australia is thousands of miles away.'

'She's coming.'

'Even the boat takes six weeks.'

90

'She's coming, I tell you.'

'And how are we going to get the money to get her here?'

Reg clenched and unclenched his fists. 'I'll get the money.'

Dottie blew her nose into her handkerchief. 'Peaches is my best friend.'

'And I'm your bloody husband,' he said sharply. He banged his fist on the table, making all the plates rattle. The sauce bottle fell over. 'Now stop this bloody racket and let's be having our tea.'

'Where d'you want it, Reg?'

Half an hour later, Michael Gilbert's cheery shout brought an angry and red-eyed Dottie from the scullery where she was washing the dishes.

'Hello, Michael.' She wiped her hands on her apron. 'What are you doing here?'

He gave her a long look and she knew he was wondering why she'd been crying. 'Reg asked me to bring some bales of hay round. You all right, Dottie?'

Michael was fond of Dottie. She joined the Land Girls on his father's farm in 1941. The Ministry of Fisheries and Food had already sent some local girls, Peaches Taylor, now Smith, Hilary Dolton-Walker (she'd ended up in Canada, he thought), Sylvie Draycot (she'd married a banker called McDonald, and lived in the New Forest somewhere) and Mary had done her bit too. There were others who came and went and he'd be hard put to recall either their names or faces, except Molly Dawson of course. She stuck out in his mind only because she'd been killed in an air raid while home on leave in Coventry. As a kid, whenever he'd looked at Dottie, he got a funny feeling at the pit of his stomach. He'd never understood it of course, but he'd made up his mind that one day he'd marry her. However, when she was eighteen and he was still only fourteen, she went and married Reg Cox. He didn't think of her in that way any more, but he was fond of her, like a sister. He didn't like to see her upset.

Dottie smiled, her eyes willing him not to ask any more questions. 'Reg is upstairs getting ready to go out.'

'Oh no, I'm not, my darling,' said Reg coming up behind her. 'I'm staying in tonight. We've got to get something sorted out about that bloody pig, haven't we?'

Dottie's heart sank. She'd been planning to run over to Peaches' house as soon as Reg left for the Jolly Farmer.

'Bring the rest of the bales down the garden, will you, Michael?' said Reg pushing past her and grabbing the first bale from Michael's hands. 'I reckon a dozen will do me. Got the chicken wire?'

Michael nodded. 'On the back of the trailer.' He lingered a second or two. Dottie was aware that he was looking at her but she wouldn't meet his gaze. 'I'll be right there.'

Silently, Dottie went back to the bowl to finish the washing up. Perhaps, she thought to herself, she could pop out while they were busy up the garden; but Reg soon put paid to that.

'When you've finished that, put the kettle on, Dot,' he called cheerfully over his shoulder. 'Michael looks like a man dying of thirst.'

The two men set to work making a pen at one end of the chicken run for the pig but first they shut the chickens in the henhouse and put the pig on a rope tied to the old apple tree. When Dottie walked up the garden with two cups of tea, Reg was missing.

'Where is he?' she asked Michael furtively.

'In the lavvy.'

Michael was at the back of the newly made pig run banging in the wooden posts. Dottie sidled up to him.

'Listen, Michael, do me a favour, will you?' She heard the bolt slide back on the lavatory door. Michael carried on banging. 'It'll take too long to explain,' she whispered urgently. 'Would you tell Peaches not to say anything to Reg but tell her I did go?'

Michael stopped banging. He readjusted a pin in his mouth and said, 'You what?'

She glanced nervously over her shoulder and realised it was too late. Reg was already coming back up the path.

'I'm sorry, Dottie,' said Michael. 'I missed that. What did you say?'

'Do you have sugar in your tea? I can't remember.'

He gave her a quizzical look. 'No thanks.'

Reg took his cup and Dottie returned to the house. She went upstairs and looked out of the window. Michael was helping Reg staple the chicken wire onto the posts. Did she have time to get over to Peaches? She could if she got her bike out, but the bike was in the shed, and Reg would see her going in there. She'd just made up her mind to chance it when Reg spotted her at the window and shouted, 'Bring us another cup of tea, Dot.'

Downstairs in the scullery again, Dottie wiped away her angry tears. Everything was going wrong. Reg wanted her to have his child and yet he didn't want her. She had upset her best friend and if she didn't explain everything to Peaches as soon as possible, she'd never repair the damage done. And on top of all that, there would be another row when she told Reg about Sylvie coming.

Twelve thousand miles away, Brenda Nichols shielded her eyes from the sun's glare with her hand as she watched the Flying Doctor's plane bank and circle the homestead. As it finally came in to land, the red earth exploded into a cloud of hot dry dust, which set up a swirling trail behind it.

Their radio call had been very specific. 'We have to make Muloorina before nightfall. Can you make sure everybody's ready to meet the doctor on the airstrip? Over.'

Brenda pressed the control button. 'This is 8 EM. Everyone is here, Doc. I have five patients for you. Baby Christopher Patterson for a Salk inoculation, little Mandy Dickson wants some cough medicine because her chest is bad again, Taffy Knowles needs you to look at his toe. He reckons a snake bit him but I think he's got an ingrowing toenail. Dick Rawlings has a cut in his finger that will need a couple of stitches and Mick Saul has another ear infection. Shall I have some tea ready for you? Over.'

'Right on, Bren.' She could hear the smile in his voice. 'Out.'

The plane taxied towards them and came to a stop. They all waited for a few minutes before the door opened and Doc Landers, wearing his now familiar brown Tyrolean hat, given to him by a grateful patient, climbed onto the steps.

Brenda had put a white sheet over the table on the veranda and it was here that the doctor set up his makeshift surgery. As usual Brenda's diagnoses were correct and it didn't take him long to dish out the medicine and insert a few stitches into the cut. As soon as he'd finished he sank back into a chair and Brenda put the kettle on.

The homestead in the Australian outback was a far cry from her nursing job in England where she had risen to the position of sister at the Royal Victoria Hospital in Boscombe. Never one to rest on her laurels, Brenda had joined the army and travelled to the Far East. When war broke out, she was in Singapore and the trouble in Europe seemed a million miles away. She had been lucky enough to fall in love with Burt Nichols in '41, a year before the Japanese overran the colony and she was safely in his hometown of Murnpeowie celebrating her marriage when the advancing forces trapped the rest of her friends and colleagues. Because they'd both come through the war unscathed, Brenda was a great believer in luck.

She thought her luck had run out when Burt got ill so soon after their return, but then she found the homestead, where they now eked out a living. Brenda put the teapot down in front of him. 'How's your mum, Doc?'

'Going for more tests.'

'Sounds ominous?' She pushed a cup of tea in front of him.

'Nobody's saying much but it sounds to me like she won't be able to take care of herself for much longer.'

'Oh, I'm real sorry about that, Doc. Does this mean you'll be leaving?'

'I'll hang around a while longer and see what the results are first.'

Brenda handed him a big piece of her legendary Victoria sponge cake. 'Did you bring any post for me, Doc?'

'A few bits and pieces,' he smiled. 'Bills mostly.'

Brenda pursed her lips. 'Nothing from England?'

The doctor shook his head. 'Definitely nothing from there.' He leaned forwards and patted her arm. 'Save yourself the trouble of worrying, Brenda. You'll never hear from that bloke again.'

'I can't let it go, Doc,' said Brenda. 'I promised the kid's mother.'

'What are we talking about?' asked Alf the pilot as he pushed his plate forward for a piece of Brenda's cake. 'Or is it private?'

'Brenda's looking after a little kid. She belonged to a friend of hers who died. She's trying to trace the kid's father.'

Alf pulled a face. 'Local, is he?'

'A British Tommy,' said Brenda. 'Got her in the family way in '42. I've got the name and address of a pub where they used to meet.'

'Blimey,' said Alf. 'What makes you think he'd even want the kid after all this time?'

'I dunno,' said Brenda. 'Maybe he won't. I don't think he's ever seen her but I just wanted to do what's right by her, that's all.'

'How long since you wrote?' asked Alf, sticking his mug out for some more tea.

'Five weeks.' She looked at the Doctor. 'That's time enough for a reply isn't it, Doc?'

'I should think so. He obviously doesn't want to know. Forget it, Bren. You've done your best.'

Brenda went to the window where she could see the children swarming around the plane. 'I can't, Doc. I promised.'

'Why don't you and Burt keep her? You both love kids.'

'I'd let her stay here, Doc, you know that, but what sort of a chance will she have around here? And besides, I have to think of my own. You told me yourself my Burt is only going to get worse. When he's gone, I'll have four to look after on my own. I can't take care of Sandy's girl, no matter how much I want to.'

'You can always put her in a home,' Alf said.

'I don't want to do that if I can help it,' Brenda sighed. 'The kid should be with her own. If I can't do anything else for Sandy, I can at least try to get her kid back with her father.'

'You've got a big heart, Bren,' said Alf admiringly.

'The war's been over for six years,' said the doctor, standing up and picking up his bag. 'How d'you know he wasn't killed somewhere?'

'Or that he's married someone else,' said Alf.

Brenda looked down at her feet. Those were both possibilities, she knew that, but something deep down inside her told her she still had to try.

They walked out to the landing strip together and the kids scattered like rabbits.

'Which one is she?'

'The little one with the ribbon in her hair,' Brenda said.

'Sweet kid,' said Alf. 'Thanks for the tea.'

'If you do hear from her dad, be careful,' Doc Landers cautioned. 'She's had a lot to contend with, what with her mother dying and all. Don't raise her hopes too high.'

'I won't,' said Brenda. 'All the best, Doc. I hope your mum turns out to be all right.'

Doc Landers gave her a mock salute.

'Best of luck,' Alf called as he closed the plane door.

Grim-faced, Brenda nodded. She knew only too well that if she were going to find Patricia a home of her own, she was going to need all the luck in the world.

# Twelve

Mrs Fitzgerald was out. She'd left a note on the kitchen table. *Dottie, give the doctor his coffee after surgery. There's some cold meat and salad in the fridge for his lunch. The downstairs windows need cleaning. M.F.*

Dottie's stomach went into an immediate knot. That meant that once surgery was over, she'd be alone in the house with Dr Fitzgerald. Apart from when he saw Gary the day he got sick, Dottie had avoided him. She couldn't risk a recurrence of what had happened when he'd given her a lift back home the night of Josephine's wedding. She had dreaded being on her own with him again, but now she had no choice.

As she went about her work, she was rehearsing over and over in her mind what she would say when she finally came face to face with him. Would he try it on again? No, he was drunk the night of the wedding. He probably regretted what he'd done. But then the thought of his podgy fingers groping around under her skirt and his whisky-saturated breath in her face came flooding back, making her feel sick.

The house was back to normal after the wedding. Keith was back in boarding school and all Miss Josephine's things had been sent to her new house in Fittleworth. In fact, her old bedroom was being converted into another guest room. Mrs Fitzgerald had chosen pale yellow walls to contrast with the new fabric she had bought in London, a bold geometric design of white 'hourglass' shapes, shot through with black on a red background. It was bang up-to-date. Ever since the Festival of Britain, contemporary lines, bright colours and geometric designs had become all the rage.

She'd asked Dottie to make a bedspread, eiderdown, curtains with tiebacks and a blind for the window, all in the same material. To Dottie, the fabric was amazing and she couldn't wait to begin work on it. She rubbed it between her fingers, loving just the feel of it. After so long using utility material or 'making-do-and-mending', it would be a real treat to cut into a fabric which had never been used for anything else before, a fabric at the height of fashion and at the forefront of modern design.

Thrilled to bits that Mariah was going to trust her with something so lovely, Dottie was determined to prove she could do a fantastic job. Mariah usually had her curtains and other furnishings done by Bentalls, so this was Dottie's big chance. Mariah had discovered Dottie's talents about six weeks ago when she'd popped round to the cottage to collect a couple of jars of jam she had been promised for her mother. Dottie invited her in, and Mariah had been amazed by the transformation in Aunt Bessie's cottage.

'Where did you buy these curtains?' she'd exclaimed. 'And that bolster cushion . . . and the fire-screen . . .?'

When Dottie confessed to making them, Mariah had found it hard to believe, but now she was confident enough in Dottie's abilities to ask her to refurbish Miss Josephine's old room. The only trouble was, she wanted it finished in time for her brother's yearly visit at the end of September.

'I'm afraid it will take a bit longer than that,' Dottie told her firmly.

Mariah had threatened to go elsewhere, but Dottie was no fool. Sending away for the job would mean they would have to send someone around to measure up (these big firms never believed your own measurements), and relying on the post. All that would take twice as long and probably cost her three times as much. In the end, they'd agreed that the room would be finished by October 11th at the latest.

Once the master bedroom had been cleaned, Dottie left the linoleum along the landing. There seemed little point in polishing it. The decorators were coming in tomorrow to start on the yellow walls and they'd be tramping back and forth.

When she got back downstairs, Dottie glanced at the clock. 10.35. The morning surgery must be nearly over. She'd make a start on the windows downstairs and then she could keep an eye on the waiting room at the same time. The doctor would want his morning coffee before he went out on his rounds.

The waiting room for the surgery was on the side of the house, so there was no need for patients to come to the house itself. They could walk up the driveway and go straight into the waiting room. The doctor would call in the next patient as the previous patient went out. It was up to Dottie to guess when surgery was finished, but before she went in she would also have to take the added precaution of listening at the connecting door between the house and the surgery to make sure no one was still in there having a consultation.

She was outside washing the windows when she saw old Sam Taylor coming down the driveway. Dottie smiled at the aged road sweeper. Out in all weathers, old Sam was a regular visitor to the surgery, especially in the winter when his cough got bad.

'Glad I seen you, m'dear,' said Sam cheerily and Dottie came down the small stepladder. 'Will you thank your Reg for me?'

Dottie was puzzled. 'What for?'

'For the tatters. He left a bag on my doorstep.'

Reg often did things for people. It was his one redeeming feature. 'Yes, yes of course.'

The old man patted Dottie's hand. 'Good man, your Reg.'

'Any more left in the surgery, Sam?' she smiled.

'Just Mrs Reid,' said Sam touching the front of his cap politely. 'She be the last.'

Dottie put down her cloth and walked indoors. She'd already poured some Camp Coffee into a cup and the milk was in the saucepan. Trying to ignore the growing tightness in her stomach, she watched it boil and then poured it onto the dark liquid, stirring vigorously. He had one sugar – she'd worked there long enough to know that – but she put the sugar bowl onto a small tray covered with a tray cloth rather than adding it herself.

As she waited outside the connecting door, she heard low voices before Mrs Reid said, 'Thank you very much, Doctor.'

The surgery door closed and Dottie knocked softly.

'Come in.'

Brisk and business-like, Dottie swept in with the tray.

'Dottie!' She was a little unsure of the tone of his voice but her throat tightened as he rose to his feet, pen in hand. Dottie laid the tray on the desk in front of him and stepped back smartly.

'I think you should know, someone saw you trying to kiss me on the night of your daughter's wedding,' she said coldly.

She saw the colour drain from his face and he glanced anxiously at the waiting room door. He was obviously worried that Mrs Reid might overhear them but Dottie wasn't too concerned. Mrs Reid was as deaf as a post. He looked back at her and seemed surprised by her boldness.

'Dottie, I want to explain . . .' he began, his voice soft and his eyes lowered.

'Touch me again,' she glared, 'and me and my witness will be round to see PC Kipling.'

He stared like a startled rabbit caught in the glare of a car's headlamps and swallowed hard.

She turned on her heel and, head held high, she swept back out of the room, and closed the door quietly. Once outside in the corridor, however, her knees began to shake and she was trembling all over. She waited a second or two until her rapid heartbeat calmed a little. A slow smile crept across her face and she closed her eyes with relief. There, that should do it. Crisis over. The dirty old basket valued his reputation in the village too much to try it on again.

'Seventy pounds!'

Reg's brow was furrowed yet again. Dottie sighed. Earlier, with Michael Gilbert's wedding less than a week away, she'd asked him if Sylvie could come, but she'd obviously chosen the wrong moment. Just as she'd feared, he'd flatly refused.

They were out in the garden in the warm evening and Reg was gathering the last of the runner beans; he planned to leave the rest to mature into seeds for next year. He had just been saying that it had been a reasonable year for the garden, despite the weather, and Dottie chose this moment to say what else was on her mind.

'That's what I said, the fare to Australia is seventy pounds.'

Dottie was picking the first blackberries from the wild branches which grew at the very end of the garden. The ground beyond the brambles was kept fallow because years of using the same few feet of land over and over again had made it unusable.

Reg stopped picking the beans and came from between the rows to stand in front of her. 'Have you been talking about my business with someone?' he challenged.

'No . . .' Dottie protested. He moved his head on one side and she knew he didn't believe her. 'Reg, I promise you I haven't said anything,' Dottie continued, 'It's just that in her letter Sylvie was talking about a friend of theirs who is going over to Australia on the ten-pound passage. She was saying what a brave thing it was and how it was a wonderful opportunity to go all that way for just ten pounds, so when I wrote back, I asked her how much the real fare was and she said seventy pounds.'

Reg looked at her, expressionless. He said nothing so Dottie ploughed on. She had to make him see how impossible his dream was going to be. 'It's going to cost us that much to get Patricia over here.'

'Then we'll save for it,' he said.

'And how long is that going to take us?' she cried desperately.

'It'll take as long as it takes!'

As she watched him striding back up the garden with the beans in his arms, her heart sank. She didn't know what to feel any more, she was so mixed up. She could see his frustration and there were times, like now, when she felt a twinge of sympathy for him, but nothing altered the fact that she didn't want this child in her home. She sighed. She'd have to talk to him again . . . make him understand how she felt. It had taken a lot of courage to stand up to Dr Fitzgerald, but she'd done it. She smiled to herself as she recalled the look on his face. Well, if she could stand up to a man like him, she could stand up to Reg. He wouldn't like it, and it wouldn't be very easy, but she'd have to try. Full of determination, Dottie picked up her bowlful of blackberries and followed him back to the house.

Reg was a man of few words; he always had been. Sylvie always said he was 'all buttoned up' but up until now Dottie had accepted that talking about things wasn't his way. At times he seemed to relish being awkward. She could put up with his moods – they didn't happen too often – but it was harder to deal with the silences and the sulks.

As she reached the back door she could see him through the kitchen window, sitting at the kitchen table with his head in his hands. She paused and all at once it hit her. This was breaking his heart. He'd had so little in life before she met him. He'd been abandoned as a child, he'd told her. He'd never known a mother's love. When Dottie had said she'd go out with him, he'd been the perfect gent. Even though Aunt Bessie never liked him, he always treated her right and he was keen to be part of the family. Look how excited he'd been on their wedding day, running around the whole house and telling her this was the first time he'd had his own home. As they lay in bed in that little guesthouse in Eastbourne, they'd talked about having children. She was being selfish, wasn't she? Just because she couldn't have children didn't alter the fact that he had a child, a child without a mother on the other side of the world, and it was breaking his heart. How could she do this to him? Just because she couldn't have what she wanted, should she deny her husband the one thing that would make him happy? All right, it upset her to think about Elizabeth Johns with Reg, but she could get over it and perhaps he was right. If Patsy came, they'd be a family at last.

Dottie smiled as a picture of Patsy formed in her mind. She'd be wearing a little gingham dress, blue and white with a pretty gathered skirt and white Peter Pan collar. She'd have white socks and a ribbon in her hair.

Reg glanced up and saw her smiling. 'What are you staring at?' he said acidly. 'Having a good laugh at my expense, are you?'

She hurried inside. 'No, Reg,' she protested. 'I was trying to imagine what Patsy looks like. Oh Reg, I'm sorry. I've been a selfish cow. We'll save up for her. We'll work all the hours God sends until we get the money.'

He rose to his feet, his whole face enveloped with a smile. 'D'you really mean it, Dot?'

'Yes, dear, of course I do.'

He took her into his arms and hugged her. Dottie snuggled into his wiry embrace. Why couldn't it be like this more often? 'But first we have to talk,' she went on.

He pushed her away, roughly. 'Oh, I might have guessed there'd be a catch.'

'It's not that,' she said, 'but we've got to make a good story for the people around here.'

'Story?' he thundered. 'What are you talking about? She's my kid, simple as that.'

'Fine,' said Dottie, 'but how's she going to feel when everyone knows she's Reg Cox's bastard?'

His face paled and he sat back down. She laid her hand over his. 'We've got to make something up, something everyone can believe, but something that won't hurt her.' She sat opposite him and waited but he seemed to have been struck dumb. 'I think the simpler we make it the better,' she went on. 'Let's just tell people we wanted to adopt a child and a friend in Australia has found us one.'

'What if the welfare people come snooping?'

'Let them,' said Dottie. 'As long as you make sure they send over all her papers with her it'll be fine. You'll have her birth certificate with your name on it, won't you? If anyone says anything, you'll be able to prove she's yours.'

'Then it'll still get out,' said Reg gloomily. 'One of them might talk and it'll be all over the village in no time.'

'I don't see why,' said Dottie. 'The welfare people aren't supposed to talk about other people's private business and, besides, once you show them you're her legal father, they'll have no reason to gossip about her, will they? As long as you don't show them our wedding certificate they'll probably assume Elizabeth Johns was your first wife. We can tell Patsy the whole story as soon as she's old enough to understand.'

'You've got it all worked out, haven't you?' he said with a sneer.

'I've done a bit of thinking, that's all. One thing puzzles me though.'

He looked up, startled.

'Was she Australian?'

'Who?'

'Elizabeth Johns. Was she from Australia? I mean, what was she doing in Burma?'

'She worked in the NAAFI,' Reg said quickly. He turned away quickly and reached for his newspaper. Blimey, he hadn't thought she'd start trying to work things out.

'In the NAAFI?' said Dottie. 'What, in Burma?'

'Leave it out, Dot,' snapped Reg. 'You know what those memories do to me.'

'Yes, I'm sorry.'

They sat for a moment without saying anything. Dottie watched him rubbing the back of his hand in an agitated way. 'I met her in India, if you must know,' he said. 'I was taken there when I was ill, remember?'

The explanation didn't really satisfy her. She wanted to ask more. What was an Australian woman doing in India? How did he meet her? What was she like? But he'd put the paper up in front of his face.

She touched his hand. 'I didn't mean to upset you, Reg. Everything will be fine.'

'Course it will,' he said, relaxing.

'Good,' said Dottie. 'Now all we've got to worry about is getting the money together for the fare.'

'I've already got that worked out,' said Reg. 'The pig can go to market. That'll fetch a bob or two. Michael Gilbert says it might fetch a tenner if we leave it till Christmas, but we've still got to feed it.'

'Reg,' Dottie said, 'we need seventy pounds.'

His face fell again.

'But you're right. We'll manage,' she said quickly. 'I've got a bit saved.'

'You?' He sounded really surprised.

She nodded. 'I've got seventeen pounds saved.' And I would have had another ten bob, she thought ruefully, if I hadn't had to pay Ann Pearce for her silence.

'Seventeen quid,' Reg gasped. 'Where did you get that kind of money from?'

'I sold some of my sewing.'

'Somebody paid you for that stupid rubbish?'

She willed herself to stay calm. 'Well, they didn't think it was rubbish when they bought it,' she said indignantly, 'and I got seventeen pounds for my trouble.'

'Pah!' he said scornfully. 'Some people have more money than sense.'

'Seventeen pounds is still a long way from seventy,' she said, glad that she hadn't told him about the fifty-four pounds she'd got in her Post Office savings bank.

'What about your friend Sylvie?' he went on. 'Can't you butter her up for a loan?'

Dottie paused. 'Well, I don't know when I shall see her again, do I?' she said cautiously. 'It's not the sort of thing you write in a letter, is it?'

Reg shrugged and picked up his paper again, shaking it irritably. Grabbing the runner beans, she took them outside into the scullery to start preparing them to bottle.

'All right then,' he called out. 'Tell Sylvie she can come.'

'Thanks, Reg,' she called back, willing her voice to stay level. 'I can ask her about the money when she comes.'

'Just for the one night, mind,' he added acidly. 'I don't want her cluttering up the place for days on end.'

Smiling to herself, Dottie licked the end of her finger and drew it down in front of her.

Dottie one, Reg nil.

# *Thirteen*

Dottie decided not to argue with Reg about Sylvie's length of stay . . . for now. As soon as he'd gone off to the pub on Sunday evening, she sat down and wrote back to Sylvie, inviting her to come Friday 7th and stay over until Sunday afternoon. As she licked down the envelope, Dottie could hardly contain her excitement.

Ann Pearce was leaning on the gate as Dottie came back from the post box.

'My gas has gone out again,' she said. 'I wondered if you might have a couple of quid spare.'

Dottie looked at her coldly. 'No, I haven't.'

'My kids will go hungry if I don't get some money,' Ann called after her receding back. 'I wouldn't want to have to take them to the doctor, would I? And you never know, if they go hungry all the time, they might get ill.'

Dottie stopped walking. This was getting beyond a joke. 'No.'

'I'd have no choice then,' Ann went on. 'I'd have to go to the doctor.'

Dottie took in her breath as she turned around slowly. Ann was staring defiantly at her, her head up and a sneer on her lips.

'Why are you doing this?' Dottie demanded. 'If you want help, ask for it.'

'I don't need your charity,' retorted Ann.

'Fine.'

Dottie turned away but plainly Ann wasn't ready to see her go.

'I'll tell the whole world about you, Mrs Bloody Perfect who isn't so perfect any more.'

Something inside Dottie snapped. 'If you're trying to scare me,' she spat, 'you're doing a pretty poor job of it. I've done nothing to be ashamed of.'

'Paid up pretty darned quick last time, didn't you?' said Ann. 'I'd hardly call that the actions of an innocent party.'

'If you want to go to Dr Fitzgerald, that's fine,' said Dottie walking back. 'I've just seen him off and I'll do the same with you.'

'Seen him off,' said Ann. 'Don't make me laugh.'

'You'll not get another penny out of me.' Dottie willed her voice not to quaver although her blood was already thumping so loudly in her ears, she felt as if the whole village could hear it.

'You bitch!' Ann shrieked.

Dottie was caught by surprise as the other woman grabbed hold of her hair. Her bun disintegrated almost immediately as Ann tugged at it with all her might. The gate was still between them but Ann mounted the bottom rung as the two of them wrestled. The pain in Dottie's head was almost unbearable. She desperately tried to prise Ann's fingers away but they seemed to be becoming more and more entwined.

By now the pair of them were screaming at the tops of their voices. Most of it was incoherent, but the occasional 'Bitch!' and 'Sodding liar!' came from Ann and 'Let go, you cow . . .' from Dottie.

The fight came to an abrupt end when Dottie managed to slap Ann across her the side of her face, which made her lose her balance. As Dottie pulled away, Ann toppled over the gate and landed in a heap in the road.

Breathless, Dottie stepped back, her head throbbing with pain and her hair spilling all over her face and shoulders like a wild woman's.

To complete her surprise, instead of jumping up and coming for her again, Ann burst into tears. For a second, Dottie was tempted to leave her but something kept her rooted to the spot, although she felt it wise to keep her distance. She was nervous that if she bent over Ann she might grab her hair and start the fight all over again. She looked around helplessly.

There was nobody was in sight. Dottie thought she saw a curtain move in the house opposite, where Vera Carter lived, but nobody came out. When she looked at Ann's house, she was horrified to see two tearstained faces staring out of the sitting room window. Ann's little children, Brian and Phyllis, made a pathetic sight. Dressed only in grubby and holey vests, their little shoulders heaved up and down as, racked with sobs, they stared at their mother sitting in the road.

Dottie closed her eyes with shame. What a thing for the children to see. Their mother and her neighbour brawling in the street like a couple of tomcats.

'Get up, Ann.'

Ann hit her hand away.

'Ann, your kiddies are watching you,' said Dottie quietly. 'Let me help you up.'

Ann struggled to her feet and Dottie helped her.

'Do you really need money that badly?' Dottie asked.

'I can't go on much longer,' Ann wept. Her guard was well and truly down. 'I get virtually nothing from the welfare. I can't get a job because there's no one to look after the kids.' She fumbled up her sleeve for a handkerchief and then blew her nose. 'You haven't a bloody clue, have you? I watch you and Mary and Peaches Smith swanning around in your pretty dresses and all you lot do is kick a dog when it's down.'

'When did I do that?' cried Dottie.

'When you reported me,' said Ann, obviously sensing the upper hand.

'But I didn't!' Dottie cried. She bit her lip. Obviously Ann

109

didn't know it was Reg who'd reported her. As far as Dottie could see, he'd done it out of spite.

'When Lennie cleared off back to his wife,' Ann went on. 'Me and the kids was left with nothing.'

'I'll lend you some money.'

But Ann wasn't listening. 'What did it matter to anybody what I was doing anyway?' She was in full swing now. 'The kids were fed and well looked after. Lennie and me was happy. We might have even got married if we could have saved up for the divorce.' She covered her face with the handkerchief.

'I'm sorry,' said Dottie. 'I didn't know.'

It was getting dark. Reg would be back home in a minute. She glanced up the road anxiously. He'd go bananas if he saw them talking together.

Ann blew her nose again and, tugging at the front of her dress, she turned towards her house, mustering what little dignity she could.

Back in her own cottage, Dottie opened her tin of savings and took out five one-pound notes. That would keep Ann going for a bit. Damn Reg and his principles. She grabbed a couple of jars of jam from the dresser and stuffed some runner beans into a brown paper bag.

As she scraped her hair back into an untidy bun, she thought better of the jam and beans. If she rushed next door laden with all that stuff, Ann would probably slam the door in her face. After all, she had her pride.

A little later when she knocked on Ann's door she heard the scampering of little feet and Brian opened the door. The grubby vest was all he was wearing.

'Hello, Brian, is Mummy there?'

Ann appeared behind him. She looked startled. 'Go in the sitting room with Phyllis, Brian,' she said sharply.

His eyes grew wide with fear and he hurried off.

'What do you want?' said Ann coldly.

'Look,' said Dottie. 'I really am sorry.' She reached for Ann's hand and pressed the rolled-up notes in it.

Ann looked down and her face flamed with colour. 'I told you, I don't want your charity.'

'It's not charity,' said Dottie. 'It's a loan. Pay me back when you can.'

'What will Reg say?'

'What Reg doesn't know, can't hurt him,' said Dottie turning to leave.

'Dottie . . .' Ann called after her.

Dottie turned. Ann's eyes were filled with tears and her chin was quivering. 'Thank you,' she choked.

# *Fourteen*

Late the following Friday afternoon, Dottie was drumming her fingers at the kitchen table. She'd been like a cat on a hot brick all day. She'd got up very early, swept the house, dusted everywhere, gone over all the rugs with the Bex-Bissell and then gone to work at the Fitzgeralds'. She'd arranged with Mariah to have the afternoon off because today was the day Sylvie was coming. Michael Gilbert's wedding was tomorrow.

Mariah had grudgingly given her the time off, but remarked that she hoped Dottie would find time over the weekend to do some more of the furnishings. Dottie couldn't wait to show Sylvie what she was doing.

Back home by lunchtime, Dottie got out the best tablecloth and her best china. A few late roses made the room smell nice and the table looked perfect, even if she did say so herself. After that, she'd started fiddling. There was a loose thread on the curtain that needed sewing in. The cushions on the easy chairs needed plumping up and once she'd done that, she thought it would be better if the floral cushion was on top of the plain one; but when she sat down at the table again, she decided the floral cushion looked a bit flash, and it would look better the other way around.

Dottie had been so excited about her friend coming. She had prepared the second bedroom with great care. The sheets on the single bed were ironed with knife-edge creases. She'd given Sylvie her best patchwork counterpane, the one she'd spent two years making, and she'd polished the sideboard to distraction. It was nowhere near the standard her friend was used to but Sylvie was never one to put on airs and graces. She may have come from a well-to-do background, but she never flaunted it.

As usual Dottie had used every spare minute she had preparing fruit and vegetables for jams and chutney. Her store cupboard boasted a large stock of plum jam, rhubarb and ginger jam, marrow and ginger jam, raspberry, blackcurrant and gooseberry jams and now she was concentrating on chutneys. She'd already prepared some marrow chutney and soon she'd be looking for the ingredients and enough jam jars to make elderberry chutney.

Her recipes weren't as good as her aunt's and rationing meant it was still hard to get the other ingredients she needed, but she could often get a few extra coupons from friends with the promise of a jar of something to come. She decorated each batch with matching jam pot covers, using any oddment of material too small to use for anything else.

She glanced at the clock. Sylvie would be here soon. The postman pushed a second-post letter through the letterbox and she jumped a mile high.

It was another letter from Australia, addressed to Reg. It was a bit fatter than last time and although she held it up to the light it was impossible to see what was inside.

A car horn tooted outside. Dottie jumped and took in her breath excitedly. 'That's Sylvie,' she said out loud, even though she was alone in the house. 'She's here.'

Dottie ran outside where Sylvie's black Humber almost filled the narrow road. As Sylvie stepped out of the car, she looked so elegant she almost took Dottie's breath away. She was wearing an emerald green dress with a wide collar with scalloped edges which lay on her shoulders. The bodice was tight over her still perfect figure and at the waist she wore a small belt. Her shoes were doe-coloured, as was the clutch bag she leaned into the car to retrieve from the passenger seat. Her auburn hair was topped by a small green hat covered in layers of green tulle and as she walked towards Dottie, her petticoats rustled under her voluminous calf-length skirts.

'Dottie, darling!' The two women embraced warmly. 'It's so good to see you again. You're looking well.'

'And you look fantastic,' Dottie laughed.

Sylvie linked her arm through hers and they walked indoors. 'I love this little house,' Sylvie said as she walked up the path, but then she gasped as she stepped over the threshold. 'Oh my goodness, Dottie! What have you done?' She turned to look at her. 'It was really sweet when your aunt was alive, but now you've made it look absolutely wonderful.'

She gazed around, taking in the neat chairs with their crisp backs, the open fireplace filled with autumn flowers and the table with its embroidered tablecloth and pretty tea service. Sylvie walked over to the dresser with its jams and chutneys, and began examining the labels.

'Have you done all these yourself? Wherever do you find the time?'

Dottie was delighted that Sylvie was so impressed. 'You must take something back with you when you go,' she said as she absentmindedly put the letter for Reg on the table. 'Tea?'

'Yes please,' said Sylvie. 'I'm gasping.'

Dottie put on the gas. The water was almost ready – in fact she'd already boiled it at least three times in anticipation of her friend's arrival.

'Where is Reg?' asked Sylvie, opening her bag and taking out an elegant cigarette holder.

'He's working until six,' Dottie called from the scullery.

'Oh good,' said Sylvie. 'That gives us plenty of time for girl talk.'

Dottie giggled. She re-emerged with the teapot and put in on the cork tablemat before covering it with a cosy. As she sat down

114

opposite her friend, Sylvie reached out and touched her hand. 'It's so good to see you again.'

Dottie looked down at Sylvie's long bronze-tipped fingernails and smooth hands and smiled shyly. 'And you.'

'So tell me,' said Sylvie lighting up her Craven A, 'How's tricks? No sign of a family yet?'

Dottie busied herself with the tea. 'Not yet,' she said quietly. 'How are your children?'

'Growing like weeds,' said Sylvie, her face lighting up. 'Hugh is seven now and off to prep school soon. Rosemary is five and a little pickle. Robin can't do enough for them. There's one thing I'll say for him, Robin has been an amazing father.'

'So you're really happy then,' said Dottie pushing the cup and saucer in front of her.

'I think so.'

Dottie laughed. 'Only think so?'

Sylvie shrugged. 'You know how it is, darling. You long for Prince Charming and finally he comes along. You get married and settle down and have his children but you always wonder if there isn't a bit more to life.' She chuckled at Dottie's confusion. 'Don't get me wrong, darling. I still love Robin. I get a bit bored, that's all.'

Dottie placed an ashtray in front of her and they sipped their tea. 'I've told Michael and Mary that you're coming.'

'I can't wait to see them,' smiled Sylvie. 'How are they?'

'Mary is all right. Still trying to lose weight.'

'Oh dear,' Sylvie chuckled. 'I'm afraid that might be a losing battle!'

'And I'm afraid you won't see Peaches,' Dottie went on. 'She can't be at the wedding.'

Sylvie seemed to pick up on Dottie's sadness. 'Why, what's wrong?'

Dottie took a minute or two to explain what had happened to Gary.

'How perfectly ghastly!' cried Sylvie. 'But I must say, I'm surprised that Reg was so concerned about you getting the disease. I never had him down as the caring type.'

'Oh Sylvie, you're not going to start saying horrible things about him, are you?'

'No . . . no of course not.' Sylvie hesitated. 'So how is Gary now? I mean, is there any sign of lasting damage?'

'They don't know yet.'

'And what about Peaches? I take it that by now you've managed to tell her you did go to see Gary?'

Dottie shook her head. 'I never seem to be able to catch her.'

'Write to her,' said Sylvie.

Dottie looked up and smiled. 'Yes, I suppose I should. I'm not thinking very straight, am I? Why didn't I think of that before?'

'How's Reg?' Sylvie said holding up his letter. 'Not thinking of going off to Australia, is he?'

Dottie could feel her face burning. She hesitated. She had to ask Sylvie about the money but this seemed like neither the time or the place. She'd only just got in the door.

'Let's get your case in first, shall we?' she said brightly. 'I'm dying for you to see your bedroom.'

Sylvie looked her very intently. She wasn't stupid. Something was wrong, something Dottie wasn't telling her, but she wouldn't press her just yet. Instead, she stubbed out her cigarette and followed Dottie out to the Humber.

It took longer to bring her things in than they thought. She might only have been staying for a couple of nights, but Sylvie had two suitcases. They were both very heavy and the stairs were steep.

'I couldn't make up my mind what to bring,' Sylvie apologised as they struggled into the bedroom. 'There's a present for Michael in that one.'

'I think he's already got a kitchen sink,' Dottie quipped as she heaved one case onto the bed.

'This is a lovely room,' said Sylvie looking around. 'You've got a real flair for decoration.'

'It was Aunt Bessie's room,' said Dottie. Seeing Sylvie's anxious glance, she added, 'but it's OK, she didn't die in here.'

'No, of course not.'

Dottie sat on the bed. 'I found her at the bottom of the stairs.'

It had come as a great shock to everybody when Aunt Bessie had fallen down the stairs eighteen months before. How ironic that it happened on the very day Reg had an extra duty at the station and Dottie was working in the Coopers' shop. Although they said her death was instantaneous, Dottie still fretted that Aunt Bessie had lain there, injured and alone before she died.

Sylvie squeezed her arm. 'It must have been awful for you. She was such a sweet old thing.'

'Not that old as it happens,' said Dottie. 'She was only sixty-one. They reckon she must have tripped at the top of the stairs. If only I had come home for lunch that day I might have saved her.'

'She died of her injuries?'

'They said she broke her neck,' Dottie said, 'and that it was instantaneous. I hope that's true.'

'Oh darling, I can't imagine how awful it was for you,' said Sylvie squeezing Dottie's elbow. 'Poor Aunt Bessie. Her death must have affected you dreadfully.'

'Me and Reg,' said Dottie. 'He was ill for weeks afterwards. He still doesn't like coming into this room. It upsets him too much. He says it makes him feel jumpy.'

Sylvie raised her eyebrow. 'What a pity Aunt Bessie won't be around for Michael's wedding,' she said sadly. 'We would have had some real laughs together.'

Dottie smiled.

Sylvie unlocked one of the suitcases. 'What's the bride like?'

'Freda? She's nice enough,' said Dottie. 'She did all the running but I think she'll make Michael a good wife. She works in the greengrocer's. That's how they met really. Her father wanted the farm potatoes, Michael delivered twice a week, and the rest, as they say, is history.'

'Is she pretty?'

'She's not exactly a beauty, if you know what I mean, but she looks a picture in her wedding dress.'

'You made it, I suppose.'

'As a matter of fact she bought it,' said Dottie, 'but I did a few alterations. They made their arrangements quite quickly.'

Sylvie gave her a knowing look and Dottie pushed her arm playfully. 'I didn't say anything and don't you say a word.'

'As if I would . . .'

'As if . . .' Dottie smirked.

'You know Michael has always been a bit in love with you, don't you?' said Sylvie.

'Don't talk daft,' said Dottie scornfully.

'It's true, darling,' said Sylvie. 'The day you got married, he was absolutely devastated. After you'd gone off on your honeymoon, we sat together in the old barn and had a long talk.'

'You're joking.'

'I'm not,' Sylvie insisted. 'He didn't like Reg very much, jealousy I suppose, but he was terrified that you'd be unhappy.'

'I had no idea.' Dottie shook her head. 'Whatever did you say?'

'Haven't a clue,' Sylvie shrugged, 'but being nineteen at the time, I'm sure I gave him the benefit of all my worldly wisdom because he soon got over it.'

They laughed.

'We ended up drinking half a bottle of cider together,' Sylvie giggled. 'He was quite sozzled by the time he left me.'

'Oh Sylvie,' Dottie laughed. 'You're incorrigible.'

Sylvie threw open her case and Dottie gasped. On top she could see a floaty evening dress in pale blue. Sylvie moved it slightly aside, revealing another in apricot satin and, underneath both of them, two day dresses. Each had matching shoes

118

and accessories. At the bottom of the case, there was a rayon nightdress, with matching bed jacket, and a pretty pair of slippers.

'Where do you manage to get all the coupons?' Dottie gasped.

'I didn't,' she said, holding up the blue gown. 'This one came from Paris.'

Dottie handed her some coat hangers. 'This one is gorgeous,' she said, hanging up the pink satin dress by its waist loops.

'Try it on,' Sylvie suggested.

'Really?'

'I was rather hoping you would like it. That's why I brought it. Try it on.'

Breathlessly, Dottie clambered out of her own clothes and slipped it on. 'It's amazing,' she said, looking at her reflection in the mirror.

'It's yours,' said Sylvie.

'Oh no, I can't . . .'

'It looks better on you than me,' said Sylvie. 'Really. You have it.'

Dottie flung her arms around Sylvie and kissed her cheek. 'Thank you, thank you.'

'Dottie, I want you to be honest with me,' said Sylvie gravely. 'Are you happy?'

Dottie turned her back. 'Can you undo me please?'

Sylvie unbuttoned the top of the dress and pulled down the zip. 'There's something wrong, isn't there? I can tell. Is it Reg? Something to do with that letter?'

'What's the time?' said Dottie glancing at the clock. 'Good heavens, it's almost five. I told Michael's mum we'd pick her up at five to take her to the village hall. Look, we haven't got time now. We really must go to the farm.'

'But you will talk to me,' Sylvie insisted.

'I will, I promise.' Dottie scrambled back into her own dress. 'I've got to get Reg's tea ready and then we really must go.'

As Dottie hurried downstairs, Sylvie laid her underwear in one of the drawers and opened her second suitcase. She couldn't help worrying about Dottie. She seemed a little strained. Something was troubling her. Was it Reg? Sylvie had never been very sure about Reg. He always seemed as nice as pie in the village, but Sylvie wasn't so sure he was the same person behind closed doors.

She took out Michael's present and laid it on the chair. Then she put the picture, a special present for Dottie, on the bedside table. She'd give it to her another time. Smiling at the photograph of the three of them, she ran her finger over Aunt Bessie's face under the glass. Even though they had all lived in the same house, Sylvie knew only too well that Aunt Bessie and Reg had barely tolerated each other.

'You never were happy with Dottie's marriage, were you, Aunt Bessie,' Sylvie said to the picture. 'You and me both. I'll tell you what though. I'll make you a promise to get to the bottom of what's troubling her during this weekend.'

Draping her cardigan around her shoulders, Sylvie turned towards the stairs. The one thing she hoped above all else was that Reg wasn't knocking Dottie about.

# Fifteen

By the time Dottie, Sylvie and Michael's mum, Edna, arrived at the village hall, Mary already had her husband Tom, along with greengrocer Cecil Hargreaves, father of the bride, and Steven Sullivan running around with trestle tables and unstacking chairs. Rose Hargreaves, Freda's mother, had brought the cake stand for the wedding cake and some candles. Some other people from the village were there too, including Maggie, young Steven Sullivan's wife, who worked in the old folks' home on the edge of the green.

Everyone was thrilled to see Sylvie again but almost as soon as they all went back to work, Sylvie tottered back to her car. 'If you'll all excuse me, I've broken my nail. I'd better go and file it before I make a start.'

'She hasn't changed,' Mary muttered as she walked out of earshot. 'Still skiving.'

Dottie gave her a hefty nudge in the ribs and that started them on a fit of the giggles.

As is the case with the users of most village halls, there was a definite pecking order. Betty Cannington was in overall charge. She had been doing village 'dos' for the past twelve years. She'd taken over from Florrie Hanson who had taken over from Emily Pulsford in 1933.

There were no written instructions and outsiders like Mrs Belski, a Polish immigrant living in the village, found it difficult to understand the workings of the village hall kitchen. She was at a loss to know who did what, but Dottie and her friends understood perfectly. Everyone knew where everything was, and that Betty was the one who had the ultimate say in where things should go and how things should be done. 'We've always done it this way,' was her watchword.

'All right if I put the cups and saucers here on the top, Betty?'

'When we did old Mrs Groves' funeral,' Betty said, 'we found it worked better if they were on this side of the urn.'

Mrs Groves had died in 1943.

Of course, whoever was organising the 'do' was allowed to put her own small stamp of change on certain things, but everyone was careful not to upset Betty, or it would be the worse for them if they wanted to hire the hall on another occasion.

Edna and Rose decided the hall should be arranged with a top table for the wedding party and two long side tables for the forty wedding guests. Sylvie, Mary and Dottie covered each of the trestles with white bedsheets decorated with bunting, while Rose and Edna worked amicably together on a small table slightly set apart from the others, on which the cake was to be cut.

'How are the kids?' Dottie asked Mary.

'Back at school,' said Mary. She put a pin in her mouth and bent down to put some of the bunting in place. 'Billy's doing his mock eleven plus in a few weeks.'

Dottie smiled. 'He's bound to pass. He's a clever boy.'

Mary swelled with pride. They stopped talking as they concentrated on fixing another loop of bunting to the sheet. 'That'll give you a bit of time to yourself then,' said Dottie, smoothing out a sheet and making sure the edges were even on both sides of the table.

'Christopher and Connie are still at home, of course. They're not quite four, but the others are all at school. I miss them when they're not there. So do the twins. The place seems so quiet.'

'I was wondering,' Dottie ventured. 'How would you feel about looking after somebody else's kids while they were at work?'

Mary looked up and stuck the pin in her finger. 'Ow! Dottie are you . . .? You're not . . .?'

Dottie looked away embarrassed. 'No,' she said quickly. 'Not me. I was thinking of Brian and Phyllis.'

'Brian and Phyllis Pearce?' gasped Mary. 'Well, I'll go to sea. I never had you and Ann Pearce down as friends.'

'I just thought she could do with a hand, that's all,' said Dottie. 'She needs a job.'

'What's brought this on, hen?' said Mary.

'The kids,' said Dottie. 'I can get her a job, easy. I know plenty of women in the village who want a cleaning lady, but she can't work with the kids in tow, and I thought to myself, Mary loves looking after kids . . .'

Mary said nothing.

'It won't be for long,' Dottie added. 'Brian goes to school next year and Phyllis is already three.'

'You can tell her I'll do it,' said Mary.

'Oh Mary!' Dottie cried. 'You're a star. I'll ask her to pay you, so you'd better work out what you want to charge her.'

'There's no need for that, hen,' said Mary, pinning the bunting to the sheet again.

'Yes, there is,' said Dottie. 'She's got her pride.'

'What will she get cleaning?' said Mary.

'Half a crown an hour is the going rate around here. If she starts at nine and works through till four when the kids get out of school, she could earn four quid a week.'

'Then tell her she can pay me a pound a week and I'll give them dinner.'

Sylvie came back.

'What took you so long?' Mary asked.

'I had to get them all even,' said Sylvie, holding out her hand to admire her fingernails. 'What do you want me to do?'

123

'Can you pin some more bunting on those tables?' asked Mary, trying not to smile.

'I'm no good at sewing,' said Sylvie.

Dottie kept her head down. If she looked at Mary again, they'd both start giggling. 'How about giving a hand in the kitchen?' she suggested. 'I think they're laying out cups and saucers.'

They were interrupted by raised voices near the top table. The mothers of the bride and groom had crossed swords with Betty. Rose wanted to place four candles on the top table.

'We never put candles near food,' Betty declared. 'It's too dangerous.'

'Don't be ridiculous,' snapped Rose. 'This is a family tradition. We always light a candle at a wedding.'

Betty pursed her lips. She was now in fighting mood. 'And while we're on the subject, we never have balloons near the hatchway, Edna,' she said sourly. 'The children might get excited and try to pop them. We can't have that when the teas are around.'

'You're determined to spoil this, aren't you, you dried up old biddy,' snapped Edna.

'Don't you dare talk to me like that . . .'

Dottie stepped in to defuse the situation. In the end, Edna agreed to move the balloons, and Betty conceded to the candles, provided Rose waited until everyone was seated before lighting them.

'As soon as the speeches are over,' said Betty, determined to have the last word, 'make sure they get blown out.'

'Of course I will,' retorted Rose, adding under her breath, 'what does the stupid woman take me for?'

By the time the men had taken down the long ladder they'd used to hang the bunting from the rafters, Mary said she'd better get back to put the little ones to bed. Tom said he'd drive her home and give Edna a lift home as well.

'See you at the church,' Mary called cheerily as they left.

Maggie had set out the big plates on the tables and Cathy, the district nurse, was helping put out the cutlery. Dottie went into the kitchen to join Sylvie who was still laying out the cups and saucers.

'That was a nice thing you did for Ann,' said Sylvie. 'Mary told me.'

Dottie shrugged. 'She needed help and I know Mary loves looking after children.'

'You're a lovely person, Dottie,' said Sylvie, giving her a hug. 'Too kind for your own good.'

Dottie laughed. 'What's that supposed to mean?'

'People don't like goodness,' said Sylvie. 'Take care it doesn't backfire on you.'

By 7.30pm everything was ready.

'You must be famished,' Dottie said to Sylvie. 'I'll get us some tea when we get in.'

'Will Reg be there?' Sylvie asked.

'I imagine he'll be at the pub by now,' said Dottie with a shake of her head.

'Then I'll take you out for a meal,' said Sylvie. 'My treat.'

Dottie hesitated.

'Come on,' Dottie cajoled. 'Even if he hasn't gone to the pub, I'm sure Reg can find himself something to do.'

Reg stood outside the bedroom door listening. The house was empty. He'd come home to find his tea in the oven between two enamel plates. The gravy had a skin on the top of it and the potatoes had started to brown. If he hadn't been so hungry he'd have chucked the lot of it in the pig bin where it bloody belonged. He knew this would happen if he let that woman into his house. She'd go filling Dot's mind with all sorts of things and she'd neglect what she was supposed to do.

After he'd eaten what he felt was the worst meal he'd ever had in his whole life (and he'd eaten some real slop during the war), he went upstairs to change. He found a clean shirt laid out on the bed but he didn't like that one. He had to turf out half the wardrobe to find the one he wanted. There was a new dress on her side. A silly frilly pink thing. He supposed Sylvia must have given it to her, but where Dot would wear the darned thing, he couldn't imagine. But then that was Sylvia McDonald all over. Always filling Dot's head with daft ideas.

On the way downstairs, he hesitated outside her room. Through the crack in the door he could see her open suitcase on the bed. A drawer was open too. He could see some things lying inside.

There wasn't a sound in the whole house, nothing except his own breathing. They must still be at the village hall getting ready for Michael Gilbert's wedding, although why on earth it should take all this time, he hadn't a clue. People expected too much at weddings these days. All those bloody sandwiches and cakes. He'd even heard her say that Edna was making jellies as well. He'd been satisfied with a glass of beer for himself and a sherry for Dot. Of course, there were no relatives on his side and he'd made Dottie keep the numbers down on hers. Like he'd told her, they didn't have the time or the money to go in for all that wedding breakfast malarky.

He reached out and pushed the door open. It creaked as it swung back and he stared into the room. Dot had made it look completely different from how it looked when that old cow Bessie was there. In fact, there wasn't a trace of her left.

He stepped onto the rug. His mouth was dry and his heartbeat quickened. This was the first time he'd been in the room in two years.

He looked into the suitcase and saw a bed jacket, some silk stockings and a book. He reached into the case and picked up one stocking. It was as light as a feather, sheer, and obviously expensive. Her underwear was in the drawer. It didn't look like anything Dot had.

Reg walked over and ran his fingers over a pair of cream

French knickers. He felt himself harden. Licking his lips, he took them out of the drawer by his fingertips and held them up to the light. He lifted them to his nose and smelled them. A sudden noise made him start. The door had clicked shut and the surprise made him brush his elbow against something on the bedside table. It fell with a clatter and a bang. Dropping the knickers, he froze in horror.

It was a photo in a silver frame. One he'd never seen before: Sylvia and a much younger Dot, their arms around each others' shoulders, smiled up at him – but it wasn't their faces that disturbed him. *She* was sitting in front of them, on a chair. She was wearing that same violet-coloured dress and she had that daft cowboy hat on. All at once her voice filled his head.

'Over my dead body, Reg Cox. Go to hell . . .'

Something touched his cheek and his skin crawled. Blind panic made him rush from the room but it was only when he reached the bottom of the stairs that he realised it was his own perspiration running in a rivulet down his face.

# *Sixteen*

Sylvie had taken Dottie to a hotel in the centre of Worthing. Overlooking the Steyne, it was almost the length of the road. Inside the restaurant, the tables were covered with crisp white table linen and they offered a silver service.

'This must be so expensive,' Dottie whispered.

'Don't worry about it,' smiled Sylvie. 'Robin's business has done really well so he can afford to treat his wife and her best pal to a meal out.'

She linked her arm through Dottie's and propelled her to a table.

In the corner of the restaurant, a pianist was playing Doris Day's song, 'Bewitched, Bothered and Bewildered'. They ordered soup with roast beef to follow. Dottie thought she had never had a better time.

As the pianist struck up 'Harbour Lights', they began to reflect.

'Robin and I lead very separate lives,' Sylvie said. 'He's very keen to do well. Did I tell you he might get onto the board of directors before long?'

'You must be so proud of him,' Dottie said.

'I suppose so,' said Sylvie grudgingly. 'It'll probably mean I'll see even less of him. Oh, Dottie, I wish I could be like you.'

'You wish you were like me?' Dottie was incredulous.

'You are so talented and you cram so much into your day,' Sylvie went on. 'I knew you were good at sewing frocks but your little house looks absolutely amazing.'

'It was the Festival of Britain that got me going,' said Dottie. 'They had one at the Assembly Hall in Worthing. I'd never seen anything like it . . . all those lovely geometric patterns and bold colours. I enjoy making clothes but furnishings are so much more exciting.' She was suddenly aware that Sylvie was staring at her.

'What?'

'Your face,' she smiled. 'It lights up like a beacon when you talk about it.'

'Sorry.'

'Don't apologise. I think you're fantastic.'

'It's only copied . . . most of it from magazines,' laughed Dottie. 'And it's all done on the cheap.'

'Well, I'm telling you, people would pay top dollar for a look like that,' Sylvie said.

Dottie smiled modestly.

'All I do,' Sylvie shrugged, 'is play bridge, shop and go to the hairdresser's. Quite frankly, darling, if it weren't for a certain person, most of the time I'd go mad with boredom.'

Dottie couldn't imagine a day with nothing to do – and what did Sylvie mean, 'a certain person'?

'I'm going to shock you now,' Sylvie went on, as if she had read her thoughts, 'I'm not unhappy . . . because I'm having an affair.'

Dottie was dumbstruck.

'He's a wonderful man,' said Sylvie, her eyes lighting up. 'His name is Bruce and he owns a riding stables. I met him when I went for some riding lessons.' She opened her bag and took out a small wallet. Inside was a picture of a rugged-looking man on a horse.

'He's very handsome,' Dottie conceded. 'Are you and Robin going to get a divorce?'

'Heavens no!' cried Sylvie. 'I'm quite happy with things the way they are. Bruce already has a wife and I have Robin.'

Dottie looked away. How could Sylvie love someone else when she was already married?

'Well,' said Sylvie. 'I've told you all my secrets. What about you and Reg? I'm making a pretty shrewd guess that you are not as happy as you like to make out either.'

'Don't be daft!' Dottie laughed.

'No, seriously,' said Sylvie. 'What about you? What do you want out of life? What are your ambitions?'

Dottie shrugged. 'I don't know. I've never really thought about it.'

'Come on,' Sylvie cajoled. 'There must be something you'd really like to do if you had the chance.'

Dottie stared deeply into her glass of wine. 'It's no good hankering after something you can't have,' she said dully.

'You're not going to wiggle out of it that quickly, darling,' said Sylvie taking a long drag of her cigarette. 'Just imagine, money no object, no ties, nothing impossible . . . what would you do?'

Her answer came quickly. 'Interior design.'

Sylvie's eyebrows shot up. 'Judging by the way you've transformed that cottage, you'd be really good at it.'

Dottie swirled the dark liquid in her glass. 'Daft idea.'

'No it's not.'

Dottie laughed.

'Seriously, darling. I think you should get some training,' said Sylvie. 'You'll have plenty of opportunity when you finally get your hands on Aunt Bessie's money . . .'

'Reg has other plans,' Dottie interrupted. 'He wants us to sell up and get a guesthouse by the seafront.'

'Blow Reg,' Sylvie retorted. 'What about you? What do you want?'

'I want him to be happy.'

'Oh, Dottie, you are absolutely impossible. You're making yourself an absolute martyr to that man.'

Dottie felt her face colour. 'I am not!'

'Then for goodness' sake, take the money, *your* money, and

do something for yourself. Look at it this way: if you succeed, you'll make the both of you rich; and if not rich you'll make a comfortable living doing something you really enjoy.'

'Sylvie, can I ask you something?'

Sylvie laid down her knife and fork and took a sip from her wine glass. 'Of course you can,' she said draining the last of it.

'This is very important but you've got to promise me you'll never breathe a word to another living soul.'

'Sounds intriguing.'

The waiter came back to the table. 'Is everything all right with your meal, Madam?'

'Fine,' said Sylvie. Then, leaning forward, she said to Dottie, 'Fire away.'

The waiter left.

Dottie explained about the letter and Patsy and then told her about the money.

After she'd filled Dottie's wine glass again, Sylvie said, 'So Reg wants me to pay the fare for this child of his to come over? The brass neck of the man! He doesn't like me but he'd like some of my money. I suppose he didn't dare ask me himself in case I refused.'

'Don't say that,' said Dottie. 'At least he's let you come and stay.'

'Probably to give himself a bargaining chip,' said Sylvie, raising an eyebrow.

'I don't understand.'

'He's let your friend come and stay, so now you have no right to refuse his child and I should dip into my purse for the privilege.'

Dottie frowned. 'Sylvie!'

There was an awkward silence.

'I can pay you back when I get my inheritance,' Dottie said desperately.

'Oh, darling,' cried Sylvie, reaching out to hold Dottie's hand, 'It's not that . . .'

The pianist seemed to be playing a little louder. Dottie found herself humming, 'when a lovely flame dies, smoke gets in your eyes . . .'

'If I do help . . .' Sylvie said.

'Oh Sylvie,' said Dottie eagerly.

'*If* I do help,' Sylvie repeated. 'It will be to help *you*, not Reg.'

The look on Sylvie's face was so serious, Dottie felt uncomfortable. Had she upset her? She wished she hadn't asked her now.

Sylvie called the waiter over and as he cleared away their plates Sylvie asked tersely, 'Coffee?'

Dottie shook her head. Oh Lord, she *had* upset her. Oh Reg, why do you always make me do these things?

'Just the bill please, waiter,' said Sylvie.

Once they were in the darkness of the car, Dottie said, 'Sylvie, if you'd rather not help out, I quite understand.'

'Don't be silly, darling,' cried Sylvie. 'Of course I'll help you. I'd do anything for you, you know that. You can't help it if Reg is being unfair.'

'He just wants his child, that's all.'

'And what about you?' said Sylvie. 'Why don't you have children of your own?'

'Reg . . . he can't.'

'What do you mean, he can't?' Sylvie frowned and when Dottie refused to look at her, she gasped, 'Good heavens! Do you mean you and Reg have never even made love? But, darling, how awful. You must leave him.'

Dottie shook her head. 'Remember what Aunt Bessie used to say? You make your bed and you lie in it.'

'Rubbish,' said Sylvie. 'We're living in the fifties, for heaven's sake. You can get an annulment straightaway if the marriage has never been consummated.'

'We did it when we were first married, before he went to the Far East,' Dottie explained.

132

Sylvie turned abruptly and crashed the gears as the car moved off. They motored back home in silence, Sylvie was struggling to keep her temper. Why was that wretched man so damned awkward? What sort of a life was he giving her friend? He was good-looking in a funny sort of way, which was why Dottie was attracted to him the first place, she supposed. She couldn't bear the thought of Reg touching her, but if Dottie loved him, surely she deserved better than this. They didn't do it . . .? Why not? Was he some sort of queer?

Dottie's thoughts had drifted back to her honeymoon. Three days. That's all they'd had, but Reg had been all right then. He was a bit rough but she hadn't worried too much about that. She was Mrs Reginald Cox and it was wonderful just being with him. It didn't matter if he was in a bit of a hurry. Everybody knew they might not have much time. So many had been here one day and gone the next. He kept saying how glad he was to have her.

'I never understood why you married him in the first place,' Sylvie said suddenly.

Dottie looked at her, horrified. 'Because I loved him.'

'Did you, darling? Are you sure?'

'Of course I did,' said Dottie defensively. 'I do . . .'

Sylvie snorted and changed gear. The car sped on.

'Come on, Sylvie.' Dottie's voice had an edge. 'Say whatever you have to. We never keep secrets from each other, remember?'

Another car came towards them and its headlights flooded the car with light.

'Let's not quarrel,' said Sylvie softly, as she glanced across at Dottie's angry look. 'I don't want to upset you. You're my dearest friend.'

Dottie looked down at her lap. 'I'm sorry. I shouldn't have snapped at you but I feel so on edge all the time. I want things to be right between me and Reg. I want to make my marriage work but it makes things so difficult when he's not happy. I know he's desperate to have Patsy and that's why I've agreed to try and help him get her over here. Perhaps if she comes here things might . . . well, you know . . .'

'It's an awfully big risk,' said Sylvie. 'And what about your life? How will you fit everything in? Your sewing, your little jobs, looking after Reg, and then Patsy . . .'

'Patsy will be at school,' said Dottie. 'I can still work during the day and I can do my sewing in the evenings when she's in bed.'

'But once she's over here,' Sylvie went on, 'how do you know that he won't shut you out altogether?'

'He wouldn't. I know he wouldn't,' said Dottie weakly. 'Oh Sylvie, I just keep thinking that if I do this for him, he may be able to . . . and then I . . . I just want a child of my own . . .'

'This gets worse . . . sewing, Reg, your job, Patsy, *and* a child of your own?'

Dottie began to cry softly.

'Don't cry. I didn't mean it,' said Sylvie, reaching across to squeeze her hand. 'Look, can't you persuade him to go to the doctor . . . or maybe you could have a word with the doctor?'

At the mention of the doctor, Dottie shook her head. 'He'd never go and I don't think I could talk to Dr Fitzgerald about something like that,' she said quickly.

'Oh, darling,' Sylvie chuckled, 'you are a little prudish at times.'

When they got back to Myrtle Cottage they were both rather surprised to find it in darkness.

'Does Reg usually go to bed this early?' Sylvie asked.

'He must be on an early shift tomorrow,' said Dottie, hanging her coat on the nail behind the door and collecting the dirty dishes.

'What, on the day of the wedding?'

Dottie shook her head. 'Oh no, of course not. He's got the day off. I forgot.' A chill ran through her body. She shouldn't have stayed out so late.

They said goodnight to each other and climbed the steep stairs, Sylvie in front clinging onto the rope banister for dear life, and Dottie right behind her to give her a sense of security. They parted with a hug on the landing.

Reg had the light off and his back to the door. Not wishing to disturb him, Dottie undressed quickly by the light of the moon filtering through the curtains and put her clothes on the chair. As she climbed into bed beside him, Reg pulled at the bedclothes and moved away.

She lay on her back staring up at the moonlight on the ceiling. Sylvie's remarks had given her a lot of food for thought. Everyone in the village thought of Reg as a pretty good egg. He often gave some of the older folk something from his allotment and of course there were his flowers at the station. He might be a bit of a loner, but people around here liked and respected him.

Dottie saw something different. The Reg she was married to was more complex. He kept her on tenterhooks all the time. She never knew what mood he'd be in. If he wanted sex, it had to be here and now or he didn't come near her for months on end. He would make remarks, small ones, but sometimes they'd hurt her very much. She always did her best for him, but somehow it was never enough. She'd always thought the way she'd been taught. Wives should be loyal to their husbands no matter what. Wives should spend their lives making their spouse's life as comfortable as possible. They should be faithful. Love, honour and obey, so the promise went. Well she'd done all that and it still wasn't enough. Just recently she'd started to think of herself as a person in her own right. Like Sylvie said, this was the fifties. Aunt Bessie may have been satisfied with that kind of life, but, for her, it was getting harder and harder to feel the same way. Surely there was more to life than this?

They'd been married since 1942, but in point of fact, they'd had very little time together. He'd gone almost as soon as the

135

honeymoon was over and because he was doing something so top secret, she hadn't even been allowed to write to him. She hadn't heard from him for years and then all of a sudden, just before Christmas 1948, he'd turned up out of the blue. He wouldn't talk about his wartime experiences, or where he'd been since the war ended. Too upsetting, he'd said. Aunt Bessie didn't like it but there it was. Reg was a changed man, who had changed even more since Aunt Bessie died.

She turned and stared at the back of his head. This wasn't what she had thought marriage would be like. Was this to be the sum total of her life? In some ways she knew him like the back of her hand. He'd gone to bed early to show her how annoyed he was that she'd stayed out late. If Sylvie hadn't been staying in the same house, there would have been a row. He'd have called her names, and perhaps even hit her. She'd have cried and then he'd have made her feel guilty, like it was all her fault. He'd have told her she wasn't good enough. She wasn't even a proper woman. She'd never be a mother because she was nothing more than a cold fish. Dottie swallowed hard as her throat tightened. If only he'd show her a little tenderness now and again. Yet even when he was nice to her, it was always for a reason. Sylvie was probably right. The only reason he'd let her stay for the weekend was because he wanted the money to get Patsy over here. She'd never know for sure, of course. Reg was deep. He never told her what he was really thinking.

All at once she remembered that other letter, the one that had come this morning. What did it say?

Her eyes were beginning to fill but she dared not cry. If he heard her, he'd be angry. He hated it when she cried. She closed her eyes. Was there anything about her he liked? How she wished Aunt Bessie was still here. Right now Dottie would have given her right arm for a crumb of affection or a cuddle.

Reg began to snore and Dottie slipped her hand under her nightie. She began to stroke herself until a warm glow washed over her. She'd better stop. It was a nice feeling but not even that took away the ache she had in her heart. If anything, it only left her even more frustrated. She was only twenty-seven and the thought of all those long lonely years stretching out before her was quite frightening.

It was no good. She had to stop feeling sorry for herself. Why get all maudlin and depressed? She had to make the best of it. She turned onto her side, away from him and, feeling under her pillow for her hankie, she blew her nose softly. Then she lay back down, willing herself not to think about it any more. There wasn't much love but she could set her mind to honour and obey. That would have to do for now.

'Oh God,' she prayed, 'give me strength. I don't think I can do this on my own . . .'

When Sylvie got into her own room and switched on the light, her suitcase was still on the bed. She moved it onto the chair and picked up a few things scattered on the top of the chest of drawers. She was surprised to see her panties draped over her hairbrush and comb. That's funny, she thought, as she tidied them into the drawer.

She arranged her face powder, hand cream, lipstick and talc into some semblance of order and fished around in her bag for a hairnet. Then she took out her nightdress, bed jacket, slippers and book.

It was quite a ritual getting ready for bed. Robin always laughed at her but it had to be done. First she undressed and put on her nightie. Then she removed all her make-up. She padded into the bathroom and turned on the taps. Only the cold-water tap was working. How Dottie put up with this primitive way of life she couldn't understand. She washed herself in the freezing water, cleaned her teeth, brushed her hair and put the hairnet right over the top.

Back in her room, she creamed her knees and her elbows. Then, sitting on the bed, she creamed her face, making sure to

137

include twenty strokes across each cheek, twenty on her forehead and twenty-five across her throat in a vigorous upward motion from the base of her neck to her chin. That was to ward off a turkey neck in later life. Next she creamed her hands and put on some cotton gloves.

It was as she climbed into bed that Sylvie noticed the picture. It was on the floor, part way under the chest of drawers. She picked it up. How did that get down there? She'd left it at the back of the dressing table.

Then it dawned on her. Someone had been in here. They'd been touching the picture . . . her panties . . . She shuddered. Reg. Who else could it be? Dear God, he'd been touching her underwear.

She jumped out of bed and opened the drawer. Everything was there but she took out the French knickers, holding them between her thumb and forefinger as if they were soiled. She threw them back into the case. She couldn't wear them. She might even destroy them. What a good job she'd brought plenty of other things. The very thought of wearing something Reg had fingered made her feel ill.

Another thought crossed her mind. If Reg had been snooping around looking at her underwear, was he really the kind of man to father a little girl? Yet she knew Dottie was counting on her help. She sat on the edge of the bed and looked at the picture again. Even though there was a war on, they had been much happier times. Dottie, her much younger self and Aunt Bessie smiled back at her.

'What do you think I should do about it?' she whispered to Aunt Bessie. But the woman behind the frame carried on smiling.

Sylvie lay down and pulled up the covers. If she did give them the money for Patsy's fare, she would have to ensure that there were some safeguards for both Dottie and the child. Reg mustn't be allowed to have everything his own way. She wished she could persuade Dottie to get shot of him, but that wasn't very likely, was it?

'I used to think it was odd that you didn't like Reg,' she told Aunt Bessie, as she turned out the light. 'But now, I'm pretty sure I don't like him either. Creepy bastard.'

# *Seventeen*

Michael's wedding day dawned dull and overcast. Dottie slipped out of bed almost as soon as it was light. By the time Reg came downstairs she had cleared up his dinner things from the night before and laid the table for breakfast.

'Hello, Reg,' she said cheerfully. 'Fancy a spot of porridge?'

'I'll go down the garden and feed the pig first,' he said pulling on his boots. 'You were late coming home last night.'

'Sylvie took me into Worthing for a meal.'

'Our food not good enough for her then?' he accused darkly.

'It wasn't like that,' said Dottie. 'We'd finished at the hall and I knew you would already be at the Jolly Farmer so when she suggested taking me out as a little treat, I didn't think you'd mind.'

'Mind? Why should I mind when my wife goes gallivanting all over the place in her friend's flash car, leaving the house in a bloody mess? Where did she take you for this little treat? Some swanky place, no doubt.'

Dottie didn't want a row and he was getting himself all worked up.

'I should have asked you first, Reg. I'm sorry. I didn't mean any harm.'

'All I can say is thank God she's going home today,' he said, 'then things can get back to normal.'

He swept past her and disappeared up the garden. Dottie

poured herself a cup of tea. Her hand was trembling. He was going to be really worked up by the time they had to go the wedding. No ... no, he wouldn't. Not with Sylvie here. He wouldn't want to make a scene in front of her. Dottie glanced at the clock. 8.15am. She couldn't worry about Reg now, she had such a lot to do. She'd have to get on.

By the time Sylvie came downstairs, the kitchen dresser was open and the enamel table inside the drop-down drawer was covered with ingredients. Dottie was well underway with baking a couple of batches of fairy cakes and a Victoria sponge.

'Did you sleep well?' Dottie asked as Sylvie came yawning into the kitchen.

'Yes, fine. Gosh, you're busy. Where's Reg?'

'Outside in the garden. Fancy a bit of porridge?'

Sylvie shook her head and sat down. 'A bit of toast and a cigarette will suit me fine.'

Dottie put some sliced bread under the grill.

'Shall I call Reg?' yawned Sylvie. She seemed to be struggling to wake up.

'He'll be busy with the pig by now,' Dottie smiled. 'He said he'd have a sarnie before we go.'

While Sylvie enjoyed some toast and a cigarette, Dottie started on the sandwiches for the wedding breakfast.

'How many are you doing?' Sylvie asked.

'I've been asked to do egg and paste.'

Sylvie screwed up her nose. 'What, together?'

'No,' Dottie laughed. 'A loaf of each. We're all sharing the cost of the reception. This is our present to him although I've already bought him a little something.'

'What little something?' Sylvie wanted to know.

'A set of fruit bowls,' smiled Dottie. 'I saw it in the market about a month ago. Very reasonable. 15/6.' She opened the cupboard under the kitchen cabinet and pulled out a small box.

141

'Very pretty,' said Sylvie, undoing the box and taking one out. 'I've brought him some bed linen.'

'You can never have enough linen,' Dottie chirped.

Sylvie took a long drag of her cigarette. 'Leave him,' she said, glancing out of the window to check Reg wasn't coming.

'What?'

'You heard me. Leave him. You're worth much more than this. You deserve to be happy.'

Dottie's eyes blazed. 'Sylvie, don't.'

'You could come back with me,' Sylvie insisted. 'Robin and I will give you a new start until you can sell this place . . .'

'I don't even own this place,' said Dottie.

Sylvie frowned. 'But I thought Aunt Bessie . . .'

'For some reason best known to herself,' Dottie retorted, 'Aunt Bessie left this cottage in trust until I'm thirty.'

Sylvie stared at her thoughtfully. 'How very frustrating for Reg.'

'And what do you mean by that?' Dottie flew back.

'Nothing,' said Sylvie innocently. 'A throwaway remark, that's all.'

Dottie continued cutting the loaf of sandwiches.

'How on earth do you get the bread so thin?' Sylvie asked. 'If it were down to me, I'd have bought a cut loaf.'

'Homemade is always nicer,' said Dottie relaxing. A little later she added, 'You're right. He is frustrated about Aunt Bessie's money. Like I told you, Reg wants us to move to Brighton and take up a seaside boarding house. We can still do it of course, but it can't be for at least another year and even then it will be difficult.'

'Why's that?'

'I can still spend the money and all that but I have to get the approval of the board of trustees for anything major until I'm thirty,' said Dottie. 'But don't say anything, will you? Reg doesn't know that bit yet. I didn't want to upset him.'

Sylvie flicked some ash from her skirt. 'I bet that'll go down like a lead balloon.'

Dottie held her tongue. She finished the loaf and turned around looking for a tin to pack them in.

'Look at me, just sitting here watching you,' said Sylvie, stubbing out her cigarette. She stood up and grabbed an apron from the back of the kitchen chair. 'Come on now. What shall I do?'

Dottie pointed to the fairy cakes cooling on the wire rack. 'Fancy putting a bit of icing on them? Time's getting on and we have to be at the hall by twelve.'

At quarter to two, as they walked the short distance from the car to the church, Dottie slipped her arm through Reg's. She was determined to show Sylvie just how happy she could be.

Michael Gilbert was already waiting in the church. He looked very different in his smart double-breasted brown pinstriped suit. His unruly hair was slicked down, although a few wayward curls had worked loose and flopped attractively onto his forehead. His weather-beaten face glowed.

'He looks incredibly handsome,' Sylvie whispered as they sat down.

Dottie nodded. She hadn't realised before how good-looking Michael was. 'I've always thought of him like a little brother,' she smiled. 'But you're right. Today he looks every inch the man.'

Tom Prior poked her in the back. 'The bugger's already proved that,' he whispered with a grin.

Dottie and Sylvie giggled. Reg picked up his hymnbook and stared ahead, stony-faced.

They waited quietly until the vicar walked down the aisle and instructed them to all stand. The organ struck up.

Freda looked a picture in her long satin dress. Defiantly, she'd worn white, though her thickening waist and the roundness of her stomach was obvious. Her dress had long sleeves and the mitre-shaped cuff had a small loop to go over her long finger on each hand. The scooped neckline was edged with lace. There was lace on the bodice reaching under the bust, ending in a large bow. Matching lace circled the hem and met at another large bow. She wore her mother's pearls, three handsome strands which no one would have guessed had come from Woolworths just before the war, if her mother hadn't told everyone last night as they prepared the hall.

Freda's wedding bouquet was enormous. Those who looked forward to dishing out acid remarks noted that it obscured her shape beautifully, covering her from waist to thigh in early autumn reds and golds.

The service brought tears to Dottie's eyes.

Reg turned and whispered, 'Remember? For better for worse, 'till death do us part?'

At the other end of the pew, Heather from the florist shop leaned forward to listen to their conversation. 'Aaaah,' she sighed happily; but Dottie didn't smile. Something about the way Reg had said it chilled her very soul.

After the service, someone got out a Box Brownie and they all posed in the churchyard for photographs.

Because hers was the only car, Sylvie had offered to drive the bride and groom the short distance to the reception. At this point, several other Box Brownies appeared and people took turns to stand next to the Humber with the bride and groom inside. Michael and Freda seemed very happy.

Rose was in tears. 'Don't they look a picture?' she said as Edna handed her a lace handkerchief. 'So romantic.'

Freda's father muttered something about Freda making sure she kept the bouquet in front of her and got a nudge in his ribs for his trouble.

'Come on, Dot,' said Reg. 'Let's pose by the car.'

He took her wrist painfully and pulled her towards the Humber. 'Take a picture of me and my old lady with the bride and groom, will you? I want to give her something to remember the day.'

The photographer lined up his camera and Dottie and Reg stood beside Michael and Freda.

'Smile, love,' Reg called out.

Dottie did her best, but her heart was thumping. What was he up to? Everybody was happy and smiling, but she could sense the undercurrent more strongly than ever.

The picture was taken. 'Thanks, mate,' said Reg as he spotted the vicar coming out of the side door of the church. 'You walk on up to the hall, sweetheart. I'm just going to have a word with Rev. Roberts,' he said. 'See if he'd like some of my chrysanthemums for the harvest festival.'

Dottie smiled nervously.

'Are you ready?' Sylvie asked.

Michael helped Freda into the car and then went round to the other door. Sylvie leaned out of the driver's window and gave her a wink. 'Don't let them get back to the hall too quickly, Dottie. I'm taking Michael and Freda the long way round.'

The wedding party cheered as she pulled out into the road and headed towards Worthing and, presumably, the seafront.

Dottie fell into step with Edna Gilbert, offering the older woman her arm. 'You never come up to the farm to see me these days, Dottie,' she chided.

'I know. I'm sorry. I'm just so busy.'

'Things all right with you and Reg?'

'Fine.' I'm becoming a good liar, she thought to herself.

'No sign of a little one yet?'

'No,' said Dottie, and seeing the expression on Edna's face, she added with a smile, 'not yet anyway.'

'You know about Freda of course?'

'You'll make a wonderful granny,' said Dottie, squeezing her arm.

Edna snorted playfully and changing the subject said, 'Here,

Dottie, I hear you're a dab hand with that sewing machine of yours. Would you come up to the farm sometime? I'd like you to do a little something for me.'

Once they returned from their romantic drive along the seafront, the bride and groom stood by the door to receive their guests.

'You look so beautiful,' Dottie told the bride as she shuffled along the line.

Michael leaned forward and kissed Dottie on the cheek. It was a featherlike touch but afterwards Dottie couldn't look him in the eye. Her heart was beating very fast. 'I wish you all the luck in the world,' she said quietly.

'Thanks, Dottie.'

She glanced up at him and felt her face flame. Reg stuck his hand out in front of Michael and the two men shook hands. Dottie hoped to God Reg hadn't seen her blushing. Why on earth had she done it? Probably because it had been so long since she'd felt such a tender touch.

The three of them were to sit together, Sylvie then Reg and Dottie, but first the women had to make sure everyone else was happy and settled. As Freda's mother lit the four candles on the top table next to the wedding cake, Dottie and Mary whipped off the damp tea towels they'd put over the sandwiches to keep them moist and began serving teas. Reg ate alone until they joined him, but he carried on a lively conversation with those nearby.

'Reg is in good form,' Sylvie remarked.

Dottie nodded. Yes, yes he was, wasn't he? She was getting herself all in a lather over nothing. He was enjoying himself that was all. How silly she'd been.

After the meal, the speeches and the cutting of the cake, someone produced a piano accordion so the men cleared away the tables to make room for dancing. Dottie, Mary and several other women went into the kitchen to start on the clearing up.

It was highly unlikely that Reg would come into the kitchen so Dottie pulled Mary to one side. 'Have you heard any news about Gary?'

Mary let out a long sigh. 'It's not good,' she said sadly. 'He's come through it, but he's lost the use of his right leg and the left one is very weak.'

Dottie put her hand to her mouth. 'Oh no.'

'Peaches has gone to live with her mother for the time being,' Mary went on. 'Gary has been moved to Courtlands.'

'That place Princess Elizabeth visited earlier this year?'

Mary nodded. 'Apparently they do special exercises for kiddies with infantile paralysis there.'

'What about the baby?' asked Dottie. 'It must be due any time now.'

'She's had the baby!' cried Mary. 'Sorry, hen, I thought you knew. She had a little girl. Mandy they call her.'

'But why didn't she let me know?' said Dottie blinking back a tear. Peaches hadn't had a reply to her letter but Dottie was sure she would have forgiven her by now.

'Don't be too cross, hen,' said Mary. 'What with the baby and Gary's exercises, she's got a lot on her plate right now.'

'Yes, yes of course,' said Dottie. 'I wonder how Gary has coped. He hasn't seen his mum for ages.'

'Funnily enough,' said Mary, 'he wasn't too bad. The hospital gave him an Ivy and Brumas and as long as they were on the bed, he was happy.'

'As a matter of fact . . .' Dottie began.

'Where do these plates go, Mary?' Edna interrupted.

'What are you doing in here?' said Mary as she took the plates from Edna. 'You're the bridegroom's mother for goodness' sake. Leave that. We'll do it. Take her back in the hall, Dottie.'

Dottie took Edna's arm. 'Come on,' she laughed. 'We'd better do what the boss says.'

Some of the men had gone down to the off-licence to buy in

some more drink. Reg had helped himself to a beer and was sitting in the corner enjoying a roll-up. The accordionist was well into his repertoire and it was time to start the dancing but nobody could find Michael. Almost immediately, the cry went up.

'Where's the groom?'

'Have you seen Michael?'

Dottie came to find Reg. 'Can you go in the gents' to look for Michael? We can't start the evening without him.'

Wearily, Reg stood up to go.

Michael was peering at his reflection in the cracked mirror in the gents'. He was quite pleased with the results. Taking his comb out of his top pocket, he re-arranged his hair so that the front flopped down in the new Teddy-boy style.

So far the wedding breakfast had been better than he expected. Almost as good as old times. Even Reg was enjoying himself.

Apart from the odd film show, Michael hadn't been in the village hall since the war years. Back in 1941, Reg had come to one of the dances they put on. Michael always enjoyed the music but he was no dancer. Reg had danced like a dream and looked so handsome in his army uniform back then that he'd whisked the best-looking girl away.

Satisfied with his hair at last, Michael stepped back to admire himself as the man himself walked in.

'I've been sent to look for you,' Reg said. 'They want to start the dancing.'

'Looks like I'm being hen-pecked already,' Michael laughed good-naturedly.

Reg said nothing.

'You all right, Reg?'

'Fine. Just gets me, times like this. I think about all me mates . . .' His voice trailed.

Michael touched his shoulder and nodded.

'It may be six or seven years ago now,' Reg went on, 'but a

thing like that stays with you, you know.' He looked up at the groom and smiled bravely. 'Sorry, mate, shouldn't have brought it up on your wedding day.'

'No, no,' Michael said. 'It's OK.' Outside, in the hall, the accordion struck up a waltz. 'Better get going then,' he said awkwardly.

When he walked back into the room, Sylvie was talking and laughing with Mary and Tom. Dottie was in the kitchen serving more teas through the hatch. She looked so beautiful in that pretty pink dress. She smiled at him and motioned towards a cup and he gave her the thumbs up.

Michael looked around for his wife, unsure as to what he should do next, but Freda had already spotted him. She came gliding towards him.

'Mike, we have to start off the dance before we can go home and get ready for our honeymoon,' she beamed.

'But I can't dance,' he murmured, looking down at his feet. 'You know I can't.'

'Nobody can start without us,' she whispered. She held out her arms and he had no alternative but to accept her invitation.

As he placed his hand across her back, he felt her tremble. She was breathing very quickly and her face was lit up with excitement.

'Just shuffle around,' she murmured closely in his ear. 'Nobody will mind.'

The embarrassment of having two left feet made him feel silly but as they moved slowly around on the inside of the circle and all his friends were nodding and smiling, he found himself enjoying it.

Freda looked attractive in her wedding dress too. It was a bit tight around the waist but that wasn't her fault. He wished he hadn't got her in the family way, but at least he had done the decent thing. He gave Freda a quick smile and pulled her closer. She was probably thinking romantic thoughts about him, but right now he was thinking that he'd just have to make the best of it.

# *Eighteen*

The reception finished at around ten and everyone, with the exception of the bride and groom, who were hopefully already enjoying their honeymoon in Bournemouth, set about with the clearing up.

To Sylvie it looked like a well-oiled machine, although it did seem a little odd that they were clambering about under the stage with trestle tables in their wedding finery. Still, it was all done with good humour and fun.

'Er, watch what you're doing with that table leg,' said Tom as he backed out on all fours. 'You nearly did me a mischief.'

'Get yer big bum out of the way then,' came the light-hearted retort from Cecil Hargreaves, the bride's father.

'You off back home, Sylvie?' asked Mary.

'I'm staying one more night,' Sylvie smiled. 'I must get back home tomorrow.'

Reg was busy stacking chairs. He turned his head sharply and looked at Dottie.

'It's so late,' she said. 'I didn't think you'd mind.'

'Course he doesn't,' said Mary. 'You wouldn't send the poor girl off on a long drive down to the New Forest at this time of night, would you, Reg?'

Reg smiled thinly. 'Of course not.'

For a second or two, Dottie felt a little of her old nervousness coming back, but then she saw the way Reg helped the bride's mother into Sylvie's car and relaxed. When it came to older people, he had a kind heart really.

Once the hall had been swept and tidied and the last of the guests had gone, Dottie and Sylvie loaded her bits and bobs into the boot alongside the rest of the wedding cake. They'd been asked to drop that into Rose Hargreaves's place on the way home. Reg and Edna sat in the back of the car chatting about roses and what to do about black spot on the leaves.

Back at the cottage, Dottie and Sylvie brought in the rest of the stuff while Reg went down the garden to shut up the hens and check on the pig. By the time he got back, Dottie had three mugs of cocoa waiting on the kitchen table. If Reg was annoyed that Sylvie was staying a second night, he wasn't saying anything.

'Can we talk about this child of yours, Reg?' said Sylvie, jumping in feet first as he walked in the door.

His head jerked up and Dottie saw something flash in his eyes. Her heart missed a beat. 'We're all tired now, Sylvie,' she said quickly. 'Perhaps this could wait until the morning.'

'Reg is off to work in the morning,' said Sylvie, 'and I have to leave early too. We've been so busy, I've hardly had time to speak to you, have I, Reg? I know it's late but we need to clear a few things up, that's all.'

Reg looked as if he was chewing a wasp. 'Things? What things?'

'You'll be glad to hear, I will loan you the money,' said Sylvie, determined to rub his nose in it. 'I'm pleased to do it for Dottie's sake, but I must insist you do two things. First you should make absolutely sure the child really is yours, get a blood test or something, and secondly, you must get someone to escort her to this country. She can't possibly be left to her own devices on either a ship or an aeroplane. It will take six weeks with one and nearly three days with the other.'

'But we don't know anyone in Australia,' said Dottie.

'Ask Brenda. Is that her name?' said Sylvie. 'Or better yet, contact a missionary society or something. They often send their people home on furlough. I'm sure someone like that would help. What do you say, Reg?'

'There's no doubt she's my kid, see,' he said stubbornly. 'And as for the other . . .' He got out his wallet and took out an envelope. Dottie recognised it as the letter that had come the day before. He thrust it at Sylvie. Glancing up at Dottie, Sylvie took it out of the envelope and read it aloud.

*Dear Mr Cox,*

*Thank you so much for your letter. Sandy told me that although you were unable to register the baby yourself, you would be delighted to acknowledge Patricia as your child. I am so glad you still feel the way you do. Sandy always made it clear that she wanted you to have everything. She never stopped loving you. Now that we have heard from you, my good friend Doc Landers has kindly offered to pay for Patricia to go to England and be with you. Accordingly, she will be travelling with him to Southampton on the* Akarda *leaving here in a couple of days with Nurse Tranter (retired) and the Doc. As luck would have it, he has to return to England to see his mother who is ill. He is very fond of children and Patricia is a lovely little girl. All things considered, she is quite bright for her age and always very happy. I feel sure you will be able to offer her far more than I can. My husband is in the final stages of an illness and with four healthy children of my own to look after, I couldn't possibly give Patricia the kind of upbringing she deserves. She has suffered so much, poor lamb. She was devoted to Sandy and was quite confused when she died.*

*Patricia has sent you another letter of her own, which I enclose.*

*May I ask that you would be kind enough to let me know*

152

*how well she is doing from time to time? Just a line or a*
*postcard will do.*
　*I remain, yours sincerely,*
　*Brenda Nichols.*

There were two other pieces of paper enclosed with the letter.
One was a copy of Patricia's birth certificate. The margin marked
for the name and surname of father was blank. Sylvie said
nothing. Reg handed her another piece of paper.

*Dear Father,*
　*I am loking forward to coming to England. When I stay*
*with Auntie Brenda I sleep with Peggy. Will I have my own*
*bed in egland? I am bringing Suzy and my best book. Your*
*ever loving daghter*
　*Patricia.*

'So you see,' Reg said with a look of triumph in his eyes, as they
read it together. 'I don't need your bloody money or your sodding
advice.'

They both stared at him. Sylvie with horror, Dottie in surprise.

'Well,' he said passing by, 'I'm off up to bed.'

He was waiting with the light on when Dottie walked into the
bedroom. She searched his face, trying to understand his mood,
but he said nothing. The bedclothes were draped around his
hips and she could see at once that he was fully aroused. She
undressed quickly and reached for her nightdress.

'You don't need that,' he said coldly.

She hesitated. She was tired. It had been a long day. She wasn't
sure that she even wanted sex, especially not with Sylvie in the
next room and the walls as thin as tissue paper, but how could
she tell him? She took a deep breath and chewed her bottom lip
anxiously. 'Reg, if you don't mind, I . . .'

He rose up in the bed and grabbed her wrist, pulling her roughly towards him.

'Reg . . .' She was desperate but she still had the presence of mind to speak quietly. 'You're hurting me.'

He pulled her down onto the bed and forced his hand between her legs. She tried to push him away. 'No, Reg, I'm tired. Please . . .'

He lifted his head. '"No, Reg, I'm tired. Please . . ."' he mimicked. 'Well, I'm not. Get your legs up, woman.'

'Sylvie will hear.'

'Then you shouldn't have invited her for another night, should you,' he hissed. 'I'm sick of her filling your head with a load of nonsense. It's about time you did something for me for a change.'

She didn't want this. She really didn't want this but her struggles only excited him more. His probing fingers dug into her tender flesh, but when she tried to cry out he forced her to submit by rolling onto her and pinning her down.

'Quiet, darling. Sylvie will hear,' he smirked as his other hand went over her mouth.

She'd never seen him like this before. He'd become a monster. The pain he was inflicting with his fingers was almost unbearable and with his crushing weight on top of her, she could hardly breathe. The more she struggled, the harder he probed. Tears filled her eyes but still he had no pity. Then he took his hand away and, sliding both hands under her buttocks, mounted her. Then the thrusting began. It was agony and it seemed endless. She bit her lip until she tasted blood in an effort not to cry out.

'Please . . . please . . .' she sobbed.

Her skin stung so much it almost took her breath away and the pain got worse with each thrust. All at once he grunted aloud, pushed himself right into her and went rigid. It was over. He looked down at her, as if seeing her for the first time. A smile played across his lips. 'That was lovely, wasn't it, darlin'? You'll soon be beggin' for more. Just like old times.'

She stared at him with a look of disgust as he lifted himself from her and turned away, his face to the wall. With a contented sigh, he pulled the bedclothes up and said, 'Turn off the light, there's a good girl.'

Slowly and painfully, Dottie climbed out of the bed and picked up her nightdress from the floor. The material felt cool and light as it fell over her shaking shoulders. Soundlessly she walked over to the door and reached for the light switch. It clicked and she was plunged into darkness. She waited a second or two until her eyes adjusted and then she went to the bathroom to bathe her burning and bruised flesh with cold water. She was so sore she could hardly bear to pat herself dry on the rough towel.

When she came back into the bedroom, the moon was shining through the curtains and room was bathed in a cold harsh light. Dottie passed her tongue over her lips, tasting the salt of her silent tears.

She climbed into bed and lay very still. She could still feel him inside her and she hated him all the more for it. Staring up at the moonlit ceiling, Dottie willed herself not to cry. She found herself wondering about Michael and Mr Malcolm. Did they treat their wives like this? How gentle was Michael with Freda? Did Miss Josephine ever lie in her bed battered and so ill used? She didn't think so, but then if she were to ask her friends, none of them would believe what Reg had done here tonight. A renegade tear rolled down her cheek and onto the pillow. She'd asked him not to but he'd done it anyway. In the eyes of the law he had done no wrong. He'd simply taken what was his by right; but as far as she was concerned, he had raped her.

When he began to snore softly, she relaxed, knowing he wouldn't want her again tonight. What about the next time? Dear God, she couldn't bear the thought of a next time. Careful not to touch him, she turned over and faced the window. He stirred in his sleep and her heart began to pound.

That was the moment she knew that she was very, very frightened.

# Nineteen

Dottie woke with a start. The bright moonlight had waxed into the dull grey of early dawn. She slid out of bed quickly, anxious not to wake Reg. Grabbing a change of clothes, she tiptoed downstairs. The clock said 5.20am.

Rather than use the bathroom and risk another encounter with Reg, she washed in the bowl and dressed by the unlit fire. She curled up in the armchair and sipped her tea. She was still sore and she had a bruise on her lip. That must have been where he pressed his hand on her face. Miserably, she cupped her hands around the tea and swirled the dark liquid. Sylvie said to leave him – but how could she? If she cleared off now, with Patsy on the way, he wouldn't be able to look after her on his own. And besides, why should *she* go? This was *her* aunt's house. If anyone should leave, it should be him. But she knew that wouldn't happen, not in a month of Sundays. She reached up onto the mantelpiece and took down the letter. The postmark was dated two weeks ago. In a few weeks, by the middle of October, the girl would be here.

She looked at the child's letter again. She had very neat handwriting, which meant she was very bright for her age. Suzy was probably the name of her dolly. Dottie wondered how she was managing onboard. She leaned back and closed her eyes. She could just picture Patsy, in her pink and white gingham dress, her blonde curls bobbing along the deck as she played hide and seek with Dr Landers. Oh dear, what if Dr Landers was too old to play hide and seek? What if poor Patsy was seasick? What if poor old Nurse Tranter fell asleep in a deckchair and Patsy climbed through the railings and fell into the sea!

Dottie opened her eyes with a start. She heard the stairs creak and glanced at the clock. 5.45. Reg was coming downstairs.

Putting her cup into the hearth, Dottie fled into the scullery intending to disappear down the garden until he'd gone. She picked up the bucket of chicken feed but when she opened the door, it was raining. Tipping it down.

'Got the kettle on out there?' The sound of his voice made her stomach churn.

'Just coming,' she called.

The teapot was only warm. She switched on the gas and poured the contents of the teapot away.

Reg appeared in the doorway. 'Been looking at Patsy's letter again, I see.'

'I'm sorry,' she said wildly. Oh hell, she'd forgotten she'd still got it in her hand when she'd heard his footfall on the stairs. She must have automatically left it on the chair. 'I didn't mean to read your letter,' she gabbled. 'I'm sorry, Reg.'

She hated to sound like this but she was scared. Scared of what he might do . . .

'That's all right,' he smiled. 'Her new mum is bound to want to look at her picture.'

He walked towards her but mercifully the kettle began to boil, so she was able to turn away and busy herself by making a fresh pot of tea. When she walked into the kitchen he was sitting at the table. He caught her by the waist as she put the teapot onto the stand.

'Bread and cheese?' she asked.

'I'd rather have you all over again.'

Dottie looked at the ceiling. 'Sylvie's up there,' she squeaked. 'She might come down.'

'I like it best when somebody's listening. Adds more spice to it.' He let her go, slapping her bottom. 'Another time, eh?'

Dottie pulled down the kitchen cabinet and got out the bread. Her hands were trembling so much as she cut the slice, she didn't get it very straight. Normally Reg didn't like it when she messed things up but today he took it as a good omen.

'Looks like I've got you all of a dither,' he smiled.

She sat down in the armchair and put her hands around a new cup of tea.

He buttered his bread thickly. 'Cheese?'

'Sorry.'

She went to get up, but he raised his hand. 'I'll get it.'

As he bent to look in the cupboard, a head appeared at the window. The tramp, under an umbrella, his knuckles poised over the glass, peered into the room. Dottie leapt to her feet and shook her head. The tramp followed the direction of her eyes.

'Let me find it for you, Reg,' she said. Bending beside him, she reached into the cupboard and drew out the cheese dish. When she stood up, the tramp had gone.

'I was looking for a piece of cheese,' Reg snapped. 'Not a bloody dish.'

I have kept the cheese in that dish ever since we got married, she thought crossly, but she said nothing. Instead, she went back to the chair and sat down. Please don't let the tramp look through the window again, she thought anxiously.

They sat in silence as Reg ate his breakfast, then he stood up and reached for his coat in the nail behind the door. 'You do the animals,' he said, coming over to her. 'The rain will most likely clear up soon.'

Flinching, she didn't know what she was expecting him to do – but it certainly wasn't to plant a kiss on the top of her head. In the minutes while he was getting his bike out of the shed, she sat very still, listening to the slow tick-tocking of the clock.

159

She was confused. How could someone be so horrible at one time and then, a few hours later, be so nice?

Reg put his head around the door again. 'Oh and Dottie,' he said pleasantly.

Relaxing, she smiled up at him. 'Yes, Reg?'

'Make sure you get rid of that silly bitch upstairs before I come home.'

As soon as she was sure he had gone, Dottie stood up and went into the scullery. She made a third pot of tea and cut a couple of doorstep slices of bread and a hunk of cheese. It had stopped raining now but when she walked outside the tramp's tin can wasn't on the windowsill. Where was he? Perhaps sheltering from the rain somewhere? Then, as she turned to go back inside, she jumped a mile high. The tramp was standing right behind her.

'Lord, you made me jump,' she cried, clutching at her chest.

He didn't move.

'I'll get your tea.'

'No,' he said quickly. 'No need.'

She'd never seen him this close up before. His face was dark and swarthy but he didn't smell. In fact, he looked quite presentable, even smart. His features were weather-beaten and he was a lot younger than she had first thought – about fortyish, with tousled hair and watery blue grey eyes. She could see at once that his eyes were filled with sadness and she wondered what had happened to him that he should have been reduced to this. She wondered if he had been in action because he was wearing an army greatcoat. Hitler and that accursed war had damaged so many people in more ways than bombs alone could.

'Can I get you anything else?' Dottie asked gently.

'The old lady in the mauve dress . . .' The sound of his voice was a surprise. Quiet, with a gentle Irish lilt. She had expected something else altogether: for it perhaps to be deeper, or a voice coated with rattling phlegm.

'What old lady? There's only me here.'

He lifted his head towards Aunt Bessie's room and then looked back at her. He didn't elaborate but gradually his gaze rested somewhere behind her head.

All at once, Dottie's blood ran cold. Reg had come back? Was he right behind her and angry because she was giving the tramp something to eat. She swung sharply around, but there was no one there.

'Don't do that!' she cried. 'You're scaring me.'

He looked at her as if she'd whipped him and she was immediately sorry.

'She fell,' he said, his voice barely above a whisper.

'Oh, you mean my aunt?' said Dottie. 'Yes, you're right. I'm afraid she died. But that was a long time ago, nearly two years.'

He touched his forehead as if trying to remember something. 'She sent me back . . .'

'She fell down the stairs,' said Dottie.

'She was kind,' he said. 'A saint.'

Dottie laughed. 'She was a wonderful person but hardly a saint.'

'She helped me.'

'I know.'

'It was my fault . . .'

The upstairs sash cord window rattled open and Sylvie stuck her head out. 'Oh, it's you, Dottie. I wondered who you were talking to.'

'I was just talking to . . . I'm sorry, I don't know your name.' She turned back to introduce him, but the tramp had gone. 'Where did he go?'

'Who?'

'The chap I was talking to. Didn't you see him?'

Sylvie shook her head. 'Is it all right to come down?'

161

'Yes, of course.'

As she went indoors, Dottie felt puzzled. His fault? Whatever did the tramp mean? Was he there the day Aunt Bessie fell down the stairs? And if so, why didn't he get help?

When Sylvie and Dottie sat down to breakfast, the atmosphere between them was a bit awkward. Dottie knew Sylvie must have heard her and Reg. It was obvious she wanted to say something but Dottie could hardly bring up the subject herself. It was too embarrassing. In the end, they both skirted around it.

'I can't believe you didn't see the tramp,' said Dottie. 'He was right beside me.'

'I heard voices,' said Sylvie, 'but it took me a couple of minutes to get to the window. Anyway, what did he want?'

'He comes round now and again for something to drink and a sandwich.'

'Robin says we shouldn't encourage that sort.'

'Reg says the same,' said Dottie, pouring Sylvie another cup of tea. 'But he's not that old. He hasn't been around for ages. I was surprised to see him looking reasonably well turned out. I keep wondering what must happen to someone, that they should have just given up on life like that.'

'Too much drink most likely.'

'I don't think so,' said Dottie. 'He doesn't smell of drink.'

Sylvie got out her cigarette case. 'What was he talking about?'

'He mentioned Aunt Bessie.'

Sylvie tapped her cigarette onto the case and looked Dottie straight in the eye. 'Did he hurt you? Reg? Last night, did he hurt you?'

Dottie felt her face flame. 'I don't want . . . it's none . . . no . . . yes . . .'

Sylvie covered Dottie's hand with hers. 'Listen, darling, I know you don't want to talk about it, but really, I meant every word I said. If you ever change your mind, ring me. Keep four pennies handy for the phone box so that you've got it day or night and I'll come. Wherever you are, I promise I'll come.'

Dottie sat very still, conscious that a large tear had rolled down her cheek and fallen onto the plate in front of her. She felt so humiliated she wanted to curl up and die. Sylvie handed her a pretty lace-edged handkerchief. Numbly she took it and wiped her eyes. 'Thank you.' Her voice was very small. The sound of the clock seemed to get louder.

Sylvie took a long drag of her cigarette and put her head back. Dottie tried not to make a sound as she cleared her nose.

'Do you have to have this child of his?'

'How will he look after her if I go?'

'That's hardly a good reason to stay,' said Sylvie.

Dottie sighed. Sylvie was right. Why should she stay here and look after Reg's daughter? This was *her* home. She wanted so much to say 'Yes, Sylvie, I'll go with you' – but if she left, Reg would get the house by default.

'This is my home,' Dottie said desperately. 'And besides, I can't let him down. Not after he's suffered so much.'

'Dottie, you can't spend your whole life trying to make someone else happy. It's time you thought about what *you* want.' Sylvie leaned towards her as if she was going to say something else, but then she seemed to think better of it.

'If Reg is happy, then I'll be happy,' Dottie said, struggling to regain her composure. 'Look, I don't want to be rude, Sylvie, but I don't see the point of going over and over the same thing and that's that. You're very kind to be so concerned but please, you're not to worry about me.'

'A very pretty speech,' said Sylvie, 'but don't forget, I slept here last night.'

Dottie's face flamed. She couldn't talk about last night. It was ... humiliating. As she rose to leave, Sylvie put up her hand up. 'Point taken, darling. If you'd rather not talk about it, we'll say no more. Like I said in the car, I care too much about you to quarrel.'

163

They finished their breakfast, making polite conversation, then Dottie helped Sylvie to pack her things. By 8.25 she was ready for the off and Dottie stood in the road to wave her goodbye.

Sylvie handed her the framed photograph of the two of them with Aunt Bessie. 'I thought you might like to have this,' she said. 'I had it enlarged and framed to remind you of the happy times we had together.'

'Oh, Sylvie!' cried Dottie. 'It's lovely. I'd quite forgotten it. She looked so funny in that old cowboy hat.'

'How did she get it?' Sylvie asked. 'I've been trying to remember . . .'

'Colonel Warren gave it to her, didn't he?'

'Of course,' cried Sylvie. 'All those American Square Dances she organised.'

They looked at each other and, smiling broadly, chorused, 'Yee-ha!'

Sylvie put her arm around Dottie's shoulder and they leaned over the photograph again. 'Dear Aunt Bessie. I always think of her in that dress.'

Dottie smiled. 'She was wearing it the day she died.' Something made her stop. She frowned thoughtfully. Something was niggling at the back of her mind, something she couldn't quite put her finger on. The tramp. He'd asked about the lady with the mauve dress. Aunt Bessie was wearing it in the photograph and she was wearing it the day she died. She shivered. The tramp must have seen her. So why didn't he raise the alarm?

'What is it?' Sylvie asked.

'Nothing,' she said, shaking the dark thoughts away. 'You'd better get going and I've got to get to work. They embraced and Dottie kissed her on the cheek. 'You're a good friend.'

As soon as she was in the car, Sylvie wound down the car windows. 'Please think about getting away from Reg,' she said. 'Don't leave it too long, and for God's sake, don't end up getting pregnant with his child.'

She roared away down the road, with Dottie staring after her. Don't end up getting pregnant . . . The words reverberated around her head. As she turned to go back inside, Dottie found herself saying, 'Absolutely not. I can't get pregnant now . . . Not now . . .'

# Twenty

Was her period late?

Dottie had never really bothered keeping tabs on her monthly cycle. Why should she? She had no reason to even think about it when Reg was unable to perform but she hadn't come on at all this month.

She was handwashing her sheets in the big tin bath outside the back door. They had already been boiled in the copper and she'd staggered out with the clean sheet in a double-handled bowl to tip it into the bath of cold water to begin rinsing. It was backbreaking and exhausting work. She would wring the sheet by hand, passing it along her forearm until one end coiled itself back into the empty bowl. When both sheets were done, she would empty the bath and refill it with cold water and add a drummer blue to whiten the sheets. After a good soak and another wringing by hand, she would fold it and put it through the old mangle before it went onto the line.

The last few golden days of autumn were fading. Already there was a nip in the air. Time had hardly moved on since Michael's wedding. He and Freda were back from honeymoon. Now at last the new Mrs Gilbert made no secret of their forthcoming happy event. Dottie had bumped into her several times in the village, her increasing girth now swathed in maternity dresses and her strained look turned into a glow. She and Michael had made a home for themselves on the farm using the old quarters used by the Land Girls during the war. Dottie hadn't seen it but she imagined it would look a darned sight better than it did back then.

Things had taken an upward turn for Ann Pearce as well. Dottie was aware that several other householders in the village were keen to find a good daily woman. They had been trying to get Dottie to work for them for ages. Colonel Harris, who was retired, and his sister, Miss Harris, a piano teacher, were two of them. Then there was Miss Edwards. Now too elderly and infirm to leave her home, she was a mine of information and was always bang up-to-date with all the village gossip.

It had been tricky approaching Ann about the job, but Dottie's decision to introduce her to Miss Edwards had been a master-stroke. The two of them hit it off straight away. Brian and Phyllis loved being with the twins all day and Mary was pleased to be able to buy a few things with the extra money Ann gave her.

Things were not so good for Dottie, however. For a few days after the wedding, Reg's demands were frequent and sickening. Sometimes she tried to fight him off, but that only seemed to enflame his passion. She had a growing dread of bedtime and spent as long as she could downstairs doing odd jobs in the vain hope that he would be asleep when she came up to bed. It didn't happen very often. Her body was so tender, she had resorted to lying to him, telling him she had her period. She'd even complained of stomach ache and that they'd gone on longer than usual, but the truth was she was late.

It was ironic that after all those years of longing for a child, even praying for one, all the years of trying to seduce Reg, now she hated the very thought of being with him. He was a brute. Dottie didn't even want to think of the things he'd done to her. He seemed to enjoy it all the more when she was crying and pleading with him to stop. And when it was all over, he would pat her like a dog and tell her what a good girl she was. It had got to the stage when she couldn't bear him to touch her.

Heaving the wet sheet back into the cold-water rinse, she knew she couldn't hold out much longer. He was no fool. He'd know she was lying. Once the sheet was submerged, she stood up and pressed her apron against her stomach. But she couldn't be pregnant. She mustn't be.

In three days, Patsy would be here. Dottie'd kept nagging him to do something about the old well, but somehow he never seemed to get round to it. It made her feel nervous. Patsy might run around the garden and . . .

Ever since she'd read the child's letter, Dottie had felt different about Patsy. More than likely, Elizabeth Johns had been a loving and caring mother. Patsy had suffered the trauma of losing her mother and now she was being shipped to a place far away from all that was familiar.

Australia was hot and barren. Dottie had once seen a picture of place called Ayers Rock and it looked an empty and desolate place. By comparison, England would seem very cold, even on a summer's day. It was true, the Worthing area was sheltered from extremes of weather by the Downs, but winters could still be very cold and sometimes they had snow. Not as deep as in the north, but enough to cause problems on the roads. How, she wondered, would a little girl used to the heat manage to cope with an English winter?

Dottie had had little time to prepare for Patsy's arrival. She was desperate to finish Mrs Fitzgerald's curtains and the bedspread, but she'd spent most evenings knitting for Patsy. Her favourite was a yellow jumper with a brown kangaroo on the front.

'Do you think she'll like this one?' she'd asked Reg. She'd held it up but he paid little attention.

As for the people in the village, Dottie had stuck to their agreed story and it had worked . . . after a fashion.

'Why the hell adopt a kid all the way from Australia?' Janet Cooper wanted to know. 'There are plenty of kids in this country who need a mum and dad. Barnardo's is bulging with them.'

'It's being done through an old colleague Reg knew during the war,' Dottie had said, but she was a hopeless liar. She could already feel her face beginning to burn.

Mary may have seemed a little disapproving as well but the next time she'd seen Dottie she'd given her a bag of clothes. 'Take what you want and give the rest back to me,' she'd said. 'We all help each other out and there are plenty of others I know that could do with a thing or two.'

Dottie smiled. So that would explain why she'd seen Phyllis Pearce wearing the jumper she'd knitted little Maureen Prior two Christmases ago.

The sheets were ready for the mangle. Dottie wiped the roller with a cloth and then passed the cloth through to check for any bits. She'd learned her lesson when, as a new bride, she'd put a sheet straight into the mangle and it came out the other side complete with a squashed spider and she'd had to rinse it all over again.

Dottie slowly turned the handle. The sheet was thick and it was hard work getting it through. There was a footfall behind her and Dottie spun around.

It was Vincent Dobbs, the postman.

'Thanks, Vince,' she said as he handed her a small pile of letters and waited while she wiped her hands on her apron.

Two bills, a letter from Sylvie (she recognised the handwriting and the Brockenhurst postmark), and a letter for Reg. She sighed. Still nothing from Peaches. Sylvie had been so sure a letter would help to heal the rift between them but Dottie had written her three letters and received not one reply. Reg didn't mind her writing so she had put her last letter behind the clock for posting on Sunday. Reg had taken it and put it in the box first thing on Monday so she would have had it, maybe second post, but certainly on Tuesday morning. She'd told Peaches all about their plans to fetch Patsy. She'd asked about Gary and even offered to help with babysitting when he got back home, but nothing. No reply. No word . . . nothing. It looked as if she'd lost one of her dearest friends forever.

Sylvie's letter was chatty and fun. After she'd told Dottie all about the children she wrote:

*Robin is as busy as ever. I have been thinking about your wonderful talent for furnishings and I was wondering if you would come here and do some work for me? I can't invite you just yet, because I am meeting my riding friend in London for a few days . . .*

Oh Sylvie, Dottie thought, you are naughty.

*. . . I will be in touch with you as soon as I get back. Don't forget, darling, if ever you are in trouble, you know where I am.*

Dottie slipped Sylvie's letter into her apron pocket as Reg came out of the house, dressed and ready for work. 'Any post?'

Dottie handed him the bills and his letter and, after a cursory glance, he pushed them into his pocket. 'What's the matter with you? You've got a face like a wet weekend.'

'I wish Peaches would write,' she said. 'I've sent her three or four letters but ever since we had that row about Gary, I haven't heard a word.'

He was looking at her with a strange expression. She frowned. 'What? What is it?' Something was wrong . . .

'You know something, don't you, Reg. Is it Gary? Has something happened to him?'

He went into his shed and took down a small tin. A few seconds later, she heard him unlocking a drawer. 'I didn't want you to see this,' he said coming back out. 'I knew you'd be upset.'

His face was so serious, her mouth went dry and her chest felt tight.

'Peaches came round.'

Dottie gasped. 'What? When? I didn't see her.'

'I found this pushed through the letterbox.' He handed her something. Tears swam in Dottie's eyes as she recognised her own letter to Peaches. It had been torn in half.

'I tried to protect you,' said Reg, 'but this makes it obvious, doesn't it? She doesn't want anything to do with you.'

'But I don't understand,' said Dottie quietly. She stared down at the pieces. 'Why didn't she read it? If only she had opened it first, it would have explained everything.'

Reg put his arm around her shoulder. 'She's not bloody worth it.'

He went back into the shed and brought out his bike. 'Well, I'm off now. See you at ten and then we'll have some fun.'

She almost retched. She had a lump in her throat and she could feel her eyes pricking. At least she still had one friend, she thought, glancing at Sylvie's letter again. Should she read it again already? No. It was something to look forward to when she finished the washing. Shoving the letter back into her apron pocket, she picked up the other end of a folded sheet and reached for the handle.

# *Twenty-One*

'People will think we're off to another wedding,' Dottie joked as Reg locked the front door on the morning they went to fetch Patsy.

It was Thursday October 11th and the weather was bright and clear. Dottie was happy. Determined not to think about her fears today, and dressed in her best clothes, she and Reg walked arm in arm to the station to catch the train to Southampton. Over her other arm, she carried a warm coat taken from the bag of children's clothes Mary had given her.

The truth of the matter was, her feelings were all over the place. She still hadn't had her period but she hadn't been sick in the morning. Could that mean it was a false alarm? Plenty of people missed a month now and again. She'd heard Peaches and Mary talk about it often enough.

Even though Reg was still rough in bed, during the daytime he'd been really nice to her, calling her 'my little wifey' and kissing her on the cheek. He'd had another letter from abroad with instructions as to where to meet Patsy when she arrived in the country. It was from Dr Landers, the man who was bringing Patsy from Australia and it had been posted in Gibraltar.

*I suspect Brenda has already told you that I am returning to England to spend some time with my widowed mother who*

*has been very unwell. Nurse Tranter is in charge of Patricia*
*but I am on hand should she need any help. Nurse Tranter is*
*a capable woman with many years of experience. She is*
*moving back to Wales to retire. We shall all be arriving in*
*Southampton. The responsibility is no hardship because I*
*have become very fond of Patricia. Despite her straitened*
*circumstances, Sandy did an amazing job with her and we*
*are all hoping that Patricia will settle down with you very*
*quickly. However, I should like to keep up contact with her,*
*and I know it will ease Brenda's mind if every now and then*
*she can have a first-hand report. Perhaps when we meet, we*
*could arrange a date at our mutual convenience for me to*
*come and see Patricia in her new home.*

*I remain yours sincerely,*
*J. Landers.*

'Bloody interfering busybodies,' Reg had grumbled. 'Everybody
wants to sticky-beak into my business.'

But this morning, as Dottie had watched him putting the
letter into his breast pocket, Reg had been very excited and she
was glad for him. Perhaps this really would be the start of a
new era in their lives. Perhaps with a child in the house he
would restrain himself a little more. Certainly he wouldn't be
able to make her do some of the things he'd wanted with Patsy
around. For a start, he'd have to stop groping her whenever he
wanted. Besides, maybe if he took it a little slower, she might
even get to like it . . . No, she would never get used to it, and
she shuddered at the thought.

'What's up?' he asked.

'Just thinking about meeting Patsy,' she said.

He patted her hand. 'Good girl,' he murmured.

Yes, she thought hopefully, perhaps he will change. Look what
happened to Tom Prior.

'I've never seen such a change in a man,' Mary had said after the birth of the twins. 'He became a father overnight to my kids and now that Christopher and Connie are here, he can't do enough for us all.'

They had reached the station.

'Off to fetch our kid today,' Reg told Marney as they stopped by the ticket office for a rail pass. As an employee, Reg didn't have to pay.

Marney cupped his illicit cigarette behind his hand and coughed. 'Best of luck, mate,' he said, once he'd recovered.

The 8.32 thundered into the station. The next time I see this platform, Dottie thought to herself, my life will be changed forever. They selected a seat and Reg took out his newspaper.

Dottie sat back and did her best to enjoy the journey. Life was so confusing at the moment. A few short weeks ago she had been dreading the thought of having a child in the house, but now it was really happening. As she gazed out of the window, she seemed to see little pockets of family life everywhere. A woman and her children waiting at the gates at Angmering to go to school, a little boy on a rope swing in a garden somewhere near Chichester, a man with a small child on his shoulders watching the trains go by at Emsworth, and a group of women with prams waiting outside a church hall for a clinic to start at Fareham.

Throughout the journey, Dottie lovingly stroked Patsy's coat. It was a very pretty cherry red trimmed with black. None of Mary's children had worn it, but she fancied it was the same one Freda's little sister used to wear. It was double-breasted and made with wool. It had black buttons and a black trim on the cuffs, a Peter Pan collar and a flared skirt. There was a matching bonnet with a turned-back brim trimmed with black and a tie under the chin. It would make a perfect frame for a halo of blonde curls. Dottie had made some knitted gloves to go with it. It might be mild for the time of year, but Dottie reasoned that, coming from such a hot place, Patsy wouldn't be used to the autumnal nip in the air.

She wondered what Dr Landers would be like. Having given the best years of his life to Australia, he was probably glad to be returning to his homeland to retire. He was obviously very worried about his poor old mother. Seeing as Nurse Tranter was returning to retire as well, Dottie hoped they hadn't found looking after a lively eight year old too tiring.

By the time they'd reached Havant, Reg was chain smoking and the tension mounted as they pulled into Southampton station. He almost lost it at the ticket barrier. He had given her the rail pass as they got on the train at Worthing and she'd absentmindedly pushed it into her bag. During the journey, it had slipped right down the bottom, and Dottie couldn't find it straight away.

The ticket collector waited patiently.

'Women,' laughed Reg. 'She's got everything but the kitchen sink in there.'

The man shared the joke as Dottie struggled to find the pass. It took her several minutes and it was only unearthed after she'd taken out her purse, lipstick, a couple of hankies, a set of keys, as well as some old letters Aunt Bessie wrote when her mother died.

'You only had the bloody thing five minutes,' Reg hissed in her ear as they left.

'I'm sorry,' Dottie said.

'Give it here,' he said churlishly, snatching it from her hand and put it in his back pocket. 'Making me look a ruddy fool . . .'

In his letter, Dr Landers had suggested they meet in the foyer of the Railway Hotel. It was an old Victorian building which, amazingly, had survived the terrible bombing in the city. Its dark red and gold interior spoke of a bygone and more opulent age. Dottie gazed in wonder at the chandeliers and the plush carpet. The foyer itself was huge. Sofas and chairs were arranged in small groups around the drinks tables. In the windows, between the heavy drapes, large aspidistras blocked the sunlight and at the other end of the foyer was a bar. Several guests and visitors sat on the bar stools enjoying a lunchtime drink. Beyond the foyer, Dottie could see the restaurant, which had white tablecloths and a silver service.

Reg looked distinctly uncomfortable and began running his finger around the inside of his collar in a desperate attempt to avoid the eye of the doorman. It was obvious he didn't know what to do, so Dottie took charge.

Marching up to the reception desk, she said, 'Mr and Mrs Cox to see Doctor Landers.'

The receptionist picked up the telephone and as Reg came to join her she noticed his collar was sticking up at the corner. She went to smooth it out for him but he hit her hand away and glared at her.

The receptionist replaced the receiver. 'Dr Landers will come down as soon as he can,' she said. 'He invites you to order a drink from the bar at his expense.'

'Thank you,' said Dottie graciously. 'I'll . . .'

'I'll have a pint of bitter,' Reg interrupted. 'She'll have a port and lemon.'

The receptionist glanced back at Dottie and she nodded. In actual fact, she would have preferred to try out one of those new Babycham drinks she'd seen advertised at the pictures but now she was too embarrassed to change the order.

'If you would like to sit down . . .' the receptionist smiled.

'Where?' Reg wanted to know.

'Anywhere you like, sir. The waiter will bring your order.'

They sat near a window, Reg following Dottie until she chose the place, her only aim to get as far away from the desk as possible.

'Why come all the way over here?' he grumbled as he sat down. Dottie ignored him, preferring to look out of the window. Her chin wobbled and her eyes were pricking.

Southampton was a busy place. She had never seen so many cars and pedestrians. Across the road, there was a bombsite, overgrown with weeds and buddleia, but in other open spaces she could see bright modern buildings going up. It all looked so light and fresh.

The barman, dressed in white shirtsleeves, black waistcoat and red bowtie brought them their drinks on a silver tray.

'Bring us another beer,' said Reg, before he'd even taken a sip. As the man walked away he said, 'I reckon he's a bloody nancy-boy,' and Dottie felt sick with embarrassment.

They sat in silence. Dottie wondered if she would know Dr Landers if she saw him. She turned her head just as a middle-aged man, balding and with a paunch walked towards them. Dottie made eye contact and smiled. She was about to stand up and hold out her hand when the woman on the table in front of them stood up, saying, 'Charles, darling.' As the pair met, they embraced each other warmly.

Dottie shifted her gaze back to the street outside.

'Mr and Mrs Cox?'

The unexpectedness of his soft voice made her jump. She turned her head and saw a dark-haired man with sparkling hazel eyes and a ready smile.

'Mr and Mrs Reginald Cox?' he repeated.

'That's right,' said Reg.

Dottie wondered why the man was giving Reg such an odd look. 'I'm Dr John Landers.'

She hadn't expected him to be so young. Well, he wasn't *that* young – thirty, thirty-five – but he certainly wasn't the balding fifty year old she'd been expecting to meet. His face was tanned and he had a line of freckles over the bridge of his nose. His teeth were white and evenly formed. He wore a lightweight cream suit made out of linen and a plain shirt, but no tie.

They all shook hands and he drew up a chair and sat beside them. 'I thought I would take the opportunity to have a chat with you before I take you upstairs to meet your daughter.'

'What's there to chat about?' Reg asked gruffly.

Dr Landers was unfazed by his rudeness. 'How was your trip?'

'We came by train,' Dottie said quickly. 'It wasn't very far. Not as far as you've come, anyway.'

Dr Landers laughed softly. Dottie looked away quickly. He was making her feel all of a flutter.

'I presume you want to take her home straight away,' he said. 'She's in good health but I expect you'll want to get her looked at by your own doctor. Anyway, I've brought all the relevant paperwork with me.' He placed a small case on the table between them. 'I won't open it now, but it's all there. Her birth certificate, her mother's death certificate, all her medical reports and the records of her childhood illnesses – you know, measles and all that stuff. By and large, she's been very healthy all things considered. Is there anything you want to ask me?'

'Brenda said Sandy left me everything,' Reg said.

Dottie was shocked but Dr Landers simply smiled. 'That's right. All the relevant papers are in the case.

Reg continued to stare.

'Has Patricia got any likes or dislikes?' Dottie asked, careful to avoid Dr Landers' eyes.

'I thought you might ask me that,' he chuckled. 'Brenda has written you a letter. She spent days getting it all down, so you can bet your boots everything is there. She's got her favourite toy, of course, Suzy. A grey elephant. Her mother gave it to her. Suzy goes everywhere with her, and even though she is very grown up in many ways, Patricia gets very upset if she can't find her.'

The waiter came back with another pint of beer and Reg took it from the tray himself and took a long drink from it.

'I'm sorry,' said Dr Landers, as the waiter hovered. 'Where are my manners? Would you like something to eat? A meal, a sandwich or something?'

He ordered a round of sandwiches and Reg excused himself to go to the gents'. He walked briskly. His cheeks prickled with rage and his nostrils flared. The toilet cubicle was occupied and Reg headed straight for the urinal. After relieving himself, he stood chewing the inside of his cheek. How much money was there then? Why couldn't the doctor tell him and put him out of his misery? Perhaps he didn't know. Yes, that was it. The solicitor had written a private letter.

Behind him, the toilet flushed and the waiter who had brought him the beer came out of the cubicle. Reg stared at him, his lip curling. The young man nodded briefly and went to the sink to wash his hands. As he put his hands under the tap, Reg stepped towards him. Their eyes met in the mirror over the sink and the waiter's face went white. In his haste to get out of the gents', the man left the tap running. Reg kicked the cubicle door.

'Bloody poofter,' he shouted after him.

'Your mother . . .?' Dottie began as Reg left for the gents'.

Dr Landers acknowledged her concern with a smile. 'Nice of you to ask, Mrs Cox. She's not too good at the moment but I'm hopeful that she will make a full recovery.'

'I'm glad.'

'Do you have any other children, Mrs Cox?'

Dottie shook her head.

'But now you've got Patricia.'

'Now I've got Patricia,' she repeated with a smile.

'I'm afraid that by the time the funeral expenses were seen to,' Dr Landers went on, 'there wasn't a lot left. When Brenda took her in, Sandy was almost destitute.'

'We'll be all right,' said Dottie. 'I have a little money coming to me next year. Patsy will lack for nothing.'

'As for the paperwork,' he went on, 'now that I've handed her over, the solicitor will write to your husband. That correspondence has to be private between him and Mr Cox until such time as you legally adopt Patricia.'

'I quite understand,' Dottie smiled.

'I know this is none of my business,' he continued cautiously, 'but I just want to say, what you are doing is marvellous. It can't have been easy for you to accept having Patricia as your own child. I must say I admire you enormously.'

Dottie felt her face colouring. 'What else could I do? She's my husband's child.'

'Ummm,' said Dr Landers leaning back in the chair. 'So it would seem.'

What did that mean? Dottie was slightly puzzled by his remark. She was about to say something when he interrupted her. 'It doesn't worry you? Taking in another woman's child, I mean?'

'Not at all,' she said but she couldn't meet his gaze and looked away.

'Tell me about Worthing, Mrs Cox.'

'There's not much to tell,' she laughed softly. 'It's on the south coast. It's thirteen miles from Brighton and they say it's full of newlyweds and nearly-deads.'

Dr Landers chuckled. 'Are you far from the sea?'

'About three miles.'

The waiter put three plates of sandwiches in front of them. 'Please,' said Dr Landers, 'help yourself.'

Their eyes met and Dottie was startled by their gentleness. 'You know, Sandy was a remarkable woman,' he went on. 'She kept a diary. We've put it in the case. It might help you to know what the child has been through, and of course, when she's old enough, I'm sure it will mean a lot to Patricia.'

Reg came back and ate his sandwiches in silence. Dottie and Dr Landers made small talk and eventually Reg finished the rest of his bitter. 'Look here, Doc,' he said. 'No offence, but I'd sooner see my Patsy than sit down here stuffing sandwiches and having a natter. We've got to get back to Worthing.'

'Yes, yes, of course,' said the doctor. 'I'll take you both up now.'

The room was on the second floor. As they walked in, a grey-haired woman wearing round, silver-rimmed glasses stood up. She was dressed in a grey skirt with a white blouse and sensible shoes.

Dottie may have got it all wrong when it came to Dr Landers, but Nurse Tranter was every bit as she had imagined.

'Where is she?' Dr Landers asked.

'She's just gone across to my room to get her toy,' the nurse said. 'I was just going to read her a story.'

Dottie noticed she was holding a book in her hand.

'Mr and Mrs Cox,' said Doctor Landers, 'Nurse Tranter. Nurse Tranter, Mr and Mrs Cox.'

All three of them shook hands. The older woman gave Dottie a warm smile but when she shook Reg's hand Dottie noticed a strange look pass between her and Dr Landers. Something was wrong. Dottie's stomach began to churn. Didn't they think he was right for Patsy? Reg was hardly being Mr Polite, was he? Was his attitude going against them?

The doctor walked down the hallway into another room and they could hear low voices. Reg was a bag of nerves. He was twitching all the time and kept turning his hat around in his hands. Every now and then, he ran his fingers along the collar of his shirt or touched the knot in his tie.

Nurse Tranter slipped the book she was holding onto a chair and waited in silence. Dottie turned her head and looked out of the window. Her heart was thumping and her legs had become like jelly now that they were so close to meeting Patsy. Supposing Patsy didn't like them? And what was that look that had passed between Dr Landers and Nurse Tranter? What would happen to Patsy if they decided she and Reg didn't measure up?

She heard a soft footfall and the door to the room creaked open but Dottie didn't move. Let Reg see her first, she told herself. This is his moment. She's his child. She forced herself to watch the people on the street below, hurrying in and out of the shops, climbing on buses, crossing the road. A man with only one leg was busking on the corner. A bus pulled up and several people got off. The bus took off again and someone ran after it, catching the central pole on the back and leaping onboard just as it gathered speed.

Behind her she heard the doctor saying, 'Here we are Patricia. This man is your daddy.'

She waited for a cry of joy, or at the very least, an acknowledgement, but there was no sound. Reg said nothing. As the ominous silence deepened, she turned her head slowly. He seemed to be transfixed. Unsmiling, he appeared to be rooted to the spot.

Dr Landers was standing in the doorway holding Patsy's hand. Dottie looked right at her.

Her hair was very dark and there was no sign of the halo of blonde curls Dottie had imagined. Instead, it was parted on the side and very curly. It was roughly cut in a pudding-basin style and she wore a large pink and white bow, which was badly tied. Her elfin face was dainty and her brown eyes were large and soft. She was thin, like Reg, but her skin was the colour of coffee cream . . . and something told Dottie it was more than a decent suntan.

Reg still hadn't moved.

'Hello, Patsy,' said Dottie awkwardly. 'It's lovely to see you. We've come a long way to meet you.'

The child regarded her carefully. 'Is that my new name?' she said looking up at Dr Landers.

'I'm sorry,' said Dottie quickly. 'Don't you like it? It's just that your father likes to call you Patsy.'

Dottie appealed to Reg with her eyes, but he continued staring.

The child looked up at John Landers. 'I like Patsy,' she said. 'Will my mummy mind if I change my name?'

The doctor shook his head. 'I'm sure she won't.'

Dottie felt a lump forming in her throat. 'Right then,' she said brightly as she glanced at the nurse. 'That's settled.' She held out her hand. 'How d'you do, Patsy?'

The child glanced back at the doctor for reassurance. Dr Landers smiled and nodded so Patsy let go of his hand and came towards her. The two of them shook hands formally. 'Are you going to look after me now?' she asked gravely.

Dottie struggled to keep her voice even. 'I should like that very much,' she smiled.

'What is your name?'

'Dottie . . . call me Auntie Dottie.'

'Mr Cox,' said the doctor, clearing his throat noisily. 'Is there anything you want to ask me?'

Reg turned his head. 'I'm sorry, Doc . . .' he began.

Dottie held her breath. Doctor Landers gave him a sympathetic look. 'You need time to think about this.'

'I think we'd better be making a move,' said Reg. 'If it's all the same to you. Our train leaves at four.'

'You're taking her?'

Reg was staring at the brown suitcase with a stony expression. The doctor turned to the nurse. 'Are her things ready?'

Nurse Tranter nodded and walked out of the room.

'I'm afraid we haven't got a coat for her.'

'That's all right,' smiled Dottie. 'I've brought one. I hope it fits.'

'Is that for me?' cried Patsy, her eyes dancing with excitement.

It fitted as if it had been made for her, and she looked so pretty. Reg took the brown suitcase, leaving Dottie to carry the suitcase with Patsy's clothes. They made their way back to the foyer.

'If it's at all possible,' said John Landers, 'I should like to keep in contact.'

Reg walked out onto the street.

'Mrs Cox,' he added in a low voice, 'is your husband all right? I mean . . .'

'Everything's fine,' smiled Dottie. 'This has all been a bit overwhelming, that's all. My husband is not very good at letter-writing, but I promise I'll drop you a line.'

The doctor gave her his mother's address and they shook

hands, then he bent to kiss the child. 'Goodbye, Patricia . . . er, Patsy. Have a lovely time.'

'Goodbye, Dr Landers. Thank you for looking after me.'

The doctor straightened himself up. Dottie noticed he had a tear in his eye.

'Mrs Cox,' he ventured, 'if I may be permitted to give you a little advice . . . It will be difficult to begin with. Don't try and solve all the problems at once.'

Dottie nodded. 'I'll take good care of her, I promise.'

'And above all,' he said, 'love her.'

'I will,' Dottie said. They shook hands, the fear and suspicion they both shared remaining unspoken.

Outside on the street, Reg was leaning with one foot up against the wall, sucking hard on a cigarette. As soon as Dottie came out of the hotel he hurried ahead of her. She grabbed Patsy's hand and the two of them began running after him. 'Reg, Reg, slow down, will you?'

'I just want to get home.'

'You've had a bit of a shock.'

Reg rounded on her. 'Bit of a shock?' he said between his teeth. 'I'll say I've had a bit of a shock.'

He stood in front of her, eyeball to eyeball, his face contorted with pent-up rage. Patsy had crashed into her side, so Dottie pressed her against her body, covering her one exposed ear with her hand. She pleaded with Reg with her eyes. *Don't say anything awful, please . . .*

'In all those letters she wrote,' he spat in low voice, 'and in all the ones I had from that Brenda woman, and the one that stuck-up doctor wrote . . .'

'Reg . . . don't . . .'

'Not one of them, not one,' he ranted on, 'had the decency to tell me that she was a bloody half-breed. '

# Twenty-Two

Patsy was in bed. Dottie poured herself a cup of tea and sat down by the fire. Anxious that the child might already be feeling the cold, she'd lit it as soon as they'd got home. Now it was 7.30 and already dark outside.

The journey home had been strained. She and Patsy had had to run all the way to the station to keep up with Reg and he'd hardly said one word all the way home. Fortunately they didn't have to wait long for the train, but he'd refused to sit in the crowded carriage with them, preferring to stand in the corridor outside, chain smoking and looking out of the window.

Dottie did her best to make Patsy feel at ease but there was one heart-stopping moment when she'd asked, 'Have I made my daddy cross?'

'No, dear,' Dottie lied. 'Daddy is just thinking about important things.'

To take their minds off the situation, Dottie told Patsy all about their home. Patsy was excited to discover they had chickens and a pig.

'My Auntie Bren has chooks,' she said. 'Uncle Burt used to tell everybody on the radio school whenever we had baby chooks. Do you listen to Uncle Burt's radio school?'

Dottie shook her head. She wasn't even sure what that was. 'You'll go to a new school in the village,' she smiled. And then she told her all about Billy Prior, and Maureen and Susan and the twins. She was about to mention Peaches and Gary but then thought better of it. Best not to confuse the child; instead, they talked about the seaside and the Downs – anything to make the journey quicker.

Dr Landers had given Patsy a book: *Five on a Treasure Island* by Enid Blyton. Dottie read it out loud, but when they reached the bit where George was taking them all out in a boat to see the wreck on the other side of Kirrin island, Patsy fell asleep on her shoulder. Dottie remained perfectly still for some time. Outside in the corridor, Reg turned around. He stared at the sleeping child until he became aware that Dottie was watching him. As her eyes met his gaze, his face coloured and he turned away abruptly. Dottie's stomach was churning. What a mess. Whatever were they going to do? Had Patsy come twelve thousand miles to this?

As soon as they arrived in Worthing, Reg strode on ahead, but this time Dottie made no effort to keep up with him. Patsy was too tired to hurry and so, for that matter, was she. By the time they reached the cottage, Reg had already dumped the child's suitcase in the middle of the kitchen floor and was nowhere to be seen.

She got Patsy some tea, gave her a wash and put her to bed in Aunt Bessie's old room. When she came back downstairs, Dottie made herself some tea and picked up the small suitcase of papers. When she tried the locks, they flew open at once.

Most of it was official stuff, including Sandy's death certificate. She'd died of breast cancer. There were several condolence cards addressed either to Brenda Nichols or to Patricia c/o Brenda. Dottie felt her throat tightening. They made sad reading. Patsy's mother was only thirty-four when she died.

Dottie unfolded another certificate and there was no denying the facts. Patricia June Johns was born on April 21st 1943. Her mother was Elizabeth Mary Johns. The space where the father's name should be was blank but pinned to the certificate was a slip of paper. *This is to certify that the father of my baby is Reginald Cox, signed Elizabeth Mary Johns.* But it couldn't possibly be right, could it? Dottie supposed that Elizabeth had been known to her friends as Sandy because of her fair hair. Reg had dark hair which he'd turned to black when he began to go grey, but how could two such people produce a coffee-coloured child with dark frizzy hair and big brown eyes? It wasn't possible. Reg couldn't possibly be Patsy's father, and yet there it was in black and white. Surely Sandy must have known who the real father was, so why did she put Reg's name on that slip of paper? And why send her daughter all this way to a man she must have known perfectly well was no relation at all?

Dottie kept all her important papers in the kitchen cupboard with the drop-down pastry-making table. She filed the birth and death certificates along with the rest of their things and sat back down with the other papers. All at once, she froze in her chair as a terrible realisation hit her. She jumped back up and pulled the certificate from its newly-filed place. Her hands were trembling and she unfolded it again.

When Connie and Christopher were born, Mary had showed her their birth certificates. They were much smaller, 'squarish' as opposed to oblong, and half the length of Patsy's. They simply said something like, 'Constance Prior, girl; date of birth, 13th December 1947; place of birth, Worthing; sub-district, Worthing'.

Patsy's was a copy of her full birth certificate and most shocking of all, it was English. Patsy had been born here . . . in this country! The registration district was Lewisham and the sub-district Lewisham.

Her heart was pounding nineteen to the dozen and she felt dizzy and sick. Reg never said he'd been in London. She'd married him in 1942 and he'd been posted just four months after they were married. So how come he was in London in 1942 and fathering a child? It didn't make sense.

She fingered her way through the other papers but they were

just nursing certificates, a first prize award for a writing competition and some old letters from England. Dottie re-filed the birth certificate and went back to the rest of the papers in the suitcase.

It felt a little intrusive opening them. The first one she looked at was signed 'Matron' who wished Sandy well in her new country. Dottie discovered that Sandy had moved to Australia at the end of 1945. Matron wrote to say she hoped Sandy would put the past behind her and make a go of this fantastic opportunity.

Dottie shook her head sympathetically. Poor Sandy. How ironic that she had gone all that way to make a new life for herself and her little girl, only to die of cancer just five years later.

There were several other letters, but Dottie could see some diaries as well. She was torn. Which should she read first, the letters or the diary? She thumbed through the letters. Looking at the envelopes, she could tell that they had been written by many different people and they were all wartime letters. She stared at one envelope for several seconds. It was addressed to Sandy at an address in London. The letter inside was signed 'all my love, Reg'. It had been posted in 1943.

There was a loud bump on the floor upstairs and Patsy called out. 'Auntie Dot . . . Auntie Dottie!'

Absentmindedly slipping the envelope into her apron pocket, Dottie hurried upstairs.

Reg hugged his pint and stared long and hard into the open fire. This was his favourite corner in the Jolly Farmer but tonight he sat with his back to the bar, hoping he wouldn't be disturbed.

'Bloody women,' he thought to himself. Now Dottie knew the kid wasn't his. How could it be? She was a bloody darkie. The father must have been one of those black Yanks. Why the hell did the silly bitch go with a darkie? Maybe the Yank got her as pissed as a newt first. Or perhaps he forced her. She was probably nothing more than a bloody bike anyway. As soon as she knew she was up the spout, she'd put his name on the birth certificate. And now he was in deep shit. How was he going to explain away this one?

He pinched the end of his cigarette and pushed it behind his ear.

'Another pint, Reg?'

Reg belched and pushed his glass towards Terry Dore, the landlord.

'Just going to the bog.'

There was a fly on the urinal. Reg aimed for it. He hoped it was a female. It was always the women that did for him. His mother had been the first. Shopping him to the ol' bill like that. If he'd had half a chance he'd have gone back there and done her in but she beat him to it, didn't she? Died while he was still in Borstal. His urine hit the fly and it rose up, buzzing angrily. He smiled maliciously as it crashed into the wall, then the window. Finishing, he readjusted his trousers and turned to go. It was then that the fly hit him on his face, near his lips. He hit out at it, cursing loudly.

Back at the bar, he made it clear to Terry he didn't want conversation. He went back to his table, and brooded some more.

He'd had a pretty good scam going. The Bomb Lark, they called it. He was part of a group of newly conscripted Royal Engineers who had been brought into London to help clear the bomb damage after an air raid. Reg had been the first to spot the lead on the roofs and told the sarge he knew a scrap metal merchant over Merton way. Everyone was up for it and a deal was struck. They'd kept the thing going for more than a month before the rozzers got wind of it. As luck would have it, Reg wasn't around the day they all got nicked. He'd had a bilious attack. Well, that's what he told the medics. In truth he'd gone back to see Joyce. Couldn't keep away from her.

His mates wouldn't tell but he knew it wouldn't be long before someone put two and two together so he went AWOL, coming down to Worthing where he met Dottie. Of course, he knew she would never agree to anything dishonest, but he didn't mind too much. She was his investment for the future so he'd spun his charm and married her. There was the promise of a nice little nest egg once she'd inherited the house from the old witch.

He never should have gone back home but he'd wanted a bit of fun with Joyce. Only they'd had a blazing row and the neighbours called the cops.

'Six months' hard labour, followed by three years' penal servitude for conspiring to loot,' that pompous ass of a judge had told him. 'A civilised society will not tolerate consistent and considerable stealing of other people's property. You are a disgrace to your uniform . . .'

He'd been beside himself with rage when they'd banged him up and because he never did learn to control his temper, he'd ended up spending a full five years in that stinking prison. Carelessness had put him there and now he'd been careless again. He never should have believed what that Brenda woman had told him. Sandy'd left everything to Patsy's father. Yeah, but he could have done without the darkie. He could feel his stomach churning. Bloody women. Every which way he turned they buggered things up for him. His mother, Sandy, bloody Aunt Bessie . . . So far, little Mrs Perfect was the only one who was still on track. All he had to do was threaten her with his fist and that was enough to keep her in check. Good job she wasn't the type to snoop around his things. All at once, his blood ran cold as he remembered that suitcase full of papers. Shit! The will. Supposing she was going through those papers right now . . .

He stood up quickly, spilling his pint. The glass fell with a clatter and rolled across the table before crashing to the floor.

He turned on his heel and walked briskly through the door, the landlord's 'You all right, Reg?' ringing in his ears.

Patsy had needed a little reassurance, that was all. Dottie tucked her up with her little elephant, Suzy, showed her where the jerry was under the bed and then lit a night-light and put it in a saucer before giving her a goodnight kiss. Now she was back downstairs with the suitcase in front of her.

Sandy's diaries were right at the bottom of the case. Three volumes, begun in 1941 and ending in 1948. Sandy hadn't written in them every day but she had jotted things down at regular intervals. The entries weren't very detailed, but even as she flicked through the pages, Dottie had a fairly good idea as to the sort of person Elizabeth Johns had been. Armed with fresh cup of tea, Dottie curled up her feet under her and turned to 1942/ 43, the years Patsy had been conceived and born.

The latch on the door lifted and Reg walked in. Dottie closed the book and looked up at him.

'Hello, Reg. Want some supper?'

'What are you doing?' he said coldly.

'I was just going through some of the papers,' she said lamely.

He snatched the book from her hand, glanced at it and then glared at her. She had never seen his eye so filled with hatred and she watched his lip curl. Her heartbeat sped up.

'I didn't mean anything by it, Reg,' she whimpered, hating herself for sounding so weak.

'Where's the will?'

'What will?'

'The money, stupid. Where's the solicitor's letter?'

Dottie frowned, puzzled. 'There isn't one.'

Reg went to throw the book onto the fire.

'No, Reg . . . don't!' she cried, grabbing it from him. 'What are you doing? Even if you don't want them, we should at least save them for Patsy.'

'What have you done with it then?'

'It's not there,' said Dottie. 'Dr Landers said the solicitor would send it along later.'

'What!' Reg exploded. 'But I need to know how much we're getting.'

'Keep your voice down,' said Dottie, glancing anxiously up at the ceiling.

'Keep my voice down,' he bellowed at the ceiling. 'The hell I will! I'm telling you, as soon as I've got the money, that little runt can go.'

'Reg, please . . .!' Dottie jumped to her feet, but he pushed her back down into the chair, snatching back the book again.

'There's no way she's my kid,' he said through his teeth, his spittle spraying her face. 'Even a dimwit like you can see that.'

'Your name is on her birth certificate,' said Dottie, pressing her back into the chair and sliding down a little.

'The bitch lied!' He hit her across the face with the book, catching her cheekbone under her left eye. Then he leaned over her menacingly, grabbing her hair and pulling her head back painfully. 'Got it?'

The pain in Dottie's head was unbearable. 'Yes, Reg.'

'I want her gone,' he said, yanking her head back again. 'I don't care how you do it, but get rid of her. Send her to a home, chuck her out on the street, anything you like, but she's not stopping here.'

'Reg, we can't,' Dottie sobbed. 'She's come all this way . . .'

He let go of her hair, lashing out at her again as he did. 'And I'm telling you, I'm not living under the same roof as a darkie.'

'If you chuck her onto the street,' Dottie cried desperately, 'Dr Landers will want the fare money back.'

Reg paused.

'It cost seventy pounds to bring her over, remember?' said Dottie. 'Where are we going to find that sort of money?'

Reg stepped back, stumbling against the suitcase on the floor.

Papers spilled everywhere. All at once he was roaring like a mad man, kicking the case around the room. He stooped down and grabbed a pile of papers, throwing them onto the fire. It took a few moments for the paper to catch alight, but all at once Sandy's writing prize burst into a flame which greedily took her nursing certificate and a couple of letters.

Dottie couldn't bear to watch, but with him in a mood like this, she couldn't do anything about it. He was making such a terrible racket, Patsy must be up there listening to all this, absolutely terrified. As he stuffed yet more paper on the fire, Dottie, her own pain forgotten, slipped upstairs to make sure she was all right.

# Twenty-Three

Janet Cooper climbed into the window of her tobacconist-cum-sweet-shop and took out the last of the old window display. It had been fairly quiet this morning, which was just as well, so she had taken the opportunity to change the window. Taking her inspiration from last week's harvest festival display in the church, she'd decided to arrange the sweets as if they were a horn of plenty. Two large sweet jars were suspended from the ceiling with wire and she'd spent hours threading toffees on cotton and sticking the ends inside the jars with gummed tape. A doll dressed up to look like a farmer raked pile of sweets on the floor of the shop window.

The shop door jangled and she backed out of the window. Her customer was Mary Prior, and she could see Edna Gilbert, her head covered with a floral headscarf, coming along the road.

'You've been busy,' Mary smiled. 'I can't believe it's that time of year already.'

'I'll be thinking about ordering the fireworks for Bonfire Night soon,' said Janet.

'Oooh, talking about fireworks,' Mary went on, 'that reminds me. We thought we'd all pitch in together and make a real show for the kiddies this year.'

Janet pursed her lips. That probably meant they'd all buy one of those great big boxes from Woolworths. She'd have to make sure she could get some decent-sized boxes at a good price.

'What can I do for you?' she asked.

'Twenty Craven A and a Walls brick please, Janet,' said Mary. The shop bell jangled again and Edna came in. 'Hello, Edna.'

'Hello, Mary, Janet.' Edna retied her headscarf and stood with her shopping bag clasped in front of her. 'No Dottie today?'

'She didn't turn up,' said Janet acidly.

'Didn't turn up? That's not like her,' Mary frowned.

'She wasn't here yesterday either.'

'Perhaps she's ill,' said Edna.

'She was well enough when she went to Southampton on Friday to fetch her little girl,' Janet said. 'Vanilla or strawberry?'

'Vanilla,' said Mary.

'I think we should have a welcome party for the little girl,' said Edna. 'Help her to feel at home.'

'We haven't even met her yet,' said Mary.

'Well, I think that's a nice idea,' said Janet, remembering she still had a box of balloons out the back. She hadn't managed to shift them since the VJ Day celebrations.

Mary nodded. 'Where shall we have it, the village hall?'

'Why not come over to the farm?' said Edna. 'We haven't had a do there since the war years. There's plenty of room in the old barn.'

'Oh I say, what about a barn dance?' Janet suggested.

'We'd need a caller,' said Mary. 'Do you know anyone?'

The other two shook their heads.

'What about Vincent Dobbs, the postman?' said Edna. 'He knows just about everyone around here. Maybe he knows a caller.'

'If we had it on the farm, there'd be no problem with babysitters,' said Mary. 'All the kids could come with us.'

Edna beamed. 'Pass the word around, but don't tell Reg just yet. You know what men are. He's bound to let the cat out of the bag. Leave it until nearer the time.'

Janet began wrapping the ice cream in layers of newspaper.

'I can't understand it myself,' she went on. 'Adopting a child is a lovely idea, but why get one all the way from Australia?'

'That's just what I said, hen,' said Mary, 'but Dottie reckoned they were doing it through a friend of Reg's.'

'It's probably a lot quicker than going through the welfare,' Edna nodded. 'I knew a girl who waited a good six months before anyone even came out to see her.'

'Let's hope that it all works out then,' said Janet, pushing the brick towards Mary. 'That should stay nice and firm for a couple of hours. That'll be one and eleven please.'

Mary handed Janet a ten-bob note. 'How's your Michael?' she asked Edna.

'Fine.'

'And Freda?' interjected Janet. 'When's it due?'

Edna's face coloured. 'Next year sometime.'

Janet handed Mary her change and gave her a knowing look. 'Now, what can I do for you, Edna?'

'A Basildon Bond pad, please.'

'Bye, Mary. And if you see Dottie on your travels,' Janet called as she opened the shop door, 'tell her she'd better turn up on Monday if she wants to keep her job.'

It was a bit of a struggle pushing the big pram. In addition to Connie and Christopher at one end and Phyllis at the other, Mary Prior had shoved a box of toys between them and a bag of clothes on the tray underneath. Maureen and Susan walked on either side of the pram, each holding onto the handle and Maureen was holding Brian's hand. Billy brought up the rear, carting another bag of clothes.

'Come on, son,' Mary puffed good-naturedly. 'We haven't got all day.'

'The 'andles have broke, Mum,' Billy complained. 'You got too much stuff in it.'

The pram went over a pothole, startling Mary and the twins

into thinking it would topple over. She grabbed at Christopher's arm and wrestled to keep the pram upright.

'You'd better get out, Christopher, love,' said Mary once she'd got it on an even keel. 'It's not too far to Auntie Dottie's now.'

She pulled him out and set him down on the pavement. Maureen caught hold of his harness and the little procession trudged on.

'It's a bit like bringing gifts to the baby Jesus, isn't it, Mum?' said Maureen.

Mary laughed heartily, her big belly wobbling up and down. 'Well, if I'm the Virgin Mary,' she laughed, 'who do you think you are? The seven kings or a load of smelly shepherds?'

'There were only three kings, Mum,' Maureen corrected and Mary laughed again.

'So there was, m'duck.'

There was no sign of life at the cottage.

'Don't tell me they're still in bed,' Mary muttered as she pushed open the gate and Maureen and Susan ran ahead of her. 'You kids keep away from that old well.'

She felt a little awkward turning up uninvited but she knew she wouldn't rest another moment until she'd checked up on Dottie. Since she'd asked around, it was apparent that nobody had seen her for days.

Billy put down his bag and rattled the doorknocker.

'I wanted to do that,' Susan complained. She pushed her brother away and, standing on tiptoe, she banged it herself.

'That's enough,' Mary scolded. 'Auntie Dottie will be wondering where the fire is.'

The door opened and Dottie stared at them in mild surprise. Mary made no reference to her black and swollen eye but Dottie stepped back, and kept half of her face behind the door in a vain attempt to hide it. Her shock at seeing them was tinged with both relief and embarrassment.

'We brought Patsy a present like the baby Jesus,' Maureen announced.

For a second, Dottie hesitated and drew back. She had spent the past couple of days licking her wounds. After smashing up the kitchen, Reg had followed her upstairs. She'd expected him to force her again but instead, he'd given her such a beating, insisting that he'd only stop if she kept quiet. He was in such a mood, the night had seemed endless. It was so difficult having to endure everything silently, but she had to. She was so afraid of frightening Patsy.

Since that Thursday, she and Patsy had stayed indoors. Dottie told herself it would be good for them to spend some time together, to get to know each other, but the truth of the matter was, she couldn't bear to go out. When she'd got up that Friday morning, her left eye was completely closed and the bruise on her cheek made it look as if she'd gone three rounds with Freddie Mills. Her body ached and she had been violently sick as well. She really couldn't face Mariah Fitzgerald so she posted a letter promising to be round with the finished curtains next week. She and Patsy had played games, done jigsaw puzzles and talked Neither of them made any reference to her face, and thankfully Reg had carried on as normal so she hardly saw him.

Now, uninvited and unannounced, Mary and her brood had turned up on the doorstep. Dottie glanced at the pram behind her. Connie held out her arms, appealing to be picked up. Dottie's heart melted. This was no time for pride. Mary was a good friend. Stepping back, she opened the door a little further. 'You'd better come in.'

She ushered them into the kitchen where Patsy was trying to master the rubber buttons on her liberty bodice. The family piled in behind their mother and Dottie introduced them.

'Patsy, this is Connie and Susan and Maureen and Christopher. This is Billy and this is Auntie Mary.'

'Hello, love,' said Mary. 'Shall I help you with that?'

Patsy shook her head. 'I can manage, thank you,' she said politely. They watched her as she pulled her dress over her head.

Dottie was suddenly aware of how untidy the room was. Not even her friends had ever seen it looking like this. She began gathering various items of clothing from the back of the chair, the table and the top of the dresser.

'Bicket?' Connie had misinterpreted her move towards the dresser. She stood in front with her hand in the air.

'Connie, that's naughty,' Maureen scolded. 'You shouldn't ask.' But Dottie had already pulled down the biscuit box. The twins sat on the floor as if they were obedient dogs waiting to beg, and Dottie offered around the broken biscuits.

Mary reappeared, staggering back through the door with the bag of toys. 'Shall I put this lot in the front room?' she asked. 'The kids can play with them while you and I have a nice quiet cup of tea in here.'

Dottie nodded. With a silent sigh she went outside in the scullery to put the kettle on. What was she going to say to Mary? She couldn't think straight. Her brain refused to function, but she'd have to say something, wouldn't she?

Ten minutes later, all the kids, including Patsy, were together in the front room, leaving Mary and Dottie alone in the kitchen. They pulled up two chairs and sat down at the table. Dottie pulled a cosy over the teapot and picked up the milk jug.

'About Patsy . . .' Mary began uncertainly.

Dottie looked away.

'She's very dark,' Mary went on.

Dottie shrugged. The two women sipped their tea, an awkward silence between them.

'Somebody sent you this,' said Mary reaching into her pocket and pulling out a letter. A bold sloping hand had addressed the envelope to 'Mrs D. Cox, c/o Mrs M. Prior'.

'It's from Sylvie!' Dottie frowned. 'Why did she address it to you?'

Mary shrugged.

Dottie reached for a knife and slit the envelope.

*Darling Dottie,*

*I hope you are well. I have written you two letters but you
haven't replied. I first I thought you might be too busy with
the little girl, but you are always so good at letter-writing and
I feel sure you would have written to me and told me all
about her so I suppose my letters have gone astray.*

'She says she's written but I haven't received her letters,' Dottie
explained to Mary.

'There's been talk in the village about missing letters,' Mary
nodded. 'Some light-fingered postman I suppose.'

'Not Vincent Dobbs surely?' Dottie gasped.

'No, of course not. Somebody at the sorting office I expect.'

'I'll read the rest later,' Dottie murmured. She pushed the
letter back in its envelope and put it in her apron pocket.

'So,' Mary asked, 'are you going to tell me how you got that
shiner?'

Dottie kept her head down. 'Does it look really awful?'

'It looks obvious, if that's what you mean, hen.'

'Somebody opened the train door too quickly,' Dottie lied.
She pushed a cup of the dark brown tea in front of Mary.

'He did it, didn't he? Reg,' said Mary, picking up a spoon and
stirring the tea furiously. 'I thought so. The blighter.'

'He didn't mean to do it,' said Dottie defensively. 'He was a
bit cross, that's all.'

'No man has a right to hit a woman,' Mary sniffed, 'so don't
insult me by making excuses for him, hen.' She threw her spoon
into the saucer with a clatter but Dottie said nothing. 'Anyway,
why was he angry with you?'

Dottie shrugged. This was so embarrassing. She wanted to curl
up and die. She was tired, she felt ill . . . not ill, sick. She rested her

hand across her stomach. Was there a baby in there? She didn't want to be pregnant. Perhaps she ought to tell Mary. She could feel the backs of her eyes pricking.

'He's saying that he only went along with the idea of having a kid because you wanted it so bad.'

Dottie looked up sharply, searching her friend's face with a mixture of horror and disbelief. 'I thought as much,' her friend said in a softer tone. 'What is it then? What's your version? He pushed you into it and then changed his mind?'

That beaten feeling crept over her again. Dottie looked down at her teacup and blinked away the tears that threatened. 'Something like that,' she conceded.

'I don't understand why you don't just kick him out.'

She looked up again, this time with a frown. 'Oh, Mary! Don't you start. Have you been talking to Sylvie?'

'Why should I talk to Sylvie?' said Mary. 'Listen, hen, this is a small place. If you don't turn up for work for two days and your old man sits in the pub with a face as black as thunder, what do you expect? People love a bit of gossip and I'll tell you right now, Janet Cooper is having a field day.'

Dottie picked up a glove belonging to Phyllis. 'And I suppose Ann Pearce has been round to your place spreading rumours as well,' she said bitterly.

'Now don't you go thinking bad things about Ann,' Mary said firmly. 'Right now she's the one friend you've got, hen. Yes, she told me, but she only came to see me because she was so worried about you. She heard him crashing around, didn't she? Shouting the odds and everything. She wanted to come round but she knows he'd do his nut if he saw her.'

Dottie's chin began to quiver and she was having difficulty in seeing.

'It's all right, hen,' said Mary gently. She patted the back of Dottie's hand.

'It's such a mess, Mary. Reg says he doesn't even want to be

201

under the same roof as her,' Dottie said quietly, 'but I can't send her back, can I?'

'What? Because she's coloured? The stupid man.'

'She's a lovely little girl,' said Dottie fiercely.

'What on earth made you choose a kid all the way from Australia in the first place?' said Mary, pouring herself some more tea.

'I didn't . . .' Dottie protested but then thought better of it. How could she tell Mary the whole story? What if Mary let slip that Patsy was supposed to be Reg's child with someone else? It would be all over the village in no time. Of course, they'd never be able to explain why Patsy had coloured blood, but then, she didn't know the whole story herself. If only Reg hadn't burned what was in that suitcase. 'I want to tell you, but I can't,' she said brokenly.

Mary moved her great bulk from the chair opposite Dottie to the one next to her and put her arm around her shoulders. 'It's all right, hen. You tell me as much or as little as you want. I won't ask any more.'

Dottie's eyes met hers with mild surprise.

'And don't look at me like that,' Mary went on. 'We're friends, aren't we? Friends don't need to pry. They just need to be there for you.'

Dottie blinked back her tears. 'Oh, Mary,' she blurted out. 'I think I'm pregnant.'

Billy burst into the kitchen. 'Can I have a drink, Mum?'

'No you can't,' said Mary irritably.

She shushed him away but Dottie stood up. 'It's all right,' she said, manufacturing cheerfulness. 'I've got some cherryade out the back.'

'Cherryade!' cried Billy.

'Get the enamel mugs out of the cupboard,' she said, blowing her nose and being very careful to keep her back to him, 'then you can go back in and make everyone sit down, Billy.'

Billy gathered the mugs and clattered his way back into the front room shouting excitedly, 'Hey, sit down, you lot. We're having cherryade.'

Dottie came out of the scullery carrying a large, bright red bottle.

'Pregnant?' said Mary. 'Oh my dear . . .'

Dottie stopped to squeeze her shoulder. 'Come on,' she said, her voice thick with emotion, 'let's see what they're up to.'

When they reached the front room, all the kids were sitting in a circle and Patsy was teaching them some kind of clapping game. Dottie and Mary stood in the doorway, Mary restraining her excited son, lest he break the game up too soon.

Patsy looked up.

'Go on, dear,' said Dottie.

'Who stole the cookie from the cookie pot,' Patsy chanted rhythmically. At the same time, she clapped her hands together once, then slapped her knees. She looked around at the children, and started a second chant, 'Maureen stole the cookie from the cookie pot.'

Maureen giggled and when she'd finished she beat out, 'I didn't steal the cookie from the cookie pot.'

'Then who stole the cookie from the cookie pot?' Patsy went on.

Dottie smiled. All of Mary's kids were having a great time, even the little ones, even though they couldn't possibly understand what a cookie was. They did it for some time until eventually Patsy turned around again.

'Cherryade!' Billy announced at the top of his voice and they all cheered.

He and Patsy organised the mugs and poured the drinks. Dottie and Mary returned to the kitchen.

'How far gone are you?' asked Mary as soon as they were alone again.

'A couple of months.'

'So there's still time to get rid of it.'

'I don't think I can do that,' said Dottie.

'I know a woman in East Worthing . . .'

'No, Mary.'

Mary curled her lip with distain. 'You mean you'd really have his child?'

Dottie rolled her eyes heavenward and pressed her lips together. 'It's my baby as well.'

'Yes, but . . .'

'I just want a child,' Dottie whispered.

Mary sat down in the chair heavily. 'I don't know what to say, hen. You've been to the doctor of course.'

Dottie shook her head. 'Not yet.'

'Then,' Mary began brightly, 'it may not be . . .'

'I'm ninety-five percent sure,' Dottie insisted. 'It happened the day of Michael's wedding.'

'You know actually when it happened?' Mary gasped.

Dottie felt her face redden. 'I can't go to the doctor, not yet. I need all the money I can get and the minute she knows I'm pregnant, Mariah Fitzgerald will ask me to go. Don't you understand, Mary? I've already got one child to provide for. I'm all she's got. Don't say anything, please.'

'All right, hen,' sighed Mary. 'But just remember I'm here for you. We both are. Tom and me.'

'Thanks for everything,' said Dottie blowing her nose again.

'I haven't done anything yet,' said Mary.

'You have,' said Dottie giving her a squeeze around her ample waist. 'You've done more than you can ever know.'

'A few toys and some hand-me-down clothes,' said Mary with a shrug.

'And a pram full of courage,' said Dottie quietly. She blew her nose again and stood up to look at herself in the mirror over the mantelpiece. 'Lord, I look a sight!' Reaching into the drawer for a comb, Dottie pulled the pins out of her hair and let it down.

'You may not realise it but your coming here has helped me make a decision,' she went on with a loud sniff. 'Patsy's been here almost a week and I'm determined she's not going anywhere else. She's my little girl now.'

'But she's not yours, is she?' Mary observed.

'I'll adopt her,' said Dottie vehemently. 'As soon as I've got enough money put by, I'm going to a solicitor.'

'But if Reg refuses to let you have her, how can you?' cried Mary. 'Besides, a woman on her own, adopting a child? It's impossible.'

'Well, she's certainly not going to be put in a children's home,' said Dottie, pulling her hair into French plait. 'This is her home. Aunt Bessie did it for me, remember?'

Mary nodded. An only child, Dottie's mother had died when she was sixteen. Rose Thornton had taken the identity of Dottie's father to the grave and so Dottie had been sent to live with her maiden aunt who owned the cottage. Dottie had told Mary many a time how alone she'd felt as she rode up the road from the station. Aunt Bessie had met her with the pony and trap, which was enough to excite any little girl, but Dottie had hardly noticed. She was terrified that Aunt Bessie wouldn't like her so she'd made up her mind to work as her skivvy if necessary. But she needn't have worried. Aunt Bessie may have been a little eccentric, but she was a sweetheart and, despite never having had children of her own, the whole village knew she had given Dottie a really happy life.

'There is a difference,' said Mary. 'That was wartime, and you two were related.'

'I don't care, Mary,' said Dottie. 'What she did for me, I shall do for Patsy.'

Mary glanced up at the clock. 'I'd better be going. Tom will be wanting his tea.'

'Oh, I forgot to tell you,' said Mary as they said their goodbyes on the doorstep. 'The whole village is having a joint bonfire for November 5th. We'll probably do it on the 3rd, that's the Saturday

205

before. We've got that bit of waste ground next to the nurseries. Bring Patsy along, won't you?'

'I might not have money for fireworks.'

'A packet of sparklers will do.'

'Me and Raymond Green are doing penny for the guy,' said Billy proudly.

'I'll look out for you,' said Dottie attempting to give him a wink. 'And if I think it's good enough, I might even give you a tanner.'

'Cor, thanks, Auntie Dottie,' Billy beamed.

Dottie hugged her friend hard. 'You're a real pal, Mary.'

'Go on with you,' said Mary giving Dottie a peck on the cheek, and whispered her parting remark in her ear. 'You keep hold of your money. You'll need all you can get from now on, hen.'

Halfway down the street, Billy looked up at his mother. 'What's the matter with Auntie Dottie's face, Mum?'

'She accidentally walked into a door,' said Mary looking straight ahead.

Christopher took his thumb out of his mouth. 'Naughty door.'

Billy said nothing. His mother always said, 'Tell the truth and shame the devil.' It wasn't often his mother lied, but he knew she was lying now.

'You're right, m'duck,' said Mary to Christopher. 'Naughty door.'

Billy could see that his mother was gripping the handlebars of the pram so tightly, her knuckles had gone white. Billy was no fool. Auntie Dottie hadn't walked into a door, had she? It was Uncle Reg. He must have hit her. Bristling with anger, Billy kicked a stone along the pavement. When he was all grown up, he'd give Uncle Reg a black eye and then he could jolly well see how much he liked it.

# Twenty-Four

When Dottie came downstairs on Thursday, her black eye was a lot less noticeable. She glanced anxiously at the shed door. Was Reg still in the shed getting his bike out?

A quick look around told her that he'd already left for work. He'd made an attempt to cut himself some sandwiches. The loaf, hacked to pieces, lay on the table beside the empty cheese dish. The shed door remained closed. He'd gone.

She moved about gingerly. She should make an effort to go back to work today. She had really enjoyed her time with Patsy. Everything was so much better when Reg wasn't around and it had given her and Patsy a chance to get to know each other. She was such a lovely child, easy-going and polite, and they seemed to have quite a lot in common. They both enjoyed sewing and Dottie had discovered a tray cloth Patsy was embroidering in the suitcase that had gone straight upstairs the day she came.

'I used to sit by Mummy's bedside when she was ill,' she said matter-of-factly, leaving Dottie with a catch in her throat. 'She was going to show me how to crochet around the edge.'

'I can do that,' said Dottie. Patsy gave her an uncertain look, and Dottie added quickly, 'But only if you would like me to.'

The evening before, they'd spent a good deal of time at it and Patsy had already made good progress. It was still in the chair where she'd left it last night before she went to bed. Dottie picked it up and fondled it between her fingers before dropping it into her sewing box.

Dottie mixed up the chicken food and walked down the garden. Clucking noisily, the chickens dashed out of their hut as soon as she opened the door. The pig grunted and put his snout over the top of the fence. He was getting so big, it wouldn't be long before he broke it down and ran amok. She'd have to mention it again to Reg some time. He'd probably forgotten all about the pig. He hardly ever came down here now.

Patsy was up and dressed when she walked into the kitchen. 'Are we going to my new school today, Auntie Dot?'

Dottie smiled. 'Yes, we are. Let's hope they've got room for you in the classroom.' As the child's face fell, Dottie was seized with remorse for having teased her. She put her hand on her arm. 'Don't worry. I'm sure they will.'

Mrs Stone, the headmistress, didn't exactly welcome her with open arms, but she did agree to have Patsy in her school.

'It just so happens,' she said crisply, 'that a pupil has just moved away. Patsy can have her place but you should have applied in writing and given me more notice.'

Dottie apologised profusely and Mrs Stone seemed placated. 'Will you have school dinners?'

Dottie's face coloured. She hadn't even given that a thought. 'Yes . . . how much are they?'

'A shilling a day,' said Mrs Stone, 'payable on Monday mornings.'

They looked around the school and Mrs Stone agreed to have her after the half-term holiday. After that, she seemed to have warmed to the child because she invited Patsy to stay for the rest of the day.

Dottie felt a lot happier now. She knew that once she'd got herself into a routine, she would be able to see her way through all her problems. All that remained now was to apologise to Janet Cooper for letting her down and then she could go on to Mariah

Fitzgerald and fit in an extra hour at the end of the day to make up for arriving at work late.

Janet gushed all over her and Mariah was eager to hear all about Patsy. Dottie told them as much as she wanted them to know and left them to guess the rest. Thankfully, nobody thought to mention Reg.

The second Sunday after Patsy came to live with them, Dottie wrote a letter to Dr Landers. As she sat at the table, she tried to imagine him sitting opposite her. She remembered his twinkling eyes and the line of freckles over the bridge of his nose and the way his face lit up when he smiled. He was a nice man. She decided not to tell him how horrible Reg had been but she did go as far as suggesting that he was having a problem adjusting to parenthood.

> *We have gone from being on our own to being a complete*
> *family overnight,* she wrote, *but you are not to worry. Patsy is*
> *very happy. She has made friends with several children*
> *around here, in particular Maureen Prior, the daughter of a*
> *dear friend of mine. Maureen is a bit younger than Patsy but*
> *they have so much in common. They play dollies and schools.*
> *Patsy has taught Maureen some Australian games and*
> *Maureen has taught Patsy how to skip. They can keep it up*
> *for hours!*

The letter was only about one and half pages long, but she kept it chatty and warm. She reasoned that if he knew Patsy was content, he would feel the same way. It came as a shock, then, to receive a letter almost by return of post in which Dr Landers asked if he could see Patsy the following Saturday.

Dottie was immediately thrown into a flat spin. What was she going to do? Try as she might to make things right between them, Reg stubbornly refused to let it happen. If he was in the house with Patsy, he would talk over her head – 'Isn't it time she was in bed?' – or dish out his instructions through Dottie – 'Tell her to get her feet off that chair.'

The solicitor's letter was a long time coming. Reg spent his evenings in the Jolly Farmer and on the days when his shifts gave him the opportunity to have time off during the day, he would go out. Dottie was never sure where he was, but a couple of times he set off somewhere all spruced up and came back very drunk. One good thing was that he hadn't been near Dottie since the night Patsy had arrived,

She knew he hated interfering busybodies as he called them, so how would he react if Dr Landers turned up? Dottie couldn't bear the thought of him ranting and raving on, demanding that the kid be taken back and telling the doctor that he didn't give a stuff about her. Though she'd been with her for only two weeks, it seemed as if Patsy had been here forever. Dottie couldn't bear the thought of losing her and she hated the thought of her languishing in some huge rambling old place, euphemistically called a children's home, more with each passing day.

No. She couldn't let that happen. She had to keep Reg and Dr Landers as far apart as possible. Having come up with a solution, she wrote back to the doctor. Once the letter was in the post, all she had to do was find the right moment to speak to Reg. It came sooner than she had anticipated. She waited until he was settled on his side of the bed and then whispered in the darkness, 'Reg, I thought I would take Patsy for a walk up to Highdown on Saturday.'

'Do what you bloody well like, woman. Now shuddup and go to sleep.'

Half-term week seemed destined to give Dottie a problem. She still had to go to work, but Patsy needed someone to look after her. Reg wouldn't help and, anyway, she wasn't happy about leaving Patsy alone with him.

Much to her relief, Janet Cooper said Patsy could come with her to the shop. Patsy helped out, doing little jobs, and Janet enjoyed basking in the limelight. Her customers bought little gifts for the child, something guaranteed to make Patsy a favourite with Janet. Patsy would thank them, and then they would linger longer in the shop, plying her with questions which she answered politely and honestly.

'Do you miss Australia?' 'What's it like?' 'Have you ever seen any of them savages?' 'Bit 'ot over there, innit?'

Sometimes Patsy didn't understand what she was being asked and most people seemed to forget that she wouldn't be able to remember much before she was five. But by the time Dottie finished work on Tuesday, she had quite a collection of colouring books, pencils and storybooks. She also had a large stash of sweets, which she stored in an old shoebox under her bed.

On Thursday, when she and Dottie went to Mary's, the first thing Patsy did was to gather the kids into a circle and share some of her booty with them.

'Isn't she a lamb, love her,' said Mary. 'I've run out of sweet coupons. They wouldn't have had any sweets this week if it weren't for her.'

Dottie was on her way to Mariah Fitzgerald's. 'It's good of you to say you'll have her, Mary,' she said. 'Are you sure it's not going to be too much?'

'No trouble at all,' said Mary. 'You'll have a cup of tea before you go?'

Dottie pulled up a chair and sat down.

'We'll be collecting stuff for the bonfire this weekend,' Mary went on. 'Tom will be on hand to help us build it properly.'

'Sounds fun.'

'Don't sound too enthusiastic,' said Mary disappointedly as she pushed a cup of tea in front of her.

'Sorry,' said Dottie. 'I've got a lot on my mind, that's all.'

'What's that?'

'Nothing really,' said Dottie. Seeing her friend's face fall, she added quickly, 'Curtains for Edna, stuff like that.'

Mary sat in the chair opposite and warmed her hands on her cup. 'Reg all right?' she said cautiously.

'Fine.' Dottie lied with ease. 'Are you having any food at the bonfire do?'

'I thought we'd do a few baked potatoes, a bit of bread and cheese, that sort of thing.'

'We'll give you a few spuds,' said Dottie rising to her feet. 'Thanks for the tea, Mary. I'll be back at one.'

Mary's parting words were, 'Don't work too hard, hen.' As Dottie walked back down the path, she let out a hollow laugh. Mariah was getting ready for a family invasion. After she'd hung the new curtains and furnishings in the bedroom, it meant a thorough clean throughout and Dottie wasn't in the mood for a hard slog.

Saturday morning heralded a crisp bright day. Dottie and Patsy dressed warmly but long before they'd finished the two-mile walk to the hill, they were already peeling off their gloves and scarves. Under her best coat, which had seen very many better days, Dottie was wearing her new bat-wing blouse. She'd managed to get it finished only the evening before but she was quite pleased with it. It was midnight blue and it went very nicely with the plaid skirt she'd made last year. Patsy was in a pretty lightweight blue woollen dress with a dainty white Peter Pan collar and dark blue appliqué leaves on the left shoulder and the right hem.

Dottie's ribs were still tender. It was probably her own fault. She shouldn't have needled him.

'You might at least ask how Patsy got on at school,' she'd snapped as she put his supper on the table the night before. 'She's your daughter, Reg. You were the one who insisted on bringing her all the way over here. The least you can do is show a bit of interest.'

'I will when that bloody letter comes.' He'd folded his paper against the HP sauce bottle and carried on reading.

Anger surged through Dottie's veins. 'That's all you want, isn't it. The money! Well, there isn't any. Sandy was broke.'

He'd glared at her for several seconds, then stood up. 'You never told me a worse thing,' he snarled.

'It's not my fault,' she shouted but he suddenly lashed out, knocking her off balance, and she'd fallen against the other chair, the wooden back digging into her ribs. Then he'd thrown his meal over her head and stormed out. Dottie shook her head at her own stupidity. She shouldn't have dropped it in his lap like that.

The walk would do them both good. Patsy was in fine form, her appetite for knowledge forming question after question.

'What are those berries?' She was pointing to the front of a cottage where a shrub, smothered in vivid red berries, covered the walls. 'Can you eat them?'

'I'm afraid not,' said Dottie. 'It's called Pyracantha and it's just to look at.'

'Pie-be-Katha?' Patsy struggled.

They spent the next few minutes saying it together, 'Pyra-can-tha,' until Patsy could say it perfectly.

'Is the King going to die?' the child suddenly asked.

The question was a bit unexpected, although the reports of George VI's operation had dominated the news on the wireless. Nobody had actually said what was wrong with him but the papers said he'd had to have the whole of his left lung removed.

'I don't know, love, but he is very ill.'

Dottie had read in the paper that the Archbishop of Canterbury had held a special service in Lambeth Palace for the King's recovery and Clement Attlee had cut short his holiday. Prime ministers don't do that unless it's serious.

'My mummy had cancer. Do you think the King has cancer? Aunt Mary says he has.'

213

'She's probably right.'

'I expect he'll die then.'

Dottie shot back with, 'We all have to die one day, love.' Oh crumbs! She shouldn't have said that. Dottie chewed her bottom lip anxiously.

Patsy looked up at her. 'Did I tell you I got eight out of ten for my spellings?'

Dottie smiled. 'That's very good,' she said, marvelling at the girl's ability to swap so effortlessly from death to spellings. 'Which two did you get wrong?'

'Government and necessary.'

At the very end of the platform on Durrington-on-Sea, Reg was waiting for the London train to Victoria. To avoid awkward questions, he had deliberately chosen to leave by another station and he'd waited until Dottie and Patsy were on their way up to Highdown Hill before setting out. He had thought long and hard about returning to his old stomping ground. He had worked hard at making a new life but just lately, the tug in his heart had become stronger than ever.

The truth was, he missed the big smoke . . . the noise, the bustle, the cries of the barrow boys, the black cabs honking their way through the narrow streets, even the bloody pigeons . . . Just lately they'd all taken on a rosy hue. He'd thought a lot about his old mates too. They'd got up to some wonderful tricks in the old days when he'd managed to avoid conscription for several months by ignoring his call papers and keeping on the move. When the authorities got closer, he'd even got some chap who'd failed his medical, a bloke with chronic asthma, to impersonate him. Paid twenty quid for the honour but he was scuppered when the bloody army doctor recognised him. In the end, Reg had been forced to respond to his 442 and he'd been put into the Royal Engineers.

In no time at all he'd gained a reputation for insubordination, but then his army days ended abruptly after he was caught for nicking the lead. Reg managed a wry smile as he remembered that pompous ass of a CO telling the judge, 'Unless the court deems it absolutely necessary, M'Lord, the army does not want him back.'

Reg stuffed his hands in his pockets and stared down the line. Where was this bloody train? By the time he got up to London, it would be time to come back again. He sighed. He'd tried the honest life and where had it got him? No money, a prissy wife and now he was stuck with Sandy's kid. It was time to move on but he didn't want to just up and leave. For a start, he had no money and nowhere to go.

The porter came out of his office and put out the boards. The train was on its way.

Reg jingled the money in his pocket. It was a stroke of luck finding the cash she'd hidden in the bottom of the wardrobe. She must have put it there for some reason but he didn't bother to ask why. As far as he was concerned, what was hers was his so he could help himself whenever he wanted. The sweets the kid had been saving would come in handy too.

The train rumbled into the station.

She was off up to Highdown with the kid. What better day for him to go to London and look up a few old pals?

As the train stopped, Reg opened the door and stepped inside with purpose.

John Landers had parked his car in the lane and was waiting for them at the top of the hill. He was dressed casually in a long-sleeved blue and white check shirt, tweed jacket and grey trousers. Dottie's heart lurched. As soon as he saw them he took off his Tyrolean hat and waved before setting off down the hill to meet them.

'Dr John, Dr John!' Patsy ran to him and he lifted her up in his arms, swinging her around as they laughed with the sheer joy of meeting again.

'You look fantastic!' he cried as he set her down. He smiled at Dottie and held out his hand in a more formal way. 'Pleased to meet you again, Mrs Cox.'

'Oh please,' she laughed nervously, 'call me Dottie, everyone does.'

'Then you must call me John,' he said softly. His eyes lingered on hers for a few seconds more, making her heartbeat quicken and then he turned his attention back to Patsy.

'I've brought a friend for you to play with,' he said. 'Someone I think you're going to like very much.'

Patsy looked around. 'Where? Where is she? I can't see her.'

John chuckled. Dottie couldn't see anyone either but as they walked back to his car, a little white head peeped out over the steering wheel.

'Oh!' cried Patsy as a delightful West Highland Terrier wagged its tail and barked excitedly.

'Come along, Minnie,' he called and the dog jumped down and bounced all around them.

'Minnie?'

'After Mickey Mouse's girlfriend,' he smiled.

'Oh, she's lovely,' cried Dottie, bending down to pat her. The dog was jumping up at Patsy, licking her face and wagging her tail so hard Dottie wondered that it didn't fall off.

'Can I play with her?' Patsy asked.

'Of course you can.' John handed her a yellow ball. 'I tell you what, she'll be your best friend for life if you throw this for her to catch.'

As the two of them bounded away, Dottie and John followed.

'I've never been up here before,' said John, breathing in the warm afternoon air. 'It's a lovely spot.'

'You get a wonderful view of Worthing from the top by those trees,' Dottie told him. 'On a clear day, you can see the Seven Sisters to the east and the Isle of Wight to the west.'

'When I told Mother I was coming here she said something about it being a radar station during the war.'

Dottie smiled. 'That's all gone now. There's just the grass, the chalk pit at the top and the Miller's Tomb.'

'Sounds intriguing,' he said.

They watched Patsy throw the ball for the dog. 'So tell me all about Patsy,' John went on. 'She certainly looks well. Do you think she's settling in all right?'

Dottie prattled away, telling him again about Maureen, Patsy's best friend, and the rest of the Prior children. She told him how much Patsy liked feeding the chickens and how she'd made a pet out of their pig, christening him Porker.

'And what about Mr Cox?' John asked. 'I got the feeling that he was a bit shocked when he saw his daughter in Southampton – does he get along with her now?'

For a second, Dottie panicked. She couldn't tell him the truth, could she? Patsy didn't seem to worry about her father's gruff behaviour and Dottie was hoping that because she was such a lovely girl she'd win him round in the end. If she told Dr Landers – John – how things really were, he might take Patsy away. Keep your mouth shut, she told herself, and it'll all come out right in the end.

'Reg is quite busy at the moment,' she said cautiously, 'but once the winter sets in, and we have those long cosy evenings by the fire, I'm sure they'll be spending a lot more time together.'

'That's good,' he said and Dottie felt a pang of guilt.

They passed the Miller's Tomb under a spreading oak tree but, just as they were going to read the inscription, a lone rider coming out of the woods distracted them.

'Patsy,' John shouted. 'Keep hold of Minnie's collar, and stand still until the lady on the horse has gone by.'

Patsy called the dog to heel and crouched down beside her. They waited as horse and rider cantered on. Dottie watched her with a smile. She was such a good girl.

Standing with his back to the ancient Iron-Age fort at the top of the hill, John was over awed by the view. The weather was fairly clear and Dottie pointed out the local landmarks; the spires of St Mary's in Goring and St Andrew's in Tarring, and the gasometer in the far distance near Worthing hospital.

'I've got a picnic in the car,' he said suddenly. 'If I had known it was so lovely up here, I would have brought it up.'

'Never mind,' she smiled. She turned towards him and as his dark brown eyes searched hers, Dottie felt her face flame.

'Tell you what!' he cried. 'You and Patsy take your time to get back to the Miller's Tomb and I'll run on down to the car and fetch it.'

'It's a long way to go back,' she protested.

'Nonsense,' he chuckled. 'If you can walk all that long way from the village, running back down the hill isn't going to kill me, is it? I'll meet you back there in ten minutes.'

He set off a steady jog. Dottie watched him go. What a lovely man. So kind. Such fun to be with. No wonder Patsy loved him. She sighed. If only Reg was like that . . .

The sound of the dog barking brought her out of her daydream, and she called Patsy back from the chalk pits where she and Minnie were playing chase. By the time they reached the Miller's Tomb, John was puffing his way back up the hill with a basket in one hand and a blanket over his arm. They spread out the blanket under a tree and Patsy and Minnie sat down on it with expectant faces.

John laughed. 'Let's see what I've got here,' he said, unstrapping the basket.

Dottie gasped with delight as he threw back the lid. He had prepared quite a spread. Chicken paste sandwiches, hard-boiled eggs, three large apples, a whole fruitcake – 'I can't take credit for that,' he smiled, 'my mother made it' – some shortbread and a flask of tea. Minnie was delighted to discover he had also packed a juicy marrowbone. She found her own corner of the blanket and set about chewing it.

They ate the sandwiches and relaxed on the blanket. 'This is my best ever picnic,' Patsy sighed happily, as she wiped some of the fruitcake from her mouth with the back of her hand.

It was for Dottie as well. John was delightful company and for the first time since Patsy had arrived, she was experiencing one of those family times she'd so long dreamed about. If time could be trapped in a bottle, she thought to herself, this would be one of those moments to capture forever, especially if she could share it with John.

'You said your mother made the cake,' said Dottie, kneeling up on the blanket to wipe Patsy's face with her handkerchief. 'How is she?'

'Funnily enough, since I've been back,' he said, 'she's rallied. She still needs to rest a lot, but she looks a lot stronger.'

'I'm glad,' said Dottie.

'Can Minnie and I play again?' asked Patsy.

'I think you should let your tea go down first,' said Dottie.

John was looking at Patsy and chewing his bottom lip. 'Dottie,' he began. 'I've told my mother all about Patsy. How would you feel if I took her to meet her?'

Dottie struggled to control her feelings. Reg would go bonkers. 'I'm not sure how my husband would feel,' she began cautiously.

'Oh please, Auntie Dottie,' said Patsy. 'I want to go to Uncle John's house.'

Dottie turned her head away. What was she going to do?

'I tell you what,' said John, as if he sensed her discomfort, 'you have a think about it. I'll give you my telephone number. If you should decide to let her come, don't worry about getting the bus or the train or anything. I'll come for you both.'

'You mean, you want me to come too?'

'Of course.'

'Thank you,' she said quietly. She had to turn away again because she had butterflies already.

'Now, come on, you two, I can't possible take any of this picnic back home or my mother will accuse me of starving you both. Have another paste sandwich.'

'I really couldn't manage another thing,' Dottie laughed. 'The whole afternoon has been wonderful.'

'So has the company,' he said, looking directly at her. Dottie busied herself tidying the plates back in the basket.

The watery sun was beginning to get lower in the sky and it was definitely getting cooler. Patsy and Minnie played one last game of 'fetch' with the ball.

'I'll give you a lift back home,' said John as he packed away the picnic things.

'No!' He raised an eyebrow and she knew she'd reacted too quickly. 'Please don't worry about us. We'll enjoy the walk.'

'At least let me take you part of the way.'

Dottie did some quick thinking. They were unlikely to bump into anyone on the way back and she *was* a bit tired. 'All right then,' she said. 'Drop us at the crossroad.'

The driver of the car behind them leaned on his horn as John slowed down.

'Damn stupid place to stop,' he shouted at the windscreen.

As he overtook the car in front, he glanced in his rearview mirror. A woman and her child were climbing out of the car and waving to the man behind the steering wheel. Michael's father, Gerald, was slightly surprised to see that the woman was Dottie Cox. She had a little girl with her. Must be the one she and Reg had adopted. He wondered vaguely what she was up to. The three of them seemed very chummy.

As he looked ahead again, Gerald jumped as he realised he was going too fast to take the bend in the road. Braking sharply, he only just managed to get round in one piece.

Skimming the grass verge, he straightened the car again and settled down again. Should he slow down and offer her a lift? He eased his foot off the accelerator, but then he thought better of it. No. If Dottie was up to no good, she wouldn't thank him for spotting her. They would be turning the corner any minute. Concentrating on the road ahead, Gerald pressed his foot down hard and headed for home.

Funny, he thought to himself as he skirted the village. I never would have had Dottie Cox down as the type to play around.

# Twenty-Five

Reg hadn't come home last night.

When Dottie woke up in the morning, her first reaction was pure joy. She lay on her back, watching the curtains fluttering in the light breeze coming from the open window. For the first time in a long time, her bed felt warm and cosy.

The church bells began their peal and Dottie wondered vaguely where Reg might be. There was no note on the table when they got back last evening, but then she didn't expect one. She was the one who left notes. Reg never told her his plans. In fact, he hardly even bothered to make conversation these days and if he felt she had talked too much, he'd be just as likely to thump her.

For some reason, he blamed her that having Patsy hadn't worked out. He was determined that she be the one to ask the authorities to take the child away, but she was just as determined not to. Dottie was no fool. She knew something was wrong somewhere, but she didn't want to think about it. Something told her that if she tried to work it out, she would be forced to send Patsy away and she was beginning to love the child.

The wardrobe door was ajar. Reg had gone in his best suit but nothing else was missing. He hadn't packed a case or anything. She felt a little guilty that she wasn't bothered about him. He was probably lying drunk in a gutter somewhere. Ah well, if that was the case, he'd be home soon enough and until then she and Patsy could do what they liked.

Dottie jumped out of bed and pulled open the curtains. Even though it was the end of the month, it was going to be a glorious day. Spoilt for choice, she couldn't decide what to do. Jump on a bus and go to Brighton, go to the beach, walk up to Titnore woods? She wished John Landers was coming again. He'd made even a simple picnic such fun . . .

Hearing voices, she looked down into Ann's garden. Brian and Phyllis were squabbling over a ball and a sudden thought struck her. If Reg wasn't around all the time, the two of them would be firm friends. Perhaps they could all do something together. Throwing open the sash-cord window, she called out, 'Brian, ask your mummy if she could come round a minute, will you?'

The offices of Brown, Son and Knightly were on the corner of Liverpool Terrace in Worthing, in a large imposing Victorian building badly in need of repair. Reg had been putting it off since he'd got back on Monday but by Thursday he couldn't wait any longer. He'd biked down to the town in his lunch break to be shown into the waiting area which was dominated by a large settee that looked to be as old as the building. The leather was cracked and dry and some of the horsehair was coming out of one of the arms. Uncomfortable in his surroundings, Reg sat on a hardbacked chair next to a small wicker table covered in old magazines. He ran his finger around the inside of his shirt collar and swallowed loudly. The only sound in the room was the slow tick tock of the railway-sized wall clock.

He wouldn't have thought of doing this if it hadn't been for Joyce. What a stroke of luck finding her again. He'd been wandering around his old haunts when he'd bumped into Molly Scrace. Bit of a shock at first. Her hair was grey now and she wore gold-rimmed glasses, but apart from that she'd looked more or less the same.

'You still the barmaid at the King's Head?' he'd asked.

'Nah . . . but I still goes there for a glass of stout now and then.'

'Any of the old crowd still there?'

She'd named a few names, some of which he remembered but others he couldn't put a face to. 'I'm on me way there now,' she said. 'Fancy a pint?'

And the first person he saw when he walked through the door was Joyce. She'd gained some weight, but she still had that bleached blonde hair he admired so much, although close up he could see the dark roots. She was no Jane Russell but every time he looked at her something stirred in his loins. He was gutted when she told him she was with someone else now. Herbie Bawden. A bookie. Only to be expected after all this time, he'd supposed, but she'd given him the nod and they'd each made their excuses to leave, he for the toilet and she to go home and make Herbie's tea. They'd met up in the back alley.

'I can't stop long,' she'd told him but she'd lifted her skirts while he unbuttoned his flies and she stopped long enough. When it was over, he'd grabbed a handful of hair. 'I want you back.'

'You've got a bloody nerve,' she'd snapped. 'When you got locked up, I wanted to wait for you but you told me not to.'

'I was an idiot,' said Reg. He kissed her hard on the mouth.

She pushed him away. 'What about you? Have you got somebody else?'

'There's no one,' he'd lied. 'I'm on me own, or as good as.'

She'd looked him straight in the eye. 'Herbie may not be love's young dream, Reg, but he keeps me comfortable. You and I have had one for old times' sake but I'm not on the game any more.'

'I got me own house,' he boasted. Her eyes lit up. 'But I got a sitting tenant at the moment. You can move in as soon as I get rid of her.'

Joyce seemed unconvinced. She put her head back and her hand on her hip. 'And how long will that take?'

'Not long.'

'I'm not hanging about, Reg.'

'You won't have to,' he promised.

Even thinking about her in this sterile office waiting room made him shift in his seat. That woman could do things to him nobody else could do. If he was to get her back, he needed money . . . which was precisely why he was here in this office.

The sound of squeaking shoes came along the polished lino floor in the corridor and a woman appeared in the doorway. Her blouse was buttoned to the neck and her pale face looked washed out in the dark grey suit she was wearing. She peered at him over the top of her glasses.

'Mr Cox? Mr Knightly will see you now.'

He followed her down the corridor and into Mr Knightly's office.

When Reg first clapped eyes on him, he was surprised. Seeing as how his name was last on the polished brass nameplate outside the door, he had expected him to be a much younger man. Mr Knightly was about fifty or fifty-five, with heavy jowls and a very discoloured nose – probably, Reg thought, from drinking too much port after dinner.

Reg introduced himself.

'Pleased to meet you, Mr Cox,' said Mr Knightly pleasantly. 'And how is Mrs Cox? Well, I hope?'

Reg assured him his wife was the picture of health. 'She and I are planning our future,' he said, getting straight to the point. 'I want to talk to you about the terms of her late aunt's will. We got plans.'

Mr Knightly raise his hand. 'Let me stop you there, Mr Cox. I'm afraid I am not at liberty to speak to you in a business sense. Mrs Cox is our client.'

Reg's mouth tightened. 'But I'm her husband. What's mine is hers and what's hers is mine.'

'That may be so, Mr Cox, but I'm not at liber . . .'

'Yes, yes, you already said that,' Reg cut in. 'It's about the wife's inheritance.'

'As you already know,' Mr Knightly continued with a sigh, 'the house is in your wife's name so I can only accept instructions for her.'

'But that's bloody ridiculous!'

Mr Knightly gave Reg a disapproving look. 'That's not for me to say, Mr Cox,' he said sitting back down at his desk. 'All I can tell you is that, without formal instruction, I cannot do business with you. Good afternoon, Mr Cox.'

His face purple with rage, Reg had no option but to turn on his heel and march back down the corridor. Damn and blast it! That bloody Aunt Bessie was still ruling his life from the grave.

What was he going to do? He had to have money if he was going to get Joyce back but Dottie was in the way. He only put up with that kid because of the promise Sandy put in the letter. 'In my will, I've left everything to you . . .' Life would be so much better without the pair of them.

Back home that evening, Reg suddenly announced that he was going away for a couple of days at the weekend.

'But you'll miss the bonfire,' Dottie cautioned.

Reg shrugged and went back to his paper. Dottie supposed she should ask him where he was going but in truth she didn't care. Another couple of days without him would be wonderful. She was just happy to be left alone.

On Friday morning she packed him a suitcase and some sandwiches and he went off in his best suit. He didn't kiss her goodbye. She didn't care about that either. As soon as she was sure he was really gone, her heart fluttering with excitement, Dottie went to the phone box and telephoned John Landers.

By six thirty on Saturday, Tom Prior and Michael Gilbert had set up the last of the Catherine Wheels and checked that the rest

226

of the fireworks were safely stored in the big tin. The womenfolk and kids hadn't arrived yet but it was already getting dark. They had cordoned off the bonfire and Tom had laid the potatoes on a sheet of corrugated iron at the base. Earlier in the afternoon, they'd sent Steve Sullivan's terrier in to check that there weren't any hedgehogs or stray cats sleeping inside and now everything was ready for the off.

'We're having a do for Patsy later on,' Tom said.

Marney nodded approvingly. 'Any excuse for a good old shindig.'

'Mum suggested a barn dance,' said Michael. 'She's left it all to us to organise.'

'How do we go about doing that then?'

'My Freda asked the bloke who played the piano-accordion at our wedding. His brother plays the fiddle,' Michael told them. 'Apparently Don Patterson from Findon is available and he's a good caller. It should be a cracking night.'

'Oh, "my Freda" now, is it?' Tom teased.

Michael felt his face flame and turned away. Yes, surprisingly it was 'my Freda' now. From the moment they'd been married, he and Freda had got on well together. She made him feel good and he was happy.

'Terry Dore says he'll give us a barrel, so us shan't go thirsty . . .' Tom was saying.

'What about the food?' asked Michael.

'Oh, leave that to the womenfolk,' said Tom dismissively. 'We've done the most important bit.'

They carried the guy in procession from Janet Cooper's shop through the village and past the church, a crowd of elated children following behind. Patsy, her eyes bright with excitement, skipped alongside the old pram which was being pushed by Billy.

'The only time I've ever known him willing to push the

darned thing . . .' Mary muttered out of the corner of her mouth.

Dottie laughed. The two friends held the hands of the little ones. Dottie had Connie and Maureen, while Mary hung on to Christopher and Susan. Everyone was well wrapped up although the evening wasn't that cold.

When they reached the field, the children ran off and by the time Dottie and Mary came the men were hosting the guy, now tied to a three-legged chair, onto the top of the bonfire with ropes. As soon as he reached the top, albeit at a drunken angle, there was a ragged cheer from the crowd and the sound of muffled clapping from their gloved hands. Dottie and Mary gathered the little ones behind the roped-off area and waited.

'They've done it very well,' Dottie remarked.

Mary smiled proudly. 'Tom is always very careful when it comes to the kids. You will give me a hand giving out the jackets when they're done, won't you, Dottie? They won't take long. I started them off in the oven.'

Michael was given the honour of lighting the first Catherine wheel. Patsy was mesmerised as it shot out a shower of coloured sparks which eventually made it turn at great speed on the nail and she gasped with pleasure as the colours merged into one bright yellow and orange blur.

The men moved about silently lighting the positioned fireworks in a pre-arranged sequence. They held things on a tight rein, the only hiccup occurring when Billy's friend, Raymond Green, threw a jumping jack into the crowd, terrifying little Connie and making the other girls scream. Raymond was rewarded with a clip round the ear from PC Kipling and then another from his father standing nearby. Dottie picked up Connie and tried to calm her down. The child clung to her, trembling and burying her face into Dottie's coat.

Within a few minutes of the start of the fireworks, Tom plunged a lighted torch into the middle of the bonfire and it quickly took hold, the glowing embers soaring high into the night sky. When the rockets went up, everyone – including Connie – looked up, their 'Oooh's and 'Ahhh's echoing all around the field.

Dottie became aware of someone standing right behind her and a pair of gloved hands covered her eyes. 'Guess who?' said a woman's voice.

Dottie didn't need to second-guess. With a cry of joy she pulled herself away from the gentle restraint. 'Peaches!' And the two of them laughed and hugged each other with Connie in between.

'How are you? Is the baby here? What about Gary? How's he getting on?' The questions just spilled from Dottie's lips.

'Hey, steady on,' Peaches laughed. Jack took Connie from Dottie's arms and, with a wink, left them to it. 'Everybody's fine. Oh Dottie, it's so good to see you.'

'It's good to see you too,' cried Dottie. She was aware that Patsy had crept beside her and was looking up at them in mild surprise. Dottie put her arm around Patsy's shoulders. 'You haven't met my Patsy yet, have you? Patsy, this is your Aunt Peaches.'

'Hello, Patsy. I've heard all about you.'

'Hello,' said Patsy.

Maureen wiggled between them. 'Mum's got some sparklers for us to hold,' she told Patsy and the two girls ran off to find Mary.

Edna pushed a baked potato wrapped in newspaper into Peaches' hand.

'Tell me about Gary,' Dottie insisted. 'I heard they transferred him to Courtlands.'

'It's a smashing place,' said Peaches. 'He's got to stay there another four to five months, but he's breathing on his own now and he's getting stronger every day.'

'Oh Peaches,' said Dottie helplessly.

'It's all right. We've got used to it now. We're just really pleased he's got this far and the doctor is hopeful that he'll make a good recovery.'

'What about his leg?'

'It's a bit skinny,' said Peaches, picking at her potato with her fingers. 'It could have been a lot worse. At one time the doctors said he might never walk again.'

Dottie took in her breath.

'It's all right now. They say the exercises will make it strong again.'

Dottie regarded her shape. 'And I heard you had a little girl.'

Peaches smiled. 'We've called her Mandy.'

'Where is she now? Is she all right?'

Peaches nodded. 'She weighed seven pounds three ounces, and she's got Jack's eyes and my hair.'

'I'd love to see her,' sighed Dottie.

Peaches lowered her eyes. 'The fact is, Dottie, after the way I treated you . . .'

Dottie squeezed her friend's arm. 'It's all water under the bridge now.'

'I know now that you did go to see Gary,' said Peaches. 'I only found out when we took Ivy and Brumas back.'

'The bears . . .? Oh, didn't he like them?'

'He wouldn't be parted from them,' said Peaches, 'but we thought they belonged to the hospital. He kept saying, "Auntie Dottie gave them to me."'

Dottie smiled. 'I'm surprised he even remembered.'

'I didn't believe him,' Peaches went on, 'but the nurse said someone brought them in for him on that first day, and she described you. Dottie, why didn't you say? Why did you pretend you didn't go?'

'Reg didn't want me to go to the isolation hospital,' said Dottie with a sigh. 'He was convinced I would get the polio and then we wouldn't be able to have Patsy.'

Peaches squeezed Dottie's hand. 'She's a lovely little girl, Dottie. Mary said she comes all the way from Australia. She's . . . she's very dark.'

'We've got her because Reg knew someone out there,' Dottie said, repeating yet again the well-rehearsed story. It slipped off her tongue easily these days. 'If we'd gone through one of those adoption agencies, we'd have to have medicals and they'd ask questions and,' she added with a nervous laugh, 'you know how much Reg hates all that red tape!'

'It's a shame you've never had children of your own.'

'As a matter of fact . . .' Dottie said confidentially; drawing Peaches closer she whispered, 'don't say anything just yet but I think . . .'

Peaches beamed. 'Oh Dottie . . . how exciting . . .'

'Don't breathe a word,' Dottie cautioned. 'I haven't even told Reg yet.'

Peaches looked around. 'Where is Reg?'

'Give us a hand, Dottie!' came a cry.

Dottie started and then the realisation dawned. 'Oh my lord . . . Sorry, Peaches, I promised Mary I'd give her a hand dishing out the spuds.'

Reg's heart was pumping. He stared at the closed door, wondering what delectable morsels were being prepared on the other side.

When he'd arrived, Joyce had been annoyed when he told her the money was a bit tied up.

'I'm not going to be poor all my life,' she'd pouted. 'If you want me, Reg, you have to pay for it. I'm not giving up what I've got for nothing.'

When she'd said that he'd lost his rag. They'd fought like cat and dog until he'd punched her to the ground. After that, they'd had passionate, exciting and violent sex. He couldn't be without her again. She did things to him that no other woman ever did. She teased him until he was in a frenzy of desire and when she gave herself to him she didn't mind experimenting – she had no inhibitions and she'd try anything he fancied. She even came up with some wild ideas herself. She was all woman and he was putty in her hands. Why couldn't they all be like her?

All at once, Aunt Bessie's voice filled his head. 'When Dottie hears what you did, you'll be out on your ear.'

'Dot will do just what I say,' he'd boasted.

Joyce's sultry voice brought him back to the present. Wait outside the room, she'd said, and I'll give you a fantastic surprise. Naked, he felt himself harden as he stood up and walked towards the bedroom. He glanced down to admire his manhood. He could have this every night if he could get hold of some decent money. His eyes narrowed. There had to be a way of getting rich quick. Only Dot and that bloody kid stood in his way . . .

# Twenty-Six

It was Sunday, the day Dottie and Patsy were due to meet Mrs Landers, and it was chucking it down with rain. Dottie regretted insisting that John meet them at the crossroads again. They were going to get extremely wet.

She asked Ann to shut the chickens in if she wasn't back in time.

'What if Reg turns up?' Ann asked nervously. 'Where shall I tell him you've gone?'

'Reg is away until tonight,' Dottie explained. 'And I'm taking Patsy to see Dr Landers.'

Ann frowned anxiously. 'Is there something wrong with her?'

'She's fine,' said Dottie. 'Dr Landers looked after Patsy when she came from Australia. He's very fond of her.'

Her friend raised an eyebrow suggestively. 'Going somewhere nice?'

'I shouldn't think so,' laughed Dottie. 'We are to meet his old mother.'

'How disappointing,' Ann sighed. 'I hope you don't get too bored with the old fossils.'

John drove them through the autumnal lanes towards Littlehampton and on to the Sussex village of Yapton. As Patsy and John chattered away, Dottie had never felt happier. He was such a lovely man, good looking, kind . . . if only . . . She pushed

233

her daydreams aside and concentrated on the view from the car window.

There was little in the centre of the village, just a few shops and a public green. They crossed the old canal and headed along the Barnham road where his mother lived in a small cottage. Although the garden had seen better days, it was a delightful place. Of course, there was little in the way of flowers in the garden at this time of year but a few chrysanthemums and Michaelmas daisies soldiered on, and the odd rose remained even though most of the bush was little more than bare twigs. The leaves of the wisteria which grew over the front door were beginning to wilt and the geraniums were way past their best, but Dottie imagined that it was very beautiful in the spring and summer months.

As they climbed out of the car, their ears were assaulted by loud music. John knocked at the front door and Minnie barked but nobody came. Taking a spare key from under a flowerpot by the window, he opened the door and they all went in.

Laura Landers was a bird-like woman with white wispy hair and pale colourless eyes, but she was far from being a fossil. She was wearing a maroon-coloured dress with tiny white dots all over it, slightly too severe for her pale complexion, but as they all walked in to her light airy sitting room, the radio was blaring out the new Patti Page song, 'Tennessee Waltz'. Laura was dancing with a cushion in her arms and, as John entered the room, she was so surprised to see them, she almost fell over.

'Mother!' John cried rushing to her side.

'Don't fuss, dear,' she said recovering herself. 'You made me jump, that's all.'

Dottie warmed to her immediately. She was wonderful!

John went over to the gramophone to turn it off.

'I'm sorry, my dear,' said Laura clutching her chest and sinking into a chair. 'Forgive the eccentricities of a silly old woman. I'm quite puffed out now.'

'Not at all,' said Dottie. 'You dance beautifully.'

Laura Landers waved her hand dismissively. 'You mustn't flatter me or I shall want to do it all over again and, as you can see, that will only make my son very cross.' She lowered her voice conspiratorially. 'He thinks I'm already in my dotage and I should spend my days on the sofa, surrounded by cushions.'

Dottie grinned.

'Don't take any notice of her,' said John as he crossed the room and kissed his mother on the cheek. 'And you behave yourself, Mother.'

'And where's the fun in that?' the old woman protested. 'I take it this lady is Mrs Cox?'

'Call me Dottie . . . please.'

'And Patsy?'

Patsy was hiding behind Dottie's skirt.

Mrs Landers and Dottie shook hands. 'Patsy, my dear, I've heard such wonderful things about you, I could hardly wait to meet you.'

Patsy gave her a cautious stare.

'John, you didn't tell me she was so beautiful,' cried Laura. 'And what a pretty dress you have. Is it new?'

Patsy nodded. 'Auntie Dottie made it.'

Laura Landers seemed impressed. 'Then she's an excellent needlewoman,' she said, struggling to get out of the chair. 'Now I wonder, Patsy, could you help me in the kitchen?'

'I'd be pleased to give you a hand, Mrs Landers,' said Dottie.

'No, no, my dear. I'm sure Patsy is big enough to help me with the tea things, aren't you, Patsy?'

Patsy beamed, her chest swelling with pride.

They went off together hand in hand, leaving Dottie alone with John.

'She does you credit,' he said.

'Not me,' Dottie insisted. 'Her mother.'

He motioned her to sit down. 'Last time we met,' he said, 'you

235

said Patsy was happy and settled, but your husband was still finding it hard to adjust to parenthood.'

Dottie nodded. 'He still is,' she said, 'but I am hoping he will come round soon.'

'So do I.' His smile was a little disconcerting. 'I feel somehow responsible, Dottie. I made a few too many presumptions when I wrote to him. For a start, I thought he'd already seen his daughter, but according to Brenda, Sandy lost touch with him before she had the baby.' He paused. 'Do you know anything about your husband's ancestry? I mean, were his parents people of colour?'

Dottie stiffened. Please don't probe too deeply, she thought. 'Reg doesn't talk about his past but I believe he was brought up in a children's home,' she said cautiously.

John looked at her apologetically. 'You know, I only want to make sure Patsy has the very best she can.'

'Then we both want the same thing.'

Being so close to him, Dottie could hardly breathe. She certainly couldn't hold his gaze so she turned her attention to the dog, which was sitting at her feet. She bent to pat her, calling her a good girl. For a sickening minute, it reminded her of Reg. That's what he'd called her that night he raped her. If she kept her hand moving, hopefully John wouldn't notice it was trembling.

Patsy reappeared with a plate of sandwiches. She put them on the table and walked over to Dottie, then put her arm around Dottie's shoulders and her mouth next to her ear. 'We've got chocolate cake,' she whispered excitedly.

After their tea, John suggested they take the dog for a short walk.

'A good idea,' said his mother. 'I'll clear the tea things while you're gone.'

'Let me help,' Dottie said, but Mrs Landers wouldn't hear of it.

Patsy was thrilled to be holding Minnie's lead. They ran on ahead while John and Dottie walked together.

'I used to dream about this place all the time when I was in Australia,' said John, 'but it has never seemed as wonderful as it does right now.'

'Did you spend the war in Australia?'

'Heavens, no,' he laughed. 'As soon as I'd qualified, I was called up. I began my war in a corvette but then we were torpedoed. After that, it was a destroyer. We were mostly on convoy duties.'

'Not an easy time,' said Dottie recalling the Pathé newsreels she'd seen during the war.

'You could say that,' he laughed, 'but being in the navy gave me a thirst for adventure. Look, there's some more blackberries.' He pointed to a hedge bowed down with brambles. The blackberries were plump and ready for picking. 'Fancy some?'

'They'd make a wonderful pie,' she said, 'but we've nothing to carry them in.'

He took out a handkerchief and spread it on the ground. 'How about this?'

'The juice will stain it,' she cautioned.

'Like I said,' he smiled, 'the navy gave me a thirst for adventure. If you're willing to risk the wrath of my mother, so am I.'

They laughed easily and Patsy came back to see what they were doing.

'This has been a wonderful afternoon,' said Dottie as they walked back, his handkerchief bulging with blackberries. 'Your mother has made us so welcome.'

'It's been our pleasure,' said John earnestly. 'Can I ask you a very personal question?'

Dottie looked up sharply. 'What is it?'

'Are you and Reg happily married?'

She looked away, startled. 'Yes . . . yes of course we are.' Dottie blurted out, but they both knew she'd reacted far too quickly.

'I take my marriage vows very seriously,' Dottie said, trying to justify herself, but she could feel her face burning.

John Landers smiled and she knew at once that he had seen right through her. She panicked. Was he looking for a way to take Patsy away?

He leaned forward and said in a soft confidential manner, 'Listen, Dottie, if ever you need anything . . . anything . . . I want you to promise that you will come to me for help.'

'I . . .' She hesitated, then in a lower tone of voice said, 'Oh, John, you're such a kind man.'

'I mean it.'

'I know you do and I thank you,' she said shyly. 'And I want you to know that I've . . . that Patsy and I have loved every minute of this day.'

'So have I.'

Once again, Dottie could feel her face flame. Just the scent of him was enough to send her into a fluster. Patsy and the dog were lagging behind. Willing herself to remain unsmiling, Dottie called back, 'Patsy, hurry up, there's a good girl. We must go.' And they finished their walk in a rather awkward silence.

Back at the cottage, Patsy said, 'Thank you for having me.'

Laura Landers cupped her face in her hands and kissed her gently. 'And we've loved having you, my dear. It's been a wonderful afternoon.' She slipped a pound note into the child's hand. 'This is for you but don't spend it all on sweets. Buy something special.'

Patsy thanked her and Laura turned her attention to Dottie. 'I'm so pleased to have met you, my dear,' she said, kissing Dottie's cheek.

Dottie blushed. 'You went to so much trouble . . .'

'Nonsense,' said Laura. 'Now you will bring her again, won't you?'

As they sped down the road towards Worthing, Dottie sighed. If only every day could be as happy as this one had been.

## *Twenty-Seven*

When she woke next morning, Dottie was alone once again. As she lay in bed, a faint smile played on her lips as she recalled the previous day and one moment in particular. It was when Patsy had looked up at her, her face purple with berry juice.

'Have you been eating them?'

Patsy's eyes had gone wide with apprehension. 'No!'

Dottie had raised her eyebrows and put her head on one side with a sceptical expression.

'Well,' Patsy added, relaxing, 'not many,' and the air had been filled with John's laughter.

Reg still had not returned home. Where was he? Had he left her? The thought brought a rush of guilty pleasure. Now that the clocks had gone back, the mornings were dark. Dottie switched on the bedside light and lay in the bed, staring at her reflection in the mirror on the wardrobe.

As the clock ticked around to six thirty, Dottie climbed out of bed. Lifting her nightdress, she looked at her gently rounded stomach and caressed her skin. If only this child were John's. Her own words came back to haunt her. What was it she'd told him? 'My marriage vows are important to me . . .' something like that. If that were really true, then why was she so glad Reg wasn't here? Even if he never came back, a man like John wouldn't want a ready-made family. He'd want his own. How would she support Patsy and her own baby? She spread her fingers across

239

her abdomen as if she were holding the baby within. Whatever she felt about Reg, this was his baby. Patsy had no mother but she still had her father. This baby had both a father and a mother. If she pushed Reg away, what sort of a life would her baby have?

Aunt Bessie had never approved of her marriage, Dottie knew that, but on the day she'd married Reg, she had given her some sound advice. 'You've made your choice, darling,' Aunt Bessie said, not unkindly, 'now make it work.'

It was a sobering thought, but it was up to her now. Dottie resolved from here on in, for the sake of her baby, she'd better forget John Landers and make more of a go of her marriage.

Patsy called from her room, 'Is it time to get up yet, Aunt Dottie?'

Dropping her nightdress, Dottie reached for her housecoat. 'It certainly is, love. Back to school today.'

Reg flexed his fingers. Bruised and sore, the skin on his knuckles was broken. After a couple of days away from that cow of a wife and that snotty kid, he'd hatched a plan and come back to Worthing. On his way back to the cottage, he'd been waylaid. He hadn't reckoned on the bloke sneaking up on him. He'd better keep his hand in his pocket. Nobody would give him a lift if they saw the state of him.

He stood on the grass verge and stuck out his thumb. Best to get away for a few days. Lie low. With a bit of luck, no one saw him get off the train but he couldn't bloody count on it. Trouble was, it was still light. He should have gone to the pub before he went home. That way the bloke wouldn't have seen him. Who was he anyway? And how did he know his name? As far as Reg knew, he'd never seen him in his life before, although he did look a bit like that dirty old tramp who used to come sniffing around the cottage when Bessie was alive.

'Not me, mate,' he'd said but if the truth were known, he'd nearly died of shock.

'I know what you've done,' the bloke shouted after him, 'but you'll never get away with it.'

For a few seconds, Reg had been rooted to the spot but then the need for survival kicked in. He'd dashed into the shed and grabbed the first thing that came to hand. The hammer. Then he'd stalked the bloke. Caught up with him by the fields.

One whack on the side of his head with the hammer felled him like a bloody tree. He hadn't lost his touch. He'd booted and punched the body until he was sure he wouldn't be telling anybody anything and then he'd toed him into the ditch.

It didn't seem like anyone had seen him, but just to be on the safe side Reg went back to the cottage and collected his bag, hid the hammer in his shed and hit the road. He almost left the hammer where it fell but went back – PC Kipling might recognise it.

A lorry pulled up. 'Where you goin', boyo?'

'Where are you going?'

'Lewes.'

'That'll do me,' he said, climbing into the cab.


By late afternoon on Wednesday, Reg was still away and it was beginning to get to Dottie. He had never been away so long before.

After school, Dottie had arranged that she and Patsy would meet up with John again. She'd mentioned a walk along the seafront from Goring to Ferring, and he'd jumped at her suggestion to spend time with Patsy.

Mr Marney had come up to the cottage the night before.

'I've no idea where Reg is,' she told him truthfully.

Marney was none too pleased.

'He's been under a lot of strain just lately,' Dottie went on. She didn't want to make excuses for him, but how were they going to manage if Reg lost his job? 'He needed a little break, that's all.'

'You're supposed to book your holidays,' Marney snapped, 'not just take them when you fancy.'

Just before lunch, Dottie walked down the garden, looking over her shoulder every now and then in case she saw the tramp hanging around. She wasn't even sure why she was thinking about him again. He hadn't been around since that morning when Sylvie frightened him off, but last night, just before she drifted off to sleep, Dottie found herself wondering what it was he was going to tell her. Did he know something about Aunt Bessie's death?

Clucking noisily, the chickens dashed up to the wire as soon as she opened the door, clearly thinking it was feeding time again. Dottie checked inside the henhouse for eggs, slipping her hand under one hen where she sat. The egg was still warm.

The pig grunted and put his snout over the top of the fence. He was getting so big, it wouldn't be long before he broke it down and ran amok. Michael and Gerald Gilbert were supposed to be coming sometime to take him to market. Judging by the size of Porker, it couldn't be a moment too soon.

When Dottie and John met, Patsy couldn't stop talking. He heard all about Patsy's day at school from beginning to end. Eventually she ran off with the dog while Dottie and John strolled behind. It was a crisp afternoon and the cloud base was low. The tide was out and the place was deserted apart from the odd walker or two. They walked along the edge of the pebble bank, with the sea on one side and a rough area of green the other. Dottie felt so at ease in his company.

'How come you ended up in Australia?'

His face clouded. 'I needed to get away,' he said quietly. 'When I got back home . . .'

'From the war?'

He nodded. 'My wife and I were strangers. She had met someone else so in the end, it was better to part.'

'Oh, I'm sorry, John.'

He shrugged. 'These things happen. It was nobody's fault.'

'Do you have any children?'

'No . . . fortunately.'

'But why Australia?'

He laughed. 'A friend was supposed to be going but at the last minute he came down with shingles of all things. I was able to take his place. It was only supposed to be for a short time, but I ended up staying there for four years.'

'Coming back here . . .' she began. 'It must be so different.'

'I hadn't planned to come back at all,' he said. 'But my mother needed me. And now . . .' He looked directly at her. 'I'm not sure I even want to go back.'

Dottie heart was pounding. She couldn't think what to say. She knew what she *wanted* to say. 'I really enjoy being with you too. You're so wonderful with Patsy . . .' but she couldn't say that, could she? It was far too familiar and besides, she was pregnant with Reg's child for goodness' sake!

In truth, when she was with John she had never been happier. She and Patsy were becoming very close as well. Their latest venture together had been making a shoebox dolls' house. Dottie had helped Patsy cut out the windows and doors, and then Patsy had decorated the outside with flowers and the inside with pictures on the wall. They'd used matchboxes covered with scraps of material to make a bed, table and a couple of chairs. After that, Dottie had shown Patsy how to make a wool doll to go inside.

'I'll make a brown one like me and you make a pink one like you,' Patsy had said.

'I've only got some red wool,' Dottie said.

'That's near enough,' said Patsy.

Remembering, Dottie smiled to herself.

'Penny for them,' John said.

'It's nothing,' she smiled. There was another thing she wouldn't

243

tell John. Not yet anyway. Patsy was embroidering a tray cloth. It was to be a Christmas present for John's mother.

All at once, the heavens opened and it began to rain, not just fine rain but big drops, bursting with water as they fell.

'Quick,' Dottie pointed to a clump of Ilex oak trees in the distance. 'Head over there, for the Plantation.'

John grabbed Patsy's hand and they out-ran her. As Dottie raced after them, her heart bursting with the joy of watching them as they shrieked with laughter and Minnie barked and jumped at their heels. John hurried into the thickest part, searching out a large bough, heavy with green leaves, which would give them maximum shelter from the wet.

As he turned to Dottie he called out, 'Mind that tree!' But it was too late. She hadn't noticed that she was heading towards a small sapling covered in low-level newly grown branches. Dottie's head was yanked back as her hair became entangled in its branches.

'Ow!'

'Hang on a minute,' John said as she struggled to free herself. It was no use. The more she tried to free her hair, the more entangled it became. She was stuck fast.

'Ouch . . . Ow . . .'

In a moment he was by her side, doing his best to untangle her.

'Sorry . . .' His fingers moved deftly and he was being as gentle as he could. How long had he desired to touch her hair? It was like silk, sensual . . . It smelled of gardenias.

'Aah . . .'

'Sorry . . .'

'It's all right,' laughed Dottie. 'I'm just being an absolute baby. Ow!'

Their faces were very close, so close that every time he breathed out, his exhaled air, feather-like, touched her cheek and she felt more alive than she'd ever felt in her whole life.

'There,' he smiled, as a tendril of her hair flopped across her face. Their eyes met and she was aware that her heart was beginning to pound once more. She was seized by the most powerful yearning to touch him. She looked away quickly.

She felt his hand on her arm, as light as a feather. 'You know,' he said softly, 'I never knew it until now, but I think I've been waiting for something like this all my life. Is this kismet?'

She glanced up at him. 'What's kismet?'

'That you and I were destined to meet even before we were even born.'

He leaned his head against hers and she felt his lips brush her cheek. It made her weak at the knees. 'Oh John . . .' she moaned softly, '. . . don't . . . we mustn't.'

Yet she offered no resistance as he bent his head and his lips touched hers. Cupping her face in his hands, he said, 'I went all the way to Australia, and you were here all the time.'

She could feel his breath touching her mouth, as gentle as the flutter of a butterfly's wings. Her whole body was yearning for him. She closed her eyes.

'Is Auntie Dottie free yet?' Patsy's voice broke the spell instantly.

'Yes,' called John. 'She's free.'

Dottie opened her eyes. 'No, John,' she said quietly as she looked directly into John's eyes. 'Auntie Dottie isn't free.' Then, calling to Patsy she said, 'Coming.'

His fingers searched for hers as they walked towards Patsy but she drew her hand away. What madness. She should never have allowed that to happen and she hated herself for it. As they waited together under the bough of the tree for the rain to stop, Dottie could hardly breathe.

John was standing very close to her. Too close. One minute his hand was resting on the bough of a tree, the next he was playing with the curls on the nape of her neck. Blushing furiously,

Dottie tried to edge away from him but there was little space to move. 'Don't,' she pleaded softly.

'What makes it rain?' Patsy asked.

'When moisture in the cloud becomes too heavy, it falls to the ground as rain,' John explained.

Dottie's mind was elsewhere. She'd been in the Plantation a hundred times but, even with the rain pouring all around them, it had never seemed more beautiful. Had the grass always been this green? And why hadn't she ever noticed how musical the rain sounded? She could hardly bear to look at John for fear that he would try and kiss her in front of Patsy. You're a married woman, she reminded herself sternly. You mustn't encourage him. It's not fair.

'Will it snow?' asked Patsy.

'It's not cold enough for snow,' said John.

'What makes it snow?'

'That's when the rain starts off as ice crystals,' John explained. 'They fall through warmer air and land on the earth as snowflakes.'

He was so patient with her, so loving.

'Right now, the air is warm enough to melt the snowflake and change it into a rain drop.'

Inside, Dottie sighed. Damn you, Reg, damn you.

The rain stopped and they came out of the Plantation to walk to his car. The sky was still heavy with clouds but it had never seemed so vast, so empty.

She deliberately didn't meet his eye all the way back to the car, and yet she was acutely aware of him walking beside her. Patsy chattered away beside them and Minnie trotted at their feet.

He unlocked the driver's door then leaned in to open the back passenger door. Patsy and Minnie clambered in.

'Uncle John,' Patsy said. 'This is my best day ever.'

'Good. I'm really glad,' he said looking over the top of the car

246

at Dottie waiting by the passenger door. 'I think it's been my best day ever as well. And what about you, Auntie Dottie?' he said teasingly. Dottie felt her cheeks flush. 'What sort of day have you had?'

'Very nice,' she said tartly as she deliberately turned her head away.

It was only when she got back home that Dottie realised just how insane that kiss had been. Yes, John was a wonderful person, but she was married. Not only that, but she was pregnant. She hadn't told him that, had she? And even if he said he didn't care about the baby, how long would it last? He'd be here today and gone tomorrow. Men like him, professionals, weren't the marrying type, not with the likes of her, anyway. And even if he was, what would happen to his career when it became common knowledge? The doctor and a pregnant housewife flirting in the woods . . . heavens above! It was the stuff of the *News of the World*. The scandal . . . the risk . . . No, no, she wouldn't allow it.

With a heavy heart, Dottie decided she would have to write to him. She'd tell him about the baby. She'd say that she and Reg had been trying for years, and that as soon as he knew about it, Reg would be very happy. She would wish John well, and tell him now that he'd seen how happy and settled Patsy was, there was no need for him to call again. She could feel the tears beginning to form even as she thought of it.

As she got their teas, she wept alone in the scullery. She couldn't do it. Not with a letter. It felt like the coward's way out. She would tell him the next time she saw him. She would see him one more time. Just one more time and then she'd tell Reg. Only she didn't know where Reg was. He'd been gone almost a week. Where on earth could he be?

# Twenty-Eight

There had been a heart-stopping moment when Reg had looked up and thought he'd seen Dottie staring at him from the street outside. He was sitting in the fish and chip shop having a spot of tea before beginning the journey back home. He could get used to this eating-out malarky. He'd ordered a complete fry-up, two rounds of bread and butter and a mug of tea. It all went down a treat. Relaxing with a full stomach, he spread out his paper and was beginning to read when the face at the window distracted him.

At first he thought the woman outside looked straight at him. She had the same hairstyle as Dottie and wore one of those felt hats his wife favoured, but the face was different. Reg breathed a sigh of relief. The woman on the pavement had sharp features and wore bright red lipstick which was so thickly spread around her mouth it had bled onto her skin. She smiled and waved. He heard a chair scraping and, looking round, he saw a heavily-built man waving back at her. The woman hurried towards the shop door and the bell jangled as she came in. Reg turned his attention once more to his paper.

He ran his finger down the 'To Let' column. *Pleasant mod.s.d. villa close station. Blt 1936 Artistic elevation 3 sunny bedrooms bthm. Good garden, garage. Semi-detached . . .* Too close to the neighbours. He read on. *1st flr maisonette . . . modern house facing sports ground . . .* It got worse. That one would have hundreds of prying eyes. Once again there was nothing really suitable. His eye drifted down to the Property Investments column. *Bungalow for sale. Attractive property in need of some renovation. The Crumbles, an area of rustic beauty between Eastbourne and Pevensey.* He knew where that was. An area of rustic beauty? It was more like the middle of nowhere. A slow smile played on his lips.

Someone on the next table dropped the pepper pot and it went everywhere. Reg sneezed. Reaching for his handkerchief, a letter flew from his pocket and landed on the floor. A woman picked it up for him. He'd forgotten that he had that. He'd shoved it in his pocket last week when he was on his way to work and he'd bumped into Vince the postman. Addressed to Mrs D. Cox, he recognised Sylvie's sloping hand. What did she want? Bloody woman, she was always scribbling letters to Dot. He slid his finger under the seal and ripped it open.

*My darling Dottie . . .*

Reg's lip curled. A bloody lesbian, that's what she was. He read on. The first page began with women's stuff. All about the kids at school and something about making curtains. He almost didn't carry on but then he was glad he did. The second page was far more interesting.

*Robin has decided to stand as the Conservative candidate for our local council elections.* Sylvie wrote. *Major Breams seems to think that in five years time, the party could put his name forward to stand in the next general election. Just think, Dottie, I could be an MP's wife before I'm forty! We are so excited, I can't tell you. Of course I shall have to say goodbye to my special friend, but we both knew it was just a fling. From now on, I shall have to live the life of celibacy. I shall be an absolute saint!*

Reg lifted his eyes and stared into the far distance, with just a ghost of a smile flickering across his lips. It was time to go home.

What did he always say? Belt and braces. He hadn't been able to get anything out of Mr Knightly but if the bungalow plan didn't work, this snobby bitch had just handed him yet another nice little prospect for the future.

The decision to look for Brenda's address came to Dottie as she listened to Patsy's prayers that night. She knelt beside her bed, with her hands together and her eyes closed.

'Thank you for all my new friends and thank you for the fireworks. God bless Auntie Bren and Audrey and Wishbone. Please don't let Wishbone bark too much and make Auntie Bren cross, and let her remember to give Wishbone a big bone for his tea. Please bless Dr Landers and make his mother better . . .'

Dottie stared at the back of Patsy's head as the list went on and on. Was it right to keep her here? She'd grown to love the child, but she couldn't bear the thought of her growing up with Reg for a father. What if he had done a runner? She didn't look much like him, it was true, but nothing could alter the fact that Elizabeth Johns had named him as the father of her child. Patsy was his responsibility and if he had cleared off, they'd never allow Dottie to keep her.

The thought struck her that if things got really bad, Brenda might take her back. On the strength of Aunt Bessie's inheritance, she could promise to make it worth her while. She'd promised John that she would write to Brenda, but how could she since Reg had destroyed all the papers? When he'd gone upstairs that first night Patsy came home, she'd managed to pull some of it out of the fire, giving herself a nasty blister on her thumb in the process. She'd managed to hide the charred remains in the scullery but now it was at the bottom of her wardrobe, along with her Post Office book and her savings. It wasn't much. The remains of a diary, some photographs of the people from the homestead, she presumed, and some baby drawings belonging to Patsy. Everything else, including Brenda's address, was gone. And then it crossed her mind that Reg might have something in that shed of his.

'. . . and please bless Al and the new flying doctor, Amen.'

Patsy stood up and jumped into bed. Dottie leaned over her and tucked her in.

'Goodnight, Auntie Dottie,' said Patsy, deliberately turning over before Dottie could give her a kiss. Dottie felt a pang of hurt. Although they shared some really wonderful times together, Patsy still held back. Dottie had often longed for a little hug or a kiss from Patsy, but she would never force the issue.

'Goodnight, love,' she said, cheerily.

She ran downstairs quickly and glanced up at the clock. 8.40pm. She had no idea when Reg might turn up. She'd have to take a chance. She found a torch and went outside. It was very quiet. The only sound was a distant bell – an ambulance or a police car in a hurry somewhere.

Dottie pushed open the shed door. It smelled musty and damp. She shone the torch around in a high arch. Her heart was already in her mouth and she knew she'd have to be quick. If he caught her, or if he found out she'd been inside his beloved shed, she knew he was perfectly capable of beating her to within an inch of her life.

The beam from the torch fell on the big workbench with its three heavy drawers underneath. Dottie had never, ever looked inside and even the thought of rummaging through his personal things filled her with guilt. But it had to be done.

She rested the torch on the top of the bench next to a neat row of tools, and tugged at the top drawer. It opened easily. She picked up the torch and peered inside.

His cigarette papers, tobacco and his Rizla tin lay on the top. Carefully, Dottie lifted them up and caught sight of some photographs. The top one was of a naked woman in a provocative pose. She stared at it with horror. The woman was reclining on a sofa but she didn't look like one of those models artists paint.

251

More of an ageing tart with her bleached blonde hair and her bright red lips. She lay back with her legs wide apart. Nothing was hidden. She turned it over and read the inscription on the back: *Come up and see me sometime. J*

Dottie took in her breath quietly. She could hardly bear to touch it but she had to see what was underneath. In fact, she found a whole pile of pictures, each one more shocking the first, and one of them depicting that disgusting thing Reg had made her do the night he had raped her when Sylvie was here. The light danced over the pictures and she realised she was shaking. Dear God, who was this person she had married?

Pushing the drawer shut, she opened the next one down. At first she thought the drawer contained only seed packets and dried runner beans and peas ready for planting next spring, but at the back she found a book at the back full of gardening tips, all handwritten by Reg. Underneath that she found a small red box. She opened it and saw a beautiful filigree brooch in the shape of a butterfly. She took it out and held it up to the light. What a wonderful present. It would look perfect on her new dark blue blouse. She wondered when he was planning to give it to her. Christmas? Or perhaps on her birthday next year when, under the terms of Aunt Bessie's will, he thought the cottage and all Bessie's money would be hers. Dottie closed the drawer with a sigh.

The bottom drawer was much heavier. It took a supreme effort to pull it open and it was jam-packed with all sorts of stuff. On the top she found a hammer wrapped in an old piece of cloth. Dottie laid it on the top of the work surface and shone the torch into the drawer.

The hammer had been resting on some torn pieces of envelope. Whatever had stained the cloth had seeped through onto the envelope. It looked a bit like rust. The envelope contained what turned out to be another of the letters she had written to Peaches. In the excitement of making up with her again, Dottie had forgotten to ask her about those letters. Why had she torn them up without reading them?

Dottie pulled herself together. What was past was past. She wasn't here to have a personal pity party. She was here to find Brenda's address. Underneath the torn envelope she found a stack of letters from Brenda. She had written more frequently that Dottie realised. Reg must have been intercepting the post on his way to work. Could he have been tampering with all her letters as well?

The pressing need to hurry pushed it to the back of her mind. She opened the first letter. Brenda's address was in the top right-hand corner. Dottie took a piece of the torn envelope and a pencil she found on the workbench to scribble it down. She intended to put it straight back but the temptation was too great. She fanned open the letter: *I can't tell you how excited Patricia is that you are going to send for her.*

Dottie had never seen this letter before.

*I am so sorry that your wife has been so ill. I hope the new treatment will soon restore her to full health and strength.*

Dottie frowned. For heaven's sake, what lies had Reg been telling now?

There was a sound outside in the yard and a long thin shadow fell across the doorway. She jumped and her heart began to pound. Oh flip! He was back! He'd come back early, and she was here, in forbidden territory. She stuffed the letter back into the envelope and switched off the torch. As she waited in the dark, to her horror, the shadow grew longer.

Oh, God, help me, she panicked. He's coming and I'm trapped!

# Twenty-Nine

'Who's there?' The light from the kitchen made the person casting the shadow seem very tall and Dottie's throat was so tight, her words were strangled.

'Auntie Dottie . . .'

Dottie almost fainted with relief when she realised it was only Patsy.

'What are you doing back downstairs?' she demanded.

'I want to do big jobs.'

'Then why didn't you say so before!' Dottie snapped.

Patsy's eyes grew wide and her chin trembled. 'Can I go now?'

'Yes, yes,' said Dottie, her voice softer now. 'I'm sorry, love. I didn't mean to sound cross. You gave me a bit of a scare, that's all.' And while Patsy was in the toilet, she went back into the shed to push all the letters back into the drawer and replace the hammer.

Reg turned up two days later. Dottie was getting ready for bed. As he came into the room and switched on the light, her heart sank.

'Hello, Reg.'

'Hullo.' He stood at the end of the bed, swaying slightly.

Don't nag him, she told herself. Don't ask him where the hell he's been. The hard look in his eye chilled her. What was he planning to do? Her hand trembled on the bedclothes. Perhaps if she told him about the baby . . .

'Reg, I need to talk to you . . .'

He looked up at her, one leg outside his trousers. His eyes were bloodshot and she could tell he had a job focusing on her. He was drunk. Too drunk for a conversation like this. What a fool she'd been. She never should have started this now. In fact, where should she start?

'Since you've been away . . .' she began.

'Oh, here it comes . . .' he slurred.

'The thing is, Reg . . . um, that night Sylvie was here . . .'

His face darkened. 'What's that bloody woman up to now?'

'Nothing.'

He pointed his finger at her. 'You stay away from her, see? Bloody stuck-up bitch.'

'Reg, this has nothing to do with Sylvie. I'm trying to tell you something.'

He put his trousers on the footboard at the end of the bed and leaned over menacingly. 'And I'm telling you,' he said belching beerily, 'if I want to go up to London for a few days to see some of my old mates, it's got nothing to do with her.'

'I don't mind you going away, Reg. It's nice . . .'

'What d'yer mean it's nice!'

'I didn't mean it like that,' Dottie protested.

They stared at each other and Dottie's heart sank. All at once he stripped the bedclothes back and grabbed her ankles. 'Well, she ain't here now, is she?' he said as he pulled her down the bed, 'so you've got plenty of time to show me what's nice.'

The next day, Dottie slept in late. It was 7.15 when she opened her eyes and 7.45 before she tumbled out of bed. Her stomach was churning. A wave of nausea swept over her. Dottie leaned out of the bed, grabbed the potty and was sick.

'Auntie Dottie . . .' Patsy called anxiously.

'It's all right, love,' said Dottie before she threw up a second time.

She moved around gingerly. Halfway through the nightmare of last night she'd decided not to tell Reg about the baby. It would be hard keeping it from him now. She kept wishing, God forgive her, that what he was making her do would make her miscarry.

And now that she had spent time with someone like John, she couldn't bear the thought of spending the rest of her life with Reg.

As he left for work that morning, she'd pretended to sleep, sneaking a look while he dressed with a mixture of disgust, resentment and anger. She hated herself for being so scared of him. She'd been utterly terrified when Patsy's shadow fell across the shed doorway and she still shuddered at the thought of what he'd have done if he'd caught her pushing all those revolting photographs back into the drawer.

It had been agreed that today Patsy could play with Maureen and Susan.

'I want to walk to Aunt Mary's by myself,' she announced.

'I'll go with you as far as the corner,' Dottie agreed, 'and then you can go the rest of the way.'

After she'd waved Patsy goodbye, Dottie returned home to clear up her kitchen but all the time her problems were going round and round in her head. If she left Reg, who would look after Patsy? If she and Patsy set out on their own, how were they going to survive? She would get something from Aunt Bessie's inheritance in the middle of next year, but the little bit of money she had now wouldn't last that long. Perhaps she should do what Sylvie suggested and give him his marching orders, but she knew he would never go. As galling as it was, she would have to let Reg stay where he was, and as soon as she could afford a solicitor, fight in the courts to get the house back. And how long would that take? It may be the fifties, but it was still hard for a woman like her to strike out on her own.

Maybe she should go round to the sweet factory and see if

she could get a full-time job . . . but what would she do if Patsy was ill? She couldn't keep asking for time off.

In the end she decided she would have to give up the luxury of Wednesdays at home. If she charred on Wednesdays she could bring in another ten bob a week. She'd write and ask Sylvie to find her a place to stay and as soon as she could, she'd take her meagre savings and her Post Office book. She and Patsy wouldn't starve. Once the place was tidy and she'd stopped for a cup of tea, Dottie felt much better.

Upstairs, Dottie opened the wardrobe door. But when she lifted the loose board at the back, the cavity underneath was empty. The things she'd hidden from Patsy's case had gone too. Her hand flew to her mouth. Oh, no . . . dear God no! Her moneybox was gone! Frantically she searched every drawer but it wasn't there. Where was it? There was no sign that they been burgled. Reg must have taken it. She had always been safe in the knowledge that he knew nothing about her little nest egg, but who else would have taken it? Her thoughts flew to the Post Office savings book. At least he couldn't touch that. It needed her signature to draw the money out. But that was gone too. Slowly the realisation dawned. All those days off he'd had. The days he'd gone away. The overnight stays . . . he must have been using her money.

Her heart pounded and her knees went weak. She sat on the edge of the bed, hot tears springing into her eyes. How she hated him now. His vindictiveness and cruelty knew no bounds. How could he use her body one minute and be so calculating and devious the next?

Patsy had never said anything but it must be obvious even to her that he wanted nothing to do with her. He kept out of her way, ignoring her if they were together in the same room. Dottie had been careful not to make a sound last night in case it frightened her, but the child was no fool. Poor little girl. To lose her mother was bad enough, but to come here to this was even worse.

In her heart of hearts, although Dottie knew it wasn't her fault, she somehow felt responsible.

What was she going to do? She didn't need to look in her handbag to know that her purse was empty bar a few coppers. She had nothing. Not a penny. The money Mariah Fitzgerald gave her for making the curtains had gone on clothes and toys for Patsy. Oh God, what was she going to do . . .?

She began what she was sure would be a fruitless search in every handbag and every pocket. Her coat pocket and an old jacket yielded five and eleven pence ha'penny. In a bag she hadn't used since Aunt Bessie's funeral, she found a ten-shilling note. There was sixpence in her apron pocket and in another apron, one she hadn't worn for ages, she found the letter Reg had written to Sandy. She'd slipped it in there the night that Patsy had arrived. She would read it later.

It was while she was looking through every pocket that she could think of that she came across the torn pieces of Peaches' letter in another apron. Not the bit with the address on that she'd written down last night. This was the envelope Reg had said Peaches had torn up and shoved back through the letterbox. She sat on the bed again and stared at it.

A tear rolled down Dottie's cheek and she sighed. She blew her nose and stared again at the envelope. How long ago had she posted this? She studied the stamp and that's when it struck her. There was no frank. She turned it over and pieced the envelope together again. There was nothing on the back either! The letter had never even been posted. She frowned. It *must* have been. She remembered now, she'd put it behind the clock and Reg said he was going right past the post box. Perhaps the postman who was supposed to stamp it missed . . . or more likely it had never been posted at all. Her hands were trembling and she could feel the anger rising in her again. Peaches had never even received this letter. How *could* he? How could Reg do this to her? Sylvie said she had sent letters which Dottie obviously hadn't received. So it must be true. Reg had been interfering with her mail for some time.

She took out the other letter, the one Reg had written to Sandy, and turned it over in her hands. It was signed 'all my love, Reg'. Almost immediately Dottie realised it was a love letter and she felt slightly intrusive reading such a private correspondence.

*My own true love . . .*

She stopped reading and caught her breath. *My own true love,* she read again.

Dottie's eyes filled. Never once in the whole time they'd been married had Reg ever addressed her in such loving terms. Reg must have loved Sandy very much.

*I can't stop thinking about you, my darling. I have to see you again. Eric says he'll look out for you if we go overseas. We shall soon be on the move again, but I'm not allowed to say where. As soon as I can, I will write to you again. Please don't forget me, Sandy. When this war is over, we will get married. I shall never feel about anyone else the way I feel about you. Every night I lie awake remembering our last night together. Darling girl, I love you with all my heart. Take care of yourself, all my love, Reg.*

Such a pretty letter. Moved by its tenderness, Dottie wiped her eyes and blew her nose.

She needed to talk to someone, but who? What a mess. Where could she start? Dottie held her arms tightly around her middle and rocked herself gently. Oh damn you, Reg. Damn you to hell!

Fifteen minutes later, Dottie hurried into the telephone kiosk and telephoned Sylvie. As soon as Dottie pressed button B, Robin answered.

'I'm sorry, Sylvie isn't here at the moment,' he said. 'Can I take a message?'

Dottie chewed her bottom lip anxiously. 'Do you know when she'll be back?'

'I'm not sure,' said Robin. 'She's gone up to London. She's staying with an old friend.'

Dottie knew what that meant even if Robin didn't. She was meeting her lover, Bruce.

'I'll ring her tomorrow,' said Dottie.

'I'm not sure that she'll be back before the middle of next week,' said Robin. 'Her friend is leaving the country.'

'Oh.'

'Yes,' said Robin. 'It was all very sudden. Poor Sylvie was quite upset. They're very close, you see.'

Dottie hesitated, unsure what to say.

'Are you sure I can't help?' said Robin.

Dottie swallowed hard. 'Don't worry,' she said willing her voice to stay strong. 'I'll ring some other time.'

# *Thirty*

It was proving to be difficult trying to contact Sylvie. Dottie'd called three times since the weekend with no luck, and she was beginning to worry. If she had to launch out completely on her own, getting away from here was going to be more difficult than she thought. It was crucial that Sylvie find her a place to stay. Dottie didn't fancy trudging the streets of a strange town with two suitcases and Patsy in tow, looking for a room to rent. She also needed to ask Sylvie to lend her some money, now that Reg had pinched all her savings.

Dottie inserted four pennies and dialled the number. 'Hello?'

Sylvie! She was there at last. The pips went and Dottie pushed button B. 'Sylvie! Oh, it's so good to hear your voice.'

'Dottie! Robin said you had rung. Is everything all right? Has something happened?'

'I want to leave him,' Dottie said. 'Can you help Patsy and me find somewhere to live? Somewhere down your way?'

'Come and stay with us.'

'I don't think that's a good idea,' said Dottie. 'As soon as he realises I've gone, your place will be the first place he'll look.'

'All right, darling. Leave it with me.'

The pips went again. 'I've got no more money,' Dottie cried. 'I'll ring at the weekend.'

'Give me the number of the box,' cried Sylvie, 'and I'll ring you back . . .' But already Dottie was listening to the dialling tone.

*　　*　　*

261

Dottie had made up her mind that this afternoon after school would be their last with John.

The weather prevented them from going for a walk. It was drizzling. Laura took Patsy into the kitchen to prepare the tea, leaving Dottie and John alone in the sitting room. He came towards her.

'Careful,' she cautioned. 'Your mother . . .'

His gentle kiss stopped her mouth. Dottie felt a yearning far more powerful than anything she had experienced before. The voice in her head kept telling her no, no, you are a married woman, think of Patsy, think of what this might do to John's reputation . . . but her heart was begging him to kiss her again. As she closed her eyes, she felt so alive, so very, very happy.

'Oh, John,' she whispered as she lay her hands on the top of his. 'It's no use. Can't you see? We must not let this happen.'

'I've made a lemon drizzle cake this time.' Laura's voice in the passageway and the rumbling of the trolley wheels heralded the return of his mother and Patsy.

John went towards the fire and fanned his fingers.

'Are you cold, dear?' his mother asked as they crashed into the room. 'Put some more coal on the fire.'

'I'm fine,' he said gently. 'Here, let me give you a hand with that.'

'I put the icing on the sponge,' said Patsy proudly.

Dottie slipped her arm around her shoulder admiringly. 'And it looks absolutely scrummy.'

While Laura and Patsy arranged the trolley as they wanted it, Dottie glanced over the tops of their heads and smiled at John. He blew her a kiss, making her heart leap and her knees go to jelly again.

'After tea,' Laura was saying, 'you'll have to go up in the attic and get some of your old toys down for Patsy.'

'Mother,' John laughed, 'I don't think a little girl would be remotely interested in playing with tin soldiers.'

'What about the draughts board?' said Laura, piercing a crumpet with the toasting fork. 'And Ludo. We could join in with that.' She handed the fork to Patsy. 'Now hold this in front of the fire, like so, and when it's brown, we'll do the other side.'

Patsy sat cross-legged in front of the fire and before long the delicious smell of toasted crumpet filled the room.

Later on, after they'd all done the washing up, they left Laura to rest by the fire and the three of them climbed up to the attic.

'It's an age since I was up here,' said John switching on the light. 'I can imagine it's pretty disgusting.'

Considering it was a dumping ground, it was surprisingly orderly. A few cobwebs were draped between the boxes and old furniture stacked around the edges, but it was obvious it wasn't as dirty as John'd imagined it would be. Patsy spotted his old rocking horse at the back and immediately made a beeline for it. Dottie laughed aloud as she sat astride it crying, 'Gee up, gee up, you good for nothing old donkey.'

John began a thorough search. 'The boardgames should be somewhere in these boxes.'

Dottie picked over a few things. They held no memories for her, but it pleased her to think that these were all part of John's life. She tried to picture him as a small boy playing with his fort with its working drawbridge, or reading the Enid Blyton *Sunny Stories* she'd found tucked away in a box of soft toys. She wondered what he might have looked like . . . a little boy with scuffed knees and a runny nose. He must have cuddled that squashy teddy bear when he went to sleep at night . . .

'Can I have a go, Uncle John?' Patsy's voice brought her back to the here and now. She was holding up a single roller skate.

'You can have them if we can find the other one,' he laughed.

Their search became a little more earnest, but Dottie settled down on an old chaise longue with a photograph album. She opened it and there he was. She recognised him straight away. A small boy aged about ten, in big Wellington boots, and a serious expression. He was holding a fish in front of him. The caption underneath read, 'Freshwater trout caught in the Adur, 8th April 1930'. She also found a picture of a family group. She had no idea who the people with him were, apart from Laura of course, but she didn't really care. She only had eyes for John, aged about five, sitting on his mother's lap in the centre of the picture.

'Here it is!' cried Patsy. She held up another roller skate. 'Can I have a go now?'

'Not today,' he said. 'It's too dark now and it's wet.'

Dottie ran her finger over the photograph of John and a gnawing attraction engulfed her. She kissed the end of her fingers and placed them over his face.

'And here's the Ludo,' John cried. 'And a couple of jigsaw puzzles you might like to do.'

As Patsy clambered back downstairs with her trophies, John wandered over to Dottie. 'I wondered what you were looking at. Heavens above, I haven't looked at those in years.' He began pointing out some of the people. 'That's my grandmother. She died at the beginning of the war. Killed while doing canteen duty for the WRVS. And that's my friend Derek. He and I used to bike all over the country in the summer hols,' he chuckled. 'I got so saddle-sore, I couldn't sit down for a week.'

She smiled. Looking up at him, she noticed he had a cobweb complete with its tiny owner on the top of his head and reached up and lifted it away. His head was so close to hers she could feel his breath on her cheek. He smelled of crumpets and tea.

'Oh, Dottie,' he said hoarsely.

She turned her head away and stood up. 'No, John, please don't.'

He caught her arm. 'Why do you never talk about Reg?'

'It's complicated.'

She should tell him now. She should say, 'I found this letter . . . I've found out something about Reg, but I'm frightened the authorities will take Patsy away from me . . . And I'm having

Reg's baby.' She tried to tell him but her mouth wouldn't work. Instead, she looked at him with a stricken expression and felt her knees giving way.

'Dottie? What is it? What's wrong?'

Her throat tightened. She took a deep breath. 'It's no use. I must go.'

'All I'm asking is a few moments with you.'

'Don't be ridiculous, John,' she said, doing her best to be firm. 'I'm married. Think of the scandal . . . your career . . .'

'I don't give a stuff about all that,' he said fiercely.

They heard a footfall on the stairs and Patsy called, 'Are you coming?'

'We'll be right there, Patsy,' she called. She held his gaze for a second and then pulled herself away. Replacing the album in the box, she stood up and saw Patsy's head appearing over the edge of the floor.

'What are you doing?' she asked. 'We've set up the Ludo and we're waiting to play.'

'Sorry, love,' Dottie smiled. 'I got carried away looking at some old photographs. We're coming now.'

Patsy turned around and raced back down, her shoes clattering noisily on the bare wooden stairs. John caught Dottie's hand and swung her back into his arms. Gently but firmly, he kissed her. Her lips parted and his tongue filled the space between, sending her pulse racing and flooding her whole body with sensual desire. He lowered her onto the chaise longue and caressed her tenderly, kissing her eyelids, her mouth, her neck, her bare shoulder and finally opening a button at the top of her blouse to kiss the top of her breast.

'Dottie, oh Dottie . . .'

And Dottie melted in his arms.

She must stop him . . . this mustn't go any further . . . she had to stop him . . . But how could she? This was her moment. Up here among the flotsam and jetsam of John's former life, she and he were together at last. She would remember this precious moment to the day she died. She was aware of the old boxes, a dressmaker's dummy, a tennis racquet hanging from a nail driven into the rafters. Aunt Bessie once told her that when she loved someone, it would be truly wonderful, she would give herself willingly and with passion. Every part of her body was aching for him now. His strong arms pulled her close as his mouth covered hers again. Releasing her, he exposed her breast completely. Her nipple was hard as his mouth went over it and Dottie moaned with pleasure.

The thundering footsteps were back and they sprang apart. By the time Patsy reached the middle of the attic steps, John was leaning over the top. Behind him, Dottie struggled to tidy herself up.

'We're coming,' he said to the upturned anxious little face coming up to the attic. 'Put the kettle on and we'll have a cuppa while we play Ludo.'

'Granny Laura says she doesn't feel well,' said Patsy.

With an apologetic backward glance at Dottie, John rushed back downstairs.

'Drop us at the crossroads,' she said.

'Dottie, it's pitch black and it's pouring with rain.'

'Someone might see us,' Dottie whispered.

He reached across and squeezed her hand. 'Don't worry.'

She looked into the back of the car. 'Patsy's asleep.'

'Then I'll take you to your door.' He negotiated a bend in the road. 'When can I see you again?'

'I'll write.'

'Don't make this goodbye,' he pleaded. 'Please . . .'

A face appeared between them. 'Are we nearly there yet?'

Dottie jumped. 'I thought you were asleep.'

'I was pretending.'

Dottie and John exchanged an anxious look.

'Will Granny Laura be all right?'

'Yes,' said John. 'All that excitement made her very tired, that's all.'

'She's a very old lady, isn't she?'

'You'd better not let her hear you say that,' John chuckled. 'Did you enjoy yourself?'

'Ooh, yes.' Patsy held up the skates. 'When you take me there next time, I'll show you how I can roller skate.'

They'd arrived at the cottage. Dottie climbed out and opened the door for Patsy.

'Thank you, Dr Landers,' Dottie said in a business-like fashion. As she went to close the passenger door, Patsy was already halfway down the path. She turned, and John was beside her.

'Goodbye, Dottie.' He leaned forward as if to kiss her cheek but Dottie fled.

He stood beside the car dejectedly, the rain soaking his jacket, but as she opened the front door and switched on the light, Dottie didn't look back.

Dr Landers got back into the car, slipped it into gear and moved off.

Neither of them noticed the curtains of the house opposite moving. 'I reckon that Dottie Cox has got herself a fancy man,' Vera Carter told her husband as she pulled them closed.

# Thirty-One

The whistle went, bringing to an end the last playtime of the afternoon. Maureen, Susan and Patsy lined up with the others by the door.

'I know a secret,' said Maureen in Patsy's ear. Patsy turned around and gave her a puzzled look.

'The grown-ups all think we're daft,' Maureen went on, 'but we know what they're on about.'

'Ooh, Mo,' cried Susan giving her sister a poke in the back. 'You said you wouldn't tell.'

'It's all right to tell Patsy, you daft,' Maureen retorted. 'Patsy ain't going to tell, are you, Pats?'

'Tell what?' asked Patsy.

'They're doing a surprise party for you.'

'A party!' cried Patsy.

'Maureen Prior, turn around and stand still,' snapped Mrs Stone.

'Shh,' said Maureen said, nervously putting her finger to her lips. 'You mustn't let on I told you.'

Patsy's eyes grew wide. 'Why are we having a party?'

'Because you are our best friend o' course.'

Patsy gave Maureen a rib-crushing hug. 'Ooooh, thank you.'

'Don't let on, will you?' Maureen warned.

'I won't,' said Patsy, a surprise of her own forming in her mind.

268

'Patricia Cox and Maureen Prior,' Mrs Stone's voice was sharp. 'Will you both stand still!'

Dottie stared at the blank piece of paper. Where should she start?

*Dear John.*

Well, that was as good a beginning as any.

*Patsy seems to be happy but I can't go on pretending everything is fine. I'm sorry to let everybody down . . .*

She crossed that out and screwed up the piece of paper. Better to begin by asking about his mother.

She didn't want to write this letter but she had to. Even though she had agreed to one more meeting, she really couldn't go again. It had to end.

*I hope your mother is well. She was so kind to us and we did enjoy our day with you both. Patsy is still a real credit to her mother. She's no trouble and she seems to have settled down very happily.*

Dottie re-read what she'd written. She couldn't send that either. She'd made it sound like everything was perfect. If only it was. She drew out her handkerchief and blew her nose. Writing this letter was breaking her heart, but it had to be done.

She tried again.

*Reg doesn't know that we are still meeting. John, I don't know how to tell you this but I'm having a baby . . .*

269

Oh, this was hopeless. Dottie screwed up that one as well. She knew only too well that when she told John about Reg, he would be duty-bound to inform the authorities and they would take Patsy away. Poor little girl . . . she would have to face yet another radical change in her life. She had to be protected at all costs, but telling the authorities felt like a terrible betrayal. She hadn't wanted the child in the first place, but now that she was here, Dottie loved her more than words could say.

Then there was the dilemma of her own baby. How could she trust Reg when the baby came? She shuddered at the thought of him living under the same roof. What a fool she'd been to marry him. Aunt Bessie had tried to tell her but she wouldn't listen. If she'd been single she might have been able to marry John – but on the other hand, if it hadn't been for Patsy, she never would have met him.

Her head was reeling from all these 'what if's but she had to face the facts and get on with it. She would have to run away with Patsy. It galled her to leave Reg in the house, but what did it really matter, as long as she and Patsy were free?

I have made the right decision, she told herself firmly. She would move to the New Forest area, somewhere like Ringwood or Fordingbridge, and make a new start. Reg would take the cottage, but her inheritance was safe. At an appropriate time, she would come back and claim it. For the time being, no one need ever know she and Patsy weren't related. They'd all presume they were mother and daughter. She could pretend Patsy's father had been one of those coloured GIs.

Dottie picked up the pen again. Would it be better to see John face to face? Would she be brave enough to say the words when he was looking at her?

*I have something important I have to tell you. I should have talked to you yesterday but I chickened out. Is it*

*possible for you to meet me for a frank and urgent
discussion . . .*

Did that sound stupid? No, she wanted it to sound formal. It
had to.

Where should she suggest that they meet? Not here. Not with
Reg around. What about the Warnes Hotel, the place where Sylvie
had taken her for that meal? She suggested that she would meet
him there on Sunday.

She signed herself formally, 'yours faithfully, Dorothy Cox
(Mrs)' and sealed up the envelope. The post box was just
down the road, a three-minute walk away, and she had to get
it in the box before the last collection. She could be there
and back in no time. She couldn't leave Patsy alone in the
house, so she called out, 'Would you like to come to the post
with me?'

Patsy appeared in the doorway. 'Can we go and see the horses
too?' They'd noticed two mares in Michael's field a couple of
days ago.

'Good idea,' said Dottie, helping her on with her coat.

Patsy grabbed a couple of tired-looking apples from the fruit
bowl. Dottie glanced at the clock. They'd have to hurry if they
were going to catch the last post. Pulling on her old coat, Dottie
hurried out of the door.

On their way, they passed Ann Pearce coming home from
work with her two children. Positive she could hear the post van
coming, Dottie was anxious not to stop.

Ann pointed towards the flowerbed near the fence. 'Dottie, I
don't mean to be rude,' she said, 'but I've never seen that old
well in your front garden looking as bad as that before. It looks
to me like it's going to cave in any minute.'

Dottie was startled. Ann was right. Dottie hadn't really noticed
before but the ground around the old well had definitely
subsided.

'I should tell Patsy to keep away from it,' Ann added. 'You don't want her falling in.'

Dottie nodded. 'I'll tell Reg right away,' she said dully.

Ann felt uneasy as she watched her go. It wasn't like Dottie to be so casual. Come to think of it, she wasn't looking her normal self these days. Her hair looked lank and untidy and there were times when she seemed miles away. Ann shooed her children indoors. As soon as she got her wages at the end of the week, she'd buy Dottie a nice bunch of flowers and invite her and Patsy in for a cup of tea. It was the least she could do for someone who had been such a wonderful pal to her.

When she and Patsy walked back indoors about half an hour later, Reg was making some tea in the scullery. Dottie's heart almost stopped.

'I heard the gate,' he smiled. 'Come on in and sit yourself down, pet.'

*Pet?* Dottie was totally bewildered. What was he up to now? And where had he been? She hesitated. 'I have to shut up the henhouse.'

'All done,' he beamed. 'I've got us all fish and chips for tea. I thought it would save you cooking. You like fish and chips, don't you, Patsy? Take your coat off, there's a good girl, and sit up at the table.'

After all these weeks, these were the first real words of kindness he'd ever spoken to her and although they were gentle enough, Patsy looked nervously at Dottie. Dottie gave her a reassuring smile and placed her hand in the middle of her back to guide her to the kitchen table.

Out in the scullery, she got the plates out and he came to help her dish out the chips. They smelled wonderful and she suddenly realised how hungry she was.

'I've been thinking, pet,' he said as he shovelled the plates high, 'I've been a bit unreasonable just lately, haven't I?'

272

'What?'

'Well, from now on, things are going to change.'

'Oh, Reg . . .'

He put his hand up to silence her. 'No, no, fair's fair,' he went on. 'I've given you both a hard time. But I've seen the error of my ways. From now on, I shall be a good husband to you and a good father to Patsy.'

They walked into the kitchen with the three plates piled high. 'There you are, Patsy, love,' he said. 'Daddy's treat.'

'Thank you,' said Patsy warily.

'That's my first treat and in a minute I'll tell you about another one.'

Dottie slid into her chair and picked up her knife and fork. 'This looks so wonderful,' she smiled. 'There's no need for anything else.'

'Nonsense,' he laughed. 'Oh, it's no good, I've got to tell you now. Patsy's here and we're going to celebrate. Remember that place we went to on our honeymoon? Well we're going back again. It's all booked up. All three of us are going for a little holiday.'

Patsy's eyes danced. 'A holiday?'

'That's right, my love,' he beamed.

'Oh, I don't think . . .' Dottie began.

'Will we be back in time for the party?' cried Patsy.

'What party?'

Patsy went red. 'Nothing . . .'

Reg tapped the side of Patsy's plate with his knife. 'Eat up, now. Don't let it get cold.'

Dottie's head was in a whirl. He was getting Patsy all excited, and he hadn't even told her why they were going. What was this all about? She was supposed to ring Sylvie tomorrow. 'When are we going on this holiday?' she said curtly.

'Right away, pet. First thing tomorrow morning.'

\* \* \*

273

Dottie lay on her back staring at the ceiling. Reg's snores filled their bedroom but that wasn't what was keeping her awake. A holiday. She didn't want to go away with Reg but she couldn't bear to disappoint Patsy. It wasn't as if it was the height of summer either. Who goes away in November? It was terribly short notice too. She'd have to get hold of Ann Pearce in the morning and see if she could do Mrs Fitzgerald's and Janet Cooper's while she was away. She felt confident Ann would agree. After all, it was all money in her pocket and Christmas wasn't too far away. Now that Reg had promised to be a model husband and father, perhaps Dottie didn't need to feel so desperate about getting away from him. She would still leave him, but she could take her time, do it properly.

She pulled the bedclothes up to her neck and turned over. The eiderdown kept slipping over towards his side. She stuck her arm out into the cold night air and yanked it back. What she needed was a heavy weight on her side of the bed to keep it over her own shoulders.

Dottie's eyes flew open and suddenly she was wide awake. The hammer. Why had he hidden that hammer in the drawer in his shed? She didn't trust him as far as she could throw him. Dottie held her breath. More to the point, where was the hammer now?

# Thirty-Two

The clock on the mantelpiece said 2.20am and Dottie was downstairs in the kitchen. She was listening out to make sure Reg was still asleep.

She had crept out of bed and down the stairs with her heart in her mouth. Call it a presentiment, or a hunch, she didn't really understand why, but she had to make sure the hammer was still in the shed. Upstairs, a loud snore convinced her it was safe to go outside. She took her coat down from the nail on the back door. Outside, she opened the shed door gingerly, remembering that it sometimes creaked, and slipped inside. Opening the drawer, she shone the torch inside.

The hammer was still there, wrapped up in the piece of sacking. Where should she put it? She couldn't leave it where it was. She didn't trust Reg. For her own peace of mind, she had to think of some place where no one would think of looking. The chickens. She'd put it in the henhouse. She'd have to ask Ann to look after the hens while they were away. Back indoors, she scribbled a note then, pulling her coat tightly around her, Dottie hurried down to the bottom of the garden.

The pig was gone. Gerald must have taken it but she was surprised to see the door of the henhouse was wide open. Reg had said he'd done the chickens, so why was the door open? Good job she'd come down or the fox might have had them before morning. She walked inside softly so that they wouldn't

275

panic. There wasn't a sound. She switched on the torch. Every perch was empty. Where were they? Had they all escaped outside somewhere? She felt sick. They were good egg-layers, and they would have eventually made good broilers. The torchlight picked out an old sack in the corner: something drew her to it. Cautiously Dottie went over and looked inside. She gasped in horror and almost dropped the torch.

All her lovely hens were in the sack. Every single one of them. Had the fox got in during the day and Reg didn't want to tell her in case it spoiled the holiday? Foxes kill for the sake of killing, she knew that. It happened once when Aunt Bessie was still alive. The fox had got inside the henhouse and killed every single chicken. Dottie frowned. Back then there had been feathers everywhere and the fox had chewed the heads off as well. She bent to look more closely. None of the chickens in the sack had a mark on them but their necks were broken. Dottie trembled. Reg must have done it. But why? Why would he do such a thing? She couldn't understand it. He enjoyed a boiled egg as much as she did.

Reg stepped back behind the curtain. What was she doing down the bottom of the garden, stupid cow? He hadn't meant her to find the chickens, damn it. What was she up to? She'd been in the henhouse for some time. Was that bloody John Landers down there too? Surely they weren't having it off in his chicken house?

Vera had collared him as he walked up the path.

'I'm not the one to cast aspersions,' she'd said, 'but I thought you ought to know . . .'

Even while she was telling him, Reg felt the contempt rising in his mouth. Dot always thought she was a cut above the rest, what with all those ridiculous cushion covers and fancy curtains, but he'd never had her down as an unfaithful wife. Not until he'd ferreted in the dustbin and spotted some crumpled paper left in the bottom of the bin. He wouldn't have bothered with it except that it was her Basildon Bond paper, the stuff she used for important letters. He'd picked up the bits and fanned them out. Now he couldn't get the words out of his head.

*Reg doesn't know that we are still meeting. John, I don't know how to tell you this but I'm having a baby . . .*

Bitch. Slut. Apart from Joyce, they were all the bloody same. She'd been seeing that Dr Landers, he'd known that, but he hadn't suspected anything was going on. Now he was boiling with rage. He'd gone down the garden to cool off but he'd lost it altogether in the henhouse. He hadn't meant to kill them until it occurred to him that she thought more of her bloody hens than she did of him. So he'd grabbed one and then another.

His lip curled. Perhaps she was meeting the doc now. He could easily hide in the lane. Reg had done it himself often enough.

He waited until Dottie emerged from the henhouse and watched as she hurried back up the garden. His eyes narrowed. On the way down, she'd walked differently. All hunched up, her arms tightly round her. Coming back, her coat flapped open and her arms were by her side. The bitch was definitely up to something.

He leaned back into the shadows as she went into the outside lav. As he climbed back into bed, he heard her pull the chain.

'I'll just pop next door and ask Ann to look after the chickens,' smiled Dottie the next morning.

Reg was sitting in the scullery, polishing his boots until they shone. 'No need,' he said cheerily. 'I've already seen her. She'll do it for you.'

Dottie chewed her bottom lip. Should she confront him? Tell him she'd already seen the bag full of dead chickens? Better not. He'd go mad and Patsy was on her way downstairs.

277

'I've also cleared it with the doctor's wife and with the old biddy in the shop too.'

Dottie was puzzled. It wasn't like him to be so organised.

The house was practically all shut up. Reg had raked out the fire while Dottie was making the beds. He'd even packed their suitcase. Although she really didn't want to go, Dottie had to do her best to make him feel everything was completely normal.

She needn't worry about meeting John. He wouldn't get her letter until Monday now. She was sure she'd missed the post. As soon as they got back from the holiday, she would arrange to go to Sylvie's. She wasn't ready but she didn't want to be with him a minute longer than necessary.

Patsy was beside herself with excitement. 'Will we swim in the sea? Will we make sand pies like you did when you were a girl? Will we eat ice cream?'

Dottie regretted telling her all that now. 'It's too cold for all that,' she explained. 'But we'll still have a lovely time, you'll see.'

'But what will we do?' Patsy wanted to know.

'We'll eat lots of lovely food and we'll go for long walks.' Dottie struggled to make it sound exciting. 'Maybe we'll hire some bicycles and go for a bike ride.'

'But I've got nobody to play with,' Patsy grumbled. 'I wish Maureen and Susan could come.'

'Perhaps next time,' said Dottie.

'Can I take my roller skates?'

'That's a lovely idea.'

Reg stopped polishing his shoes. 'Where did she get those?' he demanded.

Patsy looked up at Dottie nervously.

'Mary gave them to her,' Dottie lied coolly. 'They used to be Billy's and the girls didn't want them.'

Reg went back to polishing his boots.

'Did you tell Ann where I keep the chicken feed, Reg?'

The look he gave her made her blood run cold. 'Stop fretting about the bloody chickens. I told you, I've seen to them.'

So he *was* responsible. He had killed all her chickens. But why? She felt more than a little anxious. She had to go along with it, but what was this all about?

He waved the brush at her and smiled. 'Come on, pet.' His voice was as sweet as honey. 'Get your coat on. We don't want to miss the train, do we?'

They were halfway to the station when Reg suddenly remembered he'd left his wallet behind the clock in the kitchen.

'You two go and get us some sweets from the station shop,' he said, digging deep into his pocket and fishing out half a crown. 'I'll meet you on the platform.'

Patsy's eyes lit up.

'What a pity you didn't notice before,' Dottie remarked. 'If we'd been in the village, I could've popped in and told Janet Cooper where we're going.'

Reg wasn't listening. 'I won't be a minute.'

Dottie watched him running back down the road. She had no idea he could run so fast. Something wasn't quite right. But what was it? She couldn't put her finger on it.

'Come on, Auntie Dottie,' said Patsy tugging her hand. 'Let's get our sweeties.'

Although the Sea View was in the rundown part of the town, Dottie was relieved to arrive there in one piece. The train journey had been uneventful but Patsy's excitement made it into an occasion. Reg had read his newspaper most of the way and then he had extended his legs and dozed off.

As soon as they arrived, the landlady had taken them up to their rooms. The furniture was very basic but the bedrooms, one single and one double next door to each other, seemed comfortable enough. Only the décor offended Dottie's eye. Nothing matched: the bedspread in the double room was patterned with

279

brown and orange squares, the curtains had red roses on them and the single room had pink curtains with brown and blue on the counterpane.

'Very nice,' said Reg.

'Breakfast is at 8 o'clock sharp and I require all my guests to be out of the room by 10.30,' said Mrs Flint as she handed Reg the keys to the rooms. 'Doors open at 5pm and the evening meal is at 6.30 sharp.'

'Thank you,' said Reg. Behind his back, Dottie and Patsy grinned at each other. They turned to go.

'I haven't finished yet.' Mrs Flint folded her arms over her chest. 'Your bathroom is on the next floor up and baths are available on Sunday, Wednesday and Friday at an extra charge of two shillings.' She glanced down at Patsy. 'No running in the corridor and no food and drink in the bedrooms. Is that clear?'

'Perfectly clear,' sad Reg.

'Then I shall expect you all in the dining room at 6.30 sharp.' She turned to go. 'By the way, there is a sing-song after the meal in the parlour. You are welcome to join in. If you go out, we expect all our residents in their rooms by 10.30 unless by prior arrangement. And,' she added as an afterthought, 'I do not tolerate drunkenness or entertaining in the bedrooms.'

As she disappeared down the stairs, Reg gave her a Hitler salute and Dottie giggled.

'You and Patsy take the double,' said Reg. 'She might be a bit nervous on her own.'

Dottie was taken completely by surprise. Patsy was delighted.

The meal was plain but well cooked and enjoyable. Dottie and Patsy joined the residents with the sing-song after dinner while Reg read a book. The other guests were a motley lot. They included a retired vicar and his wife and two elderly women, both widows, who had spent most of their latter years staying in guesthouses and small hotels around the country. The other guests were three members of a dancing troupe appearing in the local theatre and a rather brassy-looking woman with blonde hair and bright red fingernails. She kept herself to herself.

'We're off to Norfolk for Christmas this year,' one of the elderly women announced at dinner. She ran her fingers up and down her string of pearls. 'Who knows, we might even pop down to Sandringham to see the King.'

'I doubt he will be there,' observed the vicar. 'In my humble opinion, His Majesty is much too ill to travel.'

After dinner, Dottie took Patsy off to bed.

'Night-night, dear,' smiled the vicar's wife. 'Such a beautifully behaved child,' she observed to her husband as they left.

# Thirty-Three

John Landers couldn't sleep. He stood at the window of the Warnes Hotel staring out to sea. Her letter, posted last night, had arrived at his mother's cottage by first post on Saturday and had been specific enough. He'd dropped everything, booked himself into the hotel that afternoon and waited for her to come. By the time they were taking last orders in the dining room, he'd realised she wasn't coming. The meal was fantastic, but he couldn't do it justice.

In her letter she had sounded frantic with worry. It was obvious she had always wanted the best for Patsy but John had a gut feeling that Reg Cox wasn't the type to make even a halfway decent father. He'd been cold and stand-offish when he'd seen Patsy. She didn't look anything like him either.

He was no fool. Sandy was very English in appearance. Although dark-haired, with a sort of gypsy appearance, Reg was too – yet Patsy was mixed race. It was possible there had been an atavism connected to Patsy's birth, but the reversion to a former ancestral characteristic after several generations, or throwback as it was more commonly known, was highly unusual.

Sandy had had a reputation for being a bit wild in her youth. Brenda once told him that coming to Australia had been a last-ditch opportunity to make something of her life. Brenda would never betray a confidence but John had the impression from the word go that Sandy had been an unmarried mother. The father of her baby must have been a person of colour. Definitely not Reg Cox. Yet the thing that puzzled him the most was the fact that Sandy had named him so clearly. In view of her youth and the fact that she was determined to keep her child, Sandy had been given a second chance. As soon as the war ended, she'd been sent to Australia for a new start.

He dropped the curtain and climbed back into bed. As puzzling as it was, there was something else on his mind. He'd have to find out why Dottie hadn't come. She wasn't the type to let people down.

His mother was looking a lot better now. He'd found her a Girl-Friday and she was being well looked after. It was time to look around for a practice. Worthing seemed like a nice enough area and he would be near Dottie. If he could only get her to trust him. She was in his thoughts day and night and he knew now that she was someone very special. Pulling the bedclothes over his shoulders, he resolved to motor over to the village to see Dottie in the morning.

At about 10pm, Reg knocked on the door as Dottie was getting undressed. 'Can I come in?'

'Just a minute, I'm not decent.' She dragged on her dressing gown. 'It's all right now.'

The door remained firmly closed. Dottie pulled it open but the corridor was empty. She stood by his door and knocked, but he didn't answer.

'Reg? Are you there?'

Never mind. He could tell her whatever it was that was troubling him tomorrow.

On the other side of the closed door, Reg's eyes glinted with excitement. As soon as Dottie knocked he pushed the woman with him against the door and covered her mouth with his to keep her quiet. With one hand he searched for her Venus mound. She began to resist him and the old excitement began coursing through his veins. He was in for a good night. She wouldn't go all limp and submissive on him. She'd give him what he craved. He pushed his tongue deep into her mouth and winced as she dug her long red nails into the flesh around his naked waist. As Dottie's footsteps died away and her door closed, he broke away and she laughed softly at his erection.

'If only she knew.'

He ran his fingers through her blonde hair. 'I wish she did,' he said huskily. 'It would make it a lot more fun.'

'Are we really going to do it then?'

Reg drew his finger across his throat and smiled sardonically.

The woman's eyes widened. 'A knife? I don't like knives.'

Reg took a small bottle out of his pocket. 'Had it stashed away for ages,' he said. 'Phenobarbitone.'

The woman laughed softly. 'Ooh, you naughty, naughty boy, Reg. Mummy's going to be very, very cross with you.'

Ann Pearce watched the well-dressed man with the big umbrella walking round the back of Dottie's place. It was a bit early to come calling and this was the second day running he'd been there.

She was upstairs at the bathroom window which overlooked Dottie's path. She loved this room. It looked so much brighter than it had done even three months before. She'd replaced the dark green walls and brown panelling with a lovely canary yellow, and she'd done it all herself.

The man was knocking at the front door again. It was only ten past eight. What on earth did he want at this hour? She pulled the curtain completely shut and began to undress. She shivered in the early morning air but she was happy. Life was a lot better since she'd taken that job Dottie had got for her. When at first she'd been put on a fortnight's trial, she'd resented it, but now that she was working full time she didn't think it was such a bad thing after all. Miss Edwards had wanted her to do the windows and even clear out the guttering. At the end of her trial period, when she'd been offered the job at The Merton, she'd said she would only stay on one condition.

'Condition?' Miss Edwards demanded.

'I'll work for you provided I don't have to put my life at risk,' she'd said tartly. 'I am not willing to go up any ladders, not unless you make a solemn undertaking to be the sole support of my children should anything happen to me.'

Miss Edwards had first glared at her but then she burst out laughing.

'Fair enough, Ann,' she'd smiled. 'And I must say, I admire your spunk.'

Dottie had been a real pal. She and the kids had really enjoyed that day they'd all walked down to the seafront to see the new streetlights. It had been one of quite a few good days this year. She and Dottie could've spent more time together gossiping over a cup of tea if it weren't for that Reg.

Her strip-down wash finished, Ann peeped through the curtains again. Despite the rain, the man was still there. He didn't look like a debt collector or a policeman. Lord knows she'd seen enough of those to recognise one when she saw one. He'd arrived at the cottage in a car so he must be well off but why was he so persistent? Could it be that he was one of Dottie's customers? Ah yes, that was it. Dottie was making some curtains for his wife or his mother and he'd been sent to collect them. Funny. If that were the case, why didn't Dottie open the door?

Come to think of it, Ann hadn't seen Dottie since Friday. On Saturday, Ann had taken the kids up to Highdown on the bus. They'd had a wonderful time, with the kids playing in the chalk pits. It was quite cold, but it was dry. Today, Monday, it was raining hard.

Mary and Edna were coming over later to talk about the food for Patsy's surprise party. They'd begun their planning with small back-of-the-hand whispers on Bonfire Night. They had to be so careful that Dottie didn't see them. Mary was bringing the twins, but that was all right – they could play with Brian and Phyllis. The important thing was, Dottie would be at Janet Cooper's.

Now washed and dressed, Ann pulled back the curtain and the man tilted his umbrella and looked up as if he sensed she was watching him. She darted back but she knew he'd spotted her. Blast! What if he came to her door? She straightened the curtain and tidied away her soap and flannel, all the time listening for the sound of crunching footsteps on the gravel. But thankfully a few seconds passed into several minutes and the door knocker stayed silent. Cautiously she peeped again, but he'd gone.

The rain was heavier than ever and she could see Vincent Dobbs, the postman, coming along the road on his GPO bicycle. Then, out of the corner of her eye, Ann became aware of a movement by Dottie's back door. She clutched at her chest. The man was still there, sheltering under the porch.

Vincent was about eight doors up. If he had post for them, he'd be turning into Dottie's gate any minute now. There was a low rumble and as Ann took another look down into Dottie's garden her eyes grew wide.

'Oh my stars . . .' she breathed.

# Thirty-Four

By the time Ann had raced downstairs and grabbed her coat and wellies from the hall, Vincent Dobbs had reached Dottie's front garden.

'Bloody hell,' he gasped, as his hand touched the gate.

The smartly dressed man stood in the middle of the path staring down at the flowerbed. 'That's the last thing I expected to happen,' he said shaking his head.

The wet ground around the well had dropped down by several feet and part of the old well wall was exposed. On the other side, an area the size of a dining room table had disappeared altogether, taking half the flowerbed too.

Ann stared in disbelief. She always knew the old well was falling apart, but she wasn't expecting anything as dramatic as this.

'When did that happen?' Vera Carter from across the road had joined them. 'Just now,' Ann said.

'They haven't used that old well for years,' said Vera, stating the obvious. 'When Bessie had the housing taken down, I thought she'd had it filled in.'

'Does she know it's gone?' asked Vince jerking his head towards Dottie's front door. A rivulet of rain circled his postman's hat and dropped down his neck.

Ann pulled her coat tightly around herself. 'I shouldn't think so, or she'd have called somebody out by now. Want me to knock on the door?'

'She's not there,' said the smart man under the umbrella. Ann regarded him for the first time. Close up, he was very good looking, clean cut and well dressed. 'In fact,' he went on, 'I'm rather worried about her . . . er, the whole family.'

Vince frowned. 'Course they're there. Reg might already be at work but Dottie and the little girl, they'll be getting up about now.'

'They're not there,' the man insisted. Ann was aware of twitching curtains as the rest of the street gathered by their windows to see what had happened. 'I've been coming here on and off since the weekend and every time the place has been empty. When was the last time somebody saw them?'

Everybody's attention was distracted by Vincent walking along the edge of the path towards the house.

'Careful,' said Ann rather unnecessarily.

Going gingerly all the way to the door, he rattled the letterbox loudly.

Ann hurried up behind Vincent. She joined in, tapping on the windowpane. 'Dottie, are you there?'

Ann went round to try the back door. It was locked. She frowned. Dottie's back door was never locked . . . and why were the curtains still drawn? She and Vince exchanged a worried look. 'Someone better get Kipper,' he said.

The rain had eased off by the time PC Kipling, affectionately known by everyone in village as Kipper, pushed his way through the waiting crowd at Myrtle Cottage.

'There's nobody in,' Mary said. 'Ann and Vince and this gentleman here have been banging on the door for ages.'

Mary Prior had arrived a few minutes after Vince. After pushing the twins all the way from home in the big pushchair, she was wet through and out of breath and dying for a cup of tea. The shock of seeing the gathering in Dottie's garden put paid to that.

Kipper leaned his bicycle against the fence and as he looked around at the sea of faces, everybody started talking at once.

'I heard the sound of breaking glass.'

'That's 'cos Vincent Dobbs broke a window.'

'The council should come out and look at that garden. It's a real danger.'

'Well, I knew something was wrong as soon as I saw the state of the place.'

'Patsy didn't go to school today. I thought she must be ill and Dottie was looking after her.'

'If somebody doesn't do something about this soon, the whole road could collapse and take our homes with it.'

'Dottie would never go off and not tell anyone.'

Kipper put his hand in the air. 'One at a time . . . please!'

'I broke the window at the back,' Vince admitted. 'Mrs Pearce here, she climbed in.'

'I couldn't bring myself to go upstairs,' Ann began, 'in case . . . well you know, so I opened the door and Vince and Bob Carter from over the road, they went up.'

Kipper swallowed hard. 'And?'

'The place is empty,' said Vince. 'They're all gone.'

'So?' Kipper demanded. 'The place is empty, what's wrong with that?' If his sergeant got wind of this lot breaking and entering, they'd all end up in court. 'Dottie works at the Coopers' today, doesn't she?'

'I dropped in for Tom's paper on the way here,' said Mary Prior, 'and Dottie's not there. I tell you, Janet Cooper is hopping mad.'

A murmur ran around the crowd.

'Constable, it seems to me that judging by everyone's reactions, Mr and Mrs Cox going off like this is very uncharacteristic,' said the smart man.

'And who might you be?' said Kipper raising an eyebrow.

'Dr John Landers.'

'Dr Fitzgerald is her doctor,' said Ann.

'Mr and Mrs Cox and I have a connection through Patricia,' John Landers continued. 'In fact, Mrs Cox wrote and asked me to come. We had an appointment for Saturday afternoon. I've been in Worthing the whole weekend but she has made no contact, which is most odd.'

Everyone looked at Vince.

'Don't look at me,' he protested. 'I deliver every letter I get. Reg quite often takes them off me on the way to work, but if someone wrote Dottie a letter, I delivered it.'

'Dottie wouldn't go anywhere without telling someone,' Ann insisted. 'And she certainly wouldn't leave her house looking like a tip.'

'A tip?' Kipper queried.

'Everything's all over the place,' said Ann. 'Like somebody's been looking for something.' She blew into her handkerchief and Vince laid a comforting hand on her shoulder.

John Landers shook his head.

Kipper frowned thoughtfully. There was no evidence of a crime except the broken window, and yet he had a gut feeling something was amiss. Dottie wasn't the sort to do a moonlight flit. And why should she? As far as he knew, she owned the cottage herself.

'Of course, you've seen the hole,' said Vince, pointing towards the sunken garden.

Silently, the crowd parted, giving Kipper a good view of the collapsed well. A clear footprint and a skidmark went right to the edge of a deep dip.

'When did that happen?'

'We don't know, but it wasn't there yesterday,' said Ann.

Kipper strained his eyes. Sticking up from the middle of the rubble he saw what looked like some brown material. He moved a little closer, frowning. Someone laid a restraining hand on his arm.

'It's her coat,' Ann sniffed. 'The one she keeps on the nail behind the back door. We didn't really notice it before it got light.'

''Ere, Mr Kipling,' said Mary, pointing to a dark stain on the material. 'Doesn't that look like blood?'

'Are you saying she could actually be down there?' Dr Landers pushed his way through the crowd.

'I wouldn't go any closer if I were you, sir,' Kipper cautioned.

John took no notice; but as he stepped onto the edge of the dip, there was a creaking sound and some more earth fell away.

'Careful!' Kipper cried. He grabbed John's arm and John stepped back gingerly. There was a loud bang and the whole area was jolted down about six inches.

Kipper's heart missed a beat. He took a deep breath and willed himself to stay steady on his feet. Mary was right. He could see it more clearly now. There was a dark stain on the material and it certainly did look like blood.

'We all reckon she's down there, Mr Kipling,' said Vince. 'Dottie's in that well.'

'And what about Patricia?' John gasped. 'Where is she?'

'Perhaps Reg is down there and all,' Vera Carter said.

There was a horrified silence and everyone stared into the hole.

John was spurred into action. 'What we need are some planks,' he said. 'Anyone know a builder around here?'

'There's Mr Tree's,' said Ann. 'Down by the station.'

'Will you take me there?' John asked.

'I can't leave my children,' Ann said.

'I'll take you,' said Vera Carter.

John opened the front passenger door of his car and Vera slid inside. John did a three-point turn and they drove off at speed in the direction of the station.

As soon as Kipper had ascertained for himself that indeed no one was at home, he left a couple of men to guard the crime scene with strict orders not to let anyone pass until his return.

Then he went back to his police house to telephone Worthing Central for re-enforcements. That done, he bicycled like a bat out of hell to be back at Dottie's before the police car turned up.

In the meantime, the crowd was moved away. Mary went back to Ann's place.

'What do you think?' asked Ann.

Mary shrugged. 'Perhaps it's like Kipper says. She and Reg have gone away for a holiday.'

'Since when did Reg take Dottie on holiday?' said Ann.

Mary sighed. 'You're right, hen. We had to practically bully him to come with us to Littlehampton for the Carnival.'

Halfway through the morning, John Landers had a builder on site. Whoever or whatever was in that well had to be got out with care because the ground all around was so unstable.

'I told Reg he should have filled that thing in years ago,' said Terry Dore from the Jolly Farmer when he came up to have a look.

By the time Michael Gilbert brought his mother to the house at eleven o'clock, Mary was sitting in Ann's kitchen drinking tea. They left the children playing in the front room while they told Michael and Edna what had happened.

'You really think she's down that well?' gasped Michael.

'Whatever it is, something bad has happened,' said Mary.

Edna began wringing her hands. 'I can't believe it. Poor Dottie.'

Michael picked up his cap.

'Where are you going?'

'To help,' cried Michael. 'I can't sit here drinking tea if Dottie's down that well.'

As soon as they heard the front door slam, the three women went upstairs to watch the goings-on out of Ann's bathroom window. Michael joined the other men, adjusting and holding onto planks. By the time the builder was able to reach the brown coat, nobody could bear to watch.

'I don't want to look,' said Ann suddenly.

'Me neither, hen,' said Mary. She was already in tears. Edna followed them downstairs.

Ann was restless. Since they'd settled their differences, she and Dottie had become real friends. She now had a good job, her children were well fed and happy and she had smartened herself up no end – all thanks to Dottie. When Vincent Dobbs had put a comforting arm around her, it felt wonderful. It was good to know she was still attractive to men, especially a decent bloke like Vince. He'd lived with his mother until she'd died a year or two back and now he lived alone. A quiet man, he was a real gentleman.

Connie came into the kitchen where the women sat in silent thought.

'Bicket?' she asked.

Ann reached up for the biscuit tin, and all at once she had four little hands reaching out to her. 'Off you go now,' she smiled as she doled them out.

They heard a collective yell outside and Ann's blood ran cold. She glanced at Edna and Mary. They must have found her . . . Oh Dottie. She turned her head away lest the children see her tears.

'Why are you crying, Mummy?' Brian's anxious little voice forced her to pull herself together. Wiping her eyes with the edge of her cardigan sleeve, she bent to kiss him. 'It's all right. Mummy's being silly, that's all. Now off you go and play with your friends.'

'But, Mummy, what are they doing in Aunt Dottie's garden?'

'Filling up the old well,' said Ann briskly. 'Now run along.'

The children went back into the front room and the three friends looked from one to the other.

'Shall I go back upstairs?' asked Ann.

Mary chewed her bottom lip anxiously. 'If you want to, hen.'

'I don't think I can bear to look.'

All at once they heard the sound of running feet along the path outside followed by frantic knocking on her door. A lone tear rolled unchecked down Edna's cheek. Ann straightened herself up and took a deep breath. Phyllis came back out into the hallway.

'Stay there a minute, darling. Mummy's going to answer the door.' Tucking a stray tendril of hair behind her ear, Ann tugged at the front of her apron. Edna and Mary stood in the kitchen doorway.

It was Vince. His face was flushed and his eyes were bright. 'It wasn't her,' he blurted out.

Ann blinked, not fully comprehending what he was saying. Behind her, she heard Mary's cry of relief.

'Thank God,' Edna breathed. 'Oh thank God . . .'

'Then who . . .?' Mary began.

Ann put her trembling hand to her mouth. 'Oh, Vince, no. Please don't tell me it was Patsy?'

'It wasn't either of them,' said Vince breathlessly. 'It was chickens. A sack full of dead chickens!'

Mary, Ann and Edna looked from one to the other.

'I don't understand it,' said Edna. 'Who would kill perfectly good chickens and chuck them down a well?'

Michael Gilbert came up behind Vince. 'A bloody mad man, if you ask me.'

# *Thirty-Five*

After a full English breakfast, Reg suggested that Patsy and Dottie meet him at the other end of the seafront.

'I've got a bit of business to do,' he explained. 'I'll catch up with you later.'

The weather was chilly but at least it was dry. They wrapped up warm and walked to the Lower Parade towards the pier, 'One day,' Dottie promised Patsy, 'we'll come back when it's summertime.'

They'd had a pleasant day on Sunday. They hadn't done a lot but it was nice walking along the seafront and eating egg and chips in warm cafés with steamed-up windows. She liked the thought of coming again next year. Patsy would be that much older and able to enjoy 'girlie things'. The baby would be born by then too. As she'd lain in bed last night, she began thinking about this change of heart Reg was having.

Dottie didn't feel comfortable about it. It was too quick, too impulsive and yet she couldn't fault his behaviour. Had he guessed she was pregnant, or was he up to something?

Whatever it was, she was still going to leave him. When she got back home later today, she'd do what she'd planned: she'd phone Sylvie. She wished she hadn't written to John asking to meet one more time, but he probably wouldn't get the letter until today anyway. She had missed the last post on Thursday night, so it wouldn't have gone until Friday and she would already have been at the hotel on Saturday by the time it arrived at his mother's place. She would always treasure those lovely days with John but from now on she'd have to make the best of what she had. Patsy must be given time to settle down. But, oh, how miserable it was going to be if she could never see John again . . .

Wiping a renegade tear from the end of her nose, Dottie took a deep breath. She mustn't give way to this. For Patsy's sake. For the sake of the baby. As she watched Patsy roller skating ahead of her, Dottie realised that she'd never seen the little girl looking so happy before.

When Reg met them at the end of the road, he surprised her again, this time by pulling up in a car.

'Where on earth did you get that?'

'I've hired it for the day. Hop in and we'll go for a drive.'

He drove them out of Eastbourne.

Dottie frowned. 'But I thought we were going home?'

'We are, but first I've got something to show you.'

Dottie studied his profile as he drove. He'd been so different yesterday and today. What made him so unpredictable? The night of Michael's wedding had been the first time he'd forced her to have sex with him, and ever since then she'd hated the thought of him touching her. Yet since they'd been there he'd let her share a room with Patsy. The way he was behaving right now he was more like the old Reg, the man she'd promised to love, honour and obey all those years ago.

'I want us to buy a new place,' he went on. 'It's not much to look at now but I reckon you'd make a better landlady than old mother Flint.'

'She is a bit formidable, isn't she,' Dottie laughed. 'No food and drink in the bedrooms . . .'

'No running in the corridor,' cried Patsy, mimicking her perfectly.

Dottie laughed but Reg's expression didn't change. She felt the old nervousness came creeping back.

'Are we going to look at a guesthouse?' Dottie asked.

'Bungalow.'

'A bungalow!'

'It needs a bit of doing up, but I reckon it would suit us just fine.'

Dottie decided to say nothing, but she couldn't help thinking that you couldn't get many paying guests in a bungalow.

Ann Pearce was surprised to see Kipper's Austin 7 waiting outside her gate. She began to walk a little quicker. Something was up. Had he discovered something about Dottie?

As she reached the gate, Kipper stepped out of the car. 'Hello, Ann. I wonder if I could have a word?'

She nodded. Although he sounded cheerful enough, her heart was thumping and it felt like the bottom had fallen out of her stomach. She could sense that the whole road was full of twitching net curtains. 'Would you like to come inside?' she asked pleasantly. She hoped her voice didn't give away how nervous she felt.

The short walk up the path seemed like the last mile home. It was cold indoors. She hadn't been home since first thing this morning and the fire had gone out. Apologising for the temperature, she mustered what little dignity she could with a nervous smile. Kipper was business-like.

'Do you know an Ernest Franks?'

Puzzled, Ann shook her head.

'Pity,' Kipper went on. 'Apparently Dottie and her late aunt were kind to him. They left him tea on the windowsill.'

Ann frowned. 'Tea on the windowsill . . .? Oh, you mean the tramp? Oh yes, I remember him. Haven't seen him for a while though. He would put the tin on the windowsill and Aunt Bessie would fill it for him. Sometimes she gave him a bit of bread and jam. I never knew his name. Ernest Franks, is it?' She was conscious that she was babbling but she couldn't help herself. 'Why do you ask? Has something happened to him?'

'I'm afraid so,' said Kipper. 'At the moment he's in Worthing hospital.'

'I'm sorry to hear that,' said Ann. 'But at least he'll get three square meals a day.'

'He was found a few days ago,' Kipper went on. 'In a hedge. He'd been badly beaten and left for dead. It was touch and go. He's made some improvement but he's still not out of the woods yet.'

'Why are you telling me all this?'

'I wonder if you would come with me and identify him as the tramp you remember,' said Kipper. 'I need to make sure he's on the level.'

'Me?' cried Ann. 'But I hardly know the man.'

'I would have asked Dottie,' said Kipper, 'but she's not here. I've come round in my off-duty because I'd rather not make it official unless I have to.'

She realised for the first time that he wasn't in his uniform. How silly of her not to notice. Normally he rode a bicycle around the village, not the Austin 7.

'If we could go to the hospital now,' he went on, 'we could clear this up very quickly. The poor old fellow took quite a licking. Most likely he's had his brains scrambled but I need to check on a few things.'

Ann glanced at the clock. 'It just so happens that my children are with Mary Prior,' she began. 'I'd have to be back here before six.'

'It shouldn't take that long,' said Kipper.

The bungalow turned out to be one of several in a row standing behind a four-foot wall on the edge of The Crumbles, an area of wild, undeveloped and lonely land between Eastbourne and Pevensey. The only thing that marked it out from the others of a similar ilk was a windswept rambling rose clinging to the white-washed walls. As they walked up the path, Dottie looked up as the net curtain in the next door bungalow was lifted and an old woman peered out. At the same time, an old man looked out of the down-stairs window. Despite Reg's enthusiasm, Dottie could never imagine the area becoming a magnet for visitors. It was too bleak.

Although it was furnished, the bungalow was musty and damp inside. Patsy ran from room to room exploring every cupboard drawer.

'It needs a bit of work,' said Reg, 'but nothing that a lick of paint won't cure.'

'How much do they want for it, Reg?'

'Nine hundred pounds.'

Dottie was flabbergasted; yet he'd made it sound as if it were just a few quid. 'Where are we going to get that sort of money?'

He turned to her with that dark look in his eye. 'There you go again,' he hissed. 'Always trying to spoil everything.'

'No, no,' she protested. 'Believe me I wasn't, but nine hundred pounds . . . it's a lot of money.'

'We'll get a tidy sum from selling the cottage,' he said. 'Add it to your trust fund, we'll do it easy.'

Dottie gasped. 'But I don't want to sell the cottage,' she cried. A wave of anger swept over her and she spun round to face him. 'I won't do it, Reg. It's *my* cottage and I won't do it!'

Immediately, he raised his arm to hit her.

'Auntie Dottie . . . Auntie Dottie, there's a funny old pump over the sink,' said Patsy, running back into the room. 'Come and see.'

Reg snapped his arm back to his side. 'Let's not talk about money now, love,' he said, giving Dottie a deliberate smile. 'Go and see what the kid wants . . . and when you come back, I've got another surprise for you.'

Ann and Kipper pulled up in the car park outside the hospital in Lyndhurst Road. They walked in silence under the clock tower and into the long tiled corridors that smelled of disinfectant.

Ernest Franks was in a room on his own next to the men's ward. He lay on his back, with his head slightly propped up. The snow-white sheet was folded neatly over his chest and beneath his unshaven chin. He looked very different. One eye was badly bruised and the eyebrow had been stitched back together again. Ann guessed from the look of him that his nose had been broken.

As they walked into the room, he appeared to be asleep but as she drew nearer, he opened his one eye and began to cough painfully.

She sat down on the chair beside the bed. 'I'm sorry to see you like this,' she said.

'I remember you,' he said softly. 'You lived next door . . .' Ann could feel Kipper leaning over her shoulder trying to catch what the man was saying '. . . to the old one.'

'You mean Elizabeth Thornton?' she said. 'Everyone knew her as Aunt Bessie.'

He nodded his head painfully. 'She helped me.'

'She was a lovely woman.' Ann agreed.

'I was going to end it all,' he said. 'I'd come to the end of my tether. If it wasn't for her . . .' He coughed. 'I went back and left her a note. I wanted her to know it was because of her I did it.'

Kipper frowned. 'Did what?'

'Got my life back together again.'

Ernest coughed again. Ann offered him some water. He took a small sip and then sank back onto the pillow, apparently overcome by emotion.

'When I saw a newspaper cutting . . .' he choked.

Ann glanced anxiously at Kipper. The poor man wasn't making much sense, but he was clearly overwrought about something. When he'd recovered a little, he indicated that he wanted his knapsack. They found it stuffed in the bottom of

300

the locker; the sister had wrapped it in a brown paper bag. When Kipper pulled it out, it still stank of ditchwater. They laid it on the bed beside him.

Ernest had precious few possessions but they included a tattered photograph of a young woman with a small child on her knee, some dog-eared letters, a few items of clothing, his trilby hat and a black tie. At the bottom of the bag they found a faded blue rabbit with floppy ears. He seized the rabbit, pressing it to his cheek. 'My poor little Bobbie . . .'

Ann felt uncomfortable. After the war, there were plenty of people with similarly pathetic little collections of bits and pieces left over from a bombed house. Rubbish to one person, but a treasure collected from the darkness for another.

'Shall we play with bunny? You'd like that, wouldn't you, Bobbie?' He began to hum.

Ann couldn't bear it. Swallowing hard, she bit back her own tears and turned over a few of the other things spread out on the bedcovers. 'Are you looking for something, Mr Franks?' she said gently.

Eventually, Ernest pushed most of the things aside and picked up a page of folded newspaper. Kipper opened it out and they scanned each side of the page. On one side was an article about canal boats, on the other a small article headlined 'Tragic Fall'.

Ann recognised it at once as the report on Aunt Bessie's death. She didn't need to re-read it to know it said that Elizabeth Thornton had been found dead at the foot of the stairs in Myrtle Cottage, High Street, on February 15th 1949; that Dr Fitzgerald had attended the scene and had pronounced life extinct. The police and the coroner had been informed and at the inquest her niece, Dorothy Cox, had said that her aunt had been in good health when she had left for work that morning. The report went on to say that Mr Reginald Cox had come home to find the doctor and an ambulance in attendance, his wife distraught and his wife's aunt dead. The newspaper report noted that he was

301

deeply moved as he spoke of Aunt Bessie, describing her as angel in disguise who, since his return from the war, had given him both a welcome and a home. He had last seen his wife's aunt at 8.30 that morning as he left for work.

As Kipper refreshed his memory by reading the report aloud, the man became agitated.

'The bloody liar,' he hissed. He gripped the edge of his sheet and screwed it as he tried to sit up. 'He didn't go to work at 8.30. He was there, I tell you. The bastard was there!'

# Thirty-Six

The whole bungalow smelled musty and damp. The windows were boarded up and the only light came from between the open cracks. There was no electricity and the wind made an eerie sound as it whistled between the back door and the fence.

'The owner is in a nursing home,' said Reg. 'I know it doesn't look a lot right now but it'll be really nice once we've done it up.'

His eyes shone with excitement and he was animated in a way Dottie'd never seen before. Patsy ran from room to room, keeping up a running commentary as she went. 'There's some old sauce-pans on the cooker. Ugh, there's something in this one, it's all mouldy.'

Dottie stood at the entrance to the sitting room watching Reg putting down a sheet. Her mind was working overtime. Surely he couldn't be serious about this?

'I can see paw marks on this floor, Auntie Dottie,' Patsy's voice drifted towards them. 'Is there a dog here? I like dogs.'

How could she make this into a guesthouse? It would take a month of Sundays to clean it up and then it would need to be redecorated throughout. No one would want to stay in a place with nicotine-stained walls and smelly drains. The garden was a wilderness and it was miles from anywhere. She wondered vaguely how the old couple next door managed to do their shopping.

'Come on,' said Reg at last. 'Let's have our picnic.'

'Reg,' she began weakly.

He glared at her stonily. 'We'll talk about it later. Now do as I say and sit down.'

His tone was so belligerent, Dottie lowered herself down at once.

Patsy bounced into the room. 'What are you doing?'

'We're having a picnic,' said Reg.

'But . . .' the child began; then seeing Dottie's expression, she lowered herself beside her, hugging her toy elephant close.

Reg opened a duffle bag and took out some sandwiches wrapped in greaseproof paper. 'I asked the old dragon to make us some sandwiches. Hungry?'

Even the thought of eating made her feel sick but Dottie nodded. She had to get out of this somehow. How could she possibly have her baby in this God-forsaken hole. And where would Patsy go to school?

Reg threw a bag of crisps at Patsy. The child's face lit up.

Reg poured some tea from a flask and handed Dottie a mug. Dottie cupped her hands around it. Did he really want her to give up Aunt Bessie's comfortable cottage for this?

'I can see the bungalow has great potential but I'm not sure many people would like it here, Reg,' she ventured cautiously. 'It's very isolated.'

'Nonsense. This is just what people want. A nice quiet place.'

A nice *quiet* place . . . her mind echoed with emphasis.

A dark expression drifted across his face. 'Eat your sandwiches.'

She ate but they tasted like cardboard and she was struggling not to cry.

'Can Suzy and me go and look for the dog?' Patsy asked.

'Course you can, pet,' smiled Reg.

'I can't buy this place,' Dottie said quietly as soon as they were alone.

His head snapped up. 'But as soon as your inheritance comes through . . .' he began.

'It'll be tied up until I'm thirty.'

His mouth became a tight line. 'Tied up?'

Dottie explained the terms of her aunt's will. 'I can't do anything without the approval of the trustees.'

Reg held her gaze for a while and looked away. 'What a shame.' His voice was so controlled it chilled her even more. What was he up to? Her head was spinning. She could think straight.

'I don't feel so good,' she said. 'My mouth is very dry.'

'Have some more tea, dear.' He helped her with the cup and she managed another mouthful. 'Tell you what. Why don't you have a bit of a lie down? There's a bed next door. I can lay the sheet over it for you.'

She protested but he stuffed everything back into the duffle bag and helped her out of the room. Her legs were like lead.

The bedroom was cold and the windows were closely boarded up. No cracks here, but she was grateful to see the bed. He spread the sheet over the mattress and Dottie lay down. 'I'll be fine in a minute,' she said.

'Course you will, pet,' he said.


Ann gasped in horror. 'What!'

But Ernest Franks was seized by a violent coughing fit. They rang the bell and a nurse came. Between them, they hauled him into a more upright position and she re-arranged the pillows.

'You'll have to put that stuff away, Ernie,' she said pointing at the old knapsack and its contents scattered all over the bed. 'If Sister sees it, you know what'll happen. She'll have it all in the incinerator as quick as you like.'

Ann busied herself putting everything back in the brown paper bag. As she pushed in the trilby hat, her fingers touched some-thing sharp and she let out a small cry. She supposed it was his knife but she pulled out a medal. The DSO and bar. She and PC

305

Kipling shared a glance and her respect for the tramp went sky-high.

Kipper opened his notepad. 'So you're saying that Mr Cox was in the house when Mrs Thornton died?'

Ernest was in a world of his own. Bouncing the rabbit in the air, he began to sing softly. 'Run rabbit, run rabbit, run, run, run . . .'

Kipper glanced at Ann and shook his head. It was obvious that the poor man was a sandwich short of a picnic. As they turned to leave, Ernest looked up sharply. 'And that isn't his name either.'

The full import of his statement was lost as Ann exclaimed, 'Ernest, if *you* heard Aunt Bessie fall, why didn't *you* go and help her?'

'I wasn't there when she actually fell,' he said. 'She gave me my tea and she let me talk. I liked it when she let me talk.' His voice trailed. 'I could never talk to people about Eileen and my boy, nobody except her. She didn't try to shut me up. She didn't say, that's all in the past, time to move on. She'd listen. I could talk to her. I told her about my boy. My little Bobbie.' His face clouded. 'But then, *he* came back,' he said bitterly. 'He never liked me being there. Whenever he saw me, he used to shout at her. She always said she wasn't worried but I didn't want to get her into trouble so I only went there when he wasn't around.'

'But he came back that day,' said Kipper.

Ernest nodded. 'He came in the back way, down the garden path, and I scarpered out the front door.'

'Reg always used to come in the back way,' Ann remarked. She wanted to tell them that he used to stand in the lane and watch her house and that he gave her the creeps, but this wasn't the time or the place.

'So why didn't you come to the police when you heard Mrs Thornton had died?' Kipper wanted to know.

'I didn't know she was gone until a few weeks ago,' he said simply. 'She had given me a rail ticket to go back home, so that's where I went.'

'Home?' said Kipper. 'Where's home?'

'Liverpool.' His voice had dropped again. 'I went back to see where they'd put Eileen and the boy.' He laid his hand on the top of the brown paper bag. 'The neighbours saved a few things for me. This is the little rabbit my boy used to take to bed with him, a few photographs and stuff. There wasn't much left.'

'May I ask you what happened?' Ann asked gently.

'They were killed in an air raid.'

They all became very conscious of how quiet it was in the room.

'Mr Franks,' said Kipper bringing them back to the business in hand. 'We are very sorry for your loss, but you indicated that Reg Cox wasn't his name?' Ernest's face clouded with anger. 'That's because when I called out his real name, he turned around. His name is Daniel Sinclair, and we met in a courtroom in 1942.'

Ann frowned. 'That's not possible,' she smiled. 'Reg and Dottie met in 1941 and were married in 1942. Soon after that, Reg went on a special mission. It was all very hush, hush.'

The tramp eased himself up on his elbow and looked intently at her. 'And I'm telling you, Danny Sinclair was a no-good thief and troublemaker,' he said, with just a hint of the authority he'd once wielded. 'He'd been had up for stealing army blankets for the black market and then he was done for stealing lead from bombed-out houses. I should know, I was the escort at his trial.'

A little air escaped from Ann's lips. 'Reg always said he was shipped to Burma. He was one of those brave Chindits.'

Ernest relaxed against the pillows. 'One of the Chindits, my eye. By the end of 1942, he was in prison.' He pointed to his face. 'Why do you think he did this? He knew I could expose him for the rat he is, so he left me for dead.'

They became conscious of Kipper turning the pages in his notebook in his struggle to keep up with what was being said. 'Can you prove any of this?'

Ernest shook his head. 'Not now. I could have done but when he jumped me in the lane and he took everything off me.'

'That's a bit unfortunate,' said Kipper dryly.

'I wrote several times,' Ernest went on, 'but of course, she never replied. I knew that wasn't like her, so I decided to come back. I turned up a couple of months ago but everyone was going to a wedding.'

'Michael Gilbert,' said Ann.

'I didn't want to intrude so I bought a few bits for my shop in Liverpool and left.'

'Shop?' asked Kipper.

'I deal in antiques now,' Ernest went on. 'And then I found that wrapped around some trinket.' He pointed to the newspaper cutting. 'I was very upset and it niggled me, so I had to come and find out what happened to her.'

'But why didn't you go straight to the police?' Kipper asked.

'Because, fool that I was, I wanted to confront him myself.'

The nurse reappeared. 'The doctor says Mr Franks has to have his sleeping pills now.'

Ernest became agitated. 'I've got to tell you . . .' he said looking at Kipper, 'about Danny . . .' He began to cough.

'You really must rest,' the nurse insisted.

'We'll come back when you're feeling better,' Kipper soothed.

Ann put the brown paper bag back into the locker as the nurse stood over him with two pills on a small tray. Obediently, Ernest took them one by one, washing them down with a sip of water.

'You do realise, he's very poorly, don't you?' said the nurse quietly behind her hand. She raised her voice to speak directly to her patient. 'Good man. Now you lie back and try and get some sleep.'

Kipper walked briskly to the door. 'Goodnight, Mr Franks.'

Ernest didn't acknowledge him. He had closed his eyes and was relaxed on the pillow. Ann couldn't resist leaning over him and giving him a feather-like kiss on his cheek. 'Goodnight, Ernest.'

Ernest Franks sighed. 'Night, Eileen, love . . .' 'you will come back, won't you? You must know . . . Danny . . .' His eyes closed and he drifted into sleep.

On the way home, PC Kipling was apologetic. 'I shouldn't have taken you there. I had no idea what he was going to say but I would ask you to keep this to yourself.'

'It's all a bit worrying, isn't it?' said Ann. 'Especially now that Dottie and Patsy have gone missing.'

'Let's not make a mountain out of a molehill,' said Kipper. 'We don't know that they *are* missing.' Ann sat grim-faced. 'What about Ernest?'

Kipper shrugged. 'I will report it to my superiors but, despite what he's just told us, he's unreliable. Half the time he's away with the fairies, isn't he?'

They had reached Mary Prior's place. 'Thanks for dropping me back,' said Ann.

'Don't forget,' he reminded her, 'this is strictly between ourselves.'

As she jumped out of the car, Ann couldn't help feeling very worried about Dottie and Patsy.

309

# Thirty-Seven

Mary listened open-mouthed as Ann told her what had happened at the hospital. Once Edna turned up, the whole story was repeated verbatim.

'I can't see how we can do it,' said Mary. 'I mean, I don't want to sound melodramatic, hen, but even if everything is all right, who's to say she'll be back by Saturday?'

Edna shrugged. 'She'll probably walk in here, right as rain at any minute.'

'I can't stop thinking about those chickens,' said Ann.

'Whoever killed them,' said Edna. 'I'm sure it wasn't Dottie.'

'Like Vince said, it was the work of a madman.' They glanced around at each other nervously.

'Do you think Kipper will keep looking for her?' Ann asked.

Mary nodded. 'He'd make a good detective.'

They all stared miserably into their teacups. 'We can't just leave it to him,' said Mary. 'One of us ought to go and look for her.'

'Don't look at me,' said Ann. 'I'm a single mum. Can't go traipsing around the country, and besides, where would I start?'

'Nor me. I've got five kids and a husband,' Mary reminded them.

'I would if I could, dear,' said Edna. 'But my old rheumatics . . .'

'Then what we need,' Mary said, 'is someone who has plenty of time and nothing much to do.'

There was a second of silence before everyone looked up.

'Sylvie,' they chorused.

'Mummy,' said Brian, bursting into the kitchen. 'That man is outside Auntie Dottie's house again.'

John Landers was pushing a letter through the letterbox at Myrtle Cottage. He had written formally and addressed it to Mr and Mrs Cox. In it he had told them that he had just been passing the area and had called in on the off-chance that he might see Patricia. After that he wrote the usual sort of keeping-in-touch letter, asking after their health and Patricia's welfare. Even though John felt honour-bound to make quite sure that the child was well, he had made his enquiry as light-hearted as possible for two good reasons. If Dottie, as he supposed by yesterday's shenanigans, had left her husband, Reg Cox wouldn't feel in any way threatened by his visit. But if the three of them had simply gone on holiday, as everyone else supposed, they would be quick to reply, having the need to apologise for his wasted journey.

The collapsed well had now been roped off and the police had satisfied themselves that no one had fallen down the shaft.

While sitting by the open fire in the pub last night, John overheard some of the locals talking. Everyone was puzzled by the Coxs' disappearance. It was, the regulars agreed, totally out of character. Rumour had it that the detective sergeant and the detective constable hadn't been too happy about being dragged out to the village to deal with a bag containing a few dead chickens weighted down with a hammer, and after that, there had been a lot of laughter revolving around eating kippers and chicken soup.

John Landers couldn't help feeling that if the Coxs had been moneyed people, the crime of kidnapping would have been uppermost in the mind of the law enforcement officers. But, to give him his due, PC Kipling had tried to persuade the DC that he should mount an investigation. As soon as the bag had been retrieved, with (it had to be said) a great deal of open hostility and ridicule aimed towards the village bobby, the scaffolding planks had been left for safety's sake.

'Excuse me.' A neighbour looked over the fence. John recognised her from the day before.

'Good morning,' he smiled affably. 'Mrs Pearce, isn't it?'

'Yes.'

John raised his hat. 'Any news of Mr and Mrs Cox?'

Ann shook her head and John Landers became conscious of two other women standing by Ann's back door. 'I don't know if you know,' he went on, 'but I accompanied Patricia from Australia.'

'We guessed who you were,' she said, 'although from what Dottie said, we thought you would be a lot older.'

'And not so good looking,' Mary muttered near Edna's ear.

'I wonder if I might have a word with you?' John asked.

'We're not much for gossiping, if you know what I mean,' said Ann, looking around at her friends.

'I wouldn't dream of asking you to,' he said. 'And I'm not at liberty to discuss confidentialities but as friends of Mrs Cox, I wondered if you might be able to throw some light on the matter.'

'We all reckon,' said Ann cautiously, 'there's something funny going on.'

Dottie felt the bed dip but she didn't open her eyes. Her head felt as if it weighed as much as a sewing machine and her mouth tasted like the bottom of a parrot cage. A sickly sweet smell drifted towards her but she couldn't work out what it was.

She heard Reg say, 'She says she can't sell the place. She can't do bloody anything until she's thirty.'

Dottie breathed in a waft of stale cheap perfume. It wasn't one she used but she had smelled it before.

'All tied up, eh?' said a woman's voice. 'Then if you ask me, lover, she's worth more to you dead than alive.'

Sitting in Ann's kitchen, John listened to Dottie's friends as they told him how much Dottie meant to them. Ann told him in glowing terms how Dottie helped her get a job which enabled her to pull herself back out of the gutter and Mary and Edna shared a few wartime experiences on the farm. Finally, Mary told him about Dottie's love for Patsy, as they all called her.

As they talked, it dawned on John that he had fallen in love with Dottie. The revelation almost took the wind out of him, but something told him that it must remain a secret for the time being. It had probably begun when he was untangling her hair from the tree branch and even now, as he remembered, his heart ached for her. Her blue-green eyes, her soft mouth, her hair . . . such a lovely colour, like burnished bronze. His daydream was sweet. Her hair must be quite long. He wondered what it would be like when it wasn't tied up in that rather severe bun. He even remembered her smell. He never had been a man for heavy perfume, but his head felt light as he thought of her natural fragrance. She wore lipstick, but not too much, and he could even remember the laughter lines around her eyes . . .

Yes, her friends were absolutely right. Dottie wasn't the sort of woman to go off without telling anyone. She was kind and considerate. She would know that people would worry. And she certainly wouldn't risk losing her job.

Everything became very quiet. He was aware that they were all looking at him. John blinked and cleared his throat noisily. 'And what about Mr Cox?'

'He doesn't think very much of me,' said Ann. 'I keep out of his way.'

'He's a dark one, that one,' said Mary. 'He gave her a black eye once.'

John's blood ran cold. What an idiot he'd been. A dark one . . .

a black eye ... He should have insisted on proper background checks before he'd left Patricia with Reg Cox. He shouldn't have listened to Brenda's protestations that everything would be all right. His chest was filled with rage.

Edna had gasped in horror. 'Reg gave Dottie a black eye? You never said.'

'It wasn't my place to,' said Mary crisply. 'Anyway, she tried to make out it wasn't much. But I told her, no matter what you do, there's no cause for a man to hit a woman, isn't that right, Doctor? Anyway, she said he'd never done it before, and it was an accident. She reckoned he just got a bit upset about the little girl, that's all.'

'Upset?' John interrupted crossly. 'Why was he upset?'

'Because of the way she looks, I suppose,' said Mary shaking her head. 'You people are supposed to tell the parents about the child they're adopting, aren't you? I can't think why you adoption people never told him she had coloured blood in her. He should have been told before they sent her.'

They were all nodding in agreement. Clearly they had no idea that Patricia was supposed to be Reg's natural offspring, but they were unanimous about Reg's dislike of the child. His mind drifted back to Dottie. What was it like for her living with Reg?

'Are they happily married?' he asked, although he could hardly bear to hear the answer.

Mary shrugged. 'She's pregnant.'

John said nothing but it felt like the bottom had fallen out of his world. He'd thought ... hoped, that she no longer had relations with Reg.

Edna and Ann gasped. 'What? Are you serious?'

Mary nodded. 'She's having Reg's baby.'

'After all this time,' Edna said slowly, 'I don't know whether to be happy or sad.'

'I'd top myself if I was having his kid,' said Ann ominously.

John smiled grimly. 'Could they have gone to visit relatives?'

'Dottie came to live with Bessie because she didn't have a soul in the world,' said Mary. 'And I can't honestly say as I've ever seen any of Reg's relatives, have you?'

Ann and Edna shook their heads.

'And if she was going away, she would have asked me to look after the chickens,' Ann insisted. 'She loved those birds.'

'PC Kipling believes Mrs Cox killed the chickens.'

'Dottie wouldn't do that,' said Edna. 'She would only kill a chicken if it was going to be eaten – and before you suggest they might have been diseased, let me tell you, I've looked at them very carefully and there's nothing wrong with those fowl.'

'That's right,' Mary went on. 'It's such a waste. Have you seen the price of chicken these days? Dottie would have put them on somebody's doorstep if she didn't want to eat them. She wouldn't chuck them down the well. Those birds would have made a nice meal for someone.'

'What about a fox?' asked John. 'There's talk that one might have got into the henhouse.'

Edna shook her head. 'And I'm telling you, no fox has been at those chickens.'

John regarded them carefully. 'You think Mr Cox did it, don't you?'

There was an awkward silence and then Ann said, 'The truth of it is, Dr Landers, we've all got a really bad feeling about all this.'

Edna nodded. 'Something has happened to them. I can feel it in me water.'

'I'm not sure exactly what I can do,' said John, reaching for his hat. He stood to go. 'But I'll ask around. The trouble is, I'm not sure where to start.'

Thanking them for their time, he made his way back to his room at the Warnes Hotel. He was glad to have met with Dottie's friends but their concern only served to fan the flame of his own terrible sense of foreboding.

315

# Thirty-Eight

When John walked into the Jolly Farmer that night, a large crowd of regulars were huddled noisily around the fireplace. Above the chatter, John could hear someone, a man, sobbing. The landlord, Terry Dore, pushed past him with a double whisky in his hand.

'Glad to see you, Doc,' he said. 'Could you have a butcher's at one of my regulars? He's had a bit of a shock.'

'I'm afraid I haven't got my bag with me,' John apologised. 'But I'll take a look.'

He followed the landlord into the confused mêlée.

'Here you are, son,' said Terry holding out the whisky. 'Get that down your neck, and then the doc here wants to take a look at you.'

'I'd prefer it if I could look at him before he drinks alcohol,' John interrupted.

The landlord stepped aside and John Landers was suddenly face to face with a tear-stained Reg Cox. They both blinked at each other in surprise.

Reg was very dishevelled. His hair was wild and his coat splattered with mud. The collar of his shirt was greasy and clearly needed changing.

John spoke first, his tone measured. 'Everyone has been very concerned about you and your family, Mr Cox.'

Reg said nothing.

'The landlord wants me to give you a quick look, if you don't mind.'

He caught hold of Reg's limp wrist and began counting his pulse. There didn't appear to be anything physically wrong with the man but he was clearly distraught about something. When John had finished his examination, it took a couple of glasses of Terry Dore's best malt whisky before Reg could stop shaking. 'Have you come to see my Patsy?' he asked John.

'Yes, I have. Where is she?'

Reg's face crumpled. 'I don't know. I don't know.'

John struggled to make sense of what he was saying when Terry took the words out of his mouth.

'What yer mean, you don't know?' Terry demanded.

'She's been taken.'

'Taken? Taken where?'

'I don't know,' Reg whimpered.

While the people around them murmured and shook their heads, John felt as if something had gripped the pit of his stomach. 'I think it best if someone gets the constable,' he said.

'Already done, sir,' said Terry. 'I sent my lad Paul. He'll be back in a minute.'

'I'm here now,' said a deep and reassuring voice behind them. 'What's up?'

PC Kipling was in civilian clothes. They were a bit scruffy and he had one or two dead leaves stuck to his jacket. He smelled pleasantly of autumn bonfire. 'Ah, Reg. I'm glad to see you're back,' he said. 'Going off like that without telling a living soul where you were going has caused a fine how d'you do in the village, I can tell you.'

'He says his girl's been took off,' Terry blurted out.

'Took off?' Kipper snorted. 'You been watching too many of them Hollywood films, Reg.'

Reg's eyes narrowed. 'Is that a fact, Mr Kipling? Well, let me

317

tell you, I've been going out of my mind looking for them, but I can't find either of them, not my Patsy or Dot.'

John stared somewhere into space. Had she really left him? He'd known she wasn't happy almost from the moment they'd met. There was sadness in her eyes even back then. Hearing she was pregnant put a whole different complexion on things. If she was having her husband's child there must be a marriage there . . . and yet there was still something about her that made him want to make things right for her, make her laugh, protect her . . . He swallowed hard. If she had run off, would he ever see her again?

Reg downed the last of the whisky and glanced up at Terry but this time there was no response. The bar fell silent. Everything seemed rather surreal. Where was Dottie? Where was Patsy?

Reg looked down at his shoes, turning his foot this way and that so that everyone could see the mud caked on the bottom. 'Look at the state of my shoes. I must have walked twenty mile or more.'

Kipper took out his police notebook from his back pocket.

'But we all thought you'd gone off together,' said Vince Dobbs.

'We did,' Reg continued. 'I took them to the hotel where Dot and I went for our honeymoon. Sea View in Eastbourne. It's only a step from the seafront. Lovely place, top notch. She's been working so hard just lately, see – I thought I'd surprise them.'

John was conscious of the people around him exchanging sentimental smiles but he kept his eye on Reg. He wasn't normally a sceptical person but he had a growing gut feeling the man was playing to the gallery. When Dottie sent that last letter to him, she had been troubled about something. All this talk about surprises and honeymoon hotels . . . Reg had never seemed the caring, tender-hearted type before.

'We had the best time.' Reg went on. 'We walked round the town and I bought my girl a candyfloss. We spent the afternoon in the pictures and on the way back to the guesthouse, I took them into a café for fish and chips.' He stared into his empty glass.

A tall bespectacled man snatched Reg's glass from his hand. 'For God's sake, give the man a drink, Landlord.'

'Thanks, Eric,' Reg said without looking up.

'Go on then, son,' said Eric, his voice low.

John started at the top of Reg's bowed head. Something was wrong. Something was badly wrong.

Reg spread his hands and wiped his palms down the side of his trousers. 'I loved that little girl, as God is my witness, I loved her. But *she* didn't want me to have her, did she? *She* wanted her all to herself.' His voice dropped to a barely audible whisper. 'When did any of you last see all of us doing something together . . . something as a family? The truth of the matter is, she wouldn't include me. Jealous, that's what she was. Jealous as sin.'

John was appalled. Dottie jealous? *Never!* How dare he? Dottie never spoke ill of her husband. The only thing she'd intimated was that Reg was the one finding it hard to adjust to being a family.

Reg looked up at him, as if reading his thoughts. His cold stare made it difficult for John to maintain eye contact. 'She always made out like she was the perfect little housewife but Les Dixon can vouch for me,' Reg insisted with a slight curl in his lip. 'Turfed out of me own home to eat in his chip shop night after night. I tell you, Doc, I've lived a solitary life since that child came.'

John said nothing, aware that several heads were nodding in agreement.

'That's 'cos she never wanted me home of an evening.'

'You was in here every night,' Eric agreed. 'I don't think I've ever known you to miss.'

'I loved that kid. Loved her, I did.' Reg choked back another sob.

John clenched and unclenched his fists. Fraud . . . Liar!

The whisky arrived. Reg gulped a mouthful and then leaned forward, supporting his head with his hand.

Kipper bent over him and said softly, 'So where is Dottie now, Reg?'

'I told you, I don't know. I swear to God. I woke up this morning and she and my Patsy had gone. Look, I found this note.' He dug in his pocket and handed a dog-eared and crumpled piece of paper to the policeman. 'I spent the whole day looking for her. I even caught a bus up to Beachy Head. Thank God she wasn't there but the more I think about it the more convinced I am. She's done for her, Mr Kipling. I know she has.'

John felt himself sway. In God's name, what had he done? Had he hurt her? And what had he done to Patsy? Never taking his eyes from Reg for one minute, John lowered himself into a nearby chair, his heart racing.

Kipper took his time unfolding the note, taking out his glasses and calling for a better light. Grim-faced, he read it and then handed it to John.

John recognised Dottie's handwriting immediately. The paper looked as if it had been screwed up and there was a large chunk torn from the top of the page. The note itself was in ink but hastily scribbled.

*Patsy seems to be happy but I can't go on pretending everything is fine. I'm sorry to let everybody down . . .*

'Are you're sure it's from her?' Kipper asked.

Yes, John answered in his head, it's her handwriting. It was similar to something she wrote in the letter she sent him . . .

'The chambermaid found it when she turned down the sheets,' Reg said.

For the first time since Kipper arrived, John found his voice. 'If you spent the whole time together, when did she write this note?

'I dunno,' said Reg. His tone had an edge to it now. 'Yesterday, after we had breakfast. I went up to use the toilet and when I came down, they'd gone. I went to look for them. Like I say, I was out all day.'

As Kipper wrote it down in his notepad, Reg blew his nose, loudly.

'Did they take their things?' John asked.

'The suitcase was gone.'

Someone handed Reg a lit cigarette. He drew on it deeply.

'Did you check with reception?'

'Nobody saw them leave.'

'How long did you wait for them?'

'All day and all night.'

'And you didn't tell anyone around here that you and your wife were going away?'

'I told you, it was a surprise, spur of the moment.'

'So spur of the moment, you didn't even ask anyone to feed the chickens?'

Reg looked up. His eyes grew dark. 'What is this?' he snapped. 'I come here to tell you my wife and child are missing and all you can do is talk about bloody chickens?' He appealed to PC Kipling. 'Look here, Constable Kipling, I'm exhausted. I've spent the last two days searching the whole of Eastbourne for them. I've walked right along the seafront. Miles, I've walked, but I couldn't find her. I couldn't find either of them.'

'Did you contact the police in Eastbourne?' Kipper wanted to know.

'I didn't think they'd help,' said Reg looking away again. 'I mean, they'd have to have something to go on, wouldn't they? A body or something . . .' He choked back a sob.

John fixed his eyes on the floor. *What have you done, you bastard . . .*

'Now, now, don't go jumping to conclusions,' said Kipper. 'I reckon in a day or two, she'll turn up, right as ninepence.'

'You all right, Doc?' Terry suddenly asked. 'Only you look a bit peaky.'

John gave him a fleeting smile. 'I'm fine. Just trying to work out the scenario, that's all.' He took a deep breath. 'You'd better go home and get some rest, Mr Cox,' he advised. He kept his voice as even as he could but in truth he was so angry it was as much as he could do not to hit the man. 'You've obviously had a shock.'

'I think we all have,' said Reg looking directly at John. 'My wife and daughter mean a lot to a lot of people.'

John felt a shiver run down his spine.

'Michael Gilbert might still be round your place,' said Terry as everyone began drifting back to the bar.

'Michael Gilbert?' Reg looked puzzled. 'What for?'

'To fill in the well,' Terry explained. 'Oh of course, you don't know, do you? It fell in on itself Monday. We couldn't leave it like that. Too dangerous.'

Reg recovered himself. 'Has it completely gone?'

'And half the garden,' said Vince. 'One time, we thought your Dottie was in it.'

'That's right,' piped up someone else. 'We saw something sticking up in the rubble.'

John noticed that Reg had gone very pale.

'Don't worry,' said Eric quickly. 'When the police finally got hold of it, t'were only a few dead chickens.'

Reg's eyes darted from one to another but he showed no real surprise.

'You knew the chickens were in the well, did you, Mr Cox?' said John.

Reg looked at him coldly. 'Of course I did,' he snapped. 'Bloody fox got them. Chewed all the heads off. I chucked them in the well without telling her because I didn't want Dot getting upset.' He stood up and walked towards the door. As he reached it, he turned back with his hand outstretched. Grasping John's hand and shaking it vigorously he added, 'Sorry you've had a wasted journey, Doctor.'

As he let go of his hand, it was as much as John Landers could do to resist the temptation to wipe his now warm and clammy palm down the side of his trousers.

Everything seemed really far away. Dottie struggled to make herself wake up. She could hear someone banging on the door but her body wouldn't move.

And that awful smell was fading but something told her something was dreadfully wrong but she couldn't think. What did it mean? She couldn't remember. It wasn't as strong as it had been but it was still there. It reminded her of rotten eggs. She coughed but it clung to her throat and her head hurt. Oh, how her head hurt.

The banging was getting more violent. She had to make herself move but her limbs felt like lead. Her mouth tasted of vomit and there was a sort of crust around her lips. What was that smell? She could remember a heavy perfume, but it wasn't that . . .

Gas!

Her eyes flew open. Where was Patsy? They had to get out of here, but where were they? She couldn't remember that either.

She had to turn off the gas.

She could hear voices but they sounded as if they were at the far end of a long tunnel. And that banging . . . was it never going to stop? She had to sit up but when she tried to move, it felt as if someone was sitting on her chest. She thought she was in bed but she wasn't. She was lying on something hard and unyielding. Should she switch on the light and see?

Turn the gas off. Turn it off! That must be why she had such an awfully bad headache and her brain wouldn't work . . .

Now it sounded like someone was kicking the door down. Someone was breaking in and she couldn't do anything about it. She wanted to vomit again.

*Mary? Help me, Mary.*

*Is that you, Sylvie . . . Get Patsy out . . .*

*Are you there, Reg . . .*

She could hear the voices more clearly now. They were getting closer. Someone was trying to get in the room but Patsy was lying too close to the door.

'Patsy . . . move over, darling . . .

A man's voice, one she didn't recognise, cried out, 'For heaven's sake, get a move on. There's a child in here!'

# Thirty-Nine

As soon as the man spoke, it was so obvious, John wondered why he hadn't thought of it before.

It was Tuesday. He'd motored over to Eastbourne and, having found the Sea View, he'd asked the manager and several members of staff about Dottie and Patsy but drawn a blank.

'I've already told the police all this,' Mrs Flint said tetchily 'I don't know what happened to the lady.'

After walking along the seafront and stopping a few people to show them the photograph of Dottie and Patsy that he'd taken at his mother's place, he was still no closer to finding out what had happened to them. The police had, they told him, already tried all the hospitals but nobody of that name had been admitted.

By now he was almost sick with worry. People don't just vanish into thin air, he told himself – but that wasn't true. People went missing all the time, if they wanted to . . . Look what had happened after the war. Hundreds of people went 'missing'. It was their one chance of a new life, a new start.

Even though she had been so adamant that they couldn't become involved with each other for the sake of his career, he couldn't bring himself to believe she would go off somewhere without even a word. Then he thought about that kiss under the ilex oak, and those precious moments in the attic . . . He did mean something to her, he knew he did. The more he thought about it, the more positive he was that she would have contacted him if she had decided to leave Reg.

As the evening drew in, he found his way to the pier, hoping against hope that she might have brought Patsy here to see the amusements. He'd planned to show the stallholders the photograph, but most of the stalls were already closed for the winter.

He sat on the seat next to an old man. He was just about to show him the photograph when an irate woman came towards them.

'Father, I've been looking for you everywhere.'

The old man looked slightly bemused. 'Do I know you?'

'It's Ivy, you daft bat,' she chided. 'Come on now. Let me take you back home.'

'I was just putting the cat out,' said the old man as she hauled him to his feet.

'Course you were,' she said, winking at John and waving her finger around in a circle next to her head.

'Have we met somewhere before?' said the old man.

Poor old chap, John thought as they walked away. Obviously gone senile and didn't have a clue where he was. And that's when the idea hit him like a thunderbolt. He'd been to the hospitals asking for her by name but perhaps Dottie didn't know who she was. Perhaps she had lost her memory.

Sylvie sucked deeply on her cigarette holder and blew the smoke high above her head. Using the tips of her fingers in her still gloved hand, she moved a plate stained with dried egg on the top of another caked with the remains of a gravy-soaked dinner.

She had never seen Dottie's kitchen look like this before. In fact, it was a complete mess. The whole table was piled high with the debris of several days' washing up, the ashtray overflowed with dog ends and there were newspapers everywhere.

When he'd shown her in, Reg had to move a couple of very unsavoury-looking shirts from the chair on which she was now sitting. She shivered. The fire was barely alight and she could see it badly needed to be raked out and the ash pan emptied. She looked around, trying to gauge if there was some clue, something that might explain the state of her friend's mind, but she'd drawn a blank. Dottie had been gone five days and already he had reduced her neat-as-a-pin home into a tip.

Reg was in the scullery, preparing her some tea. She'd been surprised when he'd invited her inside. She'd arrived unannounced and, because there was no love lost between them, she'd expected a doorstep conversation, probably peppered with abuse.

But when he'd opened the door, his expression was more of sadness than surprise and he seemed only too glad for someone to talk to.

His first question surprised her. 'Is Dottie with you?'

As Sylvie shook her head, he'd turned away like a whipped dog, giving her the second surprise.

He'd been polite, throwing the shirts onto the easy chair next to the fireplace and holding the back of the kitchen chair as she lowered herself onto it. It had been years since she'd seen him being considerate and, for a brief minute, the old Reg was back. She remembered that it was his attentive and caring manner which had impressed Dottie so much. Back in 1942, most of the other boys used to horse around and the chaps in uniform, who were usually the worse for drink, wanted a final fling before going overseas; but Reg, for all his lack of education, had been a real gentleman. Flowers for Aunt Bessie, compliments and other considerations for Dottie, they had all added up to a very attractive package.

Sylvie had wanted to motor down to Worthing as soon as Mary telephoned but it wasn't as easy as that. First, she and Robin had an important dinner party with the bank manager, and then she had to arrange for her three-times-weekly woman to come in daily so that Robin would be well looked after while she was away.

327

When she finally got here, nobody knew what to do, but they all felt they had to do something. She had been worried herself. Dottie had promised to ring again on Sunday but she hadn't. Had Reg attacked her again? Had something happened to Patsy? According to Mary, the police from Worthing Central had washed their hands of everything, although Kipper was doing his best to be helpful.

The women had met at the farm, sitting around the big oak table in the big farm kitchen while Edna plied them with tea and buns. As Mary, Ann and Edna unfolded the story about the well and the dead chickens, it crossed her mind that in years to come, there would a logical explanation and they would laugh about it, but right now, it didn't seem so funny.

'I think I should go and talk to him,' Sylvie had said.

They'd all protested loudly.

'That's what a concerned friend would do, isn't it?' Sylvie insisted. 'If we carry on as if everything was normal, he might let something slip.'

'Oh, Sylvie,' Mary gasped. 'You know how much he hates you.'

'I'll front it out,' said Sylvie. 'It's the only way.'

'But supposing he gets angry?' Ann whispered.

'Even if he's up to something he won't do anything to me,' Sylvie had told them. 'He wouldn't dare do anything,' she added with a grin, 'except shout a little.'

She took a long drag of her cigarette as Reg came back with two cups of tea. The saucers didn't match and he'd overfilled the cups, slopping tea into them. Sylvie moved some papers out of the way and onto the chair next to her so that he could put them down. Reg put a cup down in front of her and, apologising for the mess, scooped up the rest of the papers into a ragged bundle and dumped them onto the dresser. Sylvie pulled off her gloves.

She let him talk. He was only too eager to tell his story. The trip was to be a surprise. Dottie had found it difficult to adjust to having Patsy . . . oh, she was a good little girl but Dottie wasn't used to kids, and she found it hard to accept her.

Sylvie didn't believe a word of it but wisely she held her tongue.

They'd gone to their honeymoon hotel. She could check it out if she wanted, he'd give her the address. He'd arranged to meet Dottie downstairs in the foyer and then they were going to go out. But first, he'd popped out to buy a paper and when he got back, there was no sign of Dottie and Patsy. He'd walked right along the seafront. He'd asked everyone, but no one had seen her. She'd simply vanished. He hung his head and looked so dejected, Sylvie felt compelled, for the sake of appearing to be the concerned friend, to lay a comforting hand over his.

'You and she were close,' he said, looking up at her. 'What d'you reckon? Did she have a fancy man?'

'Of course not!' cried Sylvie indignantly. 'How can you possibly think that? You know perfectly well Dottie is utterly devoted to you.'

Reg stared at her. What was that glint in his eye? And could she see a ghost of a smile on that cruel mouth? Sylvie was about to pick up her cup when she noticed her hand was trembling. She took a long drag on her cigarette instead.

'I don't know what to do,' he said, lowering his head again, but not before she saw something playing at the corner of his mouth. There it was again. It was only a fleeting movement, a twitch of a muscle – that was all, but all at once, Sylvie realised this was a game. What should she do? Go along with it or front it out?

'You can stop play-acting, Reg,' she said coldly.

His head jerked up and he stared at her with a wounded expression.

'You don't fool me,' she said, drawing on her cigarette in an attempt to look calm and in control. 'I can tell you're up to something.'

'How can you be so cruel, Sylvie?' he protested. His voice had a catch in it. 'My dear wife has . . .'

'You forget,' she went on. 'I stayed in your house the night of Michael's wedding. I heard what you did to your 'dear wife'. I wonder what the police would say if I told them you used to rape her?' His eyes narrowed and Sylvie felt her heartbeat thumping. 'So you needn't come all that perfect marriage stuff with me.'

He rose to his feet menacingly.

'Be careful, Reg,' Sylvie went on, willing her voice to stay strong. 'At least four other people, including PC Kipling, know I'm here.'

She expected him to demand that she get out but to her surprise, Reg lowered himself back down in the chair with a smile. 'Well, my dear,' he sneered. 'I don't know what you have in mind, but I would think very carefully before you start making any wild accusations. You may not have enjoyed listening to our robust lovemaking, but what a man and his wife get up to in the privacy of their own bedroom is nobody else's business but theirs.'

'It doesn't give you the right to force her.'

'I think you will find, that in the eyes of the law, I have every right,' he said silkily. 'Dottie is my wife.'

'You make me sick,' Sylvie retorted.

'But *I* believe in the sanctity of marriage,' he went on piously. 'Now, if I were to go outside of the bounds of my marriage, that would be a different kettle of fish, so to speak.'

He was staring at her in such a strange way, Sylvie could feel her colour rising. 'And what's that supposed to mean?' she snapped.

'If I were to have *a little fling* . . .' Reg said quietly. 'Just a bit of *fun*, you understand . . .'

Sylvie went cold all over. He knew about Bruce! Had Dottie told him? No, no she would never betray a trust. But how else did he know? She stubbed out her cigarette and picked up her gloves. 'I don't have to listen to all this . . .'

'And if someone, say an old friend, discovered what I was doing,' said Reg leaning into her face, 'it might be a real problem, if say, my spouse was hoping to be a Member of Parliament one day.'

'I haven't the faintest idea what you are talking about,' she said haughtily.

Reg leaned forward, his eyes glittering. 'It never did take much to get your knickers off, did it, Sylvie?'

'You are despicable,' she snapped, her lip curling with disgust.

'Now, now, my dear.'

Sylvie picked up her cigarette case and slipped it into her bag. 'Is this an attempt to blackmail me?'

'Perish the thought,' he said brightly. 'I was just supposing, that's all. A friendly warning to be careful what you say outside these four walls.'

'I don't give a stuff about you, Reg Cox,' Sylvie snapped. 'My friend is missing and I'm going to find her.'

'I wonder if Robin would be so cavalier about his marriage?' Reg mused.

As she turned to leave the room, her arm brushed against the dresser and the papers he'd thrown so carelessly on the top cascaded to the floor. As Reg bent to pick them up, Sylvie felt the blood drain from her head but she said nothing. As he opened the door to let her out, she willed her legs to move effortlessly and refused to even look at him.

'Thanks for coming, Sylvie,' he called after her. 'As soon as I hear something, I'll give you a call.'

Climbing into her car, her hand was trembling as she turned the key in the ignition. Bastard, bastard! What a hateful little prick he was. Tears were welling up in her eyes. He thought he had her over a barrel. He reckoned that she wouldn't dare to say anything because if she told the police about her fears, he would

331

tell Robin about Bruce. Well, that was a risk she would have to take. She dare not risk her affair coming out into the open, but how could she turn her back on her dearest friend? Something bad had happened to Dottie, she knew it. Those papers she'd knocked to the floor told her Reg had been going over his life policies and you only do that when you are positive that someone is dead.

Dottie moaned as the feelings came back again. Were they real or just a dream? The first time it felt as if it was real, but everything kept repeating itself.

It began with torchlight as the door had been eased open. Dottie felt a stream of cold air and a beam of light was played on her face. She had screwed up her eyes and tried to turn her head away.

'No, Ada!' a man's voice had yelled. 'For God's sake, don't switch on the light. You'll blow us all to kingdom come. Open the window and get some air in here.'

Dottie had heard the sound of someone drawing back the curtains.

'It's all right, dear.' The man's voice was close to her head.

The woman screamed. 'The window, it's nailed shut!'

There was a rushing sound in her ears and the man's voice faded away but there was no mistaking the urgency. 'Quick, get them out of here.'

'You're safe now,' said the soothing voice close to her ear. Not the man this time but a woman and Dottie realized she was actually in a bed. She tried to make sense of it all. How had she got from the room where Reg had left her to this one? She remembered being manhandled at one point. Someone had hold of her shoulders and someone else her feet. The rocking movement as they carried her turned her stomach. She had heaved and vomited. It tasted of gas and hit the floor with a light splashing sound. She remembered the sound of opening doors and then the cold air hit her and she knew she was outside. Somewhere in the distance, she could hear the sea. She remembered taking in great gulps of fresh air which was so sweet but it made her head hurt.

But she wasn't outside now, she was in the warm and in bed. There was something over her mouth. She lifted her hand and pulled it away. 'Patsy . . .' she moaned. 'Have you got Patsy?'

The woman's voice came close again. 'Keep the mask on, dear. It's oxygen. It'll help you breathe.'

She must be in hospital, but how had she got here? When she'd heard the sea, she'd tried to sit up but someone pushed her down and placed a blanket over her. 'Stay there a minute, duck,' the man had said kindly. 'The ambulance is coming.'

She had difficulty in keeping her eyes open. They felt puffy and when she did manage to force her lids up, everything looked foggy. Someone wiped her face with a cloth and she heaved again. When she rolled back she had a terrible cramp in her stomach, a pain which gripped her like a vice. She had held herself around her middle murmuring, 'Help me . . . Oh please, help me.'

Things began to fade again. She forced herself back to the present day and tried to remember. What was next? A bell. She had heard the sound of a bell getting louder and louder.

'The ambulance is here,' the man had said and Dottie had felt the relief flooding over her like giant waves. She had tried to focus her eyes on him. He was old. Who was he? Did she know him? Oh yes, he was the man she'd seen in the garden next door.

The next time she opened her eyes, a man in a uniform was holding her wrist. 'I'm just taking your pulse, love.'

Where was Patsy?

The pain in her stomach came back. She groaned as it gripped every muscle.

'What's your name, dear?'

Dottie had tried to moisten her lips with her swollen tongue.

What was her name . . .? She tried to think. What was her name? She must have one: everybody had a name. It was on the tip of her tongue but she was hanged if she could remember what it was and, oh no, the pain was coming back again.

'My baby . . .' Dottie had moaned.

'My colleague is seeing to her,' the ambulance man had said. 'Don't worry, we'll get the both of you to hospital as soon as we can.'

A moment later, Dottie felt herself being lifted then the ambulance lurched as the men jumped out. It lurched again as they came back in with another stretcher.

Patsy . . . Dottie tried to sit up. Was she all right? As soon as she'd smelled the gas, she'd tried to get her out but Patsy didn't want to move. She was so heavy and then when she got to the door it was locked. She couldn't open it. She tried and tried to turn off the gas tap but it was too badly damaged. Someone had bashed it with something. As she had struggled to remember what had happened, a picture of Reg, his pockets full of squawking chickens, and brandishing a huge hammer floated before her eyes.

The woman had stuck her head into the ambulance and shouted, 'You stupid cow!' Dottie's head had thumped and a wave of sickness had swept over her.

The woman's face was distorted with anger. 'You might want to do away with yourself,' she'd screamed at Dottie. 'But there was no need to try and take the kiddie with you!'

'I didn't,' Dottie croaked. 'Oh please, please help her.'

But instead of helping Patsy, the person beside her bed slowly turned into Reg. Dottie's mouth tasted disgusting and everything was getting swimmy again. Reg was wringing Patsy's neck.

'No, no . . .' Dottie felt so cold and clammy and she knew she was going to be sick. Reg had the tramp under his arm. With a cry of anguish Dottie flailed her arms in a vain attempt to stop him wringing his neck too. She came to for a moment and found herself back in the bed. Not the one in the bungalow. Everything around her was white and clean. 'Thank God,' she thought. 'I really am in hospital.'

'We'd better give her another shot, nurse,' said an unfamiliar male voice.

A second or two later, Dottie felt herself being gently held down. 'A sharp prick,' said the nurse, and everything went in on itself again.

# Forty

'As a matter of fact, we do have someone fitting that description,' the ward sister told John. 'Is she a patient of yours? She's in a state of deep shock. We had to sedate her. She still hasn't told us her name.'

John felt a mixture of relief and concern. 'What happened to her?'

'She'd tried to kill herself.'

'Kill herself!' He couldn't disguise his shock.

'She was admitted late Monday night.'

John frowned. She'd been here two days.

A nurse burst out of a side room and rushed towards them at breakneck speed with a trolley. John stepped neatly out of her way.

'Walk, Nurse,' the sister said sharply. 'Walk.'

'Yes, Sister. Sorry, Sister.'

'The police want to interview her once she's well enough,' the Sister continued as she walked on in front of him. 'In my humble opinion they should do something to change the law. When someone is distressed enough to attempt suicide, the last thing they want is to end up in jail.'

'The woman I'm looking for had a child with her.' John's throat was thight and his voice sounded strangled. He coughed into his hand. 'Is she here in this hospital too?'

The sister stopped walking and turned around.

'A little girl,' John continued. 'About eight, dark curly hair, brown eyes, light brown skin, very pretty.'

'In that case, Dr Landers,' she said quietly. 'I think you must prepare yourself for another shock . . .'

Dottie was lying flat in the bed with her eyes closed. Her hair was down. It lay like burnished bronze clouds all over the pillow. He'd often wondered what it would look like out of that bun of hers, but even in his wildest dreams he'd never expected it to be so beautiful. It was as much as he could do not to reach out and caress one of her curls between his fingers, but he was aware that the sister was still right behind him and still watching. Dottie looked so small, so fragile. Her skin was pale, like parchment, her hands limp by her side. Thank God she was alive . . . It was as much as John could do to control his emotions.

'I think I would like to sit here with her for bit.' He drew up a chair. Several times his mouth formed a word. 'Hello?' 'Mrs Cox' 'Dorothy' but he couldn't bring himself to speak.

'You said she was a patient?' the sister said.

John cleared his throat noisily. 'Actually, Sister, you said that. Mrs Cox . . . Dottie . . . is a friend.'

'Oh, I'm sorry,' said the sister. She seemed slightly embarrassed. 'I think I'd better tell her doctor you are here,' she said, bustling out of the room.

As he touched her hand, his heart ached for her. My poor Dottie . . . what you've been through. He leaned forward. 'Dottie . . . Dottie, it's me. John.'

Dottie opened her eyes and her heart lurched. *Oh John . . . you've come at last* . . . She gave him the faintest of smiles but one look at his anxious expression and it all came flooding back. She didn't want to think about it. Patsy . . . Patsy was in the same ambulance as her. She remembered that awful smell, the smell of rotten eggs, then someone banging the door and Patsy lying on the floor. What happened? Why couldn't she get out?

337

John was talking softly to her. His voice was soothing but she couldn't grasp what he was saying . . . no wonder. His body looked just the same but he had a chicken head. As she closed her eyes there was a rushing sound in her ears and Reg was standing at the end of the bed with a bag under one arm and a hammer in his hand. She could hear someone calling her name . . . 'Dottie, Dottie . . .' but when she tried to move she was afraid of treading on the chickens. The pain was back too. A gripping pain which left her breathless. Then Reg came towards her and she cried out, 'No, Reg, no!' but she could feel him tugging at her arms and pinning her down and everything fell away once more.

The pips went and John pressed button B. 'PC Kipling?'

'Yes?'

'John Landers. I wonder if I could meet you for a chat. It's about Mrs Cox and Patsy. I think there is far more to this than meets the eye.'

'What makes you say that, sir?'

'I've found Dottie. I've been with her all afternoon. She's in hospital, very ill and somewhat confused. Patsy has been taken to the children's hospital but I haven't seen her yet.' John heard the policeman take in his breath. 'I shall be on my way back to the village shortly and I should appreciate it if I could be present when you tell Mr Cox.'

When Dottie opened her eyes again, John was asleep in the chair beside the bed. Dottie watched the rise and fall of his chest for some time. His hand was on top of hers and as she stirred, so did he.

'Dottie . . .' he said, sitting up.

Her eyes were filling with tears again. Why was she so emotional all the time? What was she going to say to him? He'd entrusted her with Patsy and she'd let him down. She'd tried to shut it out since she came here. She wouldn't even tell them her name, but she'd have to face it now. She'd have to find out . . .

'I'm sorry about Patsy . . .' She croaked.

He took her hand and squeezed it gently.

She tried to lick her lips but they felt as big as bricks. Sensing her need, he picked up a glass of water at her bedside and raised her head with his hand. The water tasted strange. Metallic. Everything still tasted of gas; but at least the liquid was cold and she could feel it trickling down her parched throat. He eased her head back down onto the pillow. 'I – I don't remember what happened.'

'It's better if you get some rest now. We'll talk about it later.'

There was something in her arm. She moved it slightly and then realised she was attached to a blood drip. Why were they giving her blood?

She smiled at John. 'Reg took me to see a bungalow.'

'Reg was with you?'

A picture of a dark and stuffy room filled with gas came into her mind. Her eyes grew wider. 'They got Patsy and me out, but I didn't even think about Reg. Is he all right?' She tried to sit up, pulling at the sheets with light fluttery movements.

'Stay calm,' John said, his hand firmly against her shoulder. 'Don't get so agitated. Reg is fine. He's back home.'

'Back home?' Dottie fell back against the pillow and closed her eyes. Her befuddled brain was trying to understand.

'Don't talk about it now,' he said gently. 'Give yourself a little chance to recover.'

'But I need to know what happened.'

There was a long pause and then he said, 'They tell me you tried to commit suicide with Patsy.'

'*What*? But that's not true!' cried Dottie, her fingers screwing the sheets into a tight ball. 'I promise you on my mother's life it's not true. I don't want to die. Not now.' Her voice trailed and she turned her head away despairingly. 'Why would they think I would try to do a thing like that? I couldn't. I wouldn't.'

'It's all right,' said John, gripping her hand.

Dottie looked back at him, her eyes swimming with tears. 'Everybody keeps telling me it's all right but they won't tell me anything. I know Patsy came with me in the ambulance, but I haven't seen her yet. Where is she? Please take me to her, John.'

'Dottie . . . you must try and stay calm.'

Her hand flew to her mouth. Patsy was dead, wasn't she? That was why no one was telling her. She'd guessed she was very poorly when they put her in the ambulance but no matter how many times she'd asked, no one would actually tell her. A heaviness settled on her chest, a crushing ache that seemed to suck the life from her. She opened her mouth and at the same time her throat closed, yet somewhere in the room, she could hear a heart-rending howl, a cry that sounded like a wounded animal. It seemed to go on and on until she heard the sister running.

The portly gent pressed a coin into Reg's hand and gave him a curt nod. Reg touched the edge of his cap and thanked him. Tight-fisted git. He must have a bob or two if he could afford to travel first class and the case he'd just lugged out to the waiting taxi weighed a bloomin' ton, yet judging by the size of the coin as he turned it over in his hand, he had only given him a measly tanner for a tip. Reg hurried back onto the platform and slammed the train door.

'Is this the Portsmouth train?'

Don't people ever read the bloody boards, he thought acidly. He spent long enough writing out all the names of the stations. Irritated, Reg turned in the direction of the voice, intending to be rude, but he was pleasantly surprised by the owner, an attractive blonde, no more than twenty-five, with an hourglass figure and an alluring expression who was gazing up at him expectantly.

'It certainly is, Miss,' said Reg, pausing to open the door again.

She didn't acknowledge him again but as he closed the door, he was left standing in a waft of expensive perfume. One day when he'd got the money from the sale of the cottage he'd get himself a woman like that.

'Mind the doors.' The guard blew his whistle and the train gathered steam before it thundered away.

'Reg.' Kipper was standing at his elbow and he had Dr Landers with him. 'Could you step this way for a moment?'

'I was just about to . . .'

'It's all right, Reg,' said Kipper gently. 'Marney will see to your duties.'

He could see Marney, his head down, hurrying along the platform.

Kipper was wearing that serious but sympathetic express of his. The same one he wore when Marjorie Thompson's husband came to see where she'd jumped in front of the Bournemouth express.

Ah, thought Reg, they'd found the bodies at last. About time too. It had taken longer than he'd thought. He hoped they didn't expect him to identify them. They'd look pretty grim after being shut up in that stuffy atmosphere for a couple of days. What if the place had rats? He braced himself as he followed the two men into the station master's office. He knew he'd have to make this look good but he was confident he'd be fantastic. He'd practised it enough times. That was where so many people slipped up. They didn't practise receiving the bad news.

He'd been brilliant when they'd found that old cow Bessie. He should have been on the bloody stage. Walking into the office, he was surprised to see that they'd arranged three chairs in a semi-circle. He sat in the chair Kipper indicated to him and John Landers closed the door.

Outside, they could hear Marney calling, 'The train approaching platform two is the 9.16 to London Victoria, calling at . . .'

Reg glanced at the station master. He sat behind his desk,

his eyes lowered and his hands on the desktop, the fingers tightly laced. Kipper positioned himself behind a chair, gripping the back. Everyone waited until John sat down.

'What is this?' Reg asked nervously. This was all a bit more formal than he'd expected. Perhaps they weren't going to tell him they'd found Dottie and Patsy after all. Had they rumbled that he'd been tampering with the mail? Perhaps he'd been too greedy. After all, they had reported rather a lot of damaged bags in the past year.

'It's your wife and daughter,' said Kipper gravely.

Reg widened his eyes the way he thought a concerned husband would.

'We've found them,' Kipper went on. 'They were in an old bungalow . . .'

'A bungalow? Whose bungalow? What were they doing there?'

'We don't know yet,' said Kipper.

Reg looked away. Damn. He was so nervous he'd asked the wrong question. That was question two. He went back to the plan. 'Are they all right?' He tried to sound anxious, doing his best to make it look as if he could hardly bear to hear the answer.

'I'm afraid . . .' Kipper began.

'Oh, no, no . . .' Reg moaned. 'Are you sure . . .?'

'The neighbours called an ambulance. It took a while to come. It's a bit isolated.'

Reg leaned back in his chair, his eyes closed. He didn't see Kipper open his mouth to say something more and John gripping his arm to silence him, but he did hear the station master's chair scraping back and then one of the cupboard doors opened. Good. He was getting the brandy out. Only cheap stuff but brandy all the same. They had to help him hold the cup because he was trembling too much to manage on his own.

'What happened?' Reg choked.

'They were gassed,' said John.

'She gassed herself,' Kipper corrected.

'You don't know that,' said John. 'It could have been an accident.'

Reg looked up sharply. 'She meant to do it,' he said coldly. 'She wrote a note. I gave it to you, didn't I, Mr Kipling? She said she was going to do it.'

'Yes, yes,' said Kipper. 'And that will be part of the evidence.'

Reg relaxed but as he caught John's eye, he leaned forward, holding his head in his hands. 'What happened, Mr Kipling?'

'Oh my poor little girl,' Reg moaned when Kipper had finished telling him. 'Poor Dottie. How am I going to live without them, Mr Kipling?' He began to weep. 'Why did she do it? All locked up like that. If she'd only told me how she was feeling, I could have helped her.'

'There's still time,' said John.

Reg lifted his tear-stained face and gave him a quizzical look. 'Time? Time for what?'

'You can go and see them for yourself, Reg,' said the station master. 'Under the circumstances the railway will give you some compassionate leave.'

'They're both in hospital,' said John. 'Dottie is still quite ill, but Patsy is making a good recovery.'

John watched the colour drain from Reg's face and noticed that he had developed a nervous tic under his left eye.

'Don't you understand, Reg?' Kipper said. 'It's good news.'

'Oh yes,' said Reg, downing the rest of the brandy and turning the glass in his hands. 'Really good news. It couldn't be bloody better.'

# Forty-One

Kipper got the call just before he was going off duty. Sinking fast, they said. He went straight to the hospital.

Ernest Franks rallied slightly as Kipper walked in the door.

'Got to tell you . . .' he gasped, 'before it's too late.'

Kipper went to the bedside and Ernest grabbed at his coat. 'Danny . . . he must have taken . . .' Ernest sank back on the pillow, his eyes wild.

'Take your time, sir,' said Kipper gently.

The man's breath was coming in short pants after his exertions. 'Bomb site . . . Reg Cox . . .'

'The real Reg Cox was found on a bombsite,' said Kipper. Ernest nodded. 'And Danny Sinclair took his identity?'

Ernest nodded again.

'Tell me,' said Kipper. 'Was Reg Cox a coloured man?'

Ernest nodded. 'Jamaican.'

Kipper patted Ernest's arm.

'He left him to die,' said Ernest. 'He could have helped him, but he didn't.'

'How do you know all this?' said Kipper.

Ernest took a deep breath and sighed his last word on earth. 'Military . . .'

Although Christmas was still weeks away, Billy's mum had let him go carol singing but his heart wasn't in it. The grown-ups had been getting together in little huddles for a couple of weeks. More than once, he'd heard his mum whispering, 'Shh, keep your voice down. Let's keep the children out of it,' but they weren't stupid. All of them knew something bad had happened to Auntie Dottie and Patsy. Even little Christopher was unsettled. He spent nearly all the time sucking his thumb and twiddling his hair. His dad always got cross when Christopher did that. He said he might be only four but it wasn't manly . . . but just lately he hadn't said anything to Christopher.

Billy and his mates Paul Dore and Dennis Long had walked right round the village and he was getting tired. They'd quickly realised that if they just sang outside a house, no one answered the door, but if they knocked first and sang as soon as the door opened, they'd get some money. His dad had given him the old oil lantern so that they looked more Christmassy and occasionally people kept the door open and listened. They weren't so keen on that because you'd feel a right twit singing your head off with everybody looking at you with goo-goo smiles. But they'd made quite a bit of money.

Billy's walk slowed to a crawl as his mates ran ahead. They were heading for Auntie Dottie's road. He'd never tell his mates of course, but he really missed Patsy. She was good fun . . . for a girl.

Maureen missed her as well. She kept on and on, asking where Patsy was but no one would give her a straight answer. In the end, it drove his mum nuts so she said Patsy had gone to a new home. Maureen was upset but not as upset as she would have been if she'd understood what that meant. Billy knew and he was gutted.

Paul Dore came running back. 'Hurry up, Billy,' he shouted.

Billy's heart did a cartwheel inside his chest as Dennis came up behind Paul, staggering under the weight of a pile of clothes.

'Look at this lot,' he cried. A jumper slid from the pile and unintentionally, he trod all over it. Billy recognised it at once.

345

It was Patsy's jumper. She didn't like it much but it was the one Auntie Dottie had knitted with the kangaroo on the front. His eye gravitated to the rest of the pile. There was Patsy's red coat and Auntie Dottie's pink hat, the one she wore at Michael's wedding. With an agonised roar, Billy charged up the road towards Auntie Dottie's gate.

Holding up the lantern he could see a large pile of clothing beside the dustbin. When he lifted the lid of the bin he found Auntie Dottie's sewing box and some material with pins in it. At the foot of the mound were two suitcases as well. The smaller one had a photo album in it and the other had loads of photo frames complete with pictures. Auntie Dottie and Auntie Sylvie, together with the old lady who used to live in Myrtle Cottage, smiled up at him from the top.

'Stay there!' Billy barked. 'Don't nobody touch it.'

'Where are you going?' cried Paul as he ran back down the road.

'Just stay there!'

Billy charged back to the house. The old pram stood in the doorway. He could hear his mother in the kitchen talking to Aunt Peaches. Billy emptied out the bedding and backed it towards the door.

Christopher appeared at the top of the stairs. 'Where are you going, Billy?'

Billy put his finger to his lips and manoeuvred the pram out of the front door. As the door closed, he ran like the wind back to Myrtle Cottage.

The three boys set about loading up the pram, then Billy pushed it back while Paul and Dennis took it in turns to carry the big suitcase.

'This thing is too heavy,' Paul protested. 'And we might drop the photo frames. They've got glass in them.'

'We're taking the lot,' said Billy fiercely.

The overloaded pram kept shedding articles of clothing but

Billy wouldn't let anything stay in the road. He shouted at them tetchily to 'pick 'em up,' his face heavily flushed. His two friends couldn't really understand why he was in such an odd mood.

'I thought we were going carol singing,' cried Dennis. 'If my dad sees me with this lot, he'll go mad.'

Billy glared at him. 'We can't leave it.'

'What d'you want it for?' asked Paul. 'This is all rubbish. They chucked it out.'

Billy rounded on him. 'All this stuff this belongs to Patsy.'

'Patsy . . .' Dennis pointed his finger at him and laughed. 'He's in love!'

'You shut up, Dennis Long,' shouted Billy, his eyes glistening with tears.

Paul pulled a woman's cardigan from under the pile. 'Well, this ain't Patsy's.'

'It's my Auntie Dottie's and she's coming home soon,' said Billy snatching it back.

Paul and Dennis exchanged an anxious look. 'Bet she don't,' said Dennis, 'my dad says she's a murderer. She tried to kill Patsy.'

'That's not true!' cried Billy. He launched himself at Dennis, throwing him to the ground and wrong-footing Paul at the same time. In the scrap that followed, it seemed to Dennis and Paul that Billy had the strength of ten men. Although it was two against one, Billy won easily. Twenty minutes later, hot and sweaty, and struggling to control his emotions, Billy pushed the pram into his dad's shed at the bottom of the garden. He cleared a space on the top of the workbench and began pulling at the untidy bundle. His shoulders shook as he folded each item carefully and placed them neatly on top of one another. It took him ages. That was because every now and then, he had to stop and wipe his nose on the cuff of his sleeve.

\*　\*　\*

347

'Sylvie, they've been found!' Mary couldn't contain her excitement.

On the other end of the telephone, Sylvie gasped. At first she was relieved that Dottie was alive but she listened with mounting horror as Mary told her what had happened.

'The bad news is,' Mary concluded. 'Dottie has lost her baby.'

'Baby?' Sylvie gasped. 'What baby?'

'Oh!' said Mary. 'Perhaps I shouldn't have said anything. I thought you knew.'

'She and Reg . . .?'

'Yes,' said Mary. 'I tried to talk her out of it, but she was determined to keep it. Anyway, now she's lost it.'

There was a slight pause.

'In one way, I can't say I'm sorry,' said Sylvie. 'That Reg is an absolute pig, but knowing how much Dottie wanted children, I should imagine she's devastated.'

'I'm sure she is.'

'Haven't you seen her then?'

'She's not allowed visitors. She's been haemorrhaging badly and they're giving her blood.'

'How awful.'

The two women struggled to contain their emotions.

'And Patsy?'

'She's still quite ill. Some sort of poisoning. They've got her in the children's ward. No visitors.'

'Let me know when we can go,' said Sylvie. 'And I'll take you over to see Dottie.'

'I bet that blinking Reg had something to do with this,' said Mary, darkly. Sylvie wouldn't be drawn but as she hung up she pondered Mary's words. When she'd last seen him, Reg was so sure Dottie was dead, he was even looking over his life policies. She shook her head in disbelief. Reg was a nasty piece of work, all right. He was capable of terrible things – but stooping as far as attempted murder? That was a different league altogether.

\* \* \*

Dottie looked around the room, willing her mind to think about something less painful. She felt a bit woozy, probably from that stuff they had injected into her arm. The blood drip was gone. The room was stark, the walls bare. The locker beside her bed was empty apart from a jug and a glass of water. There were some screens in the corner and the material was faded. They must have left it in the sun. Her mind drifted back to that cold sunny day on Highdown Hill. In her head she could hear Minnie barking and Patsy was laughing and happy as she ran up to the chalk pits . . . Oh, Patsy . . .

John was there again. Neither of them spoke, but he held her hand and gently kissed her fingers.

'Reg took us to see that bungalow in the car,' Dottie said eventually. 'He wanted me to buy it. It was horrible. So bleak and it was miles from anywhere. There were roses on the wall but inside it was old and smelly . . .' She was beginning to gabble. 'I didn't like it at all but we had a picnic in one of the rooms. It wasn't as much fun as the one we had on Highdown, but Reg was trying so hard and Patsy had egg sandwiches and . . .'

Something was beginning to niggle John, something he couldn't quite put his finger on. Dottie turned her face away and began to cry again. John held onto her hand, stroking it with his thumb. Suddenly aware, she pulled her hand away.

'John, I'm sorry,' she said. 'I've tried writing but it seems cowardly. I want to tell you face to face. I'm having a baby.'

She could feel a tear running across the bridge of her nose. Every part of her body wanted to say yes but she thought too much of him to let him ruin his whole life and reputation for her and the baby. The gossips would put two and two together and make five in no time.

'Listen, Dottie,' he said lowering his eyes. 'You need to know something –'

All at once, her eyes grew wide. 'My baby? Is my baby all right? I had bad pains. I am still pregnant, aren't I?'

John gripped her hand even more tightly. She couldn't believe it when he started shaking his head slowly. 'I'm terribly, terribly sorry. They did all they could but you'd been starved of oxygen for so long . . .'

'No!' Dottie stared at him helplessly. She'd lost the baby? She wasn't going to be a mother? 'No, no, you've got it all wrong.' Her other hand flew to her stomach and she pressed the flesh. It still felt a bit round but then she felt the sanitary belt around her waist and the bunny between her legs. 'My baby . . .'

John stroked her forehead. 'There will be other babies,' he said softly.

'No,' she moaned. 'I want *my* baby.' She turned her head away. First Patsy and then this . . . 'I can't bear it.'

John seemed to be fighting to control his own emotions.

'And Reg?'

'Reg knows.'

'I hate him.' Her voice was barely more than a whisper and her face crumpled as she searched in vain for a dry area of her handkerchief. 'Have you seen poor Patsy yet?'

'Not yet.' He fished around in his pockets and found a clean handkerchief.

She took it gratefully and blew her nose. 'I pushed her face by the gap under the door,' Dottie went on. 'I thought the air . . . fresh air . . .' she paused, taking in a huge racking breath, 'but I couldn't stop the gas. I did try and save her . . .' Her voice had risen to a squeak and now she was sobbing again.

He frowned. According to the sister, the police believed that Dottie had locked herself and Patsy into the bedroom and as soon as Patsy was asleep turned on the gas taps. At some point, Patsy had crawled out of bed and collapsed by the door, her face by the gap in a desperate attempt to get some fresh air. Dottie was found lying on the floor halfway between the bed and the door.

'I don't think you should try and say any more,' he said softly.

'I'm going to tell the sister to call the police. You must tell them everything you know.'

'No, no. I can't, I can't talk to the police.'

'Dottie, you have to,' he said. 'Listen. You're a strong woman and if you really care about Patsy, you must help them find out what happened to her.'

'*If* I really care?' she said bitterly. 'Surely you of all people must know how much I love her.'

'I'm sorry, I didn't mean it to sound like that,' said John. 'But you need to persuade the police that you meant her no harm.'

'You will stay with me, won't you?'

He hesitated. How would that look for her case? Would it be such a good idea?

'Please, John,' she begged. 'I need a friendly face with me when I talk to the police. It's the last thing I'll ever ask of you.'

At last he understood. She wanted him there professionally. He was a doctor. She needed his moral support. If that was so, how could he refuse?

# Forty-Two

'May I remind you that you are here purely as an observer, Dr Landers,' the sergeant said. 'Any interruptions and I shall ask you to leave.'

Dottie had been in hospital five days but today was the first day she was deemed well enough to be questioned. John stood with his back to the window, grim-faced as two policemen, Sergeant Smart and PC Connelly, sat on either side of Dottie's bed, their notebooks at the ready. Dottie, red-eyed and still very tearful, was telling them what had happened.

'Reg wanted to buy a bungalow.'

'On The Crumbles.'

'Yes, but when we got there, it wasn't very nice. It had been empty for ages. Apparently the owner had gone into a nursing home. Reg said he wanted us to run it as a guesthouse but there wasn't much room. I mean, we couldn't have many guests.'

'So you didn't like it,' said the sergeant. 'What happened next?'

'Reg brought a picnic,' Dottie went on. 'He made it quite fun. We had Smith's crisps, fig-roll biscuits and sandwiches. He put it all on a big sheet and we sat in the sitting room.'

'You all ate the same thing?'

'Yes. Patsy and I drank the tea from a flask. Reg had a beer but apart from that we all had the same.'

'Go on.'

Dottie shrugged. 'Then Patsy felt tired and Reg suggested she lie down on the bed for a while. I wasn't feeling so bright myself, so I lay down beside her. It wasn't very pleasant. I mean, the sheet smelled and the room was cold.'

'You say you didn't feel so bright?'

'My head felt funny and my mouth was very dry,' said Dottie. 'Anyway, I must have drifted off to sleep, and when I woke up I could smell gas. I tried to turn the tap off but someone had smashed it up.'

'Who?'

'I don't know! It was all right when I turned it on.'

'*You* turned the tap on?'

'Yes, of course I did,' cried Dottie.

The sergeant looked at his constable who was desperately trying to sharpen his pencil and handed him his fountain pen. 'Make a note of that, Constable. Mrs Cox turned on the gas tap.'

'The electricity was off so I put the fire on,' said Dottie. 'The room was cold.'

'When you woke up,' said John, 'was the fire still on?'

'Dr Landers!' said the sergeant reprovingly.

'No!' cried Dottie. 'The fire was out but the gas was still on.'

There was some shifting of feet and then the sergeant said, 'Go on.'

'The window was all boarded up and the door was locked. We were trapped. I couldn't get out . . . I couldn't . . .'

Dottie blew her nose and wiped her eyes. John smiled encouragingly at her.

'Did you shout for help?'

'The gas made me feel so sick, I was trying not to breathe,' she said. 'I dragged Patsy over to the door and pressed her face by the gap. Then I tried to break the wood over the window.' She held up her hands and showed them her broken nails. 'And then the gas just stopped.'

'Stopped?'

'I don't know why but it just stopped.'

'The only thing that saved you, apart from the neighbours smelling the gas, was the fact that the gas meter had run out of money,' said the Constable.

'I think I must have fainted.' Dottie blinked. 'The next thing I knew someone was breaking down the door.'

She told them that she didn't know where Reg was. He must have gone back to the hotel she supposed and, no, she couldn't understand why he'd left them there. Everything was fine between them and that night she was going to tell him that she was having his baby.

The thought of her beautiful baby made her break down and the three men waited for a few minutes while she sobbed uncontrollably. When she recovered herself, John gave her a glass of water, and Dottie reached out with a trembling hand for his. 'Thank you.'

John was acutely aware of the sergeant's gaze as he sat back down.

'Are you ready to continue, Mrs Cox?'

Dottie nodded.

'Mr Cox says he waited for you to come down from your bedroom that morning,' the sergeant continued, 'but you and Patsy had gone off without him.'

'That's not true,' said Dottie desperately. 'He told us to go ahead of him so we walked along the seafront.' She glanced at John. 'We didn't mind. Patsy wanted to try out her roller skates. When we got so far along, he met us with the car.'

'Car?'

'A hired car.'

'What sort of car?'

'I don't know. One looks much the same as the other to me. A black one.'

PC Connelly's fountain pen scribbled away.

'And you say you had no intention of killing yourself and the child?'

'No,' she cried, horrified. 'Of course I didn't.'

John couldn't get Reg out of his mind. He'd looked as if he was going to pass out when PC Kipling told him Dottie was still alive, but John couldn't work out why he might want to do his wife and Patsy harm. Why not simply walk away from them? Plenty of men did. Smart and Connelly probed into every part of Dottie's marriage and her relationship with Reg. Were they worried about money? Could they pay the rent each week?

'We don't have to pay rent,' she said. 'The house belonged to my aunt and she left it to me.'

Now at last, John began to understand what Reg was up to. Dottie had just given him the motive he was looking for. He put his hand up and took in his breath to say as much but one look from the sergeant silenced him immediately.

The questioning went on and on. Did she regret having Patsy? How did Reg feel about having his own baby on the way? Was it Reg's child?

Dottie was beginning to look exhausted. The circles under her eyes were growing darker than ever. John was just about to demand that they stop questioning her when the sergeant stood up.

'Thank you for your co-operation, Mrs Cox,' he said formally. 'We shall be in touch.'

Dottie was gazing somewhere into space. 'There was someone else.'

Connelly stopped by the door and turned around. 'Someone else you say? Where?'

'In the bungalow.'

'Who?'

'I don't know, but now I think about it, I feel sure Reg was talking to someone.'

'A neighbour, perhaps?'

'No, it wasn't him.'

They waited a moment or two, but Dottie shook her head. 'I can't remember.'

'We'll speak to you again as soon as we've spoken to the little girl,' said PC Smart.

Dottie sat bolt upright. 'What do you mean?' she demanded.

'We have to verify your story,' said the sergeant.

'No, no,' cried Dottie. 'What do you mean, talk to the little girl? What little girl?' Dottie's heart was beginning to pound.

'Patsy, of course,' said PC Connelly.

'You mean, she's alive?' cried Dottie. 'She's really alive? But that's wonderful.' She looked wildly from John back to the policeman. 'But why didn't you tell me? How is she? Is she going to be all right?'

John's mouth gaped. 'But I thought you knew. The sister said . . .'

'The sister wouldn't tell me anything,' Dottie cried.

'She's been very ill,' the constable said, his voice a little softer, 'but she is improving all the time.'

Dottie smiled and burst into tears. Oh wonderful, wonderful day . . . Patsy was alive. Alive and getting well. 'Is she asking after me?' she went on eagerly. 'When can I see her?'

'No, Mrs Cox, I'm afraid you can't,' said the sergeant coldly.

Dottie took in her breath. 'But why not?'

'Because I have given instructions that she's to have no visitors – not even you, Doctor.' The sergeant frowned. 'All that can wait until Connelly and I have spoken to her.'

Dottie relaxed back onto the pillows and began to laugh softly. 'But she's alive. I can't believe it. She's alive.'

'If you remember anything else, Mrs Cox,' the sergeant said as he headed for the door, 'let us know.'

'Give her my love, won't you?' Dottie called after them.

The door closed and John moved back to the bed. 'I am so sorry you didn't know.'

'It doesn't matter now,' Dottie sighed. 'Oh, isn't it wonderful? She's alive.'

'I think you'd better rest now.'

'They don't believe me about someone else being there, do they?'

John chewed his bottom lip. 'Perhaps if you could have been a little more specific . . .'

She looked up, willing him to touch her, hold her hand, stroke her hair, anything . . . but instead he picked up her chart from the foot of the bed and studied it.

'John . . .'

'Anyway, you're getting better all the time,' he said, glancing up. The coolness in his voice hurt.

The door burst open and PC Connelly came back into the room. 'Whoops-a-daisy,' he cried. 'Forgot me pen.' He smiled at Dottie and added, 'Now don't forget, if you remember anything else, just give us a shout.'

John headed towards the door with him, knowing full well that the pen had been left as an excuse to check on whether there was anything between Dottie and him. For a while he'd better keep up the pretence.

'I hope you make a full recovery, Mrs Cox,' he said stiffly.

The policeman held the door open for him to pass.

Dottie stared at the closing door, then lay back and stared at the ceiling.

Outside in the corridor, John fell into step with the two policemen.

'When do you plan to talk to Patsy?' he asked.

'As soon as we've got her father over here,' said the sergeant. 'She'll probably feel a lot safer with a relative.'

'I'm not sure that's a good idea,' said John. All three men stopped walking. 'Look,' John went on, 'I'm not one to cast aspersions, but I think Mr Cox may know more than he lets on.'

The sergeant gave him a strange look. 'And perhaps *Mrs* Cox does too, sir.'

'What's that supposed to mean?' John protested. 'You saw how pleased she was that Patsy had survived. I tell you, she loves that child.'

'Tell me, Doctor,' said the sergeant. 'How close are you and Mrs Cox?'

'We're friends, that's all,' John insisted.

'Could it be that she wanted more?' the sergeant suggested. 'Patients fall for their doctors all the time. Unrequited love is a very powerful thing.'

'It's not like that at all.' John went cold. 'And I can tell you now that you're barking up the wrong tree, Sergeant.'

'We'll see, Doctor. We'll see.'

They parted somewhere near the front entrance. On his way out, John passed a petite blonde woman carrying a large bunch of flowers.

'Excuse me,' she said exuding a waft of cheap perfume. 'Could you tell me the way to the women's ward?'

'Down the corridor, and turn left at the top of the stairs,' said John.

The woman smiled. 'Thank you. Much obliged, I'm sure.'

'Peaches!'

Dottie was walking down the ward between two nurses because she had asked to go to the toilet rather than have a bedpan.

Peaches followed them all into her room and waited until the nurses had put her back into bed. As soon as they were alone, the two friends embraced warmly.

'Oh, Peaches,' said Dottie tearfully. 'I was having a baby, but I've lost it.'

Peaches was shocked. 'Oh, Dottie, how awful.' She hesitated. 'But I didn't think you and Reg . . . No, no, I'm sorry.'

'I have never been unfaithful to Reg,' Dottie said stoutly.

Peaches squeezed her hand. 'Of course you haven't and I wouldn't suggest anything of the sort. Oh, Dottie, I'm so sorry about the baby.'

\*   \*   \*

A nurse bustled in with the tea trolley and to Dottie's delight, Peaches was allowed to have one too.

'How's Gary?'

'He's doing really well,' said Peaches, pulling up a chair and sitting down. 'He has to keep on with the exercises. Jack's much better at it than I am. Gary gets a bit cross about it and as you know, I'm not very patient, but his leg is getting stronger all the time.' As she relaxed in the chair, Dottie smiled at her friend. She was looking really good. She'd regained her figure after the baby and she'd obviously taken great care with her clothes. She was wearing a pretty tangerine twinset, a colour which suited her very well.

'I wish you could have brought Mandy with you,' sighed Dottie. 'I still haven't seen her.'

'I know, I'm sorry.'

'How did you know I was here?' Dottie asked when the nurse had gone.

'Jack,' said Peaches. 'He was doing a run to Worthing station and overheard Marney talking and, of course, you're in all the papers.'

'The papers?'

'Only no one realised it was you,' said Peaches. She held out her hand, headlining, 'Mystery woman and child in gas tragedy.'

Dottie pursed her lips.

'Oh, Dottie, I'm an idiot,' said Peaches. 'Listen to me prattling on . . . me and my big mouth. How is Patsy? Has she said anything?'

Shaking her head, Dottie reached for her handkerchief, wet from use. Peaches fished in her handbag and gave her a clean one. Dottie blew her nose. 'I'm not allowed to see her. Can you find out how she is? I'm so worried about her.'

'Of course, darling,' said Peaches. 'I'll go and see her on my way home. It's the least I can do.'

As Dottie grasped her hand in gratitude, Peaches chewed her bottom lip.

'You know something else, don't you?' said Dottie. 'Tell me, Peaches.'

'I don't like to say . . .'

'Tell me . . . please!'

Peaches lowered her head and stared at her own hands. 'The papers say you had something to do with what happened to Patsy.'

'But that's not true!' cried Dottie. 'The windows were all boarded up on the inside. I couldn't break them . . .' She was becoming agitated. 'Peaches, Reg left us there but I don't remember why. And when I smelled gas, I couldn't get us out.' She broke off and stared at Peaches wide-eyed.

'I'm sorry, Dottie. I wish I didn't have to tell you,' said Peaches gripping her hand. 'But, darling, Reg is telling everyone you did it on purpose.'

# Forty-Three

'If you ask me, they'll do her for attempted murder,' said Kipper.

'But we both know Reg Cox is lying,' said John angrily. 'Lying through his teeth.'

John had gone over and over everything again and again. There was something wrong with the story Reg was putting about but, no matter how hard he tried, it eluded him. The suspicions raised by Ernest Franks were still being checked out. The military moved very slowly.

'You may be right, Dr Landers,' said Kipper, 'but the law says, and I quote, 'If an attempted suicide failed, but killed someone else instead, by the doctrine of transferred malice, they are guilty of murder.' Nobody died in this incident, but it looks as if Dottie was responsible for what happened to Patsy.'

They were sitting in the police house in front of a roaring fire. The room itself was masculine, with none of the prettiness that comes with a feminine touch, but it was neat and tidy: a room with a place for everything and everything in its place.

John had just come back from Eastbourne and, although it was out of office hours, Kipper had invited him in to share 'a spot of whisky' after his long journey. John was pleasantly surprised to find that he liked Kipper a great deal. He was a thinker and maybe a tad slow to make judgements, but he was fair and he was candid.

'My God,' John breathed. 'You mean they'd actually do that? Accuse her of attempted murder?'

'I'm afraid so,' said Kipper. 'Look, I don't believe she's a killer any more than you do but all we've got in our favour is purely circumstantial evidence.'

'Dottie says someone tampered with the tap,' said John. 'Doesn't that prove something?'

'She could have done it herself.'

'And the boarded-up windows?'

'They'll say she planned it.'

'Surely you can't argue about the door being locked from the outside? How could she have done that?'

'The key was on the floor,' said Kipper. 'There is a theory that she locked the door and then pushed the key under the door.'

John frowned. 'Even so, you think differently.'

'I was too hasty when the well caved in,' said Kipper, knocking out his pipe against the hearth. 'I'm just a country copper, not a detective, but if I'm to get Worthing Central to take note, I'll have to have more than feeling and hearsay. I need good hard evidence. Ernest Franks knew the truth but that blow to the head scrambled his brain as well.'

John frowned. 'Ernest Franks?'

'He said that Reg was in the house the day Bessie Thornton died.'

John gasped and then smiled broadly. 'Arrest him, arrest him now!'

Kipper reached for his tobacco pouch. 'I can't. He died before I could get a signed statement and I'm not sure it would have been much use anyway, given the circumstances.'

John groaned and they lapsed into a troubled silence.

'I knew Reg was up to no good from the word go,' said John. 'I was watching his face when we told him his wife was alive in that office and it was obvious that he knew far more than he was letting on.'

'He's a slippery one, I'll grant you that, but what have we got so far?' Kipper went on. 'According to him, he was a devoted father, but she was a woman who found it hard to adjust to a fully grown child in the family . . .'

'More likely the other way around,' John retorted.

'He takes them off on holiday,' said Kipper, putting the tobacco pouch down on the table, 'and she walks out of the hotel. Hours later, she's drugged the child and gassed them both.'

'You knew she was having his baby, didn't you?'

Kipper looked away. 'I knew she was pregnant, but was it her husband's child, that's the burning question.'

'What's that supposed to mean?' John demanded.

'There's some talk that the baby was yours.'

'Mine! But that's ridiculous. Whatever gave you that idea?'

'You've been seen in the company of Mrs Cox,' said Kipper earnestly. He leaned forward in his chair. 'Often and alone.'

'I've only ever been with her when Patsy was around,' said John truthfully. 'Anyway, who saw me? Where?'

'I am not at liberty to say, but the gossip in the village is rife,' said Kipper, relaxing back in his chair. He began pushing the tobacco down in his pipe, reluctant to tell him that Gerald Gilbert and Vera Carter had come to him with stories of car rides, late-night lifts and walks along the seafront. And although Dr Fitzgerald assured him that Dottie was the soul of discretion, Mariah Fitzgerald considered that she had changed recently from a hard-working woman into a liability, and Janet Cooper was on the verge of giving her the sack. It seemed that her relationship with John Landers was the catalyst.

'Can I speak candidly?' said John.

'Please do.'

'I won't deny that I have strong feelings for Dott . . . Mrs Cox,' said John. 'But she and I have never . . . that is to say . . . She has always remained absolutely faithful to her husband.'

363

'For what it's worth,' Kipper said, striking a match. 'I believe you.'

John pressed his lips together and nodded. 'Just tell me what evidence you need to prove her innocence,' he went on, 'and I'll make sure you get it.'

'She talked about a hired car,' Kipper puffed, 'but nobody saw it, and Reg says he can't drive. And who wanted to buy that bungalow? She says he did, but the estate agent says he spoke to a woman on the telephone. Did Dottie write that suicide note? It certainly looks like her handwriting. And all that nonsense with the chickens. What was that all about? There was no way the fox got those birds, yet Reg was adamant.'

'Reg was obviously lying,' John observed.

'Precisely, and while you're on the subject, ask her again about her aunt's death.'

'Good God, you're not suggesting . . .'

'I'm not suggesting anything, Dr Landers,' said Kipper. He flicked the rest of the match into the fire and chewed the end of his pipe thoughtfully. 'And another thing, there's apparently some question about the true identity of her husband. You obviously did some checks on Mr Cox when you agreed to Patsy coming here. Did you come across anything?'

'I'm afraid we were governed by our hearts and not our heads as far as Sandy was concerned,' said John, grim-faced. 'This is really serious, isn't it?'

'Yes, Dr Landers, it is,' said Kipper. 'You and I may dismiss all this as hearsay and innuendo, but the Eastbourne police believe they have a watertight case.'

After his evening with PC Kipling, John had returned to his mother's house. The first thing next morning, he'd arrange an interview with the Eastbourne estate agent (he felt it better to talk to the man in person) and then he'd tackle finding the hire car.

* * *

Laura Landers had been devastated when he'd told her what had happened.

'I refuse to believe that that lovely girl would ever do anything to harm that child,' she'd said stoutly, 'or herself for that matter. And believe you me, I am an excellent judge of character.'

They'd reached the middle of December before they'd had their first really cold snap. There was even talk of snow coming. John and his mother were relaxing over a sherry before Sunday lunch when there was a knock at the door. Minnie, who had been stretched out before the log fire, leapt up and ran barking into the hallway. John went to open the door.

'Dr Landers?' The woman on the doorstep was elegantly dressed in a cream coat with a fur trim. 'You don't know me but I'm a friend of Dottie's. My name is Sylvie McDonald.'

John stepped back, holding the door wide open. 'Come in. Dottie has told me all about you.' As she raised her eyebrow, he laughed, adding, 'All good, I assure you.'

She walked in, peeling off her gloves, and he showed her into his mother's sitting room. The delicious smell of roast lamb pervaded the whole house and Sylvie began to feel quite peckish.

'This is my mother, Laura Landers,' he said, introducing them both. 'Mother, this is Dottie's friend, Sylvie McDonald.'

'Come in, my dear,' said Laura struggling to her feet. 'Sit down. Can I get you a sherry?'

John took Sylvie's coat. 'I'll get it, Mother.'

'I'm sorry to disturb you,' said Sylvie, patting the back of her hair, 'but I really need to talk to you.'

'If you'll excuse me,' said Laura, 'I'd better check the roast.'

'This whole thing with Dottie is driving me mad,' said Sylvie as John's mother left the room. She flung herself into a chair and crossed her elegant legs while Minnie flopped on Sylvie's foot, waiting for a stroke.

'I've been hoping it will all blow over,' said John. 'I'll be seeing

Dottie, probably tomorrow. I have to go to Eastbourne, and I'm hoping she'll be well enough to come home by then.'

'Are you aware,' she went on, 'that the Eastbourne police are planning to arrest Dottie as soon as she's well enough?'

John was conscious of his mouth dropping open. 'How can you possibly know that?'

'My husband has friends in high places.'

'Do you know the charge?'

'Attempted murder.'

'So it really has come to this.' He sank into his chair, his face ashen.

'Sadly, yes,' said Sylvie.

Laura came back from the kitchen. 'John? What's wrong?'

Sylvie explained.

'And they have enough evidence?'

Sylvie shrugged. 'It's her word against his and for some reason, the Eastbourne police seem to be more inclined to believe him. The thing is, Doctor, I should like to enlist your help.'

'We're just about to have lunch,' said Laura. 'Would you . . .?'

'Love to,' beamed Sylvie.

Laura made an extra place at the table.

'I was horrified to see the state she was in when I got to the hospital,' said Sylvie as they sat down together. 'The sister wouldn't let me in but when she'd gone off-duty, I managed to twist the staff nurse's arm. The others had to wait in the car.'

'Others?' said Laura.

'I took her friends with me, Ann Pearce, Mary Prior and Edna Gilbert,' Sylvie explained. 'They'd brought her presents and fruit. Everyone is very upset about Patsy but none of us can believe that Dottie could be in any way responsible.'

'I was just saying exactly the same thing to John,' said Laura, warming to Sylvie straightaway. 'Peas?'

'Thank you.'

366

'How did you find out where I lived?' asked John. He liked Sylvie's direct manner.

'From Mary Prior. Dottie told her all about you.'

'We don't want Reg to know where Dottie is,' said Sylvie, taking the gravy with a nod of thanks. 'So we're going to spirit her out of hospital tomorrow. She'll stay with Mary for one night and then I'll get her back home with me.'

'Is that a good idea?'

'The poor girl can't even think straight at the moment,' said Sylvie. 'What Dottie needs now is a good long rest.'

'I'm sure you're right,' said John. 'But why do you need me?'

'We need to get her a change of clothes and she's also asking for her aunt's picture,' said Sylvie. 'I rather think it's the one I gave her of me and Dottie and Aunt Bessie during the war. I had it enlarged and framed and gave it to her as a present for putting me up when Michael Gilbert got married.' Sylvie paused for a mouthful. The thing is, everything is in the cottage and since Reg is going around saying he'll have nothing more to do with Dottie, getting her stuff will be a bit awkward. The others won't go and ask for it because they're too scared of him so I have to be the one to help her. But Reg and I, well, let's say there's no love lost between us. I need to get in there, get her things and out without him knowing.' She took another mouthful of the roast lamb. 'This is absolutely delicious. I hadn't realised how hungry I was.'

'I need to talk to Reg about Patsy's future,' said John. 'I feel obliged to make sure she's in a safe place when she comes out of hospital. I'm not leaving her with someone who has made it clear from the start that he doesn't want her.'

'What will happen to Patsy now, John?' Laura asked.

John shrugged. 'If Dottie is arrested, she'll most likely end up in a children's home.'

Laura stopped eating. 'Oh, John, we can't let that happen!'

'I know, Mother.'

'Can't she come here, with us?'

'I'm afraid that wouldn't work, Mother,' said John laying his hand over hers. 'You are in no fit state . . .'

'Worse come to the worse,' said Sylvie determinedly. 'Robin and I will have her.'

John smiled at her. 'You're a good friend, Sylvie.'

They carried on eating and then John said, 'What if I take Reg to the Jolly Farmer and ply him with a few drinks while you do what you have to at Dottie's place?'

'Super!' cried Sylvie. 'Let's do it.'

Alone in her hospital room, Dottie sighed. All the details were slowly coming back to her. The woman in the kiosk and the man next door. The car ride and Patsy's roller skates. She'd left them on the back seat and during the picnic she'd decided she wanted them in the bungalow.

'You can't wear them in the house,' Dottie had said.

'But I need them, Aunt Dottie,' Patsy protested. Somehow or other, they were more than just roller skates to her. They were a connection with someone she loved.

'No,' said Reg.

'But I . . .'

'Leave them, I said!'

It was a frightening reversion back to the old Reg after a day of niceness and Patsy had hidden behind her, trembling.

'Come on, love,' Reg coaxed. 'Sit here and have a packet of crisps.'

The child did as she was told, but it had rather spoiled their picnic. Afterwards, Patsy had wanted to sleep so Dottie had suggested Reg take them back to the hotel.

'Can't,' said Reg, shaking his head. 'I've arranged to meet the bloke selling the bungalow. He's coming here in about half and hour.'

Remembering all this now made Dottie feel uncomfortable.

She climbed out of bed and stood by the window. It was dark on the street below. No one was about. A lone car went down the road. She watched it stop at the junction and turn left.

Dottie laid her hand on her stomach and for a brief moment mourned the loss of her child. Perhaps it was just as well, she thought. What sort of life would he have come to? She might even be in prison before long.

The thought of prison focused her mind again. Back in the bungalow, Reg had been very considerate. 'Why don't you have a bit of a lie down?' he had said. Something told her not to do it, but already it was irresistible. She didn't like being there. The bed wasn't very savoury and the room smelled but Reg said he'd keep the door open. 'It'll only be for a minute or two,' he'd assured her. 'Just until this bloke comes.'

She knew that Reg was counting on using her trust money, of course. Thank God Aunt Bessie had insisted that the trustees had to agree to whatever she wanted to spend. She was confident that they'd never agree to buy that dump. Reg would go mad when he found out of course, but she'd worry about that when the time came. She'd closed her eyes. Her head was spinning.

She'd heard the front door open and someone came in. Reg was talking to whoever it was in low tones and at the time something struck her as odd. It was only now that she recalled what was wrong. Reg had talked about a bloke coming to talk to him about the bungalow. The person outside the bedroom door was a woman.

She must have come into the bedroom at some point. Dottie could remember her heady perfume. Then there was a hissing sound – was that when the gas went out? And then she was aware of several sharp bangs . . . that must have been when he broke the tap. Someone shut the door. Come to think of it, she remembered hearing the key turn in the lock. He had definitely locked them both inside!

Dottie felt herself sway and she put her head against the

cold glass. How long had she been trying to make her marriage work? What a fool she had been. He'd never wanted her. He'd only wanted her money. A distant memory crept back into her brain. 'She's worth more to you dead than alive . . .'

She didn't want to even think it, let alone say it, but Reg had planned to kill her, hadn't he? Her and Patsy. He hated them both. She clenched her fists. Now that the baby was gone, he had no hold over her, none whatsoever. It was time to get a grip and get herself out of this mess.

Dottie shivered and climbed back into the bed. She may have worked it all out but she was still in trouble. He'd been trying to stitch her up and so far he'd done a pretty good job. She hugged her knees and rocked herself.

'You've been very clever, Reg,' she said bitterly. 'You've convinced just about everyone that I'm to blame. You think little mousey me will never stand up to you, don't you? I bet you're thinking, poor little Dottie, she's so weak, she'll be a right pushover. Well, I may have been a fool once, Reg, but not any more.' Dottie could feel the strength flowing back into her veins.

She sat up straight and, pulling a notepad out of the locker drawer, she began to list the pros and cons of her present position. She divided the page into two columns.

Reg had told the police he wasn't at the bungalow at all. That went in the problems column. Talk to the man walking his dog, went in the solution column. She'd chatted to him over the wall while Patsy was in the lavvy. Only a brief minute, but surely he'd remember the woman who'd given him a friendly wave. 'My husband's fetching us a picnic from the car,' she'd said.

'Funny place for a picnic, missus!' And they'd laughed. He was a nice man. With nobody else about, he'd remember her.

Find the roller skates. Patsy had left them in the back seat of the car. Reg must have hired the car from somewhere. There couldn't be that many places in Eastbourne where you could hire a car.

Then there was the woman at the kiosk. She and Patsy had stopped there for some sweets. They'd chatted. The woman's son had just been posted to Suez.

'I don't even know what we're doing in a place like that,' the woman said. 'They don't want us there.'

'We always seem to be fighting someone else's battles,' Dottie had said as she sympathised with her. They'd grumbled about the general election and wondered if Churchill wasn't a bit too old to be prime minister again and then she'd asked her if she'd seen Reg. 'Tall, with dark hair,' she'd told the woman. 'Very slim.'

The woman shook her head, so Dottie and Patsy had decided to retrace their steps back to the hotel, fearing that they'd missed Reg and he was still waiting back in the foyer. But a few minutes later, Reg had picked them up and as they'd driven back past the kiosk, the woman had waved.

Dottie smiled grimly. 'I'm going to nail you, Reg Cox. You're not going to get away with this. You may have won the battle but I'm going to win the war.'

# Forty-Four

'It's all gone!'

As Sylvie walked back through Mary's door, she threw her hands in the air in abject despair.

Mary carried on wiping her hands on her apron. 'What are you talking about?'

'I've just been over to Dottie's to get her things and I went right through the house,' cried Sylvie. 'There's not one thing that belonged to Dottie in the place. He's got rid of it all.'

'But why?' said Mary.

The two women were standing in Mary's kitchen. Mary was doing the ironing. The kitchen table was covered with an old blanket and then a piece of sheet. The iron was plugged into the light socket overhead.

'Whatever am I going to tell her?'

'I'd lend her something of mine,' said Mary, 'but she's only a slip of the thing.'

'I can give her something of mine,' said Sylvie, 'but that's not the point. He has no right to get rid of her things.' She reached for a cigarette and lit it with a trembling hand. 'I'll tell you what though . . .' Sylvie leaned forward and Mary was all ears, 'he's had another woman back there.'

'You're joking!'

'I'm not,' said Sylvie. 'There was a rubber johnny in the bathroom and a bottle of perfume on the dressing table. Pretty powerful stuff, and very expensive. Dottie would never use that.'

John Landers pushed the treble Scotch in front of Reg.

'Thanks, Doc,' said Reg with a familiarity which immediately annoyed John. He took a gulp and set down the glass. 'Ah, that's good. Goes down a treat.'

It was as much as John could do not to let his lip curl with disdain. For a man whose wife was about to be charged with attempted murder, he was far too relaxed.

John began with small talk. 'Are you going somewhere for Christmas?'

Reg shook his head. 'I'm not bothered about Christmas.'

John had spent the afternoon with PC Kipling, hoping that he might have found out something which might help Dottie. The only new development had come from the Eastbourne police. They had discovered that Patsy had been drugged before she was gassed.

'Auntie Dottie gave me some tea and it tasted funny,' Patsy had told them.

'Sleeping pills,' Kipper had explained to John. 'The bottle was still in the room.'

'How does that help Dottie?' John had asked.

'It doesn't,' Kipper had said as they left the police house together. 'The bottle belonged to Elizabeth Thornton – Aunt Bessie – which means that Dottie could have drugged Patsy herself.'

'Fingerprints?'

'Wiped clean.'

'Bit odd,' John remarked. 'I mean, if she planned to die herself, why bother?'

Kipper nodded in agreement. 'Personally I think someone else could have drugged them both but what we need is real, undisputed proof if we're going to convince anyone of her innocence.'

Now, sitting in front of Reg, John wished he could throttle the truth out of him, but he had to keep calm. 'How are you coping, Reg?' said John, bringing his thoughts back to the present.

'Bearing up,' said Reg. 'When it's all over, the trial and all, I'm leaving this bloody village. Too many bad memories.'

John nodded. 'Have you heard from Dottie?'

'Don't talk to me about that woman,' Reg spat. 'She tried to kill my Patsy.'

'How is Patsy?'

'Fine,' said Reg.

John was only too well aware that Patsy hadn't had any visitors apart from himself.

'When are you seeing her again?'

'To tell the truth,' said Reg quickly. 'I was planning to go tomorrow.'

You wouldn't know the truth if it bit you on the bum, thought John.

'Very nice, you giving me a drink and all, Doc,' smiled Reg. 'But was there something you wanted?'

'This is a bit awkward, Reg,' said John. Reg downed the rest of his drink and stared at his glass. John waved an arm at Terry.

'Fire away, Doc.'

'I think it might be a good idea to put Patsy up for adoption,' said John. 'What she needs right now is a mum and dad and a good home. I could handle all the arrangements for you, if you like. You needn't be involved at all. All you'd have to do was sign on the dotted line, so to speak.'

Reg stared ahead, unblinking. Terry placed another whisky in front of him. Reg looked up at him and then at John.

'What's the alternative?' asked Reg.

'I can't really see one, Reg,' said John. 'With a full-time job and no wife at home how would you look after Patsy? No, under the circumstances, if she wasn't adopted, Patsy would have to spend the rest of her life in a children's home.'

John saw something in the man's eye; just a flicker, but it chilled him to the bone. It was a look of triumph.

Reg picked up his glass. 'Nobody's adopting my Patsy,' he said maliciously. 'Not no-how.'

Dottie sat perfectly still, her cup of tea in her hand. She and Sylvie waited until the nurse left the ward with the tea trolley then Sylvie handed her a small bundle and Dottie climbed out of bed and padded to the toilet. She changed very quickly. As soon as the staff nurse rang the visitors' bell, Dottie emerged, looking every bit as smart as Sylvie always did.

The two women hurried down the corridor with the rest of the visitors and a while later they were both in Sylvie's car and on their way back to Worthing.

'He's probably put all my things in Aunt Bessie's room,' said Dottie when Sylvie told her all her own things were gone. 'He doesn't like going in there and he doesn't like me at the moment, so I reckon that's what he's done.'

By the time they arrived at Myrtle Cottage, it was very late in the evening.

'Do you want me to go in?' asked Sylvie drawing up outside.

Dottie shook her head. She froze as she thought she saw Reg coming towards her, pushing his bike, but it was just a piece of red cloth flapping on the post guarding the old well.

Dottie ran up the garden path and round the back of the house. She fumbled for the spare key she always kept under the mangle. It was still there but when she tried the door, it was already unlocked.

Dottie crept inside. All she had to do was grab a few things and Auntie Bessie's picture and then she'd go – but when she put on the light, she gasped in horror. Sylvie was right. The place had been stripped bare. Nothing of hers remained. All her jams and jellies, her lovely cushions and her pretty chairbacks, even they were all gone. There was a coat hanging on the nail behind the door but it wasn't hers; a coat with a pretty filigree brooch on the lapel. Dottie's blood ran cold. That was the brooch she'd found all that long time ago in the drawer in Reg's shed.

She crept into the sitting room, Aunt Bessie's picture wasn't there either. In fact, none of her photographs were here.

Back in the kitchen, Dottie heard a footfall upstairs. Someone else was here! Grabbing the bread knife from the table, she went to the foot of the stairs and looked up. A tarty blonde woman dressed only in a silk petticoat stood at the top.

'Oh,' she said. 'It's you.'

'Who are you?' said Dottie. 'You don't sound very surprised to see me.'

'I'm not.'

'I remember that perfume,' said Dottie slowly. 'You were staying in the B&B, and . . .' she frowned, 'you were in the bungalow.'

'I'll be more careful next time,' said the woman.

'You tried to kill me,' said Dottie bitterly.

The woman smiled and leaned back against the doorframe. 'You mean you tried to kill yourself and the kid.'

'You and Reg tried to make it look like that, but I have witnesses . . . proof.'

The woman stood up straight. 'Rubbish! No one will believe you. You're only playing the innocent to get hold of Reg's money.'

'Reg has no money,' said Dottie coldly. She stared at the woman again. 'I know you from somewhere. I've seen you before.'

'I've never seen you before,' said the woman tossing her head defiantly. 'Except in a photo.'

'That's it,' cried Dottie. 'You're the woman in the photograph. Reg has a picture of you in his shed.'

The woman smiled. 'The dirty dog,' she said. 'He told me he'd got rid of those.'

A picture of the woman, some years younger, it was true, and apart from a little more weight, looking much the same, floated before Dottie's eyes. It was the one she'd seen the night she found the hammer in Reg's shed. The woman in the photo had fewer clothes on than she did now and she was posing provocatively, but it was her all right. Dottie shuddered.

She turned away in disgust. 'Where are my things?'

'He got rid of them, chucked them away,' said the woman. 'This is his place now. There's nothing here for you, Dot Cox.'

Dottie's head swam. Chucked them away? What, all her clothes? What gave Reg the right to do that? It was all falling into place now. Being nice to her, taking her and Patsy on the trip to Eastbourne . . . second honeymoon, my eye. They'd planned it all together, hadn't they? Get her and Patsy to some isolated spot and make it look as if Dottie had planned to commit suicide and ended up killing Patsy. Two birds with one stone. Neat. And it had worked. They'd almost done it. And right now she was left with nothing, not even the clothes she stood up in.

'What the hell are you doing here anyway?' the woman said.

Dottie had never felt so angry in her whole life. She put one foot on the bottom stair and the bread knife glistened in her hand. The woman went white and Dottie could see her trembling through her transparent petticoat.

'Haven't you heard?' said Dottie coldly. 'Poor mad killer that I am, I've escaped.'

The woman snatched at her own throat.

'Oh yes,' Dottie went on. 'They've found enough evidence to prove it wasn't me who killed Patsy. They know Reg did it. And what's more, they know he wasn't alone.'

'You're lying.'

'I have never lied to anyone,' said Dottie.

For a second or two, the woman stared at her, then turning away she said, 'I'm getting out of here,' and the bedroom door slammed.

Putting the bread knife back on the table, Dottie hurried back down the path. It wouldn't be long before Reg came back and the last thing she wanted was to be arrested in her own home.

She paused halfway to the gate, sensing something menacing behind her. Her feet were rooted to the spot. She turned slowly. He was standing by the shed door and took a step towards her.

'Don't even think about it, Reg,' she said in a voice so full of strength it surprised even herself.

He hesitated. 'Yeah, you're right. You're on your way to a long prison sentence. Maybe they'll even hang you.'

He laughed softly. Dottie heard Sylvie open the car door.

'As soon as you're safely locked up,' Reg carried on, 'me and my Patsy are going to be together.'

'Over my dead body,' Dottie spat.

'My Joyce knows some people who would pay good money for a nice little totty like her. They won't worry that she's a darkie.'

Anger blazed up in Dottie's chest. Behind her, Sylvie called out her name sharply. Shaking with pain and frustration, Dottie turned on her heel and headed for the car.

By the time Tom came downstairs after Mary had called him, Dottie was sitting at the table, with her head in her hands.

'Just look at the state of her, Tom,' cried Mary. 'That Reg is a wicked, wicked man.'

Sylvie threw herself into a chair and tapped a cigarette on her holder. 'She insisted on going in for her things,' she said as if Dottie wasn't there. 'I told her it was all gone, but she would go.'

'It's all right, Sylvie,' said Dottie, sitting up and blowing her nose. 'It's not your fault.'

Tom sat down and took her hands in his. 'It's good to see you, Dottie. We've been so worried.'

'I'm so lucky to have friends like you,' she said softly.

'Couldn't you find anything, hen?'

Dottie shook her head. 'Oh, yes, I found something.' They all looked up expectantly. 'Reg's fancy woman.'

Sylvie groaned.

'You knew?' Dottie said.

'I knew he'd had a woman there,' said Sylvie, 'but I didn't expect her to still be there.'

'None of us have seen her,' said Mary. 'Not even Ann.'

'Who would have thought . . .?' Tom began.

'I wouldn't put anything past Reg,' said Dottie. She gave her friends a wry smile. 'The trouble is, I can't prove a thing.'

'Sylvie and Dr Landers have been really trying to help you,' said Mary eagerly. 'They both went back to Eastbourne again yesterday.'

'I found the owner of the bungalow,' said Sylvie. 'It wasn't for sale. It'll be demolished.'

'And the doctor found the car hire company,' Mary interrupted. 'And Patsy's roller skates on the back seat.'

Dottie wiped a renegade tear from her cheek.

'Ah, hen, don't,' soothed Mary.

'I don't deserve you,' said Dottie.

'Course you do,' said Tom. 'Wouldn't you do the same for them if they were in trouble?'

'Where are the children?' Dottie asked.

'All in bed, hen,' said Mary. 'It's all arranged. You'll be staying the night with us so you can see them in the morning.'

Dottie lifted her hand in protest as Sylvie said, 'Then I'm taking you home with me.'

'I'll just nip down to the pub,' said Tom all at once. 'See if the doc is still here.'

When he'd gone, Mary leaned over the table and took Dottie's hands. 'He's done it because he loves you, hen.'

'Who?'

'Dr Landers, of course.'

'It's no use now, Mary. It's all gone wrong,' Dottie sighed. 'I had proof that the Reg Cox who was Patsy's father wasn't the same Reg Cox I married, but it's gone. He got rid of it when he chucked out all my things.'

The kitchen door burst open and there stood Billy. He was in his pyjamas, his hair was tousled and his eyes puffy with sleep.

'Go back to bed, Billy,' said Mary.

'Auntie Dottie!' Ignoring his mother, Billy ran over to Dottie and gave her a hug. 'I knew you'd come back.'

Dottie held him tight, aware that Billy wasn't usually so free with his affections.

'Are you coming to live here with us?' asked Billy eventually.

'I can't, I'm afraid,' said Dottie. 'I have to go away. Have no choice. I'm in a spot of bother, Billy. I haven't got a home any more.' She laughed with irony. 'I haven't even got any clothes.'

Tom came back indoors. 'No sign of the doc in the pub,' he said. 'He must be back at his mother's.'

'What am I thinking about?' cried Mary. 'Anyone want a cup of tea? Let's put the kettle on, shall we?'

No one noticed Billy slipping outside. It took him only a minute or two to nip down to the shed. Tact told him to leave Patsy's pile of things but he grabbed all of Dottie's clothes and raced back up the garden path. His face shone like a belisha beacon as he leaned across the kitchen table and placed the neatly wrapped bundle in front of her. 'There you are, Auntie Dottie,' he said proudly. 'Here are your clothes.'

Dottie gasped with pleasure. 'But how . . .?' she began.

'I collected them when we were carol singing,' he said.

'What!' Tom thundered. 'You went into Myrtle Cottage and helped yourself?'

'No, Dad,' Billy protested. 'Uncle Reg put them out by the gate and me and Paul Dore and Dennis Long found them.'

'And they're wrapped in Edna's new curtains,' said Dottie.

'How on earth did you get them back here?' asked Sylvie.

'The pram,' said Billy.

'The pram!' exclaimed his parents.

'Oh Billy, you are amazing!' cried Dottie, giving him a quick hug.

Tom ruffled Billy's hair. 'Well done, son.'

It was wonderful to see her powder-blue twinset, her Prince of Wales check skirt, her pink and white check sundress with the bolero once more – but even more amazingly, on the top of her clothes, sat a photo frame. Sylvie and her much younger self smiled up at her with Aunt Bessie, wearing her silly . . . wonderful cowboy hat, sitting between them.

Dottie beamed from ear to ear. Lovingly, she wiped her hand across the glass.

'Tom,' she said quietly. 'Would you do one more thing for me? Would you get Kipper for me? Tell him to call head office. Tell him, I've got the blighter at last.' She turned the nails on the back of the frame and something fell out. 'I've got all the proof I need to expose Reg for the liar and cheat he is.'

Mary leaned over her shoulder. 'What is it, hen?'

'A love letter,' said Dottie. 'The one Reg wrote to Sandy all those years ago.' She spread it out in front of them.

"My own true love", Mary quoted. 'Ah, Dottie, that's beautiful.'

Sylvie snorted in disgust.

'Listen to this. 'I can't stop thinking about you, my darling. I have to see you again", said Dottie. 'And this bit: 'I shall never feel about anyone else the way I feel about you".

Sylvie laid her hand on Dottie's shoulder. 'Dottie, don't do this to yourself.'

Dottie looked up, her eyes sparkling. 'It's all right,' she said. 'I don't mind at all. Look at it carefully, Sylvie . . . do you think *my* Reg wrote this?'

There was a moment's silence while everyone crowded around.

'Reg couldn't have written that,' Tom suddenly declared. 'It's not even his bloody handwriting.'

Dottie gave them all a satisfied smile. 'Precisely.'

# Forty-Five

John opened the car door.

'The woman confessed she was at the bungalow as soon as the police went round.'

'You know I once found some dirty pictures of her in his shed?'

'*What!*'

'I didn't know who she was of course, but as soon as I saw her on the stairs, I recognised her.'

John had just picked Dottie up from the magistrates' court where, at a hastily convened sitting, Patsy had been placed, temporarily, in her care. The welfare people needed more time to go over the facts of the case for themselves, but they were satisfied that Dottie was completely exonerated of any wrong-doing in the bungalow. Now she and John were on their way to fetch Patsy from hospital.

He started the engine. 'Why don't you and Patsy come and stay with me at my mother's place?'

'I just want to get back home,' said Dottie. 'Now that there's a warrant out for Reg's arrest, and that woman has been locked up, there's no reason why we can't go back to the village.'

He nodded in a resigned sort of a way and the car made its way along the Brighton Road.

'I still don't like the idea of you being there on your own,' John protested.

'Why ever not?' said Dottie innocently. 'I have all my friends around me. I can shout for help if I need it . . . which I won't. The whole village knows what happened now, John. Myrtle Cottage is perfectly safe.'

'I suppose you're right,' John sighed. He leaned over and squeezed her hand. 'I just want to be there for you.'

Dottie gently took her hand away. 'Can I ask you something? Do you think Reg killed Aunt Bessie?'

'I guess we'll never really know if he intended to kill her,' said John, changing gear. 'Since PC Kipling acted on what poor Ernest Franks told him, there can be little doubt that Reg was there the day she died. Marney has confessed that he was lying when he told the police Reg was at work all that day.'

'Marney lied for Reg?' Dottie gasped. 'You're joking!'

'Don't think too badly of him,' said John. 'Reg had spun him some yarn and he genuinely thought he was just helping a mate out.'

'Did she fall or was she pushed?' Dottie mused.

'I guess we'll never know.'

'One thing is for sure,' said Dottie quietly. 'He fully intended to kill Patsy and me.'

John glanced across at her. 'Yes, I'm afraid he did.'

'I guess he wanted me out of the way so that he could get his hands on the house,' Dottie went on. 'But why kill Patsy? Why poor Patsy?'

'She was simply in the way,' said John quietly. 'My problem is trying to understand why, when it was so obvious she wasn't his child, he kept up the pretence that he was her father.'

'Knowing Reg,' said Dottie bitterly. 'He thought there was money in it somewhere.'

John reached out and gripped her hand for a second time.

'She was so happy that day we went along the seafront, John,' said Dottie. 'She roller skated the whole way. And you should have heard her giggle while we ate that silly picnic on the floor.'

'There will be other happy times,' he said, pulling up at a crossroads.

'I should have tried harder. I should have saved her.'

'How could you? You were both drugged. Those sleeping pills were quite powerful, you know. Thankfully, you'd pushed her by the door. Enabling her to breathe sweet air while unconscious undoubtedly saved her life.'

The road cleared and he pushed the car into gear. Dottie's mind drifted over the most recent events. Mary had told her that the friends were planning a surprise party for Patsy.

'Did you know about the party?'

'I didn't think they were going to tell you about it,' said John.

'I don't think they had much choice,' Dottie laughed. 'People kept turning up on the doorstep with food!'

'The last time I went to see Patsy,' John said, 'she asked me about it. She was scared she'd missed it.'

'Then it wasn't much of a surprise,' Dottie observed. 'Anyway, we'll do it another time. Too much excitement for Patsy may not be good for her so soon after being in hospital.'

They drove on in silence, each lost in their own thoughts. John was thinking about his new post. He had spent some time looking for a practice in need of a GP and had been delighted to find one in nearby Littlehampton, badly in need of a third partner. Drs Green and Noble seemed amiable enough and their practice was growing. The location couldn't have been better: Littlehampton was close to both Worthing and Yapton.

No, he had told them, he had no family commitments, but he had been nursing an aged mother who had been ill, but was now recovering. Yes, he thought he would settle in the area. Every third weekend off sounded reasonable, and he wouldn't mind being on call a little more often than the others. And yes, he could start at once. He was due to start the following Monday and after all this time, he couldn't wait to get back into the swing of things. Apart from being called upon a few times to help out as a locum and writing an article for *The Lancet*, he hadn't done very much since he came back from Australia.

He glanced over at Dottie again. He still had to tell her something else. Was she up to hearing more bad news? In the end, he decided it would be better to tell her now, while they were still alone. Mary's house was chock-a-block full with children and visitors, and once Patsy was with them it would be impossible to have an adult conversation.

Dottie was thinking about the future. She'd wondered whether to go back to work for Mariah Fitzgerald, and Janet Cooper. The thought wasn't very appealing, but she'd have to do something if she was going to support Patsy by herself. She knew what she'd like to do – her furnishings – but was she right to take a gamble at such a time as this? And what about John? Once this was all over, would she ever see him again?

'Dottie,' John interrupted. 'I found out something else. I don't know how you're going to feel about it, but I think it's important that you should know.'

She turned her head.

'I've discovered that Reg Cox wasn't even his real name. He stole it from a dead man. The real Reg Cox was killed at the end of 1942. Ernest Franks, your tramp, told Kipper.'

'I'm not surprised,' said Dottie. 'When Patsy came, you gave us a case full of papers, remember? That first night, I went through it and I came across a beautiful love letter from Reg to Sandy. I knew straight away that my Reg hadn't written it. Apart from anything else, the handwriting was a dead giveaway.'

'Why didn't you say something?'

'I didn't want to upset Patsy. She'd come all this way and I thought it would hurt her deeply if she realised from the outset that Reg wasn't her father. I kept hoping he'd come round.'

'I can't imagine your Reg writing a love letter.'

Dottie gave a hollow laugh. 'Neither can I.'

'Oh, Dottie, I'm sorry,' he said quickly, kicking himself for being so thoughtless.

'Don't be,' she smiled. 'At least we've still got it, that and a picture of Sandy with Patsy in her arms. Reg burned almost everything else.'

'A picture of Sandy with Patsy in her arms?'

'The one of her in the nurse's uniform,' said Dottie.

John frowned. 'I've seen that. Kipper showed me, but that's not Sandy. That's Brenda.'

'Brenda!'

'She brought Patsy into the world,' said John. 'That's how they met, Brenda and Sandy, on the maternity ward.'

For a moment, Dottie was completely dumbstruck. 'But Reg told me it was Sandy.' She paused. 'That proves beyond a shade of a doubt that he never knew her, doesn't it?'

'Absolutely,' John agreed.

'The real Reg must have loved Sandy very much.'

'I think he did,' said John, 'but she knew her family would never accept him. He'd lived in this country much of his life, but Reg Cox was half-caste. Ernest thought he was Jamaican but his parents came from East Africa, a place called Zanzibar. His father, Almas Jaffer, was the skipper of the *Al Said*, which used to be called the SS *Drake* and was bought for the Zanzibar Protectorate back in 1934. I found a whole article about him in *The People*.'

Dottie was intrigued. 'Really?'

'It was unusual to see a black man in those days,' John went on, 'let alone a whole shipload of them. The press invited the crew to Croydon airport and they watched West Ham play against Plymouth at Upton Park.'

'And you say this Almuck . . .'

'Almas Jaffer.'

'. . . was Reg Cox's father?'

'So it would seem,' said John. 'According to *The People*, he had two fat wives back home, one a native, the other a white missionary's daughter. Almas Jaffer brought Reg, who was about twelve at the time, back to this country to be educated. I suppose the family must have changed his name to spare their blushes.'

'And when he grew up, Sandy fell in love with him.'

'She had his child and kept it a secret because of her family, but as it turns out, he was killed in an air raid. I guess poor Sandy never knew that.'

'How sad,' said Dottie.

'It gets worse,' said John. 'I looked up the newspaper reports at the time. Apparently, as he lay on the ground, he was robbed. He was still alive when the medics got to him, but died some time later.'

Dottie gasped. 'You mean, you think Reg took his ID and left him for dead?'

John nodded. 'Looks like it.'

Dottie felt the shame. 'I can't believe the brass neck of the man!'

'Did you keep the love letter?'

'Of course. I hid it where I knew Reg would never look for it, behind the picture of Aunt Bessie. I knew, given half the chance, Reg would get rid of the picture as soon as he could, which was why I had to get it as soon as possible. Thank God for little Billy.'

'Indeed,' John agreed.

'Between us,' Dottie went on, 'Ernest Franks and I have given Kipper the cast-iron evidence he needs to prove that Reg was a fraud.'

'Oh, Dottie,' said John quietly, 'there's one more thing you don't know.'

'What?'

'Ernest Franks is dead.'

For a few moments Dottie was silent. 'Poor man. He suffered so much.' She sighed. 'Rest in peace, dear Ernest.'

'He's with his beloved Eileen and Bobbie now.' John waited

a second or two then asked. 'Do you think Reg attacked Ernest?'

'He did,' Dottie nodded, 'with a hammer. I found it all wrapped up in a piece of cloth in Reg's shed. Of course, I didn't know then but something made me hide it in the henhouse. Mary and Ann told me it was in the well, so when Reg went back to the house that morning, he must have thrown it there.'

'I guess he thought the weight of the hammer would take the whole lot, chickens and all, to the bottom,' said John. 'He couldn't have known the well was collapsing.'

'None of us expected that,' said Dottie. 'But Kipper had the hammer checked: Ernest's blood was on it. In actual fact, Ernest came to the house twice.'

'Twice?'

'The first time Ernest came back, the time he left the note on the windowsill, he had no idea Aunt Bessie was dead,' Dottie said. 'He told Kipper he'd come back to tell her he'd made a new life for himself. That's why he left a note saying '*I did it!*'

John nodded sagely.' And the second time?'

'It was because he'd seen a newspaper cutting, and he knew that Reg was lying when he told the police he wasn't there on the day Aunt Bessie died.'

'I never did work out why Reg killed your chickens,' said John.

'Who can understand a warped mind like Reg's,' Dottie observed.

The Royal Alexander Hospital for Sick Children was in Dyke Road, Brighton. They parked the car and walked quickly to the ward where Patsy was.

'Do you think she'll blame me?' Dottie asked.

'I don't think so,' he assured her. 'No, not at all.'

All the same, Dottie's hands were trembling and her knees like jelly by the time they'd made themselves known at the desk.

'Ah, yes,' said the sister. 'Nurse Doughty is just getting her dressed.'

There was a footfall in the corridor, and Patsy cried out, 'Uncle John, Uncle John.'

They turned and there she was. A little pale, but she was beaming from ear to ear and clutching Suzy, her toy elephant. John put his arms out and she ran to him. Dottie smiled as he swept her off her feet and twirled around. Then she wrapped her arms tightly around his neck and buried her head in the folds of his coat.

'Come on now, young lady,' said John. 'Let's get you home.'

Patsy pulled away from him. 'Where's Auntie Dottie?'

'I'm here, love,' Dottie squeaked. Her throat had closed and she could hardly speak.

Patsy reached around and put out her arms towards Dottie. Dottie took her from John and hugged her tightly. Oh, the joy to have her in her arms once more! Dottie's eyes brimmed with tears and she let out an involuntary sob.

Patsy leaned back and looked at her with a puzzled expression. 'Auntie Dottie, why are you crying?'

'Because I'm so happy to see you,' Dottie laughed.

Patsy put her hands on either side of Dottie's face. 'Don't cry. I was all right. I had Suzy to look after me.'

'Of course, how silly of me to worry,' said Dottie, swallowing hard. She took a deep breath. 'Come on. Uncle John is taking us home.'

As Dottie put her back on the floor, Patsy looked around anxiously. 'Where's Uncle Reg?'

Dottie stiffened. 'Uncle Reg has gone away,' she said.

'Is he coming back?'

'No.'

'Not ever?'

'Not ever.'

'Good,' said Patsy, as she skipped towards the door. 'I don't like that daddy.'

# *Forty-Six*

They reached Mary's house just as the baker's boy was making a delivery.

'Are we going to live with Auntie Mary?' asked Patsy.

'No, we're going home,' said Dottie, 'but we thought you'd like to see your friends first.'

Maureen and Susan emerged from the house and rushed down the path, crying, 'Patsy, Patsy . . .'

Billy hung back by the door. He had his hands in his pockets. He kicked an imaginary stone on the step as he watched his sisters jumping around Patsy. Dottie noticed a slight smile playing on his lips.

'Hello, Billy,' said Patsy. 'I've been in hospital.'

Billy stuffed his hands deep into his pockets. 'You all right now?'

He dug out a sweet and handed it to her. 'I've been saving it for you,' he said. 'It's got a bit of fluff on it, but I ain't sucked it, honest.'

Patsy laughed. 'Thanks,' she said, popping it in her mouth.

As they walked in the door, Mary handed Dottie five pounds. 'What's that for?'

'Gerald brought it round. It's what he got for the pig.' She grinned, 'Minus a bit of commission.'

Dottie laughed.

There was a white box on the kitchen table. 'This has just come for you.'

Maureen and Susan edged up to them. When Dottie lifted the lid she gasped. It was a cake covered in pink and white icing with a large pink rose on the top.

John caught his breath. 'Where did that come from?'

Maureen beamed. 'Patsy done it, didn't you, Pats?'

Patsy frowned crossly. 'O-oh! It was supposed to be for the 'prise party.'

Maureen's smile died and she looked apprehensive.

'Ummm,' Susan said to her sister. 'You shouldn't have told.'

'Where did the cake come from?' Dottie asked gently.

Susan and Patsy went red and stared at the floor.

'Me and Patsy went to the cake shop,' Maureen piped up. 'Patsy said for it to come today and the lady wrote it all down.'

'But how did you pay for it, love?' asked Dottie. 'You don't have any money.'

'Are you cross with me?' Patsy asked.

Dottie crouched down. 'Of course not, love,' she said. 'It's the nicest thing anyone ever gave me.' She opened her arms and Patsy went to her.

'Patsy used a whole pound note,' said Maureen. 'Didn't you, Pats? She got it off that old lady.'

'My mother,' whispered John. 'Remember . . .?'

Then Dottie remembered Laura giving the child a pound note that first day they went to the cottage. Buy something special, Laura had told the child – and she'd spent every last penny on a cake for her! Immediately the tears sprang into her eyes and she had a lump in her throat the size of a grapefruit. Her heart was overwhelmed with love for this beautiful child.

'Come on, you two,' said Mary briskly, putting her hands in the small of her daughters' backs. 'Come out to the kitchen with me.'

'Maureen told Patsy about the party, Mum,' said Susan.

'I never!' Maureen protested.

'Oh yes, you did . . . I said you'd get told off.'

'I never, Mum,' Maureen insisted.

'It's all right, m'duck. Nobody's cross with you.' Their voices faded as Mary closed the door.

Dottie reached for her handkerchief. 'Auntie Laura meant you to have that money for yourself, darling,' she said dabbing her eyes. 'But thank you for doing that. It's lovely.'

'Can I have some?'

Dottie laughed. 'Of course you can.'

Patsy wriggled out of Dottie's arms. 'Can I go and play with Maureen now?'

Dottie stood up. 'Off you go then.'

She hurried out of the room and in a short while Dottie could hear the girls giggling. Dottie looked down at the cake again.

'Oh John, I've been an absolute idiot. I didn't really want her in the first place but Patsy is such a lovely child. And I wanted so much to believe that Reg would come round. I kept thinking, perhaps not today, but there's always tomorrow.' She broke off and looked away.

'Everyone was fooled,' said John softly. 'It's not your fault that you always look for the good in people.'

'I married a monster.'

'Ah, there's one more thing I haven't told you,' said John cautiously. 'I'm not sure if you even realise, but you two were never even married.'

She frowned.

'Because he used a false name, that makes your marriage null and void,' said John. 'And besides, he already has a wife under his real name.'

Dottie raised an eyebrow.

'That woman he had in your house,' said John, 'his accomplice. Her name is Joyce Sinclair.'

Dottie let out a hollow laugh. 'How ironic,' she said harshly. 'All I ever wanted was to be a respectable married woman with a family. Now I turn out to be the bigamous wife of a would-be murderer. How far from respectable can you get?'

'None of this is your fault,' said John.

'Do you think they'll ever catch him?'

'He's as slippery as an eel, that one,' said John. 'Only one thing is for sure, he'll be far, far away by now.'

Dottie's chin quivered as she ran her finger along the top of the cake. She sighed. 'What a lovely thing to do.'

They were interrupted by a knock at the door. 'Can we come in, Uncle John?'

John grinned. 'I suppose they have been waiting a very long time,' he said glancing at his watch. 'At least fifteen seconds.'

'More than a lifetime,' she laughed.

She watched the children swarm over him. He was wonderfully patient and he'd make a terrific father one day. She glanced down at the inscription on the cake again, and for the first time in a very long time, she felt her heart soar.

The pink icing said it all. 'For Mummy Dottie.'

In the week before Christmas, Mary, Edna, Ann and Peaches decided to go ahead with the welcome party. Christmas Day fell on the Tuesday and everybody agreed that after the usual family affair, they would gather in Edna's barn for a barn dance and make it a Christmas to remember.

They spent Christmas Eve decorating the barn with paper chains.

'Whoever thought up that idea deserves a medal,' Mary declared. 'It kept the kids quiet all day.'

Janet Cooper finally got rid of the box of balloons left over from the VJ Day celebrations. Gerald, Tom and Jack swept out the barn and Michael arranged some bales of straw around the edge for seating. By the time the caller arrived, the trestle tables borrowed from the village hall groaned with leftover Christmas fare and plenty more besides.

Patsy was very excited. She and the other children had

been doing some country dancing at school and this was a wonderful opportunity to show off their skills. Even more thrilling, Dottie had given Patsy Aunt Bessie's old cowboy hat to wear.

'Where's John?' asked Mary as Dottie struggled through the door with a sherry trifle.

'On duty.'

'On Christmas Day?'

'Somebody's got to do it,' smiled Dottie. 'He said he'd try and come over later if everything was quiet, but I know he's worried about a couple of pregnant patients.'

She and John had had a long talk soon after Patsy came out of hospital. John wasn't too keen, but she'd persuaded him that she needed to be on her own for a bit. They were still seeing each other but, for the first time in her life, Dottie was making her own decisions and plans.

'What a shame,' Ann sighed. 'After all we've been through, we should all be together tonight.' Vince came up and handed her a milk stout. As she took it, he put his arm around her shoulders and she smiled up at him happily. 'Everyone should be with the people they love at Christmas.'

Dottie and Mary exchanged a grin as they left them to it. Several kids playing kiss chase dashed through the straw bales. 'Calm down,' Mary shouted.

By the time Dottie got back home that night, it was very late. Patsy was so tired she struggled to walk up the path so Michael Gilbert swept her up in his arms and carried her indoors and upstairs to her bedroom. While Dottie undressed her, Michael went back to his truck to fetch the presents.

'Are you sure you're going to be all right here on your own?' he asked.

'Michael,' Dottie chided gently. 'I'm a big girl now and I can look after myself.' But she knew why he was concerned.

394

Earlier in the evening, Mary had said anxiously, 'I think you should stay here with us tonight, hen.'

'Whatever for?' cried Dottie. 'As far as Reg knows, we're still at Sylvie's. Besides, coming back here would be the last thing he would do.'

'I'm sure your John wouldn't like you to be on your own,' Ann cautioned.

'John is a dear man,' Dottie had said, 'but I can make my own decisions. Stop worrying.'

Tom wasn't so sure either. 'Reg can be very vindictive, Dottie. I think you should do as Mary says.'

'Thank you for your concern,' said Dottie stiffly, 'but really, there's no need.'

Now that she was back home, Dottie didn't like to admit she was a little nervous.

'I'll stay if you like,' Michael said. 'I can sleep on the sofa downstairs.'

Dottie smiled. 'I'll be fine.'

'Lock all the doors,' Michael cautioned as he left.

'I always do,' Dottie smiled. She kissed his cheek. 'Don't you worry about me. You get your Freda home to bed. She looks all done in, poor girl.'

Before she went to bed, Dottie tidied up the toys and made herself a cocoa. Climbing the stairs to her room, she found that she was missing John. Having her independence was wonderful, but she wished he was here right now.

She opened the door slightly and listened to Patsy's deep rhythmic breathing. It was like music to Dottie's ears and she couldn't resist creeping in and giving her a kiss on her forehead. Patsy stirred in her sleep. As quietly as she could, Dottie crept outside. She'd leave the toys until the morning. If she tidied them away in Patsy's room, she might wake her. She put Aunt Bessie's hat on the top of the pile and left them.

Back in her own room, she wished John was here once again.

And if he was here . . . Humming to herself, she climbed into bed and turned out the light.

As soon as the door creaked open, Dottie held her breath. A tall figure was standing in the doorway with one hand on the latch. He waited, watching the bed for any sign of movement and then looked behind him towards the landing.

He stepped into the room and Dottie saw the glint of the knife in his hand. With one fluid movement, he was beside the bed and slashing at the bedclothes.

'Bitch,' he hissed. 'Bloody bitch.'

Dottie didn't move. Please, please, she prayed. Don't let Patsy hear him, don't let her wake up.

Dottie had known the minute she saw him that it was Reg. The others had been right. She wished to God she'd listened, but she hadn't and now she'd put Patsy's life in danger once again. A murderous intent had driven him back to the one place she honestly thought he'd never return. When she'd heard the key in the lock, she'd realised he'd got into the house the same way she had – he'd used the spare key under the mangle.

As soon as she'd heard him, something made her get out of bed and stuff the spare pillows under the bedclothes. She'd only just managed to stop the coat hangers rattling in the wardrobe where she was hiding as he'd come into the room. The door was shut, but she could watch his every move through the crack above the mirror.

A light went on outside and Patsy called out, 'Mummy.'

Reg sprang like a cat towards the door. Dottie's heart went into her mouth. He was after Patsy too. Stumbling out into the room, Dottie dashed onto the landing.

Patsy had opened her door wide and stood tousled-haired, rubbing her eyes in the doorway. When she looked up and saw Reg, she froze. Dottie's heart was pounding but from deep within her she found a strong and commanding voice.

'Patsy, go back into your room and shut the door . . . now!'

Patsy fled. Her door banged. Reg rounded on Dottie and his narrowed eyes seem to change colour. He was so terrifying, she thought she was going to faint.

'I'm going to kill you, bitch,' Reg snarled. 'You've ruined my life. You and that bloody aunt of yours.'

Dottie could feel her knees knocking. 'Did you kill Aunt Bessie?'

'Of course I did,' said Reg.

Dottie took in her breath.

'You should have seen her face,' Reg grinned. His eyes were bright with excitement. 'She was standing right where you are now.'

Dottie's knees went to jelly.

'Didn't take much. Just one little push.'

'Why?' Dottie squeaked.

'The stupid cow found out I was still married.' Reg kicked at Aunt Bessie's hat and stamped on it. 'Bloody bitch.'

Dottie trembled as Reg threw back his head and let out a hideous laugh. 'Know what?' he sneered. 'She never touched one bloody stair all the way down.'

A door closed downstairs and they both looked down. John Landers and Kipper were standing in the small hallway.

'So now we know, Reg,' said Kipper. 'That was as good a confession as I've ever heard.'

'Dottie, be careful!' John frantic cry coincided with Reg's loud roar as he made a dash towards Dottie. He was still standing on Aunt Bessie's hat and somehow the chinstrap had looped itself over his other foot. The little landing didn't allow him much room for manoeuvre. Reg looked down, and lost his balance. For a couple of seconds, he flailed his arms, but he couldn't seem to stop himself from falling. He let out a single cry of panic before tumbling over the top stair and there was a sickening thud as he hit his head at the bottom. Dottie turned her head away.

In the ominous silence that followed, John leaned over him. 'He's dead,' he said quietly. 'His neck is broken.'

A small voice called from behind the bedroom door. 'Mummy . . .' And anxious that the child shouldn't come out and see what had happened, Dottie dashed across the landing into Patsy's room.

# Forty-Seven

The first flurry of snow began as they drove out of Worthing. By the time they'd reached the turnoff for Yapton, it was beginning to settle. It was 1952, one year later and Christmas Eve. Dottie and John were on their way to pick up his mother for Christmas in the village. She'd left Patsy and the others back at Mary's place, busy making mince pies for the carol service in St Andrew's later that evening.

'What a difference a year makes,' John grinned.

Dottie nodded slowly, remembering last Christmas when Reg had broken into Myrtle Cottage and fallen down the stairs. Thank God John and the policeman had been there.

Kipper, anxious that Dottie would be in the house on her own, had rung John to tell him Reg had been spotted in the area. John was so frantic, he'd arranged for his colleague to cover for him while he drove over to Worthing to make sure that Dottie was all right.

The two of them had arrived just in time to see Reg enter the cottage. John was all for arresting him there and then but Kipper held back and as a result they'd heard Reg's confession. When it was all over, Dottie was surprised that she felt no grief. In fact, she didn't feel anything. She had been married to him and now he was gone.

The past twelve months had brought a complete change in all their circumstances. Gary was back home with Peaches and

Jack and Mandy. He'd made such good progress he'd been able to shed the calliper, although he still walked with a slight limp. Everyone agreed he'd made an amazing recovery.

Michael and Freda had a bouncing baby boy, birth weight nine pounds, and Dottie had been asked to be godmother.

'Imagine that,' Mary gasped. 'None of mine were more than seven pounds and that little slip of a girl gives birth to an elephant!'

In the same month, King George VI died of lung cancer. Like thousands of others, Dottie, Peaches, Ann and Mary huddled together around the wireless and wept.

In March, Dottie put Myrtle Cottage up for sale. By the time the May blossom was out, Ann and Vince were married. 'I'm Mrs Vincent Dobbs,' Ann sighed as Dottie, Peaches and Mary helped her change into her going-away outfit. She held out her left hand and the gold band on her finger glistened in the light. 'It so good to have a man to lean on.'

'There's nothing like a good wedding,' said Peaches, digging Dottie in the ribs.

Dottie felt her face colour. She and John were very close, but ever since Reg died, he hadn't even mentioned marriage. 'I want to stand on my own two feet,' said Dottie, keen to put a stop to her friends' speculation. 'I've decided I don't need a man to be happy.'

Peaches shook her head. 'Oh, Dottie . . .'

But Mary had surprised them all by saying, 'Good for you, hen.'

Dottie said nothing. Even if she had the chance to marry John, perhaps the stigma of her once living with a murderer might damage his career.

With the five hundred pounds she got for the sale of the cottage, Dottie had bought a small shop in the centre of Worthing and set up her own furnishing business. Sylvie had recommended her to all her friends and Dottie had a full order book before

Fabulous Furnishings had even opened its doors. Mariah Fitzgerald couldn't wait to tell all her friends that she had been the one who discovered Dottie. Her beautifully decorated bedroom became the talk of the Golf Club. By Whitsun, the requests were coming in so fast, Dottie was forced to close for a week to teach Ann how to measure up accurately. Mary said Dottie was kindness itself, but Dottie felt Ann simply needed a leg up. After all, she was a quick-witted and intelligent woman.

Patsy was really settled now. She and Billy had both passed their eleven plus and were doing well at school.

By the end of the summer, despite her best efforts to convince herself that he was just a friend, Dottie was still hopelessly in love with John. She deeply regretted holding him at arm's length now, but he seemed happy to leave things as they were.

As she and John drove out of town to fetch his mother, Dottie's mind drifted back to the night before when she and Mary had been filling their hot water bottles. She and Patsy had left their little flat over the shop and come to stay with the Priors for Christmas.

'John wants to help me adopt Patsy officially.' Dottie had told her.

'Oh? I didn't think it was possible for a single woman to adopt a child.'

'Apparently, because I'm a woman of independent means, I may be able to do it if I get the backing of a professional.'

'But if you and John got married,' said Mary pointedly, 'there would be no problem at all.' Dottie looked away. Mary pressed the filled bottle to her chest until the water drew level with the top and then she screwed in the stopper. 'You love him, don't you?'

'You know I do,' said Dottie.

'Well then?' said Mary.

'I think he's changed his mind,' said Dottie. She sighed. 'Maybe it's just as well. I may have been exonerated from the goings-on in Eastbourne, but in the kind of circles where he mixes, you know what they're like. They'll say there's no smoke without fire.'

'Now you're being silly,' scoffed Mary. 'Why should he care what people think? And besides, you're a rich woman, Dottie Cox. You can afford to move away and start all over again.'

'I couldn't bear to be parted from all of you!' Dottie cried. 'Where would I find such wonderful friends? Anyway, it's nothing to do with money. It's class. John has a position to keep up. He'll choose a wife who'll play the hostess and stay at home. Now that I've had a taste of running my own business, I'm not sure I could go back to all that.'

Mary had plonked herself on the edge of the kitchen table. 'Sometimes you do talk utter rot, Dottie. You're just putting up obstacles. What does it matter when two people love each other?'

'What do you mean?'

'My Tom had his own Post Office when I met him.'

'So?'

'I worried that he was just looking for a post mistress to help him,' Mary went on. 'I mean, I'm hardly Joan Crawford, am I? Just look at me.' She was dressed for bed in her nightie and plaid dressing gown; her moth-eaten slippers peeped out from underneath and her hair was in curlers.

Dottie laughed and gave her a cuddle.

'When my Tom married me,' Mary went on, 'I was a fat widow with three kids. Now I'm an even fatter wife with five kids.'

'Don't be silly,' Dottie laughed. 'Tom doesn't care a stuff about any of that. He's crazy about you. He just wanted to be with you . . . to love you . . .' Her voice trailed and Mary lifted one eyebrow.

'Precisely. And your John feels the same about you.'

'I'm not so sure . . .'

'Dottie, the man loves you,' said Mary in a slightly exasperated tone. 'For heaven's sake, relax a little. Encourage him when he's being loving towards you. You're a warm person. It's about

402

time you knew what real love is. Give him a chance. Just let him love you . . .'

Just let him love you. The words had played over and over in her mind ever since and now that she was in his car, heading towards Yapton, she couldn't think of anything else. Mary was right. He was so gentle, so caring. All through those dark and terrible days, the thought that he was still there had kept her going. They'd had some wonderful times during the past year, but did he really love her enough to want to be together for the rest of their lives? She glanced at his profile as he drove and her whole being lurched with desire. Mary had said it was about time she knew what real love was, and now at last, she knew Mary was right. But was it too late? Oh, John . . . John . . . have I been a complete idiot?

'Looks like we'll have a white Christmas,' he said, suddenly turning to look at her.

Dottie's face coloured and she looked away quickly. She was glad the inside of the car was dark. 'I hope we don't get snowed in,' she remarked light-heartedly.

'I hope we do,' he said and they both laughed.

Encourage him, Mary said. Dottie took a deep breath and her heart was in her mouth but she took a chance. She reached out and put her hand on his leg. She felt him stiffen. Oh God, she shouldn't have done it. What would he think of her? She began to take her hand away but he reached out, caught it and put it back on his leg. Neither of them spoke but they drove for several miles with his hand pressed over hers.

His mother's cottage looked as pretty as a picture postcard as they stepped out into the road. They hurried up the path. Dottie reached out for the doorbell but John caught her hand. 'Hang on a minute,' he said breathlessly. 'I've left something in the car.'

He took a few minutes to find whatever it was but eventually he ran back up the path. Although she was standing under the porch, the dormant rambling rose hanging over the roof afforded little protection from the prevailing wind. 'Hurry up,' she laughed, as she stamped her feet to keep warm. 'It's perishing cold here.'

He stopped short of the doorway and knelt on the ground.

'What are you doing?' she said; ever practical, added, 'John, you'll ruin your trousers.'

'I love you, Dottie, darling,' he said gravely. 'Will you marry me?'

She caught her breath. The sight of him, kneeling on the freezing cold pathway, the snow falling steadily onto his upturned face was almost too much. He loved her . . . he loved her . . .

'Oh, John, you're beginning to look like a snowman,' she laughed, afraid of the trembling passion rising in her veins.

'Then put me out of my misery,' he said, opening a small red box and holding it up to her. 'Please say yes. It doesn't have to be right away if you don't want it. I'll wait for as long as it takes, but please, please say you'll marry me.'

She glanced down at the diamond ring, twinkling in the moonlight. The sighing of the wind through the bare rose bush seemed to echo Mary's words. Just let him love you . . .

Shivering furiously, she looked into his dear, dear face. 'Oh, yes, John, yes.'

With a broad grin, he slipped the ring on the third finger of her left hand. It fitted perfectly. Then he stood up and opened out his coat. She went into his arms, the warmth of his body and his gentle kiss chasing away all the bitterness and sorrow of her cold and loveless yesterdays.

*Read on for an exclusive*
*short story by Pam . . .*

## Plan B

I'm wide-awake now and I'm seething. He's done it again. He's woken me up. One loud snort, the bed dips and I'm staring at the ceiling. Of course, he's totally unaware of what he's done. He's lying on his back snoring gently. I dig him in the side with my elbow and murmuring slightly he rolls over onto his side and sleeps on. I'm destined to lie awake for hours.

This is ruining our relationship. I love him a lot but I'm seriously wondering if I can go through the rest of my life with so little sleep. I get up to make myself a cup of tea.

Downstairs in the kitchen, Judy stirs in her basket and opens one eye. She gives me a sleepy wag of her tail. She's worn out too. This is the third time this week I've been up in the middle of the night and it's only Wednesday!

I sit at the table stirring my tea and staring into the depths of the cup. We've had loads of rows about it already.

'I don't snore.'

'Of course you do. Everybody snores,' I told him. 'The trouble is you do these gi-normous snorts that wake me up.'

'Nobody else has ever complained about it.'

I skirt around that one. I've no wish to wander down the back roads of his past relationships. 'Well I'm complaining about it now, so what are you going to do about it?'

It took weeks of nagging to get him to the doctor. The Doc

gave him an examination and he came home with a load of pills.

'Over twenty one quid that lot cost me,' he said chucking three packets onto the kitchen table, 'and they'll only last me a month.'

I kissed him and told him he was wonderful, but a month later we both realised the pills didn't work so I went to the chemist. The Chemist gave me some elasticated thingy to make his nostrils wider.

'I feel like a flippin' hippo,' he said once it was all strapped on, and I had to turn away in case he saw me laughing. His nostrils looked big enough to park a couple of toy cars in. But after two weeks of suffering, I was still being woken up by those snorts.

I was really excited when I found the nasal spray.

'You'll have me snorting coke next,' he grumbled.

'Don't be so ridiculous,' I snapped as I zapped his nostrils.

The spray made him sneeze for half an hour, his eyes were running and he kept blowing his nose.

'Whaddever that tuff is,' he said, sounding as if he had a heavy cold, 'I'm alerdit do it. There's no way dat I dating dat.'

I had to concede he was right, but it does nothing to solve my problem. I've got bags under the bags under my eyes and I even went to sleep on the bus yesterday. I wouldn't mind but when the driver woke me up, back at the depot, I had my legs wide apart and a huge dribble down the front of my coat. How embarrassing is that?

I read in this magazine that a dried pea sewn into the back of the pyjamas is a good remedy. The pea makes them uncomfortable so they roll onto their sides and stop snoring. It took me forever to sew the thing in place but it didn't work. After one flip around the washing machine, the pea went soggy so I didn't bother again.

I've got to convince him I'm serious about all this. I guess my last resort will have to be Plan B . . . to go without sex until it's sorted.

'Frisky night on the tiles?' my mate at work asks me later that day.

'I wish,' I begin and then I pour out my troubles.

'If he won't believe he does it,' she says giggling uncontrollably, 'make a tape recording.'

What a brilliant idea. Why didn't I think of that?

So the next night I lie awake for ages waiting for him to start snoring but in the end I'm far too tired, so I set the recorder going and drift off into the land of nod.

I wake with a start. The bed has dipped and a loud snort propels me into the grey light of the morning. There! Now I have all the proof I need. Feeling very smug, I roll over to face him, but he's gone. I can hear gentle singing in the shower and I'm left with a very uncomfortable thought running amok in my brain.

That snort. It was me. All this time, I've been waking myself up with my own snoring. For a second or two I chuckle to myself but then the full horror of my discovery dawns. There's no way I can afford twenty one quid's worth of pills every month to cure it. Supposing I'm allergic to that nasal spray? The pea in the back of the pyjamas won't work either. You're not supposed to know it's there. And as for going to bed with a hippo shaped nose . . .

He comes back into the bedroom and leans over the bed to kiss me.

'Hello gorgeous,' he says. He's all pink and damp from his shower and he smells really nice.

'You smell delicious,' I murmur.

He slips back under the sheet and wriggles towards me. I haven't solved the problem yet but as he takes me in his arms, I'm really glad I never got round to Plan B.